THE FOREVER DREAM

DREAM

Iris Johansen

BANTAM BOOKS

TORONTO • NEW YORK • LONDON • SYDNEY • AUCKLAND

THE FOREVER DREAM
A Bantam Book / May 1985

ISBN 0-553-24869-3

Published simultaneously in the United States and Canada

Bantam Books are published by Bantam Books, Inc. Its trademark,
consisting of the words "Bantam Books" and the portrayal of a rooster,
is Registered in U.S. Patent and Trademark Office and in other
countries. Marca Registrada. Bantam Books, Inc., 666 Fifth Avenue,
New York, New York 10103.

PRINTED IN THE UNITED STATES OF AMERICA

H   0 9 8 7 6 5 4 3 2 1

"Do I have to spell it out for you? I want you, damn it!" Jared said fiercely.

Tania was silent, so Jared took a deep breath and went on. "I had to stay away from you these past five days. I knew I couldn't see you without taking you, or without going through an inferno more blistering than any you've been putting me through since you appeared in my life. My control isn't strong enough to resist so much temptation!"

For a moment it didn't sink in; then her eyes widened as she felt an exuberant singing somewhere deep inside. Her lashes lowered as she reached up to touch his cheek. "You could have told me," she said softly. "How was I to know you hadn't gotten bored with our little game and opted out?"

"It's never been a game, Tania, not even in the beginning. It was too late to opt out from the first moment I saw you. I was just waiting until you were ready for me, for us. Will you let me love you now?"

THE FOREVER DREAM

Preface

The wind-driven snow was no longer an icy scourge against her cheeks, but the gentle caress of a lover. Her arms and legs felt warmer, and that hot jolt of agony she'd experienced with every step had diminished too. Oh, God, did that mean she was freezing to death?

The fear of death brought her an agony worse than the physical torment of the extreme cold and deep exhaustion of her trek. She shook her head in a childish gesture of negation: How stupid of her even to entertain such a question. Of course she wasn't freezing. She'd almost reached the foothills of this horror of a mountain, and the flickering lights below were no figment of an imagination about to be extinguished! Those lights should be coming from the village she was looking for, the village she remembered from the map she'd studied until every line, every squiggle, had been burned into memory.

She couldn't give up now that she was almost safe. She'd known it wouldn't be easy. She'd chosen to make her escape over the mountain instead of along the more civilized valley road, in the hope that Danilov would think it unlikely she'd choose such a difficult and dangerous route and would explore the more simple avenues first. But she hadn't bargained on the snow-

1

storm that had struck just as she'd crested the summit of the mountain.

Well, ironically, there was no question she was safe from Danilov now, she realized. Even he wouldn't venture into the Andes in a snowstorm to capture his runaway prima ballerina. Undoubtedly he'd prefer to have her caught and sent back to Russia to be imprisoned in the *Lubyanka* as an example to other would-be defectors. Still, she reasoned, her death on this awesome mountain would suit Danilov's purposes almost as well. Collectively and individually the dancers in the company had been warned that there would be no Baryshnikovs or Godunovs defecting to the West on this tour and further tarnishing the image of the Cultural Department.

Her feet were so numb now that it was as if they didn't exist, but she could see a trickle of blood oozing from the torn foam rubber of her left shoe. She supposed she'd better stop and wrap something around it. If only it had been safe to bribe one of the servants at the lake resort, where the company had been resting before moving on to Santiago, to buy her a pair of hiking boots. But Danilov surely would have learned of the purchase and guessed her plan. The sharp rocks and rough trail had ripped the soles of her shoes before she was even halfway up the mountain. Now, pain shooting from her lacerated feet up through her legs and into her belly and back, she wondered if avoiding the risk of getting the boots had been worth the price of fleeing without them.

She shrugged impatiently as she realized she was whimpering like a child for what might have been. There was no if, there was only the moment. She must accept that if she was going to fight her way through this storm and get off this blasted mountain. After all, it couldn't be so much farther. All she had to do was to put one foot in front of the other. But every step she took brought a stabbing agony to her chest, and her lungs were laboring as if she were running instead of stumbling like a blind woman. She gritted her teeth. One step after another. She couldn't let this damn mountain defeat her. She was strong. Her dancer's body was strong. The pain *would* go away. All pain went away . . . eventually. Who should know that better than she?

She was weaving, stumbling. She paused, slumping against the trunk of a tree. Suddenly her pain did seem to be gone, replaced by a comforting drowsiness. She looked back. Her tracks in the snow revealed a dizzy succession of circles. What an intricate and beautiful pattern her dragging steps had made. A sensation of warmth suffused her, and along with it a rush of longing for sleep. Warmth. Sleep. She pulled herself to her full height.

The warmth was death, the desire to sleep was death. It was not life holding out its arms to her, but death. She forced herself to move.

Think of life. One step after another. The lights were much closer, weren't they? *Life. Think of life.*

Wind chimes in her mother's garden. Laughter. The final exultant *grand jeté.* The stuff of life. Why couldn't she think of more things to add to the list? Her mind was as sluggish as her body. It didn't matter. She had enough to go on for now.

She concentrated on the wind chimes . . . and, faintly, their tinkling music played for her.

One more step. And another . . . another.

She experienced the exuberance that always accompanied a well-executed *grand jeté*: the joyous sensation a bird must know as it headed for the sky.

And she moved more swiftly, on a more direct course. She would not stop to sleep, when she had all that waiting for her just a little way down the path.

Path? Oh, Lord, it *was* a path, and there was a

cluster of cottages just ahead. Why did her knees feel so weak, when she wanted to run down that path toward those lights that were now so blessedly close? The snow was piled in soft, fleecy drifts here in the valley, and it was even harder to walk than it had been on the rougher terrain of the mountain. She mustn't stop. She doubted if she'd have the strength to get back on her feet if she fell into one of those cushiony drifts.

Then she was stumbling blindly up to a rough wooden door and her fist was pounding with a strength that was frantic with urgency.

The door was opened so abruptly, she had to grab the doorjamb to keep from falling into the room. The eyes of the plump, dark-haired woman who stood shivering in the door widened in surprise. "*Madre de Dios!*"

She had practiced the words in Spanish so many times. Why was her mind a complete blank now? "*Me llamo Tania Orlinov.*" That was right, but her voice was no more than a hoarse whisper. What if the woman couldn't hear her? Her gloved hands fumbled at the money belt beneath her jacket and finally got it off. She held it out to the woman, who was staring at her with an expression approaching horror on her face. She tried again. "*Por favor. Embajada americana. Santiago.*" Why didn't the woman say something? She couldn't hold the darkness off much longer. Then the woman was joined at the door by a little boy, who stared at her with big dark eyes almost as frightened as his mother's.

"*Por favor, me llamo Tania . . .*" She'd said that, hadn't she? "*Embajada de los Esta . . .*"

The darkness came down like a black velvet curtain as she pitched forward into the room. The woman's voice was barely audible behind the curtain as Tania's slight body was pulled into the room. It was a soothing croon, almost as musical as a wind chime. "*Pobrecita, morir tan joven.*"

Joven. That was young, wasn't it? She wasn't all that young. She'd be twenty-one soon. *Morir*—to die. The woman thought she was going to die! Tania felt a wave of indignation. Didn't that woman realize that after all she, Tania Orlinov, had gone through she wasn't about to be beaten now!

She pushed the curtain aside for a moment to open her eyes and gaze up at the woman's worried face. "No *muerte,*" she said firmly, despite the weakness of her voice. Then, as the Spanish woman continued to stare at her with that maddeningly mournful expression, she added, "No *muerte.* I will *not* die." The woman stared at her blankly. "I will not give up. I have—" What was the word for strength in Spanish? She gave up and used the Hungarian word of her childhood. "I have *erö.*" Her dark eyes blazed with incandescent vitality for a moment, then the velvet curtain descended once more and her eyelids fluttered shut.

Chapter 1

"You can just stop that, Jared," Nina Bartlett said, an amused smile curving her lips. "No matter how bored you are, we're going to stay until the intermission. My committee has worked very hard to make this benefit a success, and I'll be damned if I leave after simply making an appearance."

"Hardly a simple appearance," Jared Ryker commented, his wry gaze raking the crowded auditorium. "What could be more visible than a front-row box? If we were any closer to the stage, we'd be part of the show."

"I'm head of the benefit committee. Besides, I always like to be seen in the best seat in any house," Nina said complacently. "And you shouldn't complain about giving me my own way in this. Consider yourself lucky I even consented to see you tonight. What other woman would welcome you back with open arms after such a long time without a word?"

"A benefit gala wasn't precisely what I had in mind when I called you this morning," Jared said. One long, graceful hand reached out to caress her silk-gowned thigh. "I had a rather more personal gala in mind." He watched almost objectively the slow smolder begin in her dark blue eyes. Nina had always been a woman who frankly enjoyed all aspects of her sexuality. Unless she

6

had changed since he'd last seen her, it should be relatively simple to arouse her enough to have her consent to leave, he thought. His hand continued to tease her thigh with feather-light strokes. "And I promise you that the benefits to both of us will be considerable."

She drew a deep breath, and for a moment he could read in her expression the ambivalence she felt. Then she decisively removed his hand from her thigh. "Later," she promised, shaking the shining bell of her ash-blond hair. "Quit trying to seduce me here, Jared. You know very well you're going to get what you want, what we both want . . . but later. And it will start in private, not public." A smile quickly replaced the slight scowl on her lovely face. "There was never any question in your mind that you would have me, was there?"

It was a very generous admission, and for a moment Jared felt a flicker of affection for Nina Bartlett. "You've always been very kind to me, Nina," he murmured. "I suppose I *was* hoping that you'd extend that lovely kindness again tonight."

"It's the only demonstration of kindness you'll accept from any woman, isn't it, Jared? And God knows we're all willing to give you what you want." The wistfulness in the expression on her face vanished, and she was once more the sophisticate, wearing a mask of cool composure. "But at my discretion, if you please."

He shrugged. "As you like." It wasn't worth pushing it, he thought, although he knew he could make her change her mind if he was determined to do so. He was more spoiled than he'd realized by the eager women who'd catered to his every whim. But that was why he'd left the chateau, wasn't it? He was sick to death of the almost cloying subservience, the gratification of his every wish. The knowledge that a woman of Nina's honesty and independence was only a short distance away, in New York, had sent him racing out of the chateau. Yet at the first hint of resistance from her, he was reacting with an arrogance he hadn't known he possessed. He turned back to her and smiled. "Just as long as that discretion doesn't extend to our gala later."

He saw a flicker of relief cross her face the instant before she met his smile with one of her own. "You won't be disappointed," she said softly. Her gaze traveled slowly over his features. "I don't suppose you're going to tell me where you got that gorgeous tan." He shook his head, and she sighed in resignation. "I didn't think so. All you need is an eye patch and a black orchid to make you the perfect mystery man." She frowned. "What the hell is the big secret? You're always showing up unexpectedly and then disappearing just as unexpectedly. Are you working for the government?"

"You could put it that way," he said, then leaned back in the wine-velvet-upholstered chair. "Does it matter?"

"I think I'm entitled to a little curiosity," she said dryly. "Four years ago you were partners with my father in the fastest-growing pharmaceutical company on the East Coast. Suddenly you sell your shares in the company. Later you drop out of sight completely." She raised a brow. "You don't think that's a bit unusual?"

"I doubt if Phillip missed me very much or for very long. He was always the executive brainpower behind the company."

"He missed you," Nina said. "You know damn well that without you the company would never have taken off as it did. You're fantastically brilliant, Jared. A genius of your caliber comes along perhaps once in a century. What the devil can the government offer you that we can't?"

"We?" he asked. "How very proprietary of you, Nina. Do I gather that you're doing more with your time than organizing charity benefits these days?"

She nodded. "I've become a personnel manager for Bartlett's Pharmaceuticals." She shrugged. "I was bored. I needed something else in my life."

"We all do," Jared said, his eyes fixed thoughtfully on her face. "And did you find it?"

"I think so." She suddenly grinned. "It would be a very brilliant feather in my corporate cap if I lured you back to the company, however."

"Lure is such a beautifully sensuous word," he drawled, "and I've already signaled my extreme willingness to let you lure me back to my hotel suite." His clear gray-eyes twinkled. "You're sure you wouldn't want to practice your wiles on me at once?"

"I can wait. And so can you, Jared. You might even find this gala quite fascinating." She tapped her program. "Tania Orlinov is dancing in *The Piper* tonight."

"Is that supposed to impress me?" He shrugged. "I don't recognize the name."

"Where have you been, on a deserted island, for God's sake?"

Close, very close. A smile was tugging at his lips as he replied, "You might say I've been a little out of touch. Is she the new rage, or something?"

She shook her head in amazement. "That's putting it conservatively. You must have read about her. There were stories in all the newspapers and magazines when she defected from the USSR three years ago."

"As I said, I've been out of touch. I'm afraid I was a little too busy to keep up with the arts."

"Then you're probably the only one in the world who hasn't heard about the 'Piper.'"

His lips curved mockingly. "Is that what she calls herself? How theatrical."

"I think you'll agree she lives up to the title, when you've seen her perform. She's exceptionally colorful, to say the least. There's a picture of her in the program. Do you think she's attractive?"

The face that gazed up at him from the program wasn't conventionally beautiful, but for almost a minute he wasn't conscious of the fact. He'd never seen anyone so totally vibrantly alive as the woman laughing out of that sterile black-and-white photo. Her large dark eyes were framed with extravagantly long lashes and blazed with a vitality so intense that it had the force of a blow; her full lips were curved and stretched in a smile of such elfin zest that it seemed to encompass all of humor and joy.

Annoyance surged through him. For God's sake, why should that face have such an effect on him? He'd known a hundred women more attractive than Tania Orlinov. There was no reason that she should be able to disturb his cool control more than any other woman. He forced himself to focus on her face, scrutinizing her features with analytical thoroughness. The cheekbones were definitely too high and the face too thin and fragile-looking. Her chin was a little too strong, and the dark wings of her brows above those enormous eyes only increased that elfin quality. Her long dark hair braided in a shining coronet should have lent her dignity, but instead it only served to make her look like a little girl playing fairy princess.

He wasn't a man who was attracted to pixies playing dress-up, he thought impatiently. He had always pre-ferred his women to be coolly sophisticated and volup-tuously sensual. As Tania Orlinov's face reflected neither of these qualities, it was totally unreasonable to feel such an explosive physical attraction the longer he looked at her picture.

He tossed the program back into Nina's lap. "I suppose you could say she has a certain fascination if you care for the type."

"I thought you'd be a bit more enthusiastic. And I had an idea she'd be very much your type. She's quite a remarkable woman."

"Remarkable?"

"You don't find many women who'd risk climbing the Andes in a snowstorm to defect. It took a great deal of courage to attempt that gambit, let alone to pull it off." Nina shrugged. "She almost didn't make it. She was suffering from hypothermia and frostbite when she stumbled into a village at the base of the mountain. The villagers thought she'd die long before they could get medical help or summon an official at the American Embassy in Santiago."

"But she didn't," Jared said softly. Why was he feeling this absurd tingle of pride? Somehow he knew it would take an enormous force to stem the vitality of that woman in the picture.

"No, she didn't." There was a glimmer of satisfaction in Nina's expression. "You *are* interested." She chuckled. "I knew you would be. You two really are a good deal alike, you know."

His brow lifted in surprise. "I can't say I'm flattered to be compared to a half-pint ballerina," he said dryly. "I'm afraid I can't perceive any similarities."

"You both have a fire burning in you," Nina said slowly. "The only difference is that Tania Orlinov's flame is burning free and bright, while yours is obscured, barely discernible. Oh, yes, my friend, despite your cool good manners and your sophisticated conversation, all very distancing, I assure you, still I can sense the fire is there . . . deep within you."

"What hogwash! I had no idea you had such a flair for the melodramatic, Nina." His smile mocked her. "But I do think I'm a little hurt that you consider me some kind of ice man."

"You're no such thing," she snapped. "And be honest, Jared. You don't give a damn what I think about you." For a moment her features revealed a flicker of regret, before she gave him a teasing grin. "Then, too, we both know what a satyr you are. I wouldn't dare insult your virility, or I'd be ravished before we got out of the taxi tonight." He expression was suddenly alight with curiosity. "Would you like to meet her after the performance?"

He shook his head. "Why do I feel that your next step will be arranging a blind date for us? I think I should be a bit insulted that you're not even a little jealous."

"What good would it do?" she asked serenely. "I know very well my place in your scheme of things. Besides, I'm quite safe being so marvelously civilized in this case. Rumor has it she's been Tyler Windloe's mistress for the last two years. Under those circumstances, you wouldn't consider it worth the bother."

"Tyler Windloe," he echoed. "The name's familiar. Should I know who he is?"

"Perhaps. He was a steel tycoon before he became interested in the arts. He is the primary patron of the American Repertory Ballet Company, and our little Piper is its brightest star. Well, do you want to go backstage during the intermission?"

"I'll let you know after I've seen your 'remarkable' little Russian perform."

"She's only half Russian—her mother was Hungarian," Nina said. The houselights were dimming, and she added in a whisper, "And I think you're about to experience just how remarkable she is."

The experience began even before the curtains swung open. The wild, haunting strains of a flute wove their magic in the darkness, teasing the senses with their beauty. The curtain slowly opened on a set as appealing as the music, to reveal the Piper, on a moonlit hilltop silhouetted against the night sky.

The Piper was dressed only in pale gray tights, his

supple muscular upper torso completely bare. He was more Apollo than Pan, but the anomaly only made the scene more poignantly beautiful.

Then the quiet mysticism of the picture erupted with the excitement of a star-burst, as a slight, fragile figure bounded on the scene with a grace that caught at the heart. Gowned in drifts of scarlet chiffon, wearing slippers instead of toe shoes, Tania Orlinov was all flame and litheness. She was sheer artistry in motion as she portrayed the role of the young girl caught in the spell of the Piper and his music while fiercely resisting the power of his magic. Then, just as she seemed to have lost, to have succumbed, she suddenly halted center stage. Her arms lifted entreatingly, as if begging her gods for strength. She drew a deep, shaky breath, and a ripple of shock seemed to pass through her body. Her hands moved with studied slowness to the crown of her head. She took off a tight snood, and her shining hair fell to her waist, creating a wild, sensuous cloak about her. And with a deliberateness that was a silent challenge, she turned to face the Piper on the hilltop.

What came next was the most passionate dance of seduction that Jared had ever seen. She was Delilah and Salome in one as she played the enchantress and tempted the Piper down from the hilltop. In the slow and graceful adagio of the *pas de deux* that followed, she brought the Piper within her spell. Then their conflicts erupted in the maiden's and Piper's variations, where each danced to show superiority over the other. Finally, in a frenzied coda, just as it appeared she might triumph, she suddenly wilted, falling to her knees in despair, power ebbing from her. There was an unforgettable moment then, as if frozen in time, when the Piper, breathing heavily, every line of his body electrified with triumph, looked down at the fragile figure of his defeated adversary. Slowly raising the flute to his lips, he began to play once more his haunting siren call. He turned and moved back up to his hilltop while his captive rose jerkily to her feet and moved sluggishly after him, like a puppet pulled by hidden strings. The Piper paused at the crest of the hill to look back and ascertain that his captive was still enthralled, and the music of his flute became a gloating paean of triumph. His dominant figure disappeared from view as he moved down the other side of the hill, but the siren call of his mystical flute still drifted back over the maiden.

The scarlet-clad figure was poignantly fragile and alone. She drooped in despair as she reached the crest of the hill. She paused there, her head cocked, listening to the fading music of the Piper. She slowly raised her head, and there was an expression of such joyous mischievousness on her face that it came as a shock to every person in the audience! She whirled in a graceful series of turns before performing a *grand jeté* with exultant exuberance.

Then, her throat arched, her body singing with triumph, her lips parted once more in that smile of secret joyous victory, she leaped from view as she followed the Piper who thought *he* was the god.

There was a moment of dead silence before the crowded auditorium erupted into almost hysterical applause. It rose in volume as Tania and her partner appeared hand in hand to receive the adulation that was surging like a thundering wave from the audience.

"Well," Nina asked archly, her amused gaze on the absorbed face of the man next to her. "Do you want to go backstage?"

He did not hear her. He could see the rise and fall of the dancer's small, perfect breasts beneath the sheer scarlet chiffon and the glow of the perspiration that beaded her forehead as she took her bows. He had a sudden impulse to gather her small body close and wipe her brow. That strong surge of protective tenderness caught him off-balance and filled him with impatience. It was as unreasonable and unwanted as the wild desire he'd experienced while she was dancing. He pulled his gaze away from Tania Orlinov with an effort.

Nina's hand was on his arm. "Jared, *do* you want to go backstage?"

"Why not?" he asked with deliberate carelessness. "As you say, she's remarkable."

Tania shivered as the stage door down the corridor was opened, permitting cool October air to rush into the hall where she was standing outside her dressing room. She made a polite reply to the little old lady with the reserved expression and the razor-sharp eyes of a chairman of the board. What was her name? Leslie Vanning. That was it. And she *was* the chairman of the board of some cultural foundation or other, and Tyler had said she must be nice to her.

That shouldn't be difficult. There were very few people Tania met whom she didn't like. She had the idea that despite Mrs. Vanning's crustiness, the old lady would be dynamic. But tonight Tania had no desire to exert herself by probing that chilly façade.

Chilly. She wished she hadn't thought of that particular adjective. It reminded her how uncomfortable she was in the drafty hall, wearing only a flimsy chiffon costume. Well, it didn't matter. Another few minutes of accepting congratulations from the little crowd around her and she could plead weariness and disappear into her dressing room. She'd discovered early in her career that it was far easier to hold court outside her dressing room than to try to get balletomanes to leave once they were firmly ensconced.

"Tania, you were absolutely superb. It was a complete triumph for you." The voice was familiar, and she looked over her shoulder to see Nina Bartlett smiling at her with the warm sincerity that characterized her.

"You thought so?" she asked. An impish grin lit her face. "So did I." Her dark eyes were dancing. "But then, I had to be utterly magnificent tonight. Your committee charged two hundred dollars a ticket, and that audience would have torn me apart if I'd disappointed them."

Leslie Vanning was quietly edging away and Tania was turning back to say a courteous farewell when a man's tuxedo jacket was suddenly draped over her bare shoulders. Her eyes widened in surprise as she heard Nina Bartlett's amused laugh behind her, and she turned to gaze at the man who'd appeared at Nina's side.

"How very gallant of you, Jared," Nina Bartlett drawled. "I had no idea you were so chivalrous." The amusement in her voice warred with the expression on her face as she glanced at the man next to her.

She cared for him, Tania realized, experiencing a sudden rush of pity. Though she didn't know Nina Bartlett well, she'd found her very pleasant, and it was clear her companion was not a safe man with whom to become emotionally involved.

"This is Dr. Jared Ryker, Tania," Nina continued lightly. "He found your performance as fascinating as the rest of us did."

"I'm happy you enjoyed it, Dr. Ryker," Tania said. She unconsciously drew the coat that was still warm from his body closer about her as she looked up to meet eyes that were surely the coldest and most piercing that she'd ever encountered. Clear-crystal gray that was almost silver, they were doubly startling in the golden darkness of his face. Cold? No, that wasn't quite right. They reflected the smoldering intensity that dry ice might possess, which could burn at a scant touch. She was vaguely conscious of a broad forehead, wide, Slavic cheekbones, a strong chin. His lips were surprisingly sensuous in that almost brutally powerful bone structure, and there was a wryly cynical set to his mouth that was a surprise in itself. Heavy dark hair threaded with the faintest silver framed his face. "The Piper is my favorite role."

"I can see why," he drawled. For an instant there was a distinct twinkle in those icy eyes. "It not only gives you a showcase for your dancing but allows you to act as well." He raised a brow, mocking her. "I gathered from the rather surprising ending that the audience was supposed to assume that you were really the Piper in your little ballet."

She made a face. "My acting must not have been all that good if you have any doubts on that score." For some reason his mockery filled her with a strange unease and caused her voice to sharpen. "Of course I'm the Piper. Anyone could see that I was totally in control."

"Were you?" His silver gaze, narrowed on her face, inspired a queer breathlessness in her. "Then, why did you follow him?"

"It was a feint," she said impatiently. "The maiden was only pretending to give in, so that she could catch the Piper off-guard at a later time and assure herself of total victory." She had never had to explain before. Why couldn't the man see what was transparently obvious to everyone else?

"Perhaps," he said softly, his glance running over her features lingeringly, though noting her annoyance. "Or perhaps the Piper had grown bored with easy victories and wanted to keep the flame maiden as a constant challenge to ward off that boredom. It seems quite likely that a powerful sorcerer could feed a simple maiden just enough lure to make her want to follow him without converting her into a zombie." He was gazing at her inquiringly. "Don't you consider that a valid hypothesis?"

"No, I do not," she said crossly. She shrugged out of his jacket and held it out to him. She certainly wasn't cold now. On the contrary, she felt almost feverish. "It's completely ridiculous. There's no question whatever that *I'm* the Piper."

"*You?*" he asked pointedly, then took his jacket and draped it carelessly over his arm. "How can you be so sure?"

As she opened the door of the dressing room, she slanted a glance at him that was redolent of triumph and a touch of mischief. "Because *I* did the choreography, Dr. Ryker." She shut the door in his face with a soft click.

Tania leaned against the door for a moment, still feeling that quickening sense of excitement that was flooding her with a heady exhilaration. Anger and resentment were causing this sudden electrifying awareness, she assured herself. She had spoken only a few words to the man, and there was no possibility she could be attracted to an individual like Ryker. Oh, perhaps in a physical sense. There was no denying that he possessed a virile sensuality that was overpoweringly evident even at first glance.

She drew a deep breath and consciously tried to relax the muscles of her stomach that were knotted with tension. She was reacting to him like a teenager. She had known attractive men before whose sex appeal was just as potent as Jared Ryker's. She had recognized at once that he possessed a power and dominance that could be dangerous to any woman who couldn't respond with equal strength. She had even felt a touch of pity for Nina, who was obviously a little in love with him.

She moved briskly away from the door and crossed the room to seat herself at the dressing table. She had no doubt she had the strength to take on a dozen Jared Rykers. However, she had no desire to do so—not even to engage in a preliminary skirmish with the man. She liked her life very well just as it was. After spending a lifetime of dancing to other people's tunes, she was experiencing a fierce joy in playing the Piper and controlling her own destiny. She took a dollop of cleansing cream from the jar and began to remove her stage makeup. She'd had enough danger and excitement in her life in the past, and she had no need of any in the future. Let the Nina Bartletts of the world get their fingers burned playing with the fiery and enigmatic Dr. Jared Ryker.

"It was a mistake, wasn't it?" Nina asked, as the doors of the elevator swished open at the ninth floor and Jared ushered her out. When he didn't answer but merely escorted her down the plush carpeted corridor toward his suite, she added, "My fault, I suppose. My curiosity always did get me into hot water, and I wanted to see the two of you together. I think I got more than I bargained for. You haven't spoken three sentences since we left the theater."

"Haven't I?" He roused himself from his abstraction to smile down at her. "But then, when have we ever needed words?" His hand moved caressingly down the soft skin of her forearm to the pulse point at her wrist. Nina's wrists had always been exquisitely sensitive, he recalled. He could feel the leap of response beneath the gentle friction of his thumb. "You're being a bit over-imaginative, you know."

She pulled her wrist away from his touch with a sudden force that startled him. "Stop it, Jared," she said sharply. "We both know you'll have no problem seducing me when the time comes." Her blue gaze was direct. "But I find I have a curious reluctance to being a stand-in for another woman. She really turned you on, didn't she?"

He didn't pretend to misunderstand. "Yes, she

turned me on. And, yes, I'd like to go to bed with her."
His gaze narrowed. "I think you expected that reaction
from me, didn't you, Nina? It wasn't just curiosity that
led you to introduce us."

"No, it wasn't," she agreed bluntly, her lips curving
in a bittersweet smile. "I think I wanted to see you really
tied up in knots over a woman." She drew a deep, shaky
breath. "I wanted you to want something or someone
you couldn't have." She shrugged. "I didn't suspect I'd
react on such a primitive level, though."

"Do you want me to take you home?" he asked
quietly.

There was a flicker of pained indecision in her
expression before she smiled with a brightness that
didn't quite reach her eyes. "Why should I go home? I
think I have enough skill to make you forget a fleeting
attraction for a pretty little ballet dancer."

They had paused before the paneled oak door of his
suite. Now he unlocked it and stepped aside for her to
enter. She hesitated a moment, her gaze flicking up to
meet his. "Are you going to see her again?"

He shook his head. "There's no place for a woman
like Tania Orlinov in my life at the moment." God knew
that was the truth, he thought wearily. The next six
months were going to be difficult enough without an
emotional complication on the scale that the dancer
represented. She had touched him in a fashion he'd
never experienced before. She had aroused not only an
odd protective tenderness but the most intense desire
he'd ever known. Even during that brief interval in the
hall he'd had problems keeping his hands off her. He'd
wanted to brush those little bits of chiffon aside and hold
the swell of her small breasts in his hands. He'd found
himself wondering if her nipples would be as dusky pink
as the flush that had mounted to her cheeks when he'd
been sparring with her. He frowned impatiently. All he

needed was an obsessive affair with that defiant, black-eyed pixie. "No, I'm not going to contact her again."

His hand moved automatically to the light switch on the wall to the left of the door. But the living room was already illuminated by the ivory-shaded lamp on the end table across the room, and he unconsciously tensed, his muscles coiled in readiness. Then he exhaled resignedly as he recognized the fastidiously neat figure of the man in the gray Brooks Brothers suit who rose slowly to his feet and put the crossword magazine he'd been working on face down on the end table beside him.

"Hello, Betz," Jared said as he shut the door behind him. "I don't suppose I need bother to ask how you got in. Was it bribery or forced entry?" He glanced at the lock on the door. "Bribery."

Edward Betz gave him a reproachful look. His large brown eyes had always reminded Jared of a mournful Basset hound. "You shouldn't have left the chateau, Dr. Ryker. The senator was very unhappy that you hadn't obeyed his instructions."

"The senator doesn't give me instructions, Betz," Jared said softly, a thread of steel beneath the silkiness of his tone. "He suggests politely. Very politely." He turned to Nina, who was obviously filled with curiosity. "It seems I have a little business to conduct." His hand in the small of her back urged her forward. "Why don't you wait for me in the bedroom? I won't be long."

She nodded reluctantly and slowly crossed the sitting room to disappear into the bedroom. When the door had closed behind her, Jared strode forward to stand facing Betz. Carelessly he tossed the program he'd been carrying on the end table beside Betz's crossword book and loosened his black tie impatiently. "Okay, let's have it. Why the hell are you here, Betz?"

"I could ask the same of you, Dr. Ryker," Ed Betz said stolidly. "You know you shouldn't be here. It's not

safe for you in New York. There's no way we can give you
the security that's required in these surroundings. The
senator is very worried about this move of yours."

"How unfortunate," Jared said ironically, his lips
twisting. "I agreed to accept Sam Corbett's hospitality for
twelve weeks while he prepared the way with the
powers-that-be in Washington. That doesn't mean I
intend to let myself be imprisoned in his Canadian
version of Neuschwanstein. I'll go and come as I see fit."
He paused before continuing deliberately. "And I won't
tolerate your interference, Betz. If I were you, I'd go
back to Washington and tell Corbett that."

Betz shook his head, his thinning brown hair, with
its precise side part, gleaming in the lamplight. "I'm not
going back to Washington. The senator says that I'm to
replace Jenkins as head of security at the chateau." He
frowned. "This is really most inconvenient, Dr. Ryker.
That leaves Mr. Corbett temporarily without a security
chief in the capital. It would simplify matters enormously if you'd just agree to return to the chateau until
Senator Corbett can arrange for you to be safely installed
in a house in D.C."

"I regret that I'm complicating your life to such an
extent," Jared drawled, "but I'm afraid you're just going
to have to adjust to the situation and make the best of it."
Good Lord, the man was stubborn. When he'd first met
Ed Betz, he'd wondered how a man as brilliant as Sam
Corbett had ever been so stupid as to hire Betz as his
head of security. The man was so slow as to border on
retardation, and he had about as much initiative as a
slug. It hadn't taken him long to realize the qualities that
Corbett had seen and appreciated in Ed Betz, however.
Ed Betz was completely, almost fanatically loyal to his
employer, and he possessed the obstinacy and determination of a bulldog.

That obstinacy was definitely in full flower at the

moment. "It isn't as if we haven't provided you with everything you could possibly want, Dr. Ryker," Betz persisted. "We have orders that you're to have anything you ask for. You know that."

"Yes, I know that. And I'm finding that three weeks of having everything I want is two weeks too long. I'm so damned bored I'm about ready to set myself up as a target for those Chinese you're so paranoid about, just to stir up a little excitement."

"That would be very foolish," Betz said, frowning uncertainly. "You're joking, aren't you, Dr. Ryker?"

"Yes, I'm joking. I have no intention of becoming a victim any more then I intend to tolerate having my activities circumscribed." His expression was set and grim. "And now that I've made everything crystal clear, you'll have to excuse me. I have a lady waiting."

Betz's brown basset gaze was fixed on the door behind which Nina had disappeared. "Was it the women?" he asked abruptly. "We ascertained from your dossier that you would require a woman frequently. Weren't the women we supplied you with satisfactory?"

"How could they help but be 'satisfactory?' The call girls you invited to the chateau were all beautiful, talented, and willing to do anything."

"You didn't want them to be willing?" Betz asked, his brow wrinkled in puzzlement. "If you had explained that to them, I'm sure they—"

"Oh, for God's sake, will you get out of here, Betz?"

Betz's gaze wandered once again to the bedroom door. "Does she please you more? Perhaps we could persuade her to come to the chateau."

"No!" Jared drew a deep breath. There was no use letting himself become any more exasperated. Betz was as thick as an ox. "Listen very carefully, Betz. I do not want the lady at the chateau even if she'd consent to come. And charming as she is, she couldn't persuade me to stay on your mountaintop even to accommodate her. No woman could." He shifted restlessly, and his glance fell on the program on the end table. Tania Orlinov's face was gazing up at him, revealing that marvelous *joie de vivre* of hers, and for a moment it arrested his attention so completely he forgot what he was saying. He looked up to see Betz staring at him. "Do you understand, Betz?" he finished crisply.

Ed Betz nodded absently, his expression thoughtful. "Whatever you say, Dr. Ryker. You'll return to the chateau soon?"

"In a day or so." Jared was moving swiftly toward the bedroom. "Lock the door on your way out."

Edward Betz watched the door close behind Ryker, his expression still absorbed. He turned away slowly and picked up the book of crossword puzzles from the end table and the program Jared had seemed so drawn to. He studied it for a moment before tucking it carefully between the pages of his book and closing it. He turned out the top light, obediently locked the front door behind him, and quietly left the hotel suite.

"I love your body," Nina murmured softly, pushing the crisp white dress shirt from his shoulders. Her hands moved deftly to his belt. "It comes as such a lovely surprise every time. With your clothes on you look so civilized, almost elegantly thin, yet when I peel everything away you're hard and powerful." She pressed her lips to the whipcord muscles of his upper arms. "So strong. I like to know that strength is there." She was pushing his pants and briefs over his hips, her tongue licking at his nipple. "I like to know that you have the power to break me if you want to." Her soft hands were kneading the tightness of his buttocks.

My God, Jared thought, *he should be ready to*

explode by now and he wasn't feeling a damn thing! He was as unmoved as a block of ice.

"It makes me so hot to feel all that leashed violence inside you."

"Violence?" he asked, frowning. "You make me sound like the Marquis de Sade. I don't recall ever using violence on you or any other woman."

"You haven't," she said, rubbing her full breasts against the hair-roughened muscles of his chest. "You never lose control, no matter how difficult I make it for you."

He had to think of something, anything, to rid himself of this blasted indifference.

"You're the perfect lover, Jared. Gentle, considerate, and so damned skilled you drive me out of my mind." Her tongue licked delicately at the pulse pounding in the hollow of his throat.

Dark hair flowing to a tiny waist, small, thrusting breasts barely covered by sheer scarlet draperies. He felt the welcome stiffening in his loins with immense relief. Then, as he realized what he was doing, he instinctively rejected it. Nina deserved better than being used as a substitute for Tania Orlinov. She was no whore, but a woman who was expecting to receive pleasure as generous as the pleasure she was willing to give him. He wouldn't think of the dancer. He'd concentrate on the act itself, feed erotic stimuli to keep desire hot for the woman kneeling before him on the bed.

"But the violence is there waiting," she whispered, "and one of these nights I'm going to break that control and drive you a little crazy too."

Nina always found it exciting to talk as a form of foreplay, and he usually had the patience to let her have her way. But if he was going to keep this urgency and provide her with the satisfaction she deserved, there must be no delay tonight.

"I had no idea you were into force, Nina," he drawled as he pushed her back on the bed. He quickly stripped away the rest of his clothes and joined her. "I'll have to see if I can't oblige you."

Her blue eyes were wide with surprise as he gently parted her thighs and settled between them without the customary preliminaries. He thrust forward into her welcoming warmth, and she gave a gasp that was half surprise, half satisfaction, before her legs curled eagerly around his hips to help him.

As always, Nina took his manhood quite comfortably. There were many women who couldn't, who had to be carefully prepared before they were able to accept him. Tania appeared so tiny, with that fragile, pixie delicacy. He'd have to be very careful not to hurt her, to be especially gentle until she was used to him. He felt himself swell in response to the thought of that tightness surrounding him, before he realized that he was doing it again. He firmly banished Tania Orlinov from his mind and concentrated on pleasing the woman beneath his body.

There was little doubt that he'd succeeded some minutes later as he held Nina gently in his arms, his hand stroking the ash-blond hair of the head on his shoulder. "I almost did it, didn't I?" she gasped. "I could feel it in you, Jared. There was something different tonight."

"Yes, there was something different tonight," he said, his voice gentle. "Now, go to sleep, Nina."

She sighed happily as she curled up against him, her lids closing drowsily.

His hand continued to stroke her hair even after her breathing had deepened and he knew she was sleeping. His eyes were alert and wide awake in his dark face. Something different? Yes, despite all his efforts there had been something different tonight. Tania Orlinov's hold on his emotions was stronger than he'd imagined. There was no question in his mind now that she was going to belong to him. Only the timing was in doubt.

He was suddenly as impatient and restless as a boy. He didn't want to be wise and discreet. He didn't want to wait until there wasn't an object or a person on the face of the earth he couldn't have just by lifting a finger. For a little while it was probably going to be almost like being a god, he thought distastefully. He'd never wanted that kind of power. All he'd ever wanted was to be left alone so he could work in peace. He wasn't worried about the loneliness that degree of power would bring—he was used to that. He couldn't remember a time when he wasn't conscious of that aloneness, which was now a part of him. No, it was the boredom that he feared the most. Without challenge a man's mind and spirit could wither and die even if his body lived on.

He shrugged restlessly, carefully removing his arm from about Nina Bartlett's shoulders and shifting himself away from the warmth of her body. Despite his impatience he'd have to wait for his pleasure. Tania Orlinov would still be there for him in six months' time. To take her now wouldn't only be unwise, it could possibly constitute an actual physical danger for both of them.

It was an entirely sane, prudent decision, typical of his usual cool, analytical approach to life. That being the case, it was entirely illogical for him to lie awake for the next several hours, his silver eyes gazing into the darkness and his memory replaying the hauntingly melodic strains of the Piper.

Chapter 2

"A hundred thousand dollars?" Tania gasped, her eyes widening with shock. "That's what you said, isn't it?" She glanced down at the card in her hand. "Mr. Betz."

He nodded. "We realize your time is very valuable, Miss Orlinov. We expect to have to compensate you accordingly."

"I see," Tania said slowly as she sank into the padded straight chair before her dressing table. Her dark eyes were bright with curiosity as she motioned the funny little man into a wing chair across the dressing room. "How very interesting. And what am I supposed to do to earn this hundred thousand dollars?"

Edward Betz sat down in the chair she'd indicated, his highly polished black shoes placed precisely in front of him. "It will be a relatively simple task. We just want you to act as companion to a gentleman for the next six weeks. We'll issue a certified check for half the amount in advance and the remainder at the completion of the assignment."

"Companion?" she echoed blankly. She absently wiped the nape of her neck with the hand towel draped around her shoulders. This interview was becoming increasingly bizarre. Her gaze traveled warily over her visitor's conservatively dressed figure. There had been nothing in the manner of the man's approach to indicate he was something of a lunatic. That was the reason she'd invited him into her dressing room when he'd shown up after rehearsal this morning. But reasonable men didn't go around offering a hundred thousand dollars so casually. "What kind of companion are we speaking of, Mr. Betz? And why me?"

"It has to be you because the gentleman in question seems to find you totally fascinating, for some reason." He frowned, as if trying to puzzle it out. "No one else seems to be able to hold his interest. He requested video tapes of all your performances two weeks ago, and last weekend he came back to New York to see you dance." His lips tightened. "We knew then that measures would have to be taken to rectify the situation."

"I'm happy to know that I have such a devoted fan," Tania said lightly. "But I'm afraid I'm not available for private engagements, even when the inducement is so great. Your client will just have to be content with seeing my performances from the third row on the aisle."

"That's not possible." Betz's voice was clipped. "We can't permit him to return to New York." He scowled. "The remuneration is more than generous, but it's still open to negotiation. If we increase the amount, will you reconsider?"

"*More* than a hundred thousand dollars?" Her lips quirked. "I'm tempted to see just how high you'd go, Mr. Betz, but I feel I must warn you that as fantastic a performer as I undoubtedly am, you'd be grossly overpaying me."

Betz's face was expressionless. "Money is irrelevant in this case, Miss Orlinov. And it wasn't your skill as a dancer we had in mind."

"No?" She was puzzled. Then, as he continued to stare at her with the same bland look on his face, she understood. "You want me to go to bed with your client? You want me to be his mistress for the next six weeks?" It was as wildly unbelievable as the conversation that had gone before, but the funny little man nodded with perfect seriousness. It was too much for her, and she threw back her head and roared with laughter, her face alight, her dark eyes dancing. God, she was glad she'd consented to see this solemn little man, even if he was a bit crazy. She'd not enjoyed anything so much in a long time.

When she finally sobered enough to control herself, Ed Betz was still gazing at her with those expressionless, puppy-dog eyes and waiting patiently. "I'm sorry, Mr. Betz," she said, her lips still twitching. "I'm afraid I can't accept your client's offer. I make it a practice never to perform unless I can excel in a role." She cleared her throat to mask the laughter that persisted in bubbling. "In this case, I don't believe I have the required training for the job. I'm sure you'll be able to find someone else with far better qualifications if you make the effort."

He shook his head. "We've tried that," he said gloomily. "This isn't a spur-of-the-moment decision, Miss Orlinov. I've considered several other possibilities, but I've come to the conclusion that it has to be you. How much more can I give you to make you change your mind? The sky's the limit."

She couldn't suppress the chuckle any longer. The man was absolutely priceless. She shook her head firmly as she stood up. "I'm afraid that my decision is final, Mr. Betz," she said gently. "You'll have to look elsewhere."

He must have stared at her for a full minute before he got reluctantly to his feet. "You're sure I can't persuade you to change your mind?" he asked with a frown. "We're prepared to pay a great deal of money, you know."

"I have enough money for all my needs at the

moment, Mr. Betz," she said solemnly, her dark eyes twinkling. "And having money is not really one of my top priorities. As I said, you'll have to find someone who makes a specialty of that sort of thing."

"That's regrettable," he said slowly. "It's going to make things much more complicated."

"I'm afraid you'll have to excuse me now, Mr. Betz," she said softly. "I have an engagement for lunch." She waved her hand to indicate her leotard-clad figure. "And you can see that I still have to shower and dress. Thank you for dropping by." A mischievous smile tugged at her lips. "If I ever decide to change my vocation, I'll be sure to get in touch with you. Good luck in finding a replacement."

He was moving across the room to the door. "A replacement won't be possible," he muttered obstinately. "It has to be you, Miss Orlinov." The door closed softly behind him.

There was a lingering smile still on her face as Tania trailed him to the door and shot home the lock. She stripped off her leotard, slippers, and caramel-colored leg warmers before padding toward the adjoining bathroom. Lord, the man was peculiar. There was no way he could be for real, but it had been an interesting episode to brighten up a dull morning. She turned on the shower and tested the temperature quickly before stepping beneath the warm flow. It was one of the truly wonderful aspects of life that all manner of fascinating things happened. There was always something exciting just around the next corner if you took the trouble to look for it. For instance, there was her luncheon date today. A grin of delighted anticipation lit her face as she contemplated the afternoon to come.

Forty minutes later she glanced in the mirror as she was preparing to leave the dressing room. In the worn, faded blue jeans and tennis shoes she looked about sixteen. The shapeless thigh-length sweater in fuzzy pink angora was warm and comfortable, but no one would ever call it alluring. She had fixed her dark, waist-length hair in a single thick braid over one shoulder, and it contributed to her youthful air. She grinned, deeply amused. If Edward Betz's client could see her now, no further discouragement would be needed to convince him to look elsewhere for a mistress! Laughing, she shook her head and turned away from the mirror. The whole incident had been wildly ridiculous, and it was time she dismissed it from her mind. Besides, her appearance might not be calculated to rouse lust in a doddering old recluse, but she was sure her escort would find it more than satisfactory.

Barry Montclair opened the door of the charming brownstone, a grave smile lighting his thin face. "Hi, Tania. Mama's in the shower. I'm supposed to entertain you until she comes down." His voice had a gravelly hoarseness endearingly odd in a five-year-old. Then as if remembering his manners, he added with quaint formality, "Won't you please come in?"

"I'd be delighted," Tania said with equal formality as she entered the high-ceilinged, mahogany book-lined foyer. She'd always loved this old house, with its air of mellow warmth. She glanced up the gold-carpeted staircase to the upper level with a sigh of impatience. Marguerite was a perfectly delightful human being, as well as being her best friend, but she had absolutely no sense of time. Tania chided herself to be more under-standing. Marguerite took advantage of Tania's weekly excursions with Barry to snatch a few hours alone with her husband, Michael, who was the company's principal choreographer. Barry's mama was probably expending a lot of effort right now to look especially glamorous for Michael. She looked down at Barry. "And how do you suggest we go about entertaining ourselves, Master Montclair?"

He closed the door, carefully fastening the chain lock. He cocked his head consideringly. "Well, we could look at the picture book Daddy gave me yesterday. It has all kinds of dinosaurs and legends and junk. He said since you were taking me to the Museum of Natural History today, it was only sensible to have some background."

"Only sensible," she agreed solemnly, her dark eyes twinkling. Marguerite always said that Barry was five going on seventy. In addition to his precocity he was totally adorable in many other ways. In blue jeans and *Return of the Jedi* sweatshirt, his sturdy diminutive form gave the appearance of being both tough and oddly vulnerable. Barry's acorn-brown hair was shining with the silky luster found only in very young children, and she had a sudden urge to run her fingers through it caressingly. She restrained the impulse. Barry's dignity would be much affronted. "I have a better idea. Would you like to see the present I brought you?"

Barry's hazel eyes lit up with interest, and he nodded eagerly.

"Good," Tania said, walking briskly to the staircase and plopping down on the fourth step. She patted the step beside her. "Then, come over here and we'll take a look at it." She opened her large, cream-colored shoulder bag and drew out a small, cloth-covered package. "I bought it for you in Chinatown the other day." He was beside her on the step now, cuddling close to her in his eagerness, his sturdy warmth pressing into the curve of her arm. She ventured an unobtrusive hug as he quickly tore the wrapping off the gift. It was odd how infinitely dear the weight of a child could feel. Odd and rather wonderful.

A puzzled frown creased Barry's forehead. "What is

it?" His careful finger touched one of the clear crystal prisms hung on a glittering silver chain. There was a tiny, exquisitely painted violet on each prism. "What do I do with it?"

"It's a wind chime," Tania said softly, her own finger touching a prism with caressing delicacy. "We're going to hang it on a branch of the tree in your courtyard, in the back. Then, whenever the wind blows, it will make lovely music for you. Wind chimes are very special, Barry. They can do all kinds of wonderful things. They give you pleasure, they soothe away your pain. Sometimes they can even help to save your life. Wind chimes are *màgia*."

Barry's gaze was suddenly alert. "That's a foreign word, isn't it? Jamie said you were a foreigner. What does it mean, Tania?" A few years older than Barry, Jamie was the little boy who lived next door.

"It's a Hungarian word meaning magic," she answered. "And I'm not a foreigner. I'm Hungarian, but I'm soon going to be an American citizen like my friend Barry."

"Jamie says you're Russian and your papa was a colonel in the Russian Army before he was killed in Afgh—"

"Jamie is wrong," she said tersely, her face clouding. "My father may have been Russian, but *I'm* Hungarian." She drew a deep breath and forced a smile. "I'll tell you all about it some other time. Right now I think we'd better go out back and hang up these wind chimes, don't you?"

When Marguerite Montclair made an appearance in the courtyard a short while later, Tania was just climbing down from the oak tree, while Barry sat cross-legged on the ground below, supervising her descent with ponderous instructions and multiple shouts of warning as she carefully traversed her way through the branches.

Barry spared his mother a brief glance before resuming his duties. "Hi, Mom. Tania brought me a wind chime."

"So I see," Marguerite said as she watched apprehensively while Tania negotiated the last few feet of a branch before she jumped lightly to the ground. "Was it necessary to hang the blasted thing at the very top of the tree? You could have been hurt, Tania."

"Nonsense," Tania said, rubbing her hands briskly on her jeans. "I'm a world-class tree climber, and I had Barry down here choreographing my every move. You can tell Michael that in twenty years his son is going to give him some stiff competition." She grinned at Barry, who still sat on the ground, and he grinned in response. "We're an unbeatable team, aren't we?" He nodded contentedly, his eyes on the prisms glittering in the sunlight high above them. "And it had to be high up so Barry could just open his bedroom window and hear the chimes."

"I can see how vitally important that would be." Marguerite's tone was soft, revealing her warm affection for Tania. "Sometimes I think you're just as young as Barry." She reached out her hand and pulled her son to his feet. "Now that you've accomplished this major undertaking, suppose you go change your clothes and wash up, young man. Tania will wait for you here." She dropped down onto the redwood seat that encircled the tree and watched Barry run up the stone steps and inside the screen door. "Sit down and relax, Tania. Heaven knows you won't get much opportunity to do so this afternoon. Children are absolutely hyper—especially when they're out on a jaunt." She made a face. "You spoil him, you know. He takes advantage of you."

"I enjoy it." Tania sat down and stretched her legs out lazily before her. "How can he take advantage of me when I enjoy it as much as he does?" She darted her friend a mischievous glance. "You're aware, of course, that I'm completely in love with him."

"Well, I'm glad there's one member of the masculine gender who can stir a response from you," Marguerite commented. "Poor Tyler has been having a difficult enough time of it."

"You know very well I'd make Tyler perfectly miserable if I let him talk me into a commitment," Tania said with a grin. "He likes his life very much as it is. I may add a little occasional color, but my flamboyance would grate on him unmercifully if he had to put up with it on a daily basis."

"Then, why not find someone else?" Marguerite asked. "You're absolutely nuts about kids. Isn't it time that you had a child of your own?"

"Why should I bother, when I can borrow a charmer like Barry whenever I feel the urge? There's plenty of time for that later. I have a career that keeps me pretty busy at the moment." Her gaze was suddenly thoughtful. "What about you, Marguerite? From what I hear, you were considered an exceptional dancer before you married Michael. Didn't you ever regret giving it up when you became pregnant with Barry?"

"You're damn right I did," Marguerite said bluntly. "I still do sometimes." She shrugged. "It was a question of choices. You know how demanding a dancer's life is, Tania. I wanted to be with my son during these first important years. I couldn't have both." Her lips twisted. "Unfortunately, a dancer is only in her prime physically for a pitifully short time. It will be too late for me to go back to dancing by the time Barry doesn't need me any more. Hell yes, I regret it." She glanced at Tania's stricken face, and suddenly she grinned. "But not enough to give up Michael and Barry. They're a pretty potent argument for the life of domestic bliss."

"Yes, they would be," Tania said softly. "I might

almost be tempted to take the step myself to have a darling like Barry."

Marguerite's lips curved in amusement. "You're putting the cart before the horse, aren't you? I believe, even in this day of test-tube babies, a man is still essential to initiate the procedure." Marguerite's eyes were twinkling. "Can't you think of anyone you might consider for the job?"

Cool silver eyes burning in a golden, rough-hewn face. Now, what idiocy had made that mental picture emerge suddenly? Tania thought impatiently. She had seen Jared Ryker for only a few minutes, and that had been over two weeks ago. Why should she remember that face with such vivid clarity now? "Nary a one," she said lightly. "So I guess I'll have to settle for being an adopted aunt." Her face lit up with sudden mischief. "Though there is one possibility. Are you sure that rich old man you told me about is dead?"

"What rich old man?" Marguerite's brow creased in puzzlement.

"The one with all the hair and the long fingernails," Tania said vaguely.

"Howard Hughes?" Marguerite asked. "Well if he's not there's a passel of heirs and a battery of lawyers who are going to be very disappointed. Why?"

"He's the only rich old man I can think of who would be eccentric enough to pay a fortune in dollars for my small fair body." She cast a rueful glance down at her slight form in the shapeless sweater. "Though I can't imagine even him being that eccentric."

Marguerite shook her head dazedly. "You've lost me somewhere. Go back and start over. Who's offered to pay a fortune for your body?"

Her eyes dancing with amusement, Tania related in detail her interview with Edward Betz. "I may never get an offer like that again," she ended, her lips quirking. "Do you think I should have taken him up on it?"

"I think you should have socked him in the nose," Marguerite said indignantly. "I can't see why in hell you're so amused. Why aren't you insulted?"

Tania shrugged. "Why should I be? Everyone has his own set of values. That money probably meant a lot to that old man. If anything, I should be complimented."

"Tania, you're absolutely hopeless." Marguerite sighed. "You never react as I think you're going to. I'm surprised that you didn't take the old pervert up on his offer just to soothe his fevered brow."

"I might have," Tania said with a grin, "if I hadn't gotten the impression that wasn't the portion of his anatomy that was fevered." She chuckled as she got to her feet. "Besides, I had another commitment—to my favorite man. And now I think I'd better go and get him, so we can be on our way." She checked her watch. "It's almost one now. I'll drop Barry back here at five. That will give me an hour to get to my photography class."

"My God, Tania, don't you ever rest?" Marguerite asked. She frowned as her gaze traveled critically over Tania's slight form. "You look as though you're going to blow away any minute. Have you lost weight?"

"Perhaps a little, but not enough to matter." She lifted a brow. "And why should I rest if I'm not tired?"

"Because you *should* be tired, damn it," Marguerite said crossly. "Not only do you have rehearsals and actual performances every day, but you're always pushing yourself to go to some class or other. You don't even allow yourself time to breathe."

"I like to learn new things," Tania protested. "It's not as if I looked at it as some kind of chore. It's terribly exciting to learn new skills."

"You're also going to find it terribly exhausting if you don't slow down," Marguerite said grimly. She held up her hand as Tania opened her mouth to protest. "Don't tell me. I've heard it all before. There's nothing for me to worry about. This marathon of activities isn't going to faze you at all. You have *er&* Right?"

"Right," Tania said with an affectionate grin. "Besides, after tonight's performance, I'll have two weeks to rest before we start rehearsals for the new ballet. I'll be able to loll around the entire time if I please."

"Fat chance."

"Well, I admit I'd probably be totally insane if I did absolutely nothing for the entire time. But I'm planning to go up to Tyler's house party in Connecticut after the performance tonight. That will give me a long weekend in which to relax. Is that good enough?"

"It's better than nothing, I suppose," Marguerite said, making a face. She also stood up, and gave Tania's braid an affectionate tug. "Come on, let's go find Barry. Maybe after squiring an energetic five-year-old for four hours you'll change your mind about the length of your R and R in Connecticut. You may definitely need a rest cure."

She could hear the telephone ringing as she searched for her key, and she muttered a far-from-polite imprecation beneath her breath. There was nothing that annoyed her more than standing out in the hall not knowing how long the damned phone had been ringing and feeling the urgency to answer it. It would probably stop ringing just as she picked it up, she thought crossly as she threw open the door, kicked it shut behind her, and hurried to the cream-colored princess phone on the table in the foyer.

"Hello."

"Tania?" Marguerite sounded worried. "I thought you'd have been home forty-five minutes ago."

Tania tossed her purse on the table and dropped

down on the cushioned bench. "I should have been," she said as she stretched her jean-clad legs before her. "I had to sign a few autographs at the stage door."

"More than a few, I'd guess, judging from what Michael said about your performance tonight. How many curtain calls did they bring you back for?"

"Twelve," Tania said with satisfaction. "Michael was right. I was utterly fantastic."

"I don't doubt it." Marguerite chuckled. "Does that put you any closer to your goal of becoming the greatest ballerina in the world?"

"Well, it's another step in the right direction. Give me two more years and I just may get there."

"If you don't have a breakdown from exhaustion first," Marguerite said grimly. "Michael told me your relaxing little weekend has suddenly escalated into a full-scale bash, with you presiding as hostess."

"Only for tonight," Tania said in a tone calculated to soothe. "Tyler had one of his rare attacks of impulsiveness and invited everyone in the company up to Connecticut to mark the closing of our most successful engagement." She laughed. "Now, I couldn't refuse him, could I? I make it a practice never to discourage any variation in Tyler's careful routine. Are you coming to the party?"

"Have you ever tried to get a babysitter at midnight?" Marguerite asked dryly. "No, Michael and I are going to have to pass on this one. I only called to remind you not to burn the candle at both ends just so Tyler can show you off as a feather in his cap."

Tania felt a warm rush of affection. "No danger of that," she said lightly. "I only do what I want to do these days. No one uses me for anything, not even Tyler."

"Except Barry."

"Except Barry," Tania conceded softly. "That's an entirely different situation." She straightened. "Thanks for your concern, Marguerite, but I'll be fine. I'm not a bit tired. Now, I really must run. I only came home to change before driving up to Connecticut. I'll call you when I get back to town."

After she'd hung up the receiver she checked her watch and made a face. She was definitely going to be late, and Tyler wouldn't be at all pleased. She picked up her purse, paused to fasten the chain lock on the front door, and then strode briskly through the bright, modern living room toward the bedroom. She would have to rush if she wasn't to be the last guest to arrive at Tyler's party. Well, it would serve him right for assuming she'd be honored and pleased to act as hostess at this little soiree, she thought crossly. He should know by now how she detested that sort of thing.

In fact, it was possible that Tyler's impromptu party and champagne breakfast weren't really a celebration for the company. He might have thought it a brilliant stroke to surround her with her own friends while dazzling his corporate acquaintances with the glamour of an artist such as she. She hadn't the least doubt that this party of Tyler's would encompass a certain amount of business as well as pleasure. Like many self-made tycoons, he was totally unable to separate the two.

Forty minutes later she quickly finished weaving a silver-and-diamanté ribbon through her braid and fastened it with a diamond star brooch where the shining tresses nestled against the curve of her breast. The simple, but elegant piece of jewelry added just the touch of festive elegance that the simple black velvet gown needed, she thought with satisfaction. Even Tyler couldn't fault her appearance this evening.

She made a gamin face at the sophisticated beauty reflected in the mirror of her vanity table. She dusted a little powder over her nose and quickly got to her feet. That hadn't been at all fair to Tyler, she thought remorsefully. He never commented on her casual, sometimes tomboyish ensembles, but she was well aware he much preferred her more glamorous alter ego.

She plucked the black velvet cloak from its hanger in the closet and draped it about her shoulders. Well, she would see this weekend that Tyler got exactly what he wanted. She would be the charming, sophisticated hostess to his guests and wouldn't indicate by even the tiniest yawn how bored and restless she was. He deserved at least that from her, after all he'd done for her in the past two years. He'd been a warm, understanding friend and had guided her career with a firm, benevolent hand that had propelled her to the top of her profession. Yes, Tyler deserved a great deal more consideration than she gave him.

The shrill buzz of the phone caught her just as she was carrying the small blue-gray suitcase she'd packed earlier from the bedroom to the living room. Marguerite again? No, it couldn't be. It was the house phone, from the lobby. Who on earth could be wanting admittance at this time of night?

"Miss Orlinov? Dave Lennox from Ever Ready Delivery Service." The male voice was buoyantly cheerful. "We have a gift for you from Mr. Tyler Windloe. May I bring it up?"

"A gift?" Tania's brow knotted in puzzlement. "But I'm just leaving to join him now. Why wouldn't he wait to give it to me himself?"

"I really couldn't say, Miss Orlinov." The voice was politely noncommittal. "All I know is that we received a call this evening to drive out to Mr. Windloe's estate in Connecticut and pick up a package to deliver to you when you arrived home from the theater. He was quite insistent you receive it before you left."

"I see," she said slowly. Estate? That was the first time she'd ever heard Tyler's New England farm described as an estate, but who was she to argue terms?

Though she'd worked very hard to eliminate any trace of accent from her own speech in the last three years, she was still guilty of an occasional lapse in comprehension. Perhaps a small farm operated by a gentleman for pleasure, not profit, *could* be called an estate. "Then, I suppose you'd better bring it up." She pressed the security release for the door to the lobby, set the suitcase down, and sank down on the cushioned phone bench to wait.

This was the second apparently impulsive thing Tyler had done within an eight-hour period, she thought with a tiny smile tugging at her lips. Maybe her own impulsiveness was becoming contagious after all, or possibly Tyler realized that she might be a little annoyed with him and wanted to pour oil on troubled waters.

She leaned back against the padded back of the bench with a faint sigh and rested her head against the wall. Maybe she was a little tired. She certainly wasn't feeling her usual enthusiasm at the prospect of the next few days. She could usually find something to arouse her interest in any situation, but being on display as Tyler's charming little protégée was going to be quite a challenge to her imagination. Oh, well, it would only be for a few days, and she would be back in New York. Then she'd be free to pursue her own interests until it was time to resume rehearsals. Perhaps she'd take in those lectures on the Tutankhamen era that the Metropolitan was sponsoring. She felt her spirits lift at the thought and instinctively sat up straighter on the seat, her dark eyes brightening with eagerness.

That same eagerness was curving her lips in a smile a moment later when she opened the door in answer to the knock. Over the brass chain lock, she peered up into the young, clean-cut face of the delivery man. He was dressed in a uniform consisting of dark blue slacks, crisp white shirt, and a waist-length jacket with Ever Ready

Delivery Service emblazoned in gold over the right breast pocket. He held a long, white beribboned floral box.

"Miss Orlinov?" The sandy-haired man's bright blue eyes were admiring as he grinned boyishly at her. "I can't tell you how glad I am to see a smile on your face." He grimaced. "You can't imagine some of the responses we get when we deliver packages at this time of night. Our company may have a reputation for being 'ever ready,' but some of our customers don't feel the same way."

She chuckled. "I can see how you might have a problem." She slid back the chain lock and threw open the door. "Wait just a moment and I'll get you something." She started to turn back to the table where her evening bag lay.

"Fantastic." The man entered the foyer, leaving the door discreetly cracked open. "I don't get many tips on this shift, and every little bit helps. My next semester's tuition is due in a week."

"You're a college student?" she asked over her shoulder as she reached for her bag.

He nodded. "Law." He snapped his fingers. "I almost forgot. I'm supposed to wait until you open the flowers. There's another present inside, and I was told to make sure it was in your hands before I left."

"Another present?" she asked, frowning as she handed him a bill.

He stuffed the tip in his back pocket while balancing the large box in the other arm. He shrugged. "That's what the man said." He fumbled at the lid of the box. "Here, let me help you."

Long stemmed roses filled the box. They were a crimson shade so deep and vibrant that she caught her breath at the sheer beauty of them. There was a small square box elegantly wrapped in silver foil nesting among the dark ferns.

She touched one gorgeous petal with a delicate finger. "Beautiful," she breathed softly.

"What?" She glanced up to see his eyes narrowed on her face with an odd intentness. "The package is right there, ma'am. If you'll just let me see you take possession of it, I'll be on my way."

"Of course." She gave him a warm smile and reached for the package. "I'm afraid I got carried away. They're such a lovely color, aren't they?"

"Lovely," he agreed absently. "They came from Mr. Windloe's own greenhouse on the estate."

Her hand tightened on the box as her eyes flew up to meet his. Greenhouse? There wasn't a greenhouse on the farm. The bright blue eyes of the delivery man were no longer cheerful, and he suddenly looked older and harder. "I don't underst—"

The rest was lost as she was enveloped in a cool mist that seemed to spray from the silver box in her hand. She was vaguely conscious of the lovely roses falling in slow motion through the air to the carpet as the delivery man dropped the box and swiftly stepped back, a handkerchief pressed to his nose and mouth. Then all consciousness faded as she followed the beautiful crimson blossoms to the floor.

Chapter 3

Kevin looked up at him from the mat, a rueful smile on his craggy face, his blue eyes dancing. "One of these days, Jared. One of these days." He gave a pained groan as he rose stiffly to his feet. "I'm definitely going to have to give this up. It's not only excruciatingly taxing to my fragile physique, it's positive hell on my ego."

Ryker threw him a towel, watching with a grin while Kevin McCord wiped the sweat off that massive "fragile" physique. With the gleam of perspiration coating the rippling muscles of his chest, McCord looked more like a gladiator in the arena than a senatorial aide. His short auburn hair curled rebelliously about the rough-hewn toughness of his features, and only the dusting of freckles over the bridge of his nose and the open, engaging frankness of his expression saved him from appearing truly intimidating.

"You almost had me once or twice, there," Ryker said. "Next time, maybe."

"Almost isn't good enough. You're a scientist, for God's sake. Didn't anyone ever tell you that scientists are supposed to be stoop-shouldered, ninety-eight-pound weaklings? Where did you learn karate, anyway?"

"Nam. But I'm sure you're aware of that already. It's

46

all in my dossier, isn't it?" He smiled cynically. "Perhaps it was even you who compiled it, McCord."

McCord frowned. "It wasn't, as a matter of fact. Senator Corbett hires an agency for that type of investigation." He wiped his forehead. "I've studied it, of course, but I don't have a photographic memory, as you do, Jared. Some things do slip my mind occasionally." He turned in the direction of the door leading to the sauna, adjacent to the shower area. "Now I think I'm ready to bake out some of these aches and pains you've produced in my decrepit body." He sighed. "When the senator assigned me to the chateau as your aide, I never even dreamed I'd be the object of this kind of battering. I had visions of handling world-shaking correspondence and inspiring you to burn the midnight oil to make other mind-blowing discoveries. Instead, I'm a glorified sparring partner." He glowered. "You don't even play chess, Jared. Don't you know that all geniuses are supposed to play chess?"

"Sorry," Jared said solemnly, his lips twitching. "I'll try to rectify that fault at the earliest opportunity. The game wasn't exactly popular in that coal town where I grew up in West Virginia." He fell into step with McCord to cross the highly polished floor of the gymnasium. "You don't enjoy our poker games, then?"

McCord flinched. "That punishment is worse than the karate. I think I just may ask the senator to recall me to Washington . . . unless you're ready to use my other talents to a greater extent. You know you're bored as hell, Jared. Why don't you let me equip a lab for you here at the chateau? Corbett will get you anything you need or want."

"I'm well aware of that." Jared smiled grimly. "Sam Corbett is much too astute a man not to hedge his bets any way he can. It makes him distinctly uneasy that the key to a complicated piece of work is in my head, and not written on a slip of paper locked in a safety-deposit box somewhere."

"Can you blame him?" McCord's blue eyes were sober. "Your discovery will probably change every aspect of our existence as we know it. It's not very reasonable of you to insist upon carrying it around in your head. You owe it to society to safeguard that knowledge."

"But that's what I'm doing, Kevin. Safeguarding it," Jared said. "I'm keeping the key. Without it my notes, papers, models, computer printouts are of little use. As long as the last piece of knowledge is mine alone, I can control it." His facial muscles tightened to flintlike hardness. "And I *will* control it, Kevin. I'll be damned if I'll let a bunch of bureaucratic bastards get their hands on this!"

"Okay, okay." McCord threw up his hands in surrender. "No lab." He sighed. "I guess I'll just have to resign myself to the role of buddy." He rubbed the small of his back in painful reminiscence. "If my muscles will survive the strain."

Jared chuckled. It was almost impossible not to like McCord, despite the wariness he'd conditioned himself to feel in the presence of any one of the battery of Corbett's underlings who surrounded him here in the senator's stronghold. McCord possessed not only an incisive mind, but almost a quiet charm that drew people to him. God only knew, Jared reflected, how out of his mind with boredom he would have been here without McCord's presence. Not that he wasn't nearly to that point now, he thought, suddenly impatient with himself as well as the situation he was in. The offer of a lab had come at a diabolically tempting time because his need to get back to work was almost a physical ache. And he hadn't the slightest doubt that McCord understood too well.

"You'll survive, McCord," Jared said as he pushed

open the door and entered the shower area. "You may even get a rest cure in the near future. I've been thinking of flying to New York for a few days."

A troubled frown replaced the grin on Kevin's face. "Betz will foam at the mouth when he hears what you're planning. He was nearly climbing the walls when you left the chateau last time."

Jared shrugged. "Too bad. I was stumbling over one of his security men whenever I turned around in New York. That should be enough for him; if not, he'll just have to foam away."

"Believe me, he will. Betz is practically a fanatic about his precious security measures, and the senator's told him that if anything happens to you, he'll be axed." Kevin hesitated. "It's only another six weeks, Jared. Why chance it?"

"Drop it, McCord," Jared said curtly. He rapidly stripped off the loose white jacket and pants of his *gi* and reached into the shower cubicle to turn on the spray. "I won't tolerate interference from you any more than I will from Betz." He ducked into the shower and closed the frosted door.

"Whatever you say," Kevin called to him. "I'll see you at breakfast, after I bake the aches out of these muscles in the sauna." His massive shadow moved away from the translucent door.

He was feeling a few aches and pains himself, Jared realized as he soaped his body thoroughly. What Kevin lacked in skill, he made up for in sheer brute strength, and he'd been perfectly honest when he'd said the match had been closer than any that had gone before.

"Dr. Ryker." The ponderous, measured cadence to those words announced Ed Betz as surely as the solid square shadow thrown on the frosted pane. "I wonder if it would be possible to see you for a few minutes?"

Jared slammed the soap into its compartment on the

wall and let the spray wash the foam from his body. Foam. The word suddenly reminded him of McCord's description of Betz's probable reaction to his plans for this weekend, and he smiled. "I'll be out in a minute, Betz," he said politely. "Unless you'd prefer to come in."

"No, I can wait, Dr. Ryker," Betz answered with perfect seriousness.

Jared shook his head in amazement. If Betz had considered the matter of utmost urgency, Jared hadn't the slightest doubt he would have accepted his invitation. Lord, he wasn't even safe from the man under a spraying shower. Well, he might just as well get it over with and see what was on that methodical, snaillike mind. He abruptly turned off the shower and opened the door.

Betz was standing outside the stall. Dressed in one of his usual dark business suits, he offered a towel to Jared with his customary impersonal efficiency. "I'm glad you were almost finished," he commented. "I did want to get you settled before I left the chateau. I received a call from the senator asking me to try to make it to Washington by noon to coordinate the security for his trip to California next week."

"Settled?" Jared began to dry himself with the towel. "I appreciate your concern, but I don't think I'll need your help. Run along to Washington, Betz."

"As I said, I intend to do that immediately after I see you . . . er . . . happy to stay here," Betz said. "I wouldn't have considered leaving before, but now that I'm sure you'll have something to occupy you, I don't think there's any further cause for alarm." He smiled with a satisfaction bordering on smugness. "I believe you'll be very content here when you see the surprise that arrived at the chateau for you a few hours ago."

Jared was dressing rapidly, and he looked up from zipping his jeans to frown impatiently. "Stop playing cute, Betz. What the hell are you talking about?" He pulled a cream-colored sweatshirt over his head and settled it around his hips before taking a comb from the tray over the basin and starting to comb his hair. "If you're trying to be mysterious, believe me, it isn't your forte."

A little smile was tugging at Betz's lips as he met Jared's eyes in the mirror. "I have no intention of being mysterious, Dr. Ryker. In fact, I'm quite eager to show you what I've arranged for you, if you'll come along with me now."

"Certainly," Jared drawled as he threw the comb back on the shelf. "I don't think I've seen you this excited over anything but the *New York Times* crossword puzzle." He gestured mockingly. "By all means lead on, Betz."

Jared was feeling a mild flicker of curiosity as he followed the security man up a flight of stairs to a hallway on the ground floor of the chateau. Their heels clicked on the echoing parquet-floored corridor as they made their way toward the grand staircase.

The bedroom door on the second floor before which Betz paused was in a generally unused wing of the chateau. For a moment there was a glint of triumph in the usually expressionless face as he opened the door and stepped aside. "After you, Dr. Ryker."

Jared darted him a derisive glance. Betz was really carrying his little surprise to extremes.

As he entered the room, darkness enveloped him. When his vision adjusted slightly he could make out vague shapes and a general impression of the same Louis XIV elegance in furnishings that characterized the other rooms in the chateau. Then, as his eyes became fully accustomed to the lack of light, he saw the heavy emerald velvet drapes that were drawn across the French windows, blocking out the early-morning sunlight. A canopied double bed stood in the dusky intimacy of the center of the room. An occupied double bed.

Jared sighed impatiently, curiosity gone and annoyance in bloom. "Another one of your imported whores, Betz? I thought I'd discouraged that particular practice."

"Look a little closer, Dr. Ryker."

He drew closer to the bed and, casting a casual glance at the sleeping woman who occupied it, suddenly stiffened. His body was as galvanized by shock as if he'd been stroked by an electric wire.

She looked almost childlike to him in that big double bed. Her small body was obviously naked beneath the cream satin sheet that covered her to her shoulders, and the dark shining hair falling over one shoulder was braided with silver and fastened with a tiny diamond star. The long sweep of her lashes against the curve of her cheek gave her a curious vulnerability that was absent when dominated by those blazing dark eyes. The silken sheet scarcely lifted with each breath; she was sleeping deeply. Too deeply.

"I thought you'd be pleased."

Betz's voice was redolent with satisfaction, and it served to jerk Jared from his state of bemusement at the sight of Tania Orlinov. He whirled to face the other man, his eyes blazing with an intensity of anger that caused Betz to take an involuntary step backward. "You arrogant son of a bitch!" Jared's voice was hoarse with rage. "Whatever gave you the idea that you could do this to someone?" He strode nearer to the bed and picked up Tania's wrist. The pulse was slow but steady. "What the hell did you give her?"

"She'll be quite all right in a little while," Betz said soothingly from behind him. "She breathed in an innocuous gas, which knocked her out immediately. On the plane she was accompanied by a competent physician, who kept her sedated at a very safe level of drugs. She'll wake up in a few hours without even a trace of a headache."

"My God, you actually kidnapped her." Jared was charged with incredulous anger. "Didn't it ever occur to you that she's an independent woman, with the right to make her own decisions? You can't ride roughshod over a human being this way."

"It was necessary," Betz said calmly. "We offered her a great deal of money, but she wouldn't take it. We had no other option but to use force." He frowned. "You needn't worry that the method of her arrival will spoil your pleasure. We've taken precautions against something like that happening."

"Take her back to New York!"

Betz's eyes widened in surprise. "Back to . . ." He studied Jared's tense face and blazing eyes for long, thoughtful moments before he slowly shook his head. "I'm afraid we can't do that, Dr. Ryker. Aside from the fact that our actions in abducting her might be discovered and make things difficult for the senator, the reason we took Miss Orlinov in the first place still exists." He paused. "You want her."

Oh, yes, he wanted her, Jared thought grimly. Even in his anger he could feel his swelling need for her push against the fabric of his jeans. The sight of her lying there before him, her shoulders and the upper swell of her breasts rising from the satin sheets, was like a delicate loving hand stroking him. His eyes turned compulsively to the pulse point his thumb was absently stroking even now. Her hand. He drew a deep breath and carefully laid her arm back on the counterpane. "It's the mark of a civilized man that he does not always take what he wants, even if he can have it. That quality separates us from the Neanderthal. Take her back to New York, Betz."

"No. The situation hasn't changed, so it would be unreasonable to undo all our work at this stage." He frowned. "I don't understand the problem, Dr. Ryker. It's been obvious that the reason you've been taking these hazardous trips to New York was Miss Orlinov. Now the trips are no longer necessary. You have her here in the chateau."

"And have you informed Sam Corbett of your solution to your little problem?" Jared asked caustically. "I think he'd regard your reasoning as simplistic, to say the least."

Betz shook his head. "I didn't consult him, but I don't think he'd have any major objections. My instructions were to take any measures necessary to protect you." He paused. "*Any* measures, Dr. Ryker."

"Delightful," Jared said bitterly. "You wouldn't consider your attitude a bit ruthless?"

"You have the reputation of being a bit ruthless yourself, upon occasion. You should have no problem understanding our position." Betz meticulously straightened his discreetly-patterned tie. "Now I really must be on my way. I'll probably be back within a few weeks, but if you need anything, you need only inform Mr. McCord, of course."

"Of course," Jared echoed ironically. "If I want another woman abducted or a murder committed, I'll just tell Kevin."

Betz's lips curved in an uncertain smile. "You're being humorous?" He shrugged and turned away. "I'm sure after consideration you'll realize this action can only be to our mutual benefit." He was moving swiftly toward the door. "Until you come around to a more logical way of thinking, however, I should warn you that I've left instructions with my staff that under no circumstances is Miss Orlinov to be allowed to leave the chateau." He paused at the door. "Oh, one more thing. I know that you've mentioned your disgust at the cloying willingness of some of the other women we've provided for you. I did think, though, that you might find rebelliousness or resistance on Miss Orlinov's part not to your liking." He smiled. "I wanted to make sure you and she started out on the right foot, so I had the doctor give her an injection of paradynoline."

Paradynoline. A potent illegal drug whose side effects were aphrodisiacal. "You really are a bastard, aren't you, Betz?" Jared said, his lips twisting. He hadn't the slightest doubt that the man knew exactly how that piece of information would affect him. His stomach muscles contracted from a jolt of pure lust at the thought of Tania's waking to find him beside her, and desiring him as much as he desired her.

"I do what I think is necessary."

"Betz!"

The security man turned to look at him inquiringly.

Jared's gaze was once more on Tania's sleeping face, fixed with compulsive fascination on the parted pinkness of her lips. She looked so damn young and innocent. Her skin had the clear, silky sheen of a child's. "Who undressed her?"

"The doctor and I. Why?"

Jared reached out a hand and touched the curve of Tania's cheekbone. "Don't ever touch her again, Betz," he said thickly. "You'd better make damn sure that no one ever touches her again."

A smile of infinite satisfaction touched Edward Betz's lips as he softly closed the door behind him.

The first sensation of which Tania became aware was of dreamy languor; the second was of molten heat, which was surging through her in a restless tide. Her dark head thrashed on the satin pillow as she resisted the sensations burning through her with a strange, fitful fury.

"Shh, easy." The voice was a dark velvet murmur. "Relax and flow with it, little Piper."

She lifted heavy lids to meet glowing silver eyes that were oddly warm, despite their color. They seemed to blaze in the shadowy darkness of his face, just as the vitality of his slender, jean-clad body appeared to shimmer like a flame in the dimness of the bedroom. Somehow it seemed perfectly natural to open her eyes and see Jared Ryker sitting in an elegant tapestry-covered wing chair beside her bed. As natural as any dream could be, she thought hazily. For there could be no doubt whatever that this was a fantasy, though a strangely tactile one. Her hand rubbed lazily against the smooth satin of the sheet that covered her.

The man was frowning. "Do you know who I am, Tania?"

Of course she knew who he was, but it was most inconsiderate of a fantasy figure to demand that she rouse herself to answer when it took so much effort. "Ryker," she said, the word sounding slurred and far away, even to her own ears.

He smiled grimly. "Well, that's something, anyway. How do you feel?"

She smiled dreamily. "Wonderful." Then her face clouded in confusion as she once more felt that hot electric surge of sensation go through her. "No." She shook her head vaguely. "I don't know. Something."

She heard a murmured curse from the man in the wing chair, and suddenly he was sitting beside her on the bed, his hands gathering hers in a warm, secure clasp. A *very* tactile dream, she thought contentedly, as her own hands tightened on his. "Listen, Tania, and try to understand. What you're feeling is going to get worse when some of the sedation wears off." His gray eyes were holding hers with compulsive force, as if trying to pierce the veil that was enveloping her senses. "I'd give you something to put you out again, but I can't risk it without knowing precisely what they used on you. It would be too dangerous. Do you understand?"

The face looking down at her was oddly taut and

strained. There were graven lines on either side of his beautifully cut mouth hinting at a power and sensuality, that aroused her even through the dark haze surrounding her. Yes, a beautiful mouth.

Then his hands were on her bare shoulders, shaking her. "Do you understand?"

Understand what? She'd forgotten what he'd been saying. But he obviously wasn't going to leave her alone until she answered him. "I understand," she said. It wasn't nearly so slurred this time, she thought with a vague sense of pride.

"I hope to hell you do," he muttered, exhaling slowly. One hand left her shoulder to run restlessly through his dark hair. "Look, I'm going to help you in the only way I can. Trust me, okay?"

She nodded happily, her dark eyes dreamily content. Why had she been so wary of him at that first meeting? she wondered. There was nothing to be afraid of in the dark, intent face of the man above her. Then the hot tide flowed over her again, and she gasped at the aching need it left in its wake. She knew a wrenching emptiness in her loins, and the tips of her breasts were suddenly so sensitive that the touch of the satin sheet against them was almost painful.

Ryker murmured an obscenity that would have shocked her if she hadn't been lost in an intensity of sensation that was tearing her apart. "So help me God, if I had Betz here right now, I'd strangle him," he snarled savagely, his eyes blazing. He leaned forward and gently brushed her forehead with his lips. "Hold on, sweet, it's going to be all right in a little while. I'll take care of it."

Then he was on his feet, pulling the cream sweatshirt over his head and tossing it carelessly on the wing chair. He turned to face her, his hands working swiftly at his belt. "Do you know how many hundreds of times I've thought of having you like this?" he asked thickly. "With that strong, lovely body naked and willing to take me into you? I think I know your body now better than my own. I've watched those video tapes of your performances until I've almost worn them out." He slid his jeans and briefs over his hips, his gaze still fixed on her flushed, dreamy face. "I know how you move, how your expressions change like quicksilver. I love those flyaway eyebrows. I've wanted to run a finger over them more times than I can count." He smiled, his harsh face oddly tender. "You're always laughing. Even when the role calls for you to be sad and pensive, the laughter is lurking, waiting to burst free. I think that touches me more than anything else about you."

He stepped out of his loafers and moved closer to the bed, totally naked now, his lean, whipcord body gleaming like polished gold in the dimness of the room. He shook his head. "No, that's not true. It's the totality of you that obsesses me." His face became grim. "Even an unimaginative bastard like Betz recognized the signs that you'd become special to me."

Betz? The name was vaguely familiar, wasn't it? Then she dismissed it as unimportant, as her gaze ran admiringly over Ryker's naked body. She was accustomed to male beauty in her partners, and she generally appreciated it with the impersonal attitude with which she viewed a beautiful painting. Ryker's body wasn't as graceful and symmetrical as many she'd seen, but it possessed a lean, muscular tension radiating a leashed power that sent a tingle of excitement through her. Her gaze traveled from the springy mat of dark hair on his chest to the hard, muscular stomach and down to the soft nest of hair that cradled the root of his manhood.

"Do you like me, little Piper?" His voice was as darkly mellow as cognac. "Do you want to feel me inside you as much as I want to be there?"

This fantasy was beginning to seem more real by the minute, Tania thought vaguely as Ryker sat down next to her on the bed. Not that it mattered. She was infinitely content to have it so. It was as if Ryker were weaving a golden gossamer web of sensuality about her.

"I wonder if you're comprehending even half of what I'm saying to you." He sighed heavily, filled with frustration. His hand gently smoothed the hair at her temple. "It wasn't supposed to be like this, damn it. I was going to wait until it was safe to come to you, and try to make you want me as much as I want you." He grimaced. "Well, Betz blew that all to hell, so we're going to have to make the best of it."

The warmth of his hips against the thin satin sheet was causing the throbbing between her thighs to accelerate to a cadence of need like liquid fire. Her hand lifted lazily from the sheet to rest on the soft mat of hair on his chest. She smiled contentedly as she felt his heart jump beneath her hand and saw him inhale sharply. It was nice to have one's fantasies respond so satisfactorily.

"I love to have your hands on me." His voice was a low, husky growl, and his eyes were closed in a face that was taut with an almost painful pleasure. "I don't know if I'm going to be able to pull this off, Tania Orlinov." His lids swept up, and the silver eyes were a fresh shock as they looked down at her with a glazed absorption. "I'm in a hell of a box. If I take you now, when you come out from under the drug, you're going to be angry as hell with me for taking advantage of you when you were helpless." He reached up and touched her hand that was curled intimately in the thatch of hair on his chest. "And if I don't take you, you're going to spend the next few hours being uncomfortable as the devil."

He lifted her small hand and kissed the palm lingeringly, his warm tongue probing the soft center with a thoroughness that made her heart leap in response.

"You taste so good," he said softly. "I can't let you hurt when I can do something about it, love." The expression on his face was an odd mixture of sensual longing and stern control as he looked down at her. "So I'm going to give you what you need, and maybe I can salvage something to build on along the way. Before you go back to sleep you're going to know my body so well that every breath I take will be your breath; you're going to know how your touch excites my every muscle and tendon. You're going to know how your tongue can make me shake like a kid with his first woman." He sucked tenderly at the sensitive tips of her fingers. The warm moisture of his mouth tugged erotically at her senses. He released her fingers. "I'm going to make sure of that, because once the anger starts, that memory may be the only weapon I have." His lips curved in a bittersweet smile. "Are you ready for me, little Piper?"

She nodded slowly, her dark eyes cloudy in smoldering response to his words. A flicker of pain crossed his face. "Tell me," he demanded. "Say the words. For God's sake, let me know you're at least aware of who the hell is making love to you."

A troubled frown creased her brow. He was doing it again. "Ryker," she said, a note of impatience in her slurred voice. "You're Ryker." She hoped that would satisfy him, for she was suddenly tired of dream images who talked and explained things she couldn't be bothered to think about. Her body was burning up, her hips shifting restlessly on the counterpane. He had promised to help her. Why wasn't he doing it? "Help me, Ryker," she whispered.

"I will, Tania," he murmured. "I will, love." His lips closed on hers with a gentleness that caused her to give a little whimper of pleasure. So sweet, so warm. His tongue was warm, too, as it pushed past her lips to explore the moist darkness of her mouth. He took his time, exploring every cranny and nook, running his tongue over her teeth and the warm smooth wall of her mouth before enticing her tongue to play the most erotic of games with his own.

When he lifted his head, she could feel his warm breath caressing her lips as he murmured, "You taste honey-sweet. I want more of you." His lips dipped down once again, this time catching her tongue in his mouth and using gentle suction and delicately nibbling with his teeth in a kiss so erotically intimate that she groaned. Her hands slid over the steel smoothness of his shoulders in a feverish search before curving about his neck and burying themselves in the thick crispness of the hair at the nape of his neck. His mouth still on hers, he reached out with careful gentleness and slowly slid the satin sheet down to her waist.

She caught her breath as the silky material caressed her nipples, which were already peaked and distended. His lips released her tongue, and he drew a deep, ragged breath. His gaze traveled slowly down her throat and shoulders to the fullness of her breasts, with their flowering pink crests. "Poor baby, they're very sensitive now, aren't they?" he asked hoarsely. "I'll be careful not to hurt you."

His head bent, and his tongue suddenly darted out to stroke a puckered nipple. She gasped, her hands clutching at his hair as a hot shudder shook her. Then his tongue was gently licking the entire surface of her breast in light, teasing strokes. She was breathing in broken little gasps as the swirls of sensation rushed over her. His teeth nibbled gently at the other nipple. He raised his head. "You liked that? God, so did I! That first night at the theater when you were taking your bows, your breasts were moving in the same little gasps beneath that scarlet chiffon. There was a bead of moisture in this pretty little hollow. It nearly killed me not to bend down and lick it away."

His tongue buried itself between her breasts while his hands tenderly cupped their fullness. Then he began a slow rhythmic contraction and release, his long, strong hands dark and virile against the pale skin of her breasts. It was a sensation so incredibly voluptuous that she felt an explosive knot gathering in intensity in the apex of her thighs. Then his lips and teeth were toying with her nipple while the erotic massage accelerated in lightning, quantum leaps.

"Ryker." She could barely breathe, her head moving back and forth on the pillow with feverish restlessness. "Ryker, I nee—"

"I know," he murmured. "I know, Tania. Let it come, just let it come, pretty Piper."

And it did come. It exploded within her like a heat-guided missile, her body convulsing against him in the force of that release. She was vaguely conscious of his hands leaving her breasts to curve around her and draw her securely into his arms. His fingers moved in soothing circles on her naked back as he held her in an embrace as warmly comforting as a fire in the winter. "Better?" His lips brushed the pulse in her temple softly. She could feel the tension drain out of her as she collapsed against him, her breathing as shallow as if she'd just run a marathon.

One palm was cupping the back of her head, while he rocked her like a beloved child. "You'll feel fine for a few minutes now," he said thickly. "Then it will start to build again." His lips brushed the lobe of her ear. "Don't worry, love, we'll take it step by step."

Why should she worry? she wondered. She had never felt so full and safe and secure in her entire life as she did in the arms of this stranger. No, that wasn't right. Fantasy figures couldn't be strangers when they were created from your own imagination, could they? Ryker could be anything she wanted him to be, do anything she wanted him to do. But at the moment the dream sequence was proceeding with such complete satisfaction that she was content to drift along in its wake.

"Sit up, love. I want to look at you." He was pushing her away, and then the satin sheet was flipped aside and he was pulling her to her knees on the bed. She felt a wave of sudden dizziness, and she sank back on her heels. Then it was gone. She looked up to see the quick concern on Ryker's face. "Okay?"

She smiled and nodded, blissfully content. Somehow that instant of protective concern had caused a heart-catching swell of emotion deep inside her, and his smoldering gaze as it ran lingeringly over each curve and shadow of her body brought that feeling to a radiant maturity.

"Beautiful," he said huskily, his hand running over the curve of her hip with utmost care, as if she were infinitely fragile and would shatter at the slightest pressure. "So tiny and delicate, yet I can feel the supple strength of you under my hands. I knew you'd look like this." His hand moved across the softness of her belly to rub gently against the springy dark down. "Such a lovely soft nest. Do you know how often I've thought about how it would feel against me?" His eyes were hooded, a flush mantling the golden darkness of his face. "Come here."

She edged closer to him on the bed and suddenly he was parting her legs and lifting her into his lap so that she was facing him. She gave a little shocked gasp when she felt the aroused length of him pressing against the intimate heart of her womanhood, and it was echoed by Ryker's guttural groan as he crushed her to him with a force that robbed her of breath. "Sit very still, love," he gasped, and she could feel his heart pounding as if it were about to break through the wall of his chest. "Don't even breathe. I think, in this case, realization of this particular fantasy wasn't such a good idea." Then, as if unable to resist the temptation, his hips moved in an indulating movement against her. "But Lord, it's fantastic."

Fantastic? That was an understatement, she thought feverishly. She felt as if a hot liquid was rushing through every part of her, and her lungs were laboring so hard that it came close to actual pain. She felt him stiffen against her and the muscles of his thighs and buttocks lock with the effort he was making at control. His breath was coming in rough gasps, and she could feel the dew of perspiration beneath her hands, on his shoulders.

"No!" The word was almost an explosion. Then he was lifting her off his lap and onto the bed. He backed away from her hurriedly. "Not now. Not this time." He was sucking air into his lungs as if he were starved for it. "Though so help me God, I may be elevated to sainthood if I make it through this."

She was staring at him in bewilderment. Why had he pushed her away just when she was coming so close to the rapture he'd shown her before? She didn't like Ryker's expression: The tenderness and vulnerability were now completely gone—and she wanted them back.

"Don't look at me like that, damn it," he bit out tersely. His eyes were harried as he ran his hand through his hair in exasperation. "You don't even know what's happening. Hell, you probably don't even know who I am."

The man seemed to be obsessed with that idea, she thought crossly. She knew very well who he was. In fact, at this moment she felt as if she knew him better than she'd ever known anyone before in her life. "I do know you," she said indignantly. "I told you." Her fingers touched his lips. "You're Jared Ryker." Her fingers wandered down to test the pounding of his heart. It leaped with a very satisfying response. She chuckled. Then, feeling extraordinarily mischievous, she let her hand swoop down to curve around his tumescence. An expression of shock accompanied the little jerk he gave in her small hand, and her dark eyes danced. "Ryker," she said triumphantly.

"I think the sedation must be wearing off a little," he said, making a wry face. "Which may present an entirely new batch of problems." He gently pried her hand away. "God, how I love to hear you laugh." Two fingers traced the smile that still lingered on her lips. "I'm happy as hell that part of you is back with me, at least."

What was he talking about? He was speaking as if she were in never-never land, when she felt more alive now than she ever had in her life. Perhaps too alive, she thought dizzily as a wave of molten heat assaulted her senses. Her throat felt suddenly dry, and she shook her head as if to clear it. "I fee—"

He drew her into his arms. "I know," he said, his tone gentle despite the thread of desperation running through it. "God, I hope you can go to sleep after this. I'm not used to this particular kind of torture, love." He bent her backward, so that she was once more reclining against the pillows. His voice was a velvet growl. "Come along, little Piper. Let's see you dance to the music of *my* flute."

He was beside her on the satin sheet, his lips covering hers with a passionate urgency that caused her instantly to open to him. At first with yearning submission and then more active aggression, her tongue was suddenly exploring his mouth and finding it as exciting as he had found hers. Moist warmth, the clean smoothness of his teeth, and that lovely skilled tongue that promptly engaged the invader in a sensual minuet caused her to arch against him with a little breathless moan.

He lifted his head, and a teasing smile lit his face. "Oh, no," he said huskily. "Much as I'd like to linger awhile, I have other gardens to explore. I want to know all of you, Tania Orlinov."

Then his lips were moving over her taut midriff and down to the softness of her belly. The breath seemed to rush out of her body as she felt the warm moistness of his tongue stroke delicately at her navel while his hands moved in a rhythmic massage over the silky skin just below. He gently spread her thighs, one leg coming between her own. The fine hairs that coated his hard, muscular leg felt deliciously abrasive against the softness of her inner thighs, but the position was so submissive, so vulnerable, that she instinctively tried to close them against him.

His eyes were half shut, their glitter almost molten, as he lifted his head to gaze down at her. "Don't close me out, love." His fingers started a rhythmic stroking that sent a soaring response to every nerve in her body. Her hands reached out blindly to close on his shoulders.

She could hear his harsh, labored breath above her, but she was so lost in the haze of desire he was weaving about her that she was scarcely conscious of anything but the feeling within her. "Lord, it's almost worth it just to watch you and know that I can make you respond like this." His fingers suddenly rotated with a skill that caused her to jerk against him. His voice was oddly husky. "You're so damn beautiful." Then the broad hard line of his cheek was against the softness of her belly and he was rubbing it back and forth with slow, sensual pleasure. "So soft and sweet." His tongue darted out to stroke lazily. "You taste like all the good things on the face of the earth." His hands slowly curved around to cup her buttocks in the strong warmth of his hands. "Do the flowers in your garden taste as luscious, little Piper?" Then his hands were lifting her and he was discovering for himself.

She couldn't believe it. No sensation could be that intense. His tongue and lips worked with heated skill, until she was clutching at the dark silkiness of his head in an agony of need. Her body was being honed to a feverish pitch of hunger, and her reaction was so extreme that it was inevitable that that hunger would have to reach satiation swiftly. This time when the explosion of feeling came she was expecting it, but it didn't alter the fantastic delight she experienced in its aftermath.

She was vaguely conscious of Ryker moving, shifting to lie beside her on the bed. When he pulled her in his arms and settled her head in the hollow of his shoulder, it seemed so perfectly right and natural that she cuddled as contentedly close as if she had done it every night of her life. She was suddenly so weary that every muscle of her body felt leaden, and she was conscious of a lassitude that was blurring her senses and causing her mind to reject all thought.

She was in a state of languor so profound that it came as a little shock to realize the man holding her was far from being so relaxed. She gradually became aware that the arms holding her were coiled with tension and his heart was pounding beneath her ear. Her head moved uneasily on his shoulder, her dark braid splaying over his hair-roughened chest like a caressing hand. His breath constricted in his lungs, and she felt his heart give a little jerk. Even through the veil of exhaustion that was rapidly enveloping her, the knowledge that the man who now seemed an intimate extension of herself was not equally content filled her with a nagging sense of unhappiness. Then her lips curved in a relieved smile as she realized just how ridiculous she was being. None of this was real. Soon she would wake up and shake her head ruefully at the vividness of her fantasy.

"I'm glad one of us is happy," he muttered. His lips traced the winged darkness of her brow in a fairylike caress. "Go to sleep, pixie. I don't think I can take much more without going crazy." He reached for her hand and pressed it against his breast so that she could feel the leaping cadence of his heart. "Do you feel that? It's for you, love." He carried her hand to the muscles of his belly, which were painfully knotted. "And that's for you too." His voice was a soft velvet murmur in her ear.

He lifted the hand to his lips and brushed a gentle kiss on the delicate veins at her wrist. "When you wake up in a fury and start hating my guts, remember that, little Piper. I was the one who was used, not you. I took nothing from you but the knowledge of that lovely body and gave you comfort and pleasure in return." He released a long, shaky breath. "God, I hope you remember that."

But memory as well as consciousness vanished as her eyes closed and she fell peacefully asleep.

Chapter 4

*T*he heavy velvet drapes were no longer drawn, and the late-afternoon sun streaming through the French windows danced over the highly polished surfaces of the exquisite furniture. Tania opened her eyes to a scene at once alien and familiar.

From the emerald-velvet canopy above her head, to the petit-point tapestry of the wing chair drawn close to the bed, to the cream and spring green of the antique rug on the floor, her gaze flew to the vacant pillow next to her own, and the indentation caused the adrenaline to pump through her system.

The truth hit her with the force of a blow. My God, it had all been real! The man who had held her until she fell asleep in his arms had been no fantasy figure. Jared Ryker's strong, sensitive hands had explored every curve of her body with such intimacy, his lips had . . .

"No!"

She threw the satin sheet aside and jumped out of bed. She was naked . . . exposed, vulnerable. That vulnerability stoked the fury building in her. Dammit, she had been kidnapped!

She jerked the sheet from the bed and wrapped it carelessly around her. It was impossible. Things like this just didn't happen in the United States. And where the devil was she? With swift, impatient strides she crossed the room, threw open the French doors, and stepped out onto a stone balcony.

Mountains. Her gaze swept the horizon. Towering snow-crested peaks appeared to ring the house she was in. A chill greater than the one that whipped the satin sheet against her body settled into her spirit.

God, how she hated mountains. After the horror of her experience in the Andes, she had sworn she'd never set foot on a mountain again. And yet here she was, apparently in some sort of turreted stone castle that was nestling on top of one of the bloody things, and ringed with an entire range of other forbidding peaks. And all compliments of the arrogant Jared Ryker!

A growl of pure rage rose from her. How could anyone have the nerve to do what he'd done to her? It was all rushing back to her now with a vividness of detail that caused the color to burn her cheeks. Her thoughts quickly scuttled away from the more intimate physical details of those hours in Ryker's arms, to fasten on the words that would bring light to the confusion still afflicting her.

He had mentioned the name of that funny little man whose offer had so amused her. Betz. The connection was too obvious not to be made immediately. The staggeringly lucrative offer to become the mistress of a recluse for a six-week period had been made on behalf of Jared Ryker. The pitiful old eccentric of her imagination had been wild fabrication. Eccentric, Ryker might be, but there was nothing old or pitiful about him—though he might be a subject for considerable pity before she got through with him!

"Miss Orlinov?"

She whirled to face the tall, broad-shouldered man standing at the French doors. He was dressed in tan khakis and a brown crew-necked sweater. There was an appealing smile on his face that lit his blunt, craggy features, set off by a crop of thick red hair.

"I knocked, but I guess you didn't hear me," he said. "My name is Kevin McCord." He grimaced. "I made the mistake of complaining to Jared earlier about the lack of challenge in my duties as an aide. He said facing you and trying to soothe your ruffled feathers would be a task worthy of a member of the Security Council of the United Nations." His bright blue eyes were mournful. "One of these days I'll learn to keep my mouth shut."

"Where is he? Where's Ryker?" Her voice was shaking with fury.

McCord took a step back in the bedroom. "I have a note for you from him," he said in a deep, soothing murmur. "You'll see him shortly. Now, why don't you come back inside and hear me do my stuff?" His gaze went over her sheet-wrapped form, and his face darkened in concern. "You shouldn't be out here dressed like that. The wind's damn sharp."

"Your concern is touching," she said caustically as she strode toward him like a small, vengeful Valkyrie, her dark eyes blazing. "Considering it's thanks to your employer's very criminal actions that I'm not only here, but dressed—" she drew a deep breath before continuing between her teeth, "or should I say undressed in this fashion? And I don't want to see Ryker shortly, I want to see him *now!*"

McCord gestured to the blue-gray suitcase on the carpet beside him. "I'm sure you'd feel much happier and more secure tackling him dressed in something besides that sheet," he said. "That's why I brought your suitcase up. I understand that Jared ordered a complete wardrobe to be sent to the chateau in the next few days, but I thought you'd be more comfortable in your own things for a while."

"Do I have to tell you what Dr. Ryker can do with his wardrobe?"

McCord shook his head, his blue eyes twinkling. "I have an excellent imagination, and probably a more extensive vocabulary than you in that area, Miss Orlinov. I think I'll let you take that up with Jared yourself. However, I should warn you that the man can be more than a trifle intimidating when something annoys him." He gestured to a polished cherrywood door. "There's an adjoining bath that should have everything you need. Why don't you go shower and change into something more fitting your warlike mood? A lovely thing like you draped only in a satin sheet can be quite distracting when you're having a serious conversation."

"I'll do that," she said grimly as she bent down to pick up her suitcase. She marched toward the door he'd indicated. "Unfortunately, I neglected to pack anything that would do my feelings full justice. Suits of armor and battle-axes went out of style several centuries ago." She cast him a glance that was as razor-sharp as the ax she'd just mentioned. "I'll have a few things to say to you, too, Mr. McCord. I'll be back in fifteen minutes. Wait for me." The door of the bathroom closed behind her with a decisiveness that, if not exactly a slam, was ominous enough to make McCord flinch.

With a rueful sigh he dropped into the tapestry-covered wing chair, stretched out his khaki-clad legs before him, and prepared to wait.

In less than the fifteen minutes she had designated, Tania was back in the room, dressed in jeans and a brilliant orange-and-cream ski sweater. She had removed the silver ribbon and diamond clip that had fastened her braid and arranged it in the severe coronet that had made Ryker think of a little girl playing dress-up. It was just as well that she wasn't aware of his comparison at the moment, for it would have goaded her rage.

"Now," she said coldly, halting before McCord's chair. "Where's Jared Ryker?"

"We'll get to that presently," he said, rising politely to his feet. "But first I have to try to do the job I was assigned."

"And what is that?"

His lips curved in a grin. "Explanations and reassurances are supposed to be the name of the game. Actually, I think Ryker wanted me to take the fine edge off that temper before he had to face you. He's not considered a genius for nothing, you know."

"No, I didn't know," she snapped. "I know nothing about the man except that he's an arrogant hedonist with no respect for anything but his own wishes. Your employer may think he's rich enough to play king of the mountain here in his own private castle, but I think he'll find kidnapping not quite so amusing when I press charges once I get back to civilization." Her hands clenched at her sides. "How can he possibly think he can get away with it? I have friends and career commitments. People aren't going to just stand by and do nothing about my disappearance."

"Betz is amazingly thorough, and enough money can buy almost any form of cover-up." His lips twisted cynically. "Everything from forged notes to a telephone call that your own mother couldn't tell wasn't from you. And for the record, Jared Ryker isn't my employer," McCord added quietly. "Nor does he own the chateau. You might say we're both on loan. The chateau belongs to Senator Corbett." He raised a brow inquiringly. "Perhaps you've heard of him?"

Who in the United States hadn't heard of him? Tania wondered, stunned. A wealthy industrialist with a political family background so prestigious that it was thought by many analysts to be only a matter of time before he was catapulted into the presidency. Son of a Supreme Court judge and grandson of an ambassador, he possessed a keen intelligence combined with a boyish charisma that was quickly making him a power to be reckoned with. That Sam Corbett could have anything to do with an act so politically damaging and criminal as kidnapping was utterly outrageous.

McCord must have read the skepticism in her face. "It's all quite true," he said. "And I assure you that Sam Corbett isn't usually involved in anything so asinine as this piece of business. I've been his aide for the past two years and never been involved in anything more criminal than trying to dissuade a traffic cop from giving the senator a parking ticket. Please believe me when I tell you that your abduction wasn't planned by either Jared or the senator. The action was taken by Betz, the senator's head of security, on his own initiative." He shrugged. "Unfortunately, it's too late now to do anything about it."

"I think there's a great deal you can do about it," Tania said, her eyes flashing. "To begin with, you can release me and return me to New York."

He shook his head regretfully. "I honestly wish that were as easy as it sounds, but even the senator would agree that course is closed to us. You'll have to stay until they're ready for Ryker in Washington. We'll try to make certain that you have every comfort while you're waiting, and suitable compensation once you've returned to New York."

"Suitable comp . . ." Her words were choked off by sheer fury. "And just what do you consider compensation for kidnapping and drugging me, Mr. McCord? Perhaps, like your charming cohort, Mr. Betz, you'd like to add another hundred thousand or so and have me hop into your friend Ryker's bed in gratitude?" Her voice rose. "This is incredible. How could Ryker's whim cause a man as powerful as Sam Corbett to jump through hoops? To do such a callous and outrageous thing?"

"As I said before, bringing you here wasn't Jared Ryker's idea, Miss Orlinov." Kevin paused. "But I think you should know he wields a power that dims Corbett's by comparison. I wouldn't anger Jared if I were you."

"I risked my life to escape from a country run by dictators, Mr. McCord," she bit out. "It's a breed I know well, and I've never been afraid of anything that I know well enough to battle."

"But then, you've never been up against a battle of this magnitude," he said softly. "For starters, all Ryker would have to do was lift a finger and the U.S. government would return you to those dictators you mentioned."

Tania's eyes widened. "Impossible. I defected and claimed asylum. In two years I'll be a United States citizen. He couldn't—"

"He could," Kevin said softly. "I'm not saying he'd do it, but he definitely could, Miss Orlinov. A power struggle is shaping up on a scale that's never been known before, and Ryker is the prize everyone will be battling for. Neither Russia nor the U.S. would bat an eye at giving him anything his heart desires."

"Or his body desires?" she asked caustically.

"That too."

"Who the hell *is* Jared Ryker? What has he done? Created some sort of superbomb, or something?"

"You might say that." There was a curiously bitter smile on Kevin McCord's lips. "It certainly has the same potential for explosion. It's not my place to discuss Ryker's work with you, I'm afraid. He's already given instructions that you're to be kept as much in the dark as possible regarding the project. He thinks it may prove safer for you."

"It's a little late for him to express concern," Tania said curtly. "I've been kidnapped, drugged, and now you say I have every chance of being deported unless I submit to Ryker's every wish. You can't expect me to believe that he's worried about my safety."

He shrugged. "I know it's hard for you to accept that no one here is really a threat to you if you'll only try to cooperate."

"Not even Jared Ryker?"

"Ryker's not an easy man to know," he said slowly. "He keeps a hell of a lot of what he's thinking and feeling under wraps. Perhaps in his position I might do the same." His likable, rough-hewn features were thoughtful. "He's probably tougher than any man I've ever run across, but I think that if he'd let anyone get close enough he'd be a friend you could trust to hell and back."

"I'm sure he'd be grateful for your character endorsement, but I'm afraid I can't appreciate it," Tania said. "Nor do I intend to submit meekly to the kind of treatment I've been subjected to." Her dark eyes were smoldering. "Now that I've listened to what you've had to say, am I to be allowed to see the great man?"

"Why not?" He reached into the back pocket of his khakis and pulled out a folded piece of paper. "I've done my duty. Let him take some of the flak." He handed her a note. "There's one other thing I should explain before I let you go." His blue eyes were suddenly serious. "Betz's security staff may be unobtrusive, but you'll find them very much in evidence if you make an attempt to leave the chateau. They're efficient and more than a little lethal if need be. There's not a servant or guard in the chateau who's not completely loyal to Betz." His voice was ominously soft. "Don't make the mistake of thinking that we're not entirely determined about this, Miss Orlinov."

Tania felt a tiny chill run through her as she met McCord's steady gaze. The threat was couched in the most courteous of terms, but it was a threat nonetheless. She raised her chin defiantly. She had faced threats before and come through victorious. This was just another challenge to be met. She unfolded the note and scanned it quickly. The message was terse, scrawled in bold black script.

If you want to see me, I'll be at the birch grove.
                                            Ryker

If she wanted to see him? Oh, yes, there was no question that she wanted to see Dr. Jared Ryker!

She glanced up at McCord. "Where is this grove he waits in?"

"You go through the courtyard and the formal gardens to a small stand of birch trees," McCord supplied. "I might have known Jared would choose his favorite place on the grounds." She was already striding quickly to the door. "You'd better take a jacket—temperatures in the Laurentians this time of year aren't exactly balmy."

"Laurentians. That's Canadian, isn't it?" She glared at him over her shoulder. "You mean I'm not even in the United States any longer?"

"You're only a few hours in flight time from New York," he said soothingly. "The senator decided the chateau's seclusion would be safer for Ryker. Not many people are even aware that he owns it. He inherited the property from his great-grandmother, who was French-Canadian, and he thinks it's more politically advantageous to stress his American antecedents."

"It may not be as safe as he thinks," she said grimly. "And you don't have to worry about my being cold, Mr. McCord. At the moment I'm generating enough heat to melt the snow off those damned mountain peaks out there." This time the door's closing was definitely a slam.

By the time she'd crossed the courtyard and the extensive formal gardens, Tania was even more enraged. McCord should have furnished her with a road map. She'd lost her way twice in the chateau's winding corridors before she'd found her way down that sweeping staircase that would have done justice to a czarist palace. At least the paths in the garden had been laid in a more orderly pattern.

The birch trees were bare of foliage, their white branches lifting with stark asceticism against the azure of the sky. The little grove appeared to be on the very edge of the mountain itself, and offered a spectacular view of the valley below. There was a tranquil beauty here that would have been soothing under other circumstances. Now she scarcely noticed her surroundings, her attention focused on the slender, graceful figure of the man who was seated on the ground, leaning against the trunk of a birch tree.

He didn't see her, his head turned toward the valley below. The preoccupied expression on his brutally powerful face gave her a little jolt of shock. She hadn't allowed herself to think of Ryker's actual physical presence since the moment she'd regained consciousness. Now, like a double exposure, she had a brief searing memory of Ryker's expression as it had been only a short time ago, his eyes glazed and hot, his face heavy with sensuality, his naked muscular body hard with desire. Superimposed against that vision was the Jared Ryker before her now, his expression almost as coolly ascetic as his surroundings. Faded jeans molded the strong line of his thighs as he sat with his knees drawn up, his arms linked loosely around them. A dark blue flight jacket that was zipped halfway revealed the cream-colored sweatshirt beneath.

Warm color flooded her cheeks as she had a sudden memory of him pulling that sweatshirt over his head and throwing it carelessly aside. It was possible he felt the emotional turbulence that thought was generating, for he suddenly stiffened as if she had spoken, his crystal-gray gaze flicking warily to where she was standing.

"Hello," he murmured. There was no surprise in his face. "I thought you'd be here a long time ago. Kevin must have been more eloquent than I'd thought possible to keep you from venting your righteous rage on me before this. Come and sit down."

His manner was as calm as if he were inviting a chance acquaintance out for a sociable drink! The swift indignation that surged through her immediately dispersed the odd shakiness that had afflicted her at the sight of him. She strode swiftly to stand before him. "It would take more than McCord's 'eloquence' to do that," she said, her voice trembling with anger. "How can you sit there so calmly after what you've done to me? Don't you have the least notion of right and wrong?"

His eyes were regarding her gravely. "I'm sure Kevin made it plain to you that I had no prior knowledge that you were being brought here. It was a complete surprise to me to find you in that bed this morning."

"But it didn't stop you from taking advantage of the situation," she said hotly. She bit her lip vexedly as she saw his mouth curve in an amused smile. She hadn't meant to mention those blindingly sensual hours she had spent in his arms. She'd wanted to confine their conversation to a straight demand for her immediate release. Yet she hadn't been in the man's presence for two minutes before her unruly tongue had placed them both on exactly the terms of intimacy she'd wished to avoid.

"I didn't take advantage of you, little Piper," he drawled. "As Betz would say, I did what was necessary.

And I hope to God I never have to do anything that painful again. I must have walked ten miles after I left you, just to forget the taste of your breasts and the way you felt cuddled against me."

"Necessary?" She felt her cheeks burn with shock at the casualness with which he referred to those intimacies. "I'm afraid I can't agree with you. I don't think many people would regard taking sexual license with an unwilling woman as necessary."

"Sit down." He reached up, grasped her hand, and pulled her to her knees beside him. "That's better. All I could see from that angle was the pert little thrust of your breasts beneath your oversized sweater. I assume the sweater was meant to discourage my lust? I'm still in no condition to withstand any provocation, intentional or otherwise." His glance lingered on her breasts before returning to her face. "The whole point is that you weren't unwilling, sweet. That was what made the whole episode so damnable." His expression became grim. "That idiot Betz had you injected with paradynoline."

"Paradynoline?"

"A drug whose side effects are like an aphrodisiac," he supplied tersely. "Betz wanted to make sure you kept me happy and eminently satisfied while he was away from the chateau."

To her amazement her first reaction to this disclosure wasn't anger, but relief. She hadn't wanted to admit even to herself that the needs of her body could turn her into the voluptuary whom she remembered with uncomfortable clarity. The knowledge of her physical dependence on Ryker during those hours chafed unbearably at her sense of independence. It was much easier to accept the fact it had been a chemical, rather than the man himself, that was responsible for that sensual enslavement. It even served to lessen her anger toward him.

"Charming," she said caustically. "Is that his usual method of assuring you of your mistresses' compliance?"

"No, he usually finds money to be the most potent aphrodisiac. I understand he tried that first with you."

She nodded. "I thought you were some rich, perverted old recluse." She tossed her head. "Two out of four isn't bad."

"Actually, you did better than that," he drawled. "Though not in the same class as Corbett, I'm considered moderately wealthy." There was a glint in the icy gray of his eyes that might have been a twinkle. "As for the other designations, many scientists have a tendency to be recluses, and I certainly can't deny I've had any number of lewd thoughts since that night I saw you dance *The Piper*."

"I've been told that my performance arouses a number of interesting reactions, but I never thought it would inspire a kidnapping," she said lightly. Suddenly she realized she was actually indulging in a form of playful verbal sparring with the man who had, if not actually kidnapped her, certainly been the catalyst! She belligerently squared her shoulders. "Since you claim that all of this was done against your wishes, perhaps you'll tell me how you're going to make amends. According to your 'eloquent' friend, McCord, you're the one who has everyone bowing and scraping at your every command. Why don't you just tell them to let me go back to New York?"

"I can't do that. Even if I succeeded in convincing Corbett that security could still be maintained if we let you go, it just might be more dangerous for you. At least I can keep an eye on you here." He shrugged. "No security system is fail-safe. If there were a leak, there are certain parties who might decide it would be very advantageous to have a lever in the form of a woman I'd displayed an interest in." His lips tightened grimly.

"There's no way I'm going to let that happen to you, Tania." For a moment there was a glint of ruthlessness so savage in his eyes that it caused a little shiver to run through her. The next moment it was gone, replaced by quick concern. He straightened, his hand going to the zipper of his jacket. "You're cold," he said, frowning. "Why the hell didn't McCord see that you were properly dressed before he let you go?" He was slipping out of the jacket. Ignoring her protests, he draped it over her shoulders and thrust her arms into the sleeves. There was a curious tenderness in the little smile that touched his lips as he zipped it to her chin and carefully turned up the collar. "We wouldn't want you to risk getting sick, would we? Kidnapping is a serious enough crime. Causing you to come down with a cold in the head would be completely unforgivable."

"Completely," she agreed softly, her gaze fixed in compulsive fascination on Ryker's face. Why was that face so compelling? she wondered absently. It wasn't so much the bold prominence of the bone structure, but the vitality that pierced the guarded wariness of his expression. She shook her head to clear it and edged away from him. "You're absolutely refusing to release me, then?"

"I told you why I couldn't do that," he said. He paused. "But even if your safety weren't in question, I probably wouldn't let you go now."

"But you said—"

"I said a lot of things that were coolly logical," he interrupted, a trace of weary impatience shadowing his face. "What I didn't say was that, while Betz may have jumped the gun, it probably would have come down to this anyway. It was only a matter of time before I came for you." His gaze was steady on her bewildered face. "For once, Betz had the perception to read me correctly. I am obsessed by you."

Tania inhaled sharply. A wave of heat coupled with a liquid languor—that sensation she'd known only a few hours before—surged through her. No, it had been the drug, she thought frantically, it had been that para— something or other. She would not let herself be dominated sexually by Jared Ryker. "You want to go to bed with me?" she asked, keeping her voice steady.

Ryker's lips quirked with amusement. "Actually, that particular euphemism isn't quite explicit enough in this case. I've already been to bed with you." His voice became velvet-soft. "I want to be inside you. I want to hear you gasp with pleasure every time I thrust in and out. I want to feel you tighten around me and hold me as if you never want to let me go."

Tania could feel her nipples harden beneath the wool sweater as she listened. Her mouth was dry, and she moistened her lips nervously. "I think you're being more than explicit enough," she said, and to her annoyance there was a thread of shakiness in her voice. "I think I get the picture."

"No, I don't believe you do," he said. "That's only the physical aspect. If that was all there was, I might have given in to temptation this morning and taken everything I wanted from you." His slender finger reached out to touch one winged brow with great delicacy. "This isn't just a yen, little Piper. This is a full-fledged obsession."

She tried to laugh, but the sound came out as a rush of breathlessness. "Impossible. We only met the one time, even if you've seen me perform more than that. What you feel can't be more than a fleeting desire."

"I didn't think so either at first," he said quietly. "I thought it was because I was so damned bored that you had such an effect on me. I told myself that a few weeks in the sack with you was all I wanted." The tips of his fingers were now tracing the other brow with equal gentleness. "I tried to persuade myself I was only curious when I ordered Kevin to get me every article and story ever written about you." He smiled. "And of course I wanted the video tapes merely because I appreciate your skill as a dancer, as an artist."

"I didn't know about the articles," she said dazedly. The gentle stroking of her brows had a mesmeric effect on her. The action was almost totally sexless, as if he were stroking the plumage of a bird that might take fright and fly away any second.

"It didn't satisfy me for very long," he continued, as if she hadn't spoken. "I found myself trying to find out everything I could about you. I even compiled a list of your actual quotes so that I could build a picture in my mind of what lay behind that pixie face." He shrugged. "It wasn't enough. I began to leave the chateau and fly down to New York to watch you perform in person." His lips twisted. "It made Betz more than a little nervous."

"Just what are you trying to tell me? If you don't believe this is a passing fancy, what the devil do you believe it is?"

"I wish I knew," he said. "All I know is that it's not going to go away soon. It's going to be a long time before I'm going to be willing to let you leave me even for a little while." His smile was curiously bittersweet. "As I said, it's an obsession."

"But you can't do that," she protested, brushing his hand away from her face. "You can't keep me here against my will."

"From what they tell me, there's very little that I can't do," he said cynically. Then, as she would have spoken, he held up his hand. "But that doesn't mean I'm about to pressure you into anything. I've always believed that the only efficient method of wielding power is to persuade rather than bludgeon."

"How very condescending of you," she said tartly.

"And I assume that I'm to be 'persuaded' to occupy your bed?"

A smile that was surprisingly boyish warmed his dark face. "God, I hope so, sweetheart. I'm certainly going to make every effort to have it happen." Then the smile slowly faded. "Hell, yes, I'm going to try to seduce you. I want you so much I'm aching from it. But that's not all I want by a long shot. In the next weeks I'm going to learn you inside out. How you think, what foods you like, the memories and experiences that make you what you are." He grimaced. "Who knows? You may get lucky. Perhaps after I know everything about you, the fascination will fade a little and I'll be willing to let you go. It would probably be better for both of us if I did."

"And if it doesn't?"

"Then I hope I can make you want to stay with me until it does," he said quietly. "I know you want me. Those particular physical signals are pretty unmistakable. I can build on that. By the time it's safe to let you go, I have every intention of making very sure you have no desire to do so." There was a flicker of sadness in the depths of his eyes. "And if the charm of my company doesn't do the trick, I have a wild card that most assuredly will. You might say it's an offer that you can't refuse."

"You expect me to just sit still while you try to seduce me, after the way I've been treated?" Her dark eyes were flashing fire. "In spite of your research you don't know me very well if you think I'll submit meekly to your neat little plans."

"I know you well enough to realize that you can't resist a challenge," he drawled, his gaze narrowed on her face, flushed with indignation. "I have no doubt that you'll fight me tooth and nail both mentally and physically. But have you considered that an intimacy exists in battle that's as primitive as a sexual confrontation? I can build on that too."

She felt a tiny thrill of excitement run through her as she met the cool confidence of his gaze. Perhaps he did know her after all. Certainly the gauntlet he'd thrown down might be impossible for her to resist picking up. She was filled with heady exhilaration as she contemplated doing battle with him. She'd never been beaten yet, and Jared Ryker would prove an antagonist more worthy than she'd ever encountered.

"Let me understand you," she said carefully. "You refuse to let me go?"

"Yes."

She felt a tingle of emotion that might have been satisfaction. She knew herself well enough to realize it quite probably was. Now that she'd decided to accept his challenge, she would have been disappointed if Ryker had withdrawn it. "And this battle you're talking about," she said briskly, "what are the terms?"

He grinned with frank enjoyment as he observed her face come alive with eagerness. "Seduction, not force. You set the boundaries. Fair enough?"

She nodded with satisfaction. "More than fair," she said. "You're going to wish you'd been a great deal less generous before this is over, Ryker."

"I might at that," he said wryly. "Are you always this happy when you're contemplating an enemy's demise?"

"Always. But then, I always enjoy myself no matter *what* the circumstances. I decided a long time ago I could only be defeated if I let that joy be taken away from me." The smile she gave him was almost affectionate. "I intend to have a very good time taking you on. Would you like me to detail my battle plans for you?"

"I can hardly wait."

"My first priority will be to escape," she said calmly. She scowled as she regarded the mountainous terrain surrounding them. "I do wish you'd chosen some other obstacle for me to overcome. I've had it with mountains."

"Sorry," he said solemnly, though his lips twitched with amusement. "I'll keep that in mind in the future."

"Do that," she said, grinning mischievously. "That is, if you get the chance, of course. You may have changed your mind about the pleasure of my company by that time. I'm going to make your life perfectly miserable, you know."

"For instance?"

She pretended to consider. "Well, I don't approve of sexual teasing, but I've decided to make an exception in your case. If you think you're aching now, you're in for a shock. I'm going to drive you out of your mind, Jared Ryker." Her dark eyes narrowed determinedly. "And through it all you're going to know that you're never going to get what you want. Never."

There was a glint of admiration in Ryker's eyes as he said softly, "We'll see, little Piper. Remember, you're not doing the choreography this time. The moves may not be what you expect."

"But that always makes the dance that much more exciting. And a triumphant finale is even more satisfying."

He chuckled, and for an instant she thought she saw a flicker of pride in his face. "You're going to be a joy and delight, Tania Orlinov." He stood up and reached out a hand to pull her to her feet. "The crown of thorns and stinging nettles you have in mind for me just might be worth it." He slipped an arm affectionately around her waist and turned her in the direction of the chateau. "Now, though I know it's abominable tactics to reveal one's weaknesses to the opposition, I have to confess I'm freezing my ass off without that jacket." He made a face. "I've spent most of my time the last few years on an island I bought in the Caribbean, and it didn't equip me for autumn in the Laurentians. Let's get back to the chateau and get some hot coffee."

She obediently fell into step with him, and they made their way through the formal gardens in an oddly companionable silence. It wasn't until they'd nearly reached the courtyard that she noticed that Jared was scowling.

"Windloe," he said abruptly. "Are you still his mistress?"

Her momentary surprise was quickly replaced by satisfaction as she noticed the smoldering of Ryker's eyes. So the cool man of science had a jealous streak. It was a good thing to know.

"I don't think I'll answer that." Then, as his expression grew stormy, she said softly, "Stinging nettle, Ryker. Just a little touch of stinging nettle."

Chapter 5

The next morning Tania was up at six, as was her custom, did her stretching and warm-up exercises, and was out of the shower by seven. She was feeling remarkably fit, she realized with surprise as she quickly dressed in a pair of dark corduroy slacks and a cowl-necked cashmere sweater in a delicate shade of peach. She seemed to have recovered completely from the effects of the drugs she'd been given and was as vigorous and full of zest as usual.

In fact, she'd felt almost as well last evening, but she hadn't been able to convince Ryker of the fact. After coffee in the library, he'd insisted she return to her room and be served dinner there. When she'd protested, she'd been met by an implacability fully as strong as her own determination.

It hadn't seemed worthwhile to argue the point last night, but Ryker wouldn't find her equally compliant today. He was about to discover she'd meant everything she'd told him and that she was a force to reckon with. However, before she could start to wage open warfare, she'd have to reconnoiter her surroundings as well as her antagonists and determine their strengths and weaknesses.

She left her bedroom and found her way downstairs

with a good deal less difficulty than she'd experienced yesterday. That small victory caused her spirits to brighten. Knowledge and optimism were already easing her path in this bizarre situation.

She was met at the bottom of the grand staircase by the same broad-shouldered young man in the dark jacket who'd served coffee in the library last evening. What had Ryker called him? George, that was it. She smiled. "Good morning, George. I don't believe we've been introduced. I'm Tania Orlinov, and I'm going to be here a while." She made a face. "I guess that piece of information is redundant. I understand you've already been told to make quite sure that I don't leave."

George's expression of surprise vanished swiftly. "George Brady, Miss Orlinov," he supplied politely.

"I'm very happy to meet you, George." Tania beamed cheerfully at him. "I just wanted to tell you that I have no intention of being here for very long, but I hope we'll be friends while I am. No hard feelings, okay?"

"Okay." George seemed a little dazed. Then, with an obvious effort, he gathered his faculties to say, "I was told to show you the breakfast room as soon as you came down. Mr. McCord and Dr. Ryker have already eaten."

So she wasn't the only one who started the day with the rising sun, she thought. The early start of the two men was a trifle inconvenient at the moment, though. She'd hoped to see McCord at breakfast and put a few questions to him.

"I'll have breakfast later," she said. "Will you tell me where Mr. McCord is, please?"

He glanced at the grandfather clock in the stairwell. "He's usually in either the gymnasium or the sauna at this time of the morning. But I don't know——"

"Thank you," she interrupted firmly, giving him a dazzling smile. "Now, will you tell me how to get there?

I really must get someone to draw me a map of this monstrosity."

He hesitated briefly before shrugging his shoulders and proceeding to give her the directions she required.

The large gymnasium was empty when she arrived, so she headed directly to the door at the far end of the room, which led to an area well equipped with everything from steam and sauna rooms to a good-sized whirlpool. She paused before the birch door that obviously led to the sauna. So much for the shower she had taken earlier, she thought wryly as she stripped off her clothes and wrapped herself in one of the large bath towels she found folded and stacked on a shelf by the door. Then she opened the door and stepped into the cubicle.

"What the hell!"

Kevin McCord had been lying full length on the long bench across the room, but sat bolt upright as he glanced up to see her standing just inside the door. The room was bathed in a rosy glow from the red light that was the only illumination in the cubicle, but she had an idea that McCord's face would have been scarlet anyway. His arms dropped to shield his loins. She'd thought only women acted with that instinctive modesty when surprised in the nude.

She couldn't quite keep the laughter from her voice as she said, "I'm sorry to disturb you, Mr. McCord, but I thought we should have a talk." Her lips were twitching. "Perhaps you'd feel more comfortable with a towel. Would you like me to get you one?"

"Please." His answer was somewhere between a gulp and a gasp, and it caused the smile to linger on her lips as she left the cubicle to return with the towel. She crossed the few yards to the bench, carefully circumventing the pewter tray of hot coals in the center of the room, and handed him the towel before dropping down on the bench beside him.

He stood up and wrapped the towel around him with lightning swiftness. The glance he shot her as he resumed his seat was almost comically wary. "Couldn't it have waited until I was out of the sauna? You caught me a little unprepared."

Which might be to her advantage. "How was I to know that you'd be nude?" she asked with a grin. "But don't worry about it. I wasn't at all embarrassed."

"I'm glad to hear that," he drawled. "Are you always this precipitous?"

"Most of the time. When I have something on my mind, I like to take care of it right away and get on with other things." She leaned her head back comfortably against the wall behind her. "Where is Ryker this morning?"

He shrugged. "Probably off on one of his long rambles around the estate. He does a lot of walking, says it helps him to think." He lifted his brow. "Is that why you invaded my privacy and caused me to react like I was thirteen years old again? You were looking for Jared?"

She chuckled. "Did I do that?" Her dark eyes were twinkling. "Actually, I noticed the shock had a much more mature effect. Though I noticed your complexion turned a lovely shade that almost exactly matched your hair."

For a moment he looked indignant, but then he shook his head and smiled. "You're a very unusual woman, Miss Orlinov. I don't think I've ever met anyone quite like you."

"That's because there isn't anyone else like me," she said calmly. "I'm unique. I work very hard at it." Then, as he chuckled, she continued, "And no, I didn't want to see Ryker. It's you I wished to speak to."

"Now, why does that make me feel so nervous? I haven't felt this on edge since the senator had me arrange a *sub rosa* meeting between the President and Castro."

"There's nothing to be the least bit nervous about," she assured him kindly. "All I want is the answer to a few questions."

His expression was immediately cautious. "I told you I had instructions not to talk about Jared's work, Miss Orlinov. I can't disobey those orders."

"Tania," she urged. "How can I pump you and find out all I want to know if you're so formal? And I don't give a damn about Ryker's bomb or whatever. That doesn't pertain to my situation."

She could see the tension leave the man next to her as he, too, relaxed and leaned back against the wall. "Well, I'm glad of that at least. I have an idea you'd be as tenacious as our friend Betz if you put your mind to it. Pump away, Tania. I'm entirely at your disposal."

"Good. Now, what do you know about Jared Ryker?"

"As much as anyone, I suppose," he said slowly. "I've gone over his dossier. What precisely do you want to know?"

"Everything," she said briskly. "You can start with his background. Where was he born?"

"In a small town in West Virginia," he answered. "His father was a coal miner, who died of black lung disease when Jared was sixteen. His mother had divorced Jared's father when Jared was ten, giving him custody of Jared and a younger sister, Lita. His sister died a short time after Jared's father did."

"So he was virtually alone from the time he was sixteen," Tania said thoughtfully. "He mentioned that he was moderately wealthy. How did this come about with a background like his?"

"You wouldn't ask if you knew Ryker a little better," McCord said wryly. "I'd say he decided one day that it would be nice to be rich and set about accomplishing that end. He can be remarkably singleminded when he wants something." Then, as she continued to regard him patiently, he asked, "You want the details?"

"I want the details," she said emphatically.

He shrugged. "Jared is fantastically brilliant. Not only does he have an IQ that's out of sight, but he has a photographic memory. Probably what's even more valuable is the fact that his thinking is so original. He has the ability to shed preconceived theories and look at problems with an entirely fresh viewpoint. With his drive and genius it was inevitable he'd be offered every scholarship going, even the Rhodes." He glanced at her. "More?"

"More."

"He has several doctorates, including one in medicine, but he specializes in cellular chemistry. He spent three years in Viet Nam, which he doesn't like to talk about. As for money, after working for a large pharmaceutical company for a few years, he and Phillip Bartlett went into partnership to start their own firm. Several years ago he sold his shares in the company and disappeared from view, presumably to do some private research of his own. He's thirty-eight, doesn't play chess, and is positively lethal in a karate match, as I can testify." He lifted a brow inquiringly. "Now that you've completely stripped me of information, are you satisfied?"

"Not quite. What about women?"

McCord's face resumed its former cautiousness. "I think Jared might place any discussion of that subject in the same category as his work."

"Nonsense! I'm not one of his mistresses. And even if I were, I wouldn't throw a jealous scene and make him uncomfortable. All I want is information." And a little ammunition, she thought.

His expression retained its wariness. "He's never been married, but is very sexually active. He seems to have a preference for blondes." He paused deliberately. "And I believe that should conclude our little question-and-answer session."

There was a glint of steel in the blue of Kevin McCord's eyes and a firmness about his lips that caused Tania to look at him with fresh speculation. There was obviously more to the senator's aide than the likable charmer he appeared to be on the surface. If this was so, she'd be wise to probe a little further.

"Okay, no more questions about Jared Ryker," she agreed cheerfully. "Now let's start on you."

He chuckled. "Lord, you never give up, do you? I think I'm beginning to feel sorry for Jared."

Her first response was an impudent grin. Then she said, "You should. But I'm probably not going to be any threat to you, so there's no reason at all not to answer my questions about you."

"The key word there is 'probably,'" he said, and sighed ruefully. "Any woman who'd barge in on a naked man just to give him the third degree is capable of anything. What do you want to know?" Then, as she opened her lips, he held up his hand. "Don't tell me. Everything, right?"

She nodded serenely.

"Well, at least it shouldn't take as long as Jared's biography. I'm very boringly middle class, I'm afraid. I grew up in Bakersville, California, attended the University of California at Berkeley, and spent two years in the Peace Corps. I moved to Washington, D.C. five years ago and worked at several positions before I became Sam Corbett's aide. That was almost two years ago." He scowled at her. "And I have no intention of revealing my sexual preferences."

"That won't be necessary. I think I have quite enough to go on."

His face was suddenly serious. "I admire your tenacity, but don't think anything I've told you will help you escape, Tania. If it would, you'd never have gotten it out of me. I've been pumped by experts in the past, including members of the press." He smiled. "The only reason I let you do it is because I thought you'd be more at ease here if you knew something about us. It must be frightening to be snatched and left alone with no one but strangers surrounding you."

Tania felt a twinge of warmth for McCord. Despite the toughness she could sense in him, there were likable qualities to the man.

"I wouldn't worry too much about me, Kevin. I'm very adaptable."

"I gathered as much," he said. "But everyone needs a little help sometime or other. As much as it's within my power to give it, I will."

"I don't intend to be here very long. But I may take you up on your offer. I've decided to accept Ryker's offer of the wardrobe. It may come in handy. I'll also need a barre and mirrors installed in the gym." Her lips tightened. "I have no intention of missing practice and losing muscle tone even for the short time I'm here."

"No problem. I'll have them installed today." He made a face. "Though I can't say I'm going to enjoy working out in front of those mirrors. A man of my size has a tendency to have all the physical appeal of a pregnant ox."

"Oh, I don't know." The glance she slanted at him was teasing. "My first impression of you was more that of a bashful ostrich."

"Ouch, that hurt! Not the image a virile young

executive wants to project. It really was unfair of you to catch me off-guard. I'm usually positively dripping with poise and *savoir-faire*."

"That's not what I'm dripping with at the moment," Tania said as she stood up and moved toward the door. "I'm definitely starting to glow. I think I'll leave you to it and hop in the shower. Thank you for your cooperation. You've been very helpful."

"Any time," Kevin said politely. "It's been an experience, Tania. However, next time you have one in store for me, I'd appreciate a little advance warning."

"I'll remember that." There was a rush of cool air in the cubicle as she opened the door, then closed it carefully behind her.

Thirty minutes later she'd showered, dressed, and was proceeding to the next item on her agenda. Now that she'd learned as much as she could reasonably hope to at the moment about two of the principal inhabitants of the chateau, it was time to get a fix on her physical surroundings. She didn't expect the task to be easy after her experience with those winding corridors yesterday. As she explored, her surmise proved to be depressingly correct.

The chateau was enormous, but the size wouldn't have been difficult to deal with, for the plan of the central part of the building was simple and symmetrical. It was the additions put in at various times and apparently willy-nilly, that made the layout confusing.

Many of the rooms on the second floor were not used, and her own quarters were set off in a separate wing from those occupied by the other members of the household. The lower level was also vacant, and seemed to have housed a scullery and servants' quarters in the past.

The first floor, however, was as beautifully cared for and lavishly furnished as a museum. From the magnificent chandelier that dominated the foyer to the seventeenth-century tapestry that graced the wall of the formal dining room, the entire chateau was steeped in the glory of old-world culture and elegance. She opened the door to the spacious library, where they'd had coffee last night. A nineteenth-century clock on the mantle ticked loudly in the otherwise serene and lovely book-lined room. How was one supposed to be able to concentrate on one of those beautifully bound books with that annoying noise in the background? She'd definitely be doing her own reading in her room.

The exterior of the chateau was her next target. She studied closely the formal garden and courtyard that she'd walked through the day before. The outer perimeter of the estate was smaller than she would have thought. The chateau was bordered on three sides by cliffs that dropped with breathtaking steepness to the valley several hundred feet below. The only exit from the castle appeared to be the winding gravel road that led from the courtyard and disappeared around a curve some distance down the mountain. That road was sure to be well guarded if security was as tight as McCord had indicated yesterday. Of course, there were the possibilities offered by a concrete pad at the rear of the chateau to consider. It was obviously used for helicopter landings and, if escape by road turned out not to be feasible, she'd have to focus on the potential of that landing area.

"Don't you ever wear a coat?" Ryker's voice drew her quickly out of engrossed study of the serpentine path down the mountain. He stood only a few feet away, and the scowl on his face matched the tone of voice he'd used.

"Don't worry. I'm not going to appropriate your jacket again." She turned back toward the chateau. "I was just going to return for breakfast. I think I've worked up an appetite now."

"I imagine you have," Ryker said, catching up with her. "I could almost see the wheels go round while you were gazing down that road. Forget it, Tania, you'd never make it."

"We'll see. There's always a way out. One just has to find it." She wrinkled her nose. "Though I did notice that neither you nor McCord appeared to be exaggerating about the security measures here. On my little stroll I counted at least eight supposed servants who look more like Olympic weight lifters. How remarkable that such big men can move so gracefully and swiftly through that oh-so-convenient shrubbery."

"It's the ones who don't look quite so intimidating whom you have to watch out for. They have more of a tendency to resort to firepower, since they don't have brawn to rely on."

"Firepower?" Tania asked, her eyes widening with shock. She didn't know why that casual comment surprised her. Of course there would be weapons here that brought pain and death. How could there not be in a situation where a hundred thousand dollars in bribe money was considered trifling and kidnapping was a simple means to an end?

Ryker's hand on her arm was swiftly reassuring. "Don't be afraid. Nothing like that is going to happen to you. I've passed the word you're to be treated with kid gloves."

"I wasn't afraid," she said in hot denial. "And I don't need or want your protection, Ryker. I can take care of myself."

"I don't doubt it. A woman who can climb up and down a mountain in a snowstorm has very impressive credentials."

"Well, it was very small, as snowstorms go. But it

was a *very* large mountain." She chuckled. "You're right, though, my credentials are impeccable."

He opened the front door and stepped aside for her to enter. "Give it up, Tania. I'm not as much afraid of the security boys hurting you as I am of your doing something foolish and hurting yourself."

"You think I'll fall off your mountain, perhaps? I'm a ballerina, remember? We're very sure on our feet." She darted him a barbed glance. "And I make it a practice not to do anything foolish. Which is more than I can say for you, Ryker. Kidnapping is considered very foolhardy by most individuals."

"I told you I had nothing to do . . ." He shrugged resignedly. "I suppose it was too much to hope that you'd mellow overnight. So much for the 'sweet council of sleep.'"

"Much too much to hope, Ryker. I'm exactly of the same mind as I was last night." She glanced at him over her shoulder as she walked to the center of the foyer. "By the way, what's your favorite color?"

"Color?"

"What's your favorite color? You must have one. Everyone does."

He frowned. "I've never thought about it. I guess I have a preference for bright colors. Why?"

"Nothing." She started toward the breakfast room. "Just curious, Ryker. Just curious."

The tangerine gown would not only be considered bright, but brilliant, and it was certainly the most seductive garment Tania had ever worn offstage. Made of chiffon so soft and sheer it was like petals drifting about her, the gown clung and undulated with every step and every breath she took. She cast a rueful glance down at the neckline, which plunged to the waist before being caught in a matching tangerine cummerbund. She'd have to be very careful of those breaths or she'd come out of the gown entirely. Her hair was in its usual lustrous braid, and she fastened it with her own diamond star. It was quite remiss of Ryker not to supply her with a fresh selection of jewels to go along with the fabulous wardrobe that had arrived this afternoon. She grinned at the thought. She'd have to speak to him about that, she decided as she hurried toward the staircase.

The crystal chandelier glowed softly at this late hour. Sweeping down the last few steps to the broad foyer, Tania could imagine that she was going to a glittering ball in the long-ago past instead of a rendezvous with Ryker.

Actually, rendezvous wasn't the right word. It implied collusion on the parts of both parties, and this meeting was entirely her idea. By discreet questioning of McCord at dinner, she'd learned that Ryker could usually be found in the library poring over a weighty tome into the wee hours. She'd waited to leave her room until after midnight so she could be sure he'd be alone. No, "rendezvous" definitely wasn't the word for it: "Stalking Ryker" was a more appropriate description of her maneuver.

She drew a deep, steadying breath as she paused outside the cream double doors of the library. She'd never done anything like this before, and for a moment a quiver of uncertainty went through her. But she staunchly repressed that small self-doubt, assuring herself there was nothing to be apprehensive about. This was just another role to play, just another move to be made in the battle with Ryker. She threw open the library doors, flamboyantly entering the room and drawing the doors closed behind her, breasts thrust forward, head held high as her hands lingered on the doorknobs at her back.

Ryker was lounging in a Queen Anne chair across the room, his feet propped up on the matching ottoman. He was still casually dressed in the dark cords and hunter-green turtleneck sweater he'd worn at dinner. His expression as he looked up from his book to gaze at her with lingering thoroughness was curiously enigmatic. "Very beautiful. You should have given me some warning and I'd have dressed for the occasion."

"That's what McCord said. He didn't like being caught off-guard, either."

Ryker smiled. "He told me about your foray into the sauna. He was irritated that you'd rattled him like that." He paused. "However, I can't say that your appearance tonight is exactly a surprise. I was expecting a skirmish. I just wasn't expecting you in such full and potent battle regalia."

"You were expecting me?"

He shrugged. "I've studied your expressions a great deal over the past two weeks. I ought to recognize that air of repressed excitement about you at dinner." He smiled. "It's exactly the same look you have the split second before you execute one of those *grand jetés* with such exceptional elevation. What does one call that ability to rise so lightly, to hold position in the air?"

She drifted toward him, the brilliant panels of her gown floating about her. "*Ballon.* It's a special quality of elevation—and it applies equally to the way a dancer lands. If one has *ballon* she comes down softly, smoothly." She stopped before him and fluttered a panel of her gown. "Is this bright enough for you, Ryker?"

"Yes, it's bright enough," he said, his gaze on the neckline. "What there is of it. It's quite a change from the slacks and sweater you wore at dinner."

"I admit I thought about wearing it for dinner. But I decided there'd be no purpose to it. It would have much more impact on you when we were alone."

"And that's the purpose, I assume."

"But of course," she said, and punctuated her words

with a throaty laugh. "After going over the chateau's defenses, I decided it might take awhile longer to escape than I'd thought. It was only practical to initiate plan two." With one swift movement she was on his lap. "Would you like to kiss me, Ryker?"

He inhaled sharply, and she could feel his muscles stiffen against her. "Stinging nettles, Tania?"

"Stinging nettles." She nestled closer and brushed her lips in the lightest of caresses on the plane of his jaw. "Do you like this perfume? I don't remember the name of it, but I thought it was quite seductive when I sprayed it on."

"Quite seductive."

The scent of her hair was delicately, pungently floral, and he found it more heady than a heavier perfume could ever be, as she rubbed her cheek back and forth against his shoulder like a sinuous little cat. She felt as boneless as a cat, too, as she curled even closer to him. He carefully kept his expression bland, but he couldn't keep the knowledge of his body's arousal from her.

Her response was a triumphant smile as her arms curved around his neck. She brought his head down so that his lips met her own. It was a light, teasing kiss, and, like her perfume, its very delicacy made it the more tantalizing.

His lips opened hungrily to take more of her, his arms slipping around her back to pull her tight to his chest.

She drew back immediately and shook her head. "Oh, no, Ryker. This time I am playing the flute. I set the boundaries, remember?"

His eyes narrowed. "I remember. Are you going to tell me just what those restrictions are, or am I to find out for myself?"

"It's very simple," she said, smiling with infinite

sweetness. "I initiate, you respond." The tip of her tongue teased his lower lip. "But that's all you do. You don't move, or touch, or even kiss me unless I tell you to. How's that for a challenge, Ryker?"

"Entirely worthy of you, Tania," he said, casting a wry glance over his shoulder at her hand stroking his back. "Also worthy of the torturers of the Spanish Inquisition."

"But you're *so* strong and self-disciplined, Ryker." She moved her breasts against him with sinuous grace and heard him catch his breath. "Anyone can see how cool and controlled you are. A little exercise like this shouldn't bother you at all."

"Shouldn't it? Then something is seriously wrong. It bothers the hell out of me."

Her laugh was soft, a contented purr. "There you go again, admitting your weaknesses. You should really watch that, Ryker. You're not going to give me any contest at all."

Her hands slid up to his neck, around and down his chest. She tugged his sweater free from his belt. "I want to touch you. You won't mind sitting *very* still while I do that, will you?"

Her hands were exploring the taut muscles of his midriff before wandering up his chest to curl playfully in the soft thatch of hair there. Then one of her hands moved to the side. "Your heart is pounding so hard, Ryker. I can feel it jumping against my palm. Are you so excited?"

He didn't answer. His face was lightly flushed and his body rigid with control.

Her fingers brushed his tiny nipples before plucking at them with gentle provocation, which caused the drumming of his heart to increase. She felt a slight shudder run through him as her head lifted and her lips searched for his. She continued the gentle plucking while she kissed him slowly. She pulled away. The muscles of his forearms were bunched beneath his sweater as his hands closed on the arms of the chair with white-knuckle force.

"That's right, Ryker, don't touch me. You have to keep your word, you know. If you don't, then I win the game." Her tongue plunged into his mouth with all the erotic skill he'd taught her yesterday. Suddenly her hands left his chest and pulled the sweater down. The next minute she'd slipped off his lap and turned to face him, her eyes glowing with triumph. "Not that I won't win anyway. It's all just a matter of time."

She could see the pulse throbbing jerkily in his temple, but when he spoke his voice was level. "I gather the exercise is over for tonight?"

She nodded as she made an effort to steady her breathing so that he wouldn't notice those heated moments hadn't left her as unshaken as her words implied. "For the moment."

"I'm surprised that you're letting me off so lightly."

She backed away from him with seeming casualness, wishing now that the chiffon of her bodice wasn't quite so sheer. The thrust of her taut nipples must be clearly visible against the material. "It's just the beginning, the opening scene," she said with a bright smile. "I have to keep something in reserve for the next time." She paused. "And there *will* be a next time. Are you hurting, Ryker?"

"Oh, yes, I'm hurting," he said. "Maybe even enough to satisfy you, little Piper. You play a very mean flute."

"It will get worse," she assured him. "Unless you'd care to send me back to New York."

"Not a chance. I can take anything you can throw at me, Tania." His lips twisted. "I'm not saying it won't rip the guts out of me, but I'll be able to take it."

"It's a little early to be so confident," she said, a thread of exasperation in her voice. Though there was no mistaking the fact of Ryker's arousal, her victory wasn't as complete as she would have liked. The man possessed a strength of will that was even greater than she'd imagined. "Tell me that after a week."

"If you like," he said absently, his gaze narrowed on her face with an absorption that made her a little uneasy. "Your visit should be even more interesting than I first thought."

"Interesting? Oh, yes, I fully intend to make things interesting, if not entertaining, for you, Ryker."

"That isn't quite what I meant," he said. "I thought I knew you very well, but I've discovered today that beneath that gamin charm, you're not quite what you seem. You're carrying a defensive shield that I'd wager is hiding all sorts of fascinating secrets. It will be something of a challenge to see if I can't pierce that shield."

She felt a sudden rush of panic that she was quick to hide. That strength of will was evidently accompanied by a perceptiveness that was frightening. "You'd better prepare to be disappointed." She turned and sailed regally toward the door. "I'm not going to give up, you know," she said over her shoulder. "Not ever. You're going to lose, Ryker. I'll not let any man dominate my life ever again. I have *erb*. *I'm* the Piper now, and I intend to remain the Piper." The door closed behind her with an emphatic click.

Jared expelled his breath and got slowly to his feet. He crossed to the small portable bar against the far wall and poured himself a brandy. My God, his hands were shaking! With a deliberate effort he steadied them and drank half the brandy in one swallow. Well, what the hell had he expected? He'd been an inch away from throwing that sexy pixie down on the carpet and raping her.

Great heavens, she was a tough little bitch. Yet even

while she was tormenting the hell out of him, he'd been aware of a fugitive admiration for the determination and flawless execution of the moves she'd made tonight. He wasn't sure, however, he'd be able to retain that same attitude if she kept up her campaign, as she almost certainly would.

He refilled his glass and carried it back to the chair by the fire. Still, it hadn't been a total loss, despite the frustration that was eating at him. She had let something slip before she'd walked out of the room that he had an idea could be a key to the puzzle that was Tania Orlinov. Who was the man who had dominated her so completely that even the thought could arouse such fierce hostility?

He dropped down into the chair and raised his drink to his lips. He'd try to think about this piece of the puzzle—and not the fever of need she'd stirred in him. He put his head against the high back of the chair. It was going to be a long night, he realized. There was no use going to bed just to lie there thinking of a chiffon-clad siren with the hunting instincts of a tigress on the prowl. He'd stay and fight it out down here, where the brandy was readily available as an aid to forgetfulness.

And what the hell did *erb* mean? He'd have to get Kevin to work on that in the morning.

Chapter 6

"**S**he's done it again." Kevin put the elegant receiver of the French phone back in its cradle and turned to face Jared, who sat in a fireside chair.

Kevin's exasperated announcement was met by Jared's amused chuckle.

"Well, she was due. It's been three full days since the last attempt. What did she try this time?"

"Just guess who the security guards discovered in the routine search of the utility van at the checkpoint? Tania, of course. She hid in the back in a large cardboard box that normally holds emergency spare parts. Monday afternoon is the time Murphy always drives down to the town in the valley to replenish the supplies for the chateau."

"That's something of a surprise," Jared said, and grinned. "I thought she'd try the helicopter next. There was a distinctly speculative look on her face when those dispatches were delivered to you a few days ago."

"I'm glad you're so amused," Kevin said grimly as he crossed the length of the library to drop into a chair across from Jared. "I don't think Betz's security boys are finding it funny. This is her fifth escape attempt in two weeks, Jared. They're getting nervous."

"You're always telling me how tough and efficient

Betz's men are. They should have no problem keeping an eye on one fragile ballerina."

"Fragile, hell!" Kevin's expression was sour. "If you'll remember, that fragile little ballerina lowered herself about fifty feet by a rope from her balcony to the courtyard below one night last week." He ran his hand distractedly through his red hair. "Where the hell did she get hold of a rope?" He scowled. "I don't know why I'm surprised. The way you've let her run all over the chateau, she probably has a stash of everything from picklocks to crowbars."

"More than likely," Jared agreed, his lips twitching. "I wonder how she managed to smuggle herself into the van? Tania's nothing if not inventive." He lazily stretched out his long legs in front of him. "Is she on her way back to the chateau?"

Kevin nodded. "She should be here in a few minutes. Murphy was calling on the van's mobile phone as they were 'escorting' her back here. Two of the perimeter guards are riding with her." His expression was suddenly grave. "Can't you convince her to stop these escape attempts, Jared? Edgy men are dangerous."

Jared's position didn't change, but he stiffened imperceptibly. "Then, you'd better issue tranquilizers to those 'edgy' men. I'd be very displeased if Tania received even a tiny bruise from one of those nervous gentlemen."

"Do you think that I wouldn't be displeased too? Good Lord, it's impossible not to like the imp even while she's driving you crazy." He sighed morosely. "The lady has the determination of a pit bull. She's completely incredible. One moment she's laughing and joking and acting as if her stay at the chateau is as much fun as a kid's visit to Disneyland and the next she pulls something like this."

Jared could feel the tension ebb out of him. It wasn't fair to get up-tight with Kevin, who echoed his own anxiety about Tania's safety. It was obvious Kevin had developed a genuine fondness for her in the past weeks. But then, who at the chateau had been able to withstand her gamin charm? She treated even the guards who had recaptured her time after time with a philosophic good nature that resulted in both their baffled amusement and that nervousness Kevin was so concerned about.

"Well, our charming Mr. Betz will be back on the scene tomorrow and security will be reporting directly to him instead of you."

"Thank heaven for small favors," Kevin said fervently. "I can't say that Betz is one of my favorite people, but I'll welcome him with open arms." He darted a keen glance at Jared's impassive face. "And I think you will too. You've been as finely drawn as a violin string since Betz delivered his little surprise package to you."

It was a more accurate simile than Kevin knew, Jared thought wryly. He wasn't only as taut and drawn as a sensitively tuned instrument, but well played by that mischievous pixie who seemed to be dominating all of their lives. Stinging nettles. There was no doubt she'd been the painful irritant she'd warned him she'd be. She was uncanny in finding ways to insinuate herself through his defenses and launch an attack where he was most vulnerable. He'd quickly regretted revealing how her past relationship with Windloe disturbed him. Lately she'd been dropping references to the man with deliberate frequency, watching with narrowed eyes for a reaction. After the first few times he'd carefully guarded against giving her a response, but he couldn't quash the abrasive signs, much less the primitive emotion itself.

It was one thing to decide clinically that jealousy could have no possible place in the future he'd helped to shape. It was quite another to try to apply it to Tania.

Just the thought of Windloe with her, his hands cupping her breasts, his tongue . . .

He shifted restlessly and drew a deep breath, deliberately blocking out the image. He was a civilized, self-disciplined man, not a caveman. The electrifying rage he felt was a primitive impulse that could be sublimated. He'd never experienced jealousy before that dark-haired nymph had entered his life. It was possibly the newness of his reaction that had caught him off-guard and given Tania that minor victory.

He looked up to see Kevin regarding his moody abstraction with a curious alertness. He straightened slowly in his chair, his expression instinctively resuming its accustomed wariness. "There's no denying Tania can be a handful," he said lightly. "But you can't say it's been boring."

"No, I can't say that," Kevin agreed, pulling a face. "I find myself lying awake at night wondering what she'll try next."

"The helicopter," Jared drawled, his lips quirking. "Almost certainly the helicopter."

"I'll keep that in mind."

The door of the library was opened with explosive vitality. "Good afternoon, gentlemen," Tania said as she breezed into the room. "It's very chilly out today. Is there any coffee?"

"On the desk," Kevin said testily, trying to frown sternly. She smiled serenely at him and strode briskly across the library to the desk. Dressed in jeans and a dark windbreaker, her slight figure looked even smaller than usual, and there was a black smudge on her cheekbone that gave her a raffish appeal. "I'm surprised that you didn't wear something warmer, or didn't you know the back of the van wasn't heated?"

She shrugged. "I knew, but I couldn't take the chance of wearing anything bulkier. It was a tight squeeze in that box as it was." She reached for the carafe of coffee and then halted abruptly as she noticed that her hands were smudged with grease and dirt. "I seem to be a little disreputable at the moment. Will one of you do the honors?"

"I will," Jared said as he stood up and strolled toward her. He filled one of the cups on the tray, added a dollop of cream, and handed her the cup and saucer. His gaze was searching. "Are you all right?"

"Of course," she answered, her dark eyes dancing. "Other than a slight stiffness from stuffing myself into that box like a pretzel, I'm fine." She took a sip of the hot coffee and gave a sigh of contentment. "There's nothing that tastes as good as hot coffee on a cold day."

"And the guards?"

"The epitome of gentlemanly conduct, as usual. I quite enjoy our little encounters."

"Give it up, Tania," Jared urged quietly. "Can't you see that it's hopeless?"

She shook her head. "Nothing is hopeless. These little setbacks are just learning exercises." She grinned. "For example, I now know that there's a checkpoint I wasn't aware of before, where it's located, and how it's manned. Not bad for a dull Monday afternoon."

A reluctant smile tugged at the corner of his lips, and again there was that odd glimmer of pride. "Not bad." One hand reached out to caress the thick braid on her shoulder. "And this time you escaped with no more consequences than a dirty face. That may not be the case next time, Tania."

"The guards?" She shrugged. "They're so frightened of displeasing you that they're no threat." Then she frowned. "My face is dirty too?" One grimy hand went instinctively to her cheek. "Where?"

"I'll get it." He reached into his back pocket and

drew out a clean white handkerchief. "You'll only make it worse."

She stood quite still, accepting his ministrations like an obedient child as he drew a step closer and carefully wiped at the smudge of grease on her cheekbone. She smelled of crisp cold air, a light floral perfume, and motor oil, and her dark eyes were gazing up at him with the bold challenge he'd become accustomed to in the last weeks.

"I want to be alone with you this evening," she murmured, so that only he could hear.

"I thought you would." He was rubbing gently at her cheek. "I recognize the pattern."

"Of course you do," she said swiftly. "You're a brilliant man, Ryker. So you'll send Kevin away and teach me more about the intricacies of poker?"

"Yes, I'll send Kevin away." His lips twisted wryly. "And then we'll play 'games,' little Piper."

"Good." She stepped back, took one last sip of coffee before replacing the cup and saucer on the tray on the desk. "Now I must go to my room and shower away this grease." She wrinkled her nose distastefully. "I smell like a garage."

"I was finding it quite erotic," Jared said as he threw the soiled handkerchief carelessly on the desk.

"Were you?" Her gaze was speculative. "I'll remember that."

"I'm sure you will. I've discovered you have a mind that's exceptionally retentive where such matters are concerned."

She was moving swiftly toward the door, and her glance back at him sparked with mischief. "Have you discovered that, Ryker? I must be making even more progress than I thought." She gave a jaunty little wave that included both men. "I'll see you at dinner."

* * *

It took longer than usual for Tania to dress that evening. There was not only the acrid scent of oil to shampoo from her hair, but she wanted to take special pains to erase every trace of the tomboy from her appearance. She must be everything that was womanly and desirable, the complete antithesis of the grease monkey in the library. It was a necessary preliminary for the games that were to come.

As she finished weaving her hair in its accustomed single braid, she gave her reflection in the vanity mirror a critical appraisal before nodding with satisfaction. She'd debated about wearing a gown but decided the silky brocade of these Chinese lounging pajamas had a more tactile allure; then, too, this particular shade of sunshine yellow gave her olive skin a little of its glowing radiance. A brush of pink lip gloss and a little powder and she was ready to launch her evening campaign.

The last two weeks had been just as stimulating as she'd suspected at first they would be. The conflict between her and Jared struck sparks that made her feel breathlessly alive. It had been a heady victory when she'd scored even the smallest dent in that wariness with which he armored himself against her.

She frowned at a twinge of uneasiness so intense it was close to pain. What was the matter with her? She was zestfully enjoying their passage of arms. She certainly didn't want Ryker to lower his shield and let her know the man behind it. As long as he stood firm, unable to be overcome, captured, she could whip about him like a flame, circling his quiet strength and singeing and stinging at will. Playing dangerously. She must on no account let herself give in to this odd hunger to *know* Jared Ryker . . . know what he was feeling, thinking. It was becoming increasingly difficult of late to smother that hunger to know when she was in his presence.

More than once she'd felt, too, a wild impulse to

lower her own guard and see what would happen. Thank heaven she'd come to her senses before she'd actually gone that far. Ryker as an antagonist was a delight, but in any other role might prove too dangerous to handle. She'd already caught herself enjoying his wry humor more often than she liked to admit. His brilliance was unquestionable, and he had an aura of intense inner strength that was enormously appealing and reassuring. Good Lord, only a short time before she'd been discovered in that van this afternoon she'd actually felt a bit sad at the thought that she might escape!

A few hours later she was scowling at Ryker across the card table. During dinner and in the hours since, he'd been more punctiliously polite and withdrawn than ever before. He'd scarcely spoken to her in the last hour except to make courteous replies to her remarks. His attention presumably was concentrated entirely on the cards in his hands, and the only sound in the library was the crackling of the logs in the fireplace. No, there was also the sound of that blasted clock on the mantle. The steady, dull rhythm was like sandpaper on her nerves.

She cast a glowering look at the openwork time-piece beneath its crystal dome. "Do you keep that thing around to distract the other players' attention from their cards? Why the devil don't you put it away somewhere?"

He raised a brow. "You don't like it?"

She threw her cards down on the table. "It's too loud. It gets on my nerves." She pushed back her chair and stood up.

His gaze followed hers to the crystal-domed clock on the mantel. "I don't agree with you," he said softly. "I find it very satisfying."

"Satisfying?"

He shrugged, and tossed his cards carelessly onto the green baize top of the table. "Perhaps you'll also find it satisfying shortly." He smiled. "Tastes have a way of changing with circumstances, I've found."

"I can't imagine developing a sudden liking for that antique monstrosity. . . . And the only change of circumstances that would appeal is if this chateau had a moat I could throw it in."

"You never know," he said, his gray eyes resting speculatively on her face. "You seem to be a trifle on edge this evening. I've never seen you upset by something so trivial."

"It's the trivial things that have a way of chipping away our resistance," Tania said, as she moved purposely toward the fireplace. "We think they're too minor to bother with, and suddenly we find we've been weakened before we know it." She carefully lifted the crystal dome off the clock. "That's why it's always best to stem an annoyance at its source." She switched off the clock's mechanism, and there was an abrupt but very welcome silence in the room. "There, that's better."

She heard Ryker's sudden chuckle and turned to see his usually guarded expression had changed. His face was alight with humor and genuine enjoyment. "Little Piper, you're a treasure and a joy to me."

"What's so funny?" she asked, puzzled. Ryker seemed to be deriving inordinate amusement from her simple act of defiance.

"Nothing." He shook his head, a smile still tugging at his lips. "I was just thinking that we're more alike than you know. Our reasoning processes run along remarkably similar lines."

"Do they?" she asked. It appeared this was Ryker's evening for being cryptic. "Well, I'm glad I didn't upset you by stopping your blasted clock."

"No, you didn't upset me." His smile widened. "I stopped one myself once. It can be very satisfying, I know."

His dark face was illuminated with an expression of gentle warmth and humor that made it almost boyish, and his eyes were glowing with tenderness as he gazed across the room at her. Tania felt an odd ache start in her chest, and she was suddenly conscious of a melting sensation that filled her with a vague fear.

Fear?

She drew a deep breath, and her back stiffened at the thought. Of course it wasn't fear. She was just in an oddly vulnerable mood tonight. It would be gone tomorrow and she'd have regained her usual calm.

She smiled sweetly, her dark gaze narrowed on his face. "It wasn't my intention that you notice how much alike we are, Ryker," she said softly. "Tonight I wanted you to be more aware of our differences." She could see the grin fade slowly from his face and the mask of wariness return. She would *not* feel this twinge of pain. "I dressed very carefully to that end, and you haven't even told me you like the way I look."

"You're very lovely," Jared murmured, his gaze running over her lingeringly. "You're like a Chinese princess in that outfit. I don't think you need me to tell you that."

She was walking toward him, her movements as consciously alluring as any she'd ever made on the stage. "It helps. I like to know that you think I'm attractive. To know that I can stir you." She was next to his chair now, and her smile was deliberately provocative. "And I can stir you, can't I, Ryker?"

"There's no doubt about that," Jared said. She could see the imperceptible tensing of his muscles beneath his charcoal crew-necked sweater and the hollow of his cheeks deepen as his expression became taut. Why did it bring her so little satisfaction?

"You know why I wanted to be alone with you tonight?"

"I'd be pretty dense not to. As I said, I recognize the pattern. Every time you suffer a minor defeat, you come to me and make sure I have one too." His lips twisted. "And mine is far more physically painful than any of yours have been, I assure you. Sometimes I don't sleep all night after one of our little sessions. Does that please you?"

It should have pleased her, but for some reason it didn't. "Of course it does," she said firmly as she moved even closer to his chair. Her hand reached out to stroke his dark hair. Its heavy crispness curled around her fingers with a sensuality that was pleasing. "That's the purpose of the entire exercise. To make you so miserable that you'll want to let me go."

"Is it?" His gray eyes regarded her steadily. "Perhaps that was your reasoning in the beginning, but I think the situation has changed a little. I've noticed a few new and different nuances lately."

She shook her head vehemently, her hand unconsciously clenching in his hair. "Nothing has changed," she said quickly. "Why should it?"

"You tell me. Or better still, come here and show me. I think I've developed a few masochistic tendencies in the last two weeks. I've noticed lately that I sometimes actually enjoy the pain you inflict, little Piper. I embrace it like a lover and hug it to me like that Spartan boy in the legend with the fox that gnawed at his vitals."

Her hand in his hair was trembling. "Then perhaps I'd do better to stop," she said with a shaky smile. "I seem to be defeating my purpose." Her hand would have dropped from his hair, but he stopped her, his own hand swiftly grasping her arm.

"But you wouldn't want to take my word for it," he said silkily. "What if I were lying to you? You wouldn't want to give me victory by default, would you? Come close and sharpen those needle teeth on me, vixen."

She responded to that challenge in her usual fashion. Her chin lifted in defiance. "They don't need sharpening, thank you. I haven't found you all that tough in the past."

With a swift jerk that caught her off-balance he pulled her into his lap. "But as I mentioned before, circumstances and attitudes have a way of changing."

She could feel the warm length of his arousal burning like a brand through the material that separated their bodies, and she felt a little flicker of triumph. "Not all that much," she said demurely, gazing at him through the veil of her lashes. She pressed close, rubbing the softness of her unconfined breasts against him. "You desire me."

"Do you want me to say the words?" he asked calmly. "I desire you. Does that give you pleasure, sweetheart?" His hand was gently massaging the tendons in the hollow of her back through the brocade. "I don't mind giving you your little victories. Defeat isn't easy to accept, but it is even harder for you than for me." His palm lazily covered her small breast, and the sudden vibrant warmth caused her heart to beat crazily. "Would it help if I told you what it does to me to feel the way you harden and swell in my hand? That it causes an ache to start that goes all the way down to the soles of my feet?" His head bent slowly, and his lips opened to gently suckle at her other breast through the fabric. "You never wear a bra, do you, love?"

Her hands tightened spasmodically on his shoulders. "I'm not exactly voluptuous," she said breathlessly. "I don't really need one."

His hand in the small of her back arched her forward, and his tongue stroked her nipple teasingly through the silk. "I'm glad," he said thickly. "Even when it's driving me crazy, I like to know you're ready and waiting for me." He blew gently on the damp material and smiled at the instant pucker of response. "And you *are* ready for me, little Piper. Didn't anyone ever tell you that a huntress can get caught in her own snare when she plays a game like this?"

"No! It's not like—"

"Oh, but it is," he interrupted. "Do you think I'd have let myself be used in these torrid petting parties if I hadn't thought it would be worth my while in the end? I'm a bit old for this kind of refined torment." He grimaced. "It's a wonder I haven't gone completely gray putting up with your little games. The only thing that kept me from going insane was that I knew what you were doing was conditioning yourself."

"Conditioning?" she asked, her expression stormy. "Conditioning me for what, pray?"

The hand on her breast was stroking her soothingly. "For me," he said softly. "I wanted you to grow accustomed to knowing what it was like in my arms, to feel how natural it was to have my hands and lips loving you. You're at home with me now. You'd miss this as much as I would."

She was too honest not to admit there was every possibility he might be right. She did have a strange feeling of homecoming in his arms, even when she was enveloped in a need so intense she was dizzy with it.

Her hands were suddenly on his shoulders, pushing him away. "No," she said sharply. "Let me go. I don't want this." She tried to wriggle off his lap, but suddenly found his arms holding her in a firm, but gentle prison. "You said I could set the boundaries."

"And you've been doing just that," he said, pulling her inexorably closer until she was cradled against the broad wall of his chest. "But we both know that referred to sexual boundaries." His hand was smoothing the fine hair at her temple with a gentle hand. "This is entirely different. I'm not trying to seduce you, Tania."

Wasn't he? Perhaps not in the carnal sense, but there were other ways to entice that were even more beguiling. She felt again that melting tenderness, that strange aching hunger to reach beyond that wall of reserve and touch him. But he wasn't a man to give without demanding in return, and how could she give him that? Her own barriers had been up too long to yield to probing without pain. Yet his arms felt so warm and secure about her. Her cheek instinctively nestled closer against the rough wool of his sweater.

"This isn't any good, Ryker," she said wearily. "I don't know what you want from me."

"Yes, you do," he said quietly. "I told you I want to know everything about you. I want you to open to me and let me inside." He paused. "I guess what I'm saying is that I want to be your friend. I can wait for the other. I've developed a good deal of patience over the years and find generally that anticipation only sharpens the pleasure." His hand moved to the nape of her neck, gently massaging the taut muscles. "But since you've been here, I've begun to want something more. If I read the signs correctly, I think you have too."

She tensed unconsciously. The yielding he was speaking of wasn't physical. And the surrender he was asking was much more frightening. Her hands clenched on a fold of his sweater. "And will you open to me as well?"

"As much as I can," he said, his tone of voice grave. "As much as it's safe. We can't go on as we have been, you know. We've reached the point where it's almost as painful to stand still as move on to the next step."

"And what is the next step, Ryker?" she asked. She raised her head to meet his gaze. "I don't think either one of us can afford that kind of vulnerability. We're much safer going on as we have been."

He smiled as he leaned forward to brush a kiss on

the tip of her nose. "We may not be prepared for a permanent disarmament, but we might settle for a temporary truce. That shouldn't damage our fortifications too drastically. Will you give that to me, little Piper?"

"It would be a mistake," she whispered. All her life she'd avoided the pain that went with being that close to anyone. The friendship he was talking about was not the casual camaraderie with which she filled her life. She could handle that and still protect the core of privacy that kept her free. There was every chance Ryker would trespass on that very private territory. If there was one thing she'd learned about him in the last two weeks, it was that he never did anything halfway. "I don't think I could do it."

"You can do anything," he said, his eyes twinkling. "You're the Piper, remember? You have *er'b*."

She suddenly knew with certainty that he was right. Why shouldn't she take what she wanted? And what she wanted was an intimate knowledge of Jared Ryker. If she had to let him breach her own walls to attain that goal, she could always rebuild them later. For a woman with *er'b*, it would be child's play. "You're right," she said, her dark eyes dancing. "I can do anything, Ryker."

"Of course you can," he agreed promptly. "Now, do you suppose you could begin by calling me Jared?" He grinned. "Ryker sounds a bit militant, and I could use a change of pace after the hostilities of the last two weeks."

"Jared."

His name on her lips sounded oddly intimate, and he felt a little shock of sensation surge through him. He drew a deep breath, carefully keeping his expression from registering pleasurable emotion. He could sense the hesitancy and fear behind Tania's impudent acceptance, and he didn't want to disturb the fine balance between them. Strange how he was beginning to catch those vibrations emanating from her almost as if they were his own. Now those vibrations indicated the need for very delicate handling if he was going to coax her into his hand.

"That's better," he said lightly. "See how easy that was? There won't be any problem at all if we take it one step at a time."

The simple phrase caused her spirits to lift and banished the last vestige of uncertainty. They were the words that had given her strength during her ordeal in the Andes. She had a sudden fleeting memory of Jared in bed with her murmuring those words as he held her in his arms in an agony of sympathy on her first morning at the chateau.

"All right, Jared," she said quietly. "One step at a time."

"Good." He gently pushed her off his lap and stood up. "Now, why don't we celebrate our truce by taking a stroll up to the birch grove?" His eyes twinkled. "As usual, after a few hours in your very desirable presence, I feel a definite need to cool off."

Chapter 7

The night was crisp and clean, and the moonlight cast a pale glow over the valley below that made it look as unreal as a picture in a fairy tale. It was an indisputably lovely sight but Tania felt a shiver run through her just the same.

Jared looked down at her in quick concern. "You're cold? I thought surely that jacket would be enough. Do you want to go back to the chateau?"

She shook her head. "I'm fine. A goose walked over my grave, I guess." She suddenly chuckled. "What odd sayings you Americans have." But so descriptive, so very descriptive, she added to herself. Her gaze traveled restlessly over the rough terrain. "I can't say I share your fondness for this spot. In the daylight it's all right, but at night it's too harsh, too cruel."

He stopped, and his eyes searched her shadowed face. "Is it the mountains? You said before that they bothered you."

"Probably." She shrugged wearily. "I don't know." She paused beside the slender birch tree on the very edge of the precipice. She had an evanescent memory of her first glimpse of Jared leaning against this tree, so remote and strange, like the mountains around him. She shot him a swift, defensive look. "I'm not frightened, you understand."

"I'd never make the mistake of thinking such a thing," he said, his lips quirking. "Never you, little Piper."

Was she afraid? No, of course not. She just didn't like bloody mountain ranges. But it was suddenly intolerable that Jared would think she was. On their almost silent stroll from the chateau, she had been conscious of an odd closeness with the man by her side. It was as if there were a living cord binding them together.

"I'm tired," she said abruptly. She deliberately dropped down on the ground and leaned back against the white birch. "I think we should rest before we go back to the chateau." She cast a carefully casual glance at the rugged outlines of the mountains closest to them. "They're really quite pretty, aren't they?"

There was a gentle smile of amused comprehension on Jared's face as he sat down beside her. His arm drew her close in a sexless embrace that offered only warmth and comfort. "But they're not to everyone's taste. I can see how you could prefer other surroundings. I think you would have liked my island. Not a mountain on the entire three miles."

She remembered that Jared had mentioned he'd spent the last few years on an island in the Caribbean. She hadn't given it much thought, but now she was curious. "Would have?" she asked. "Why the past tense? Don't you own it any longer?"

"I sold it before I came back to civilization. It had served its purpose and furnished me with the privacy I needed to do my work." His voice lowered. "There wasn't a chance in hell I'd be let alone on the island once I went public. I needed a wall around me the size of Fort Knox."

"So you approached Sam Corbett?"

He nodded. "He had a ready-made security system, political contacts, and credibility. He also had the reputation for being fairly honest." He smiled cynically. "As honest as any politician."

There was an element of hardness in his voice that disturbed her. She hadn't realized how quickly she'd become accustomed to that gentleness of tone in the last few hours. She instinctively moved to distract him from the subject that had brought that abrasiveness to the forefront. "You're right, I probably would have enjoyed your island," she said lightly. "And not only for the lack of mountains. I much prefer a little foliage on my trees." She raised her hand to indicate the grove that surrounded them. The slender white birches looked strangely ghostly in the moonlight, their branches stretching toward the sky in a loveliness as stark as the mountains themselves. "I always hated the time when the leaves would fall and there would be nothing to protect the trees." Her face was dreamily reminiscent. "There was a tree in my mother's garden that was very old and gnarled, but it had the most beautiful glossy green leaves imaginable. I used to gather them and sew them into chains that I'd wear as a necklace or crown."

"Your home was in a small village just outside Moscow, wasn't it?" he asked, careful to display only an idle interest. "The autumn is short there; the winters are extraordinarily cold. There must have been many, many days when the trees were as bare of leaves as these."

"Yes, but it didn't really matter, for then there were always the wind chimes."

"Wind chimes?"

She nodded, her gaze fixed on the valley below, but not really seeing it. "Every year when the leaves would start to fall, my mother would hang wind chimes from a branch of a tree. It became a little tradition with us. She had brought them from Hungary with her. She told me that her father had given them to her when she was just a little girl herself." She closed her eyes. "I loved those wind chimes. No matter how ugly or harsh everything was, they were always beautiful. They glinted and shimmered in the sunlight like icicles, and their music. . . ." she paused, searching for words, "their music was like a blessed balm when things became too much to bear."

"And did they get that way very often?" he asked quietly.

Her eyes opened, and he inhaled sharply at the desolation he saw there. "It was never any other way," she said simply. "My mother was a whore, you know."

He felt himself stiffen with shock and then mentally cursed the instinctive reaction. Now that she was at last opening to him, he wanted nothing to inhibit the flow. "I don't understand," he said gently. "According to what I've read, your father was a colonel in the army and brought your mother with him when he returned from his tour of duty in Hungary. The magazines played it up as a grand passion."

"It was a passion, all right." Her smile was bitter. "He probably desired her greatly at the start. My mother was quite beautiful, you see." Her lips tightened. "She was also very simple and very gentle. She was perfect for my father."

"Perfect?"

"What could be more ideal for a destroyer than the quintessential victim?" she asked. "They were really quite a pair."

He was silent, afraid even the most casual comment would cause her to close within herself.

"After my mother died, I tried to look at him objectively. I tried to tell myself that he couldn't be as bad as I thought he was." She shook her head. "It didn't work, because he *was* that bad. I don't know what made him like that, and I don't even care anymore. No one has the right to drain all the joy from life, the way he did. He was like a vampire, devouring all the good things in life."

"Your mother?" he prodded.

"My mother was in love with him." Her lips twisted. "I told you she was simple. She'd let him do anything he wanted with her. When he took her from her home and family in Budapest to a strange country, he didn't even marry her. He set her up as his mistress in a cottage outside Moscow and visited her when the mood took him. I was born there, two years after she left Hungary."

"You were illegitimate, then?"

"To put it politely. My father rarely was so courteous. From the time I was old enough to understand, he made sure that I was aware that I was a bastard whose birth never would have happened if my mother hadn't been so stupid that she couldn't remember to take the pill." She smiled sadly. "She was always afraid to admit it even to me, but I don't think she'd really forgotten. I think her life was so hellish by then that she wanted something of her own. Someone to love who would love her back. It wasn't a great deal to ask."

"No, it was very little."

"My father didn't feel the same way. He thought she should be punished for the inconvenience and expense she'd caused him." She drew a deep, shaky breath. "So he decided to see that he was compensated for some of that expense. He started to send her other officers to 'entertain.' At first they were only high-ranking officials he wanted to impress or curry favor with. Later he wasn't so discriminating."

"Why didn't she just leave him and return to Hungary?"

"By that time he'd found I was useful for something after all," she answered. "He'd threaten to take me away from her and she'd do anything he wanted." Her voice was suddenly fierce. "Do you know how it made me feel when I realized that I was the scourge he was whipping her with? I wanted to kill him! Whenever he was around, it was as if I were burning up inside, as if a poison were eating at me." Her dark eyes were blazing. "Then I realized that was what he wanted, what he was feeding upon. He wanted to be able to inflict pain, anger, unhappiness—any of the negative emotions—wherever he could, because it increased his feeling of power. The only way I'd ever be able to defeat him was to rob him of that satisfaction." She drew a ragged breath. "So I began to sublimate the pain and the hate and concentrate on finding some element of joy in everything around me. God, it was hard sometimes."

She unconsciously nestled closer to him. His arm about her had gradually tightened in an attempt to pour strength and support into her. He could feel his throat tighten achingly, as if her remembered pain was his own.

"But it worked. I could see that it was working and I was getting stronger with it. He had control of every aspect of my life, but he couldn't take that away if I didn't let him." He eyes flashed. "And there was no way on earth I was going to let him do that. He'd already destroyed my mother, but he wasn't going to do that to me. I wasn't a victim. I have *er'b*!"

My God, and how she must have needed that strength. She was small and fragile even now, and he could imagine what a big-eyed slip of a child she must have been. Lord, he'd never counted on the tenderness that was flooding him with every word she spoke in that husky, intense little whisper. He felt as if he were melting inside, and it hurt damnably.

"How did you begin dancing?" he asked, hoping to ease her away from the more painful memories.

"My mother arranged for lessons in the village while my father was on one of his tours of duty outside the country." Her smile displayed a savage satisfaction. "By the time he returned, it was too late. I'd exhibited what they called 'exceptional promise,' and had been sent to the cultural department at Moscow and been accepted at the Bolshoi School. The cultural department is very prestigious and powerful in Russia, and he wouldn't have been able to withdraw me without showing cause." The smile faded. "He did manage to salvage a minor victory. He wouldn't allow my mother to go with me. He placed me in a foster home near the academy, and I was permitted to go back to visit her only twice a year. That was a lovely two-edged sword he could turn. It hurt both my mother and me." She shrugged wearily. "After a while, though, I don't think it really mattered anymore to her. She didn't care about anyone or anything that happened. He had won, you see. Her spirit was totally destroyed." There was a long silence that was fraught with raw tendrils of emotion so extreme it could almost be felt. Tania's eyes were bright with unshed tears as she stared blindly before her. He wanted to draw her into his arms and cradle her there. He wanted to reach out and take her pain into himself. He wanted to do anything that would erase that agony of desolation.

"Will you let me hold you, little Piper?" he asked, his voice suspiciously husky.

At first she seemed not to hear him; then her gaze moved dazedly to meet his own. "Oh, yes." Then, as he carefully enfolded her in his arms, she murmured, "Thank you, Jared."

He swallowed hard to relieve the ache that was tightening his throat at that polite, almost humble, acceptance. "You're welcome, sweetheart." His lips brushed her temple gently. "It's my pleasure."

Her arms slid around his waist, and she cuddled close with a touching childishness. Indeed, she felt more like a child at this moment than she ever had in her life. It was so good to be held and cosseted in arms that seemed to embody all the security and all the caring she had never known. Strange, she hadn't realized how much she'd missed those qualities until they were suddenly available to her. She'd been so lost in memories of that time long ago that it all seemed wonderfully right and natural.

His hands were massaging her back in soothing little circles. "Just relax, love. I'll take care of you."

Yes, he'd take care of her, she thought contentedly. She could trust Jared to hold back the darkness of those memories. He was strong. So very strong.

Strong. The word sent a sudden tingle of shock through her that pierced the dreamy euphoria and caused her to stiffen in his arms. Jared *was* strong, possibly the strongest man she'd ever known, and there lay the danger. "No," she murmured, shaking her head frantically. "No, let me go." Her hands were pushing at his chest. "I won't let you do this to me."

For a moment his grasp tightened around her, and she thought he was going to ignore her plea. Then his arms loosened slowly, before letting her go entirely, and she hurriedly moved away from him. He was too close. And she suddenly felt cold and lonely outside his arms. He made no move to follow her, but his gaze narrowed thoughtfully on her tense face.

"What is it?" he asked quietly. "Why are you so frightened?"

"I'm not frightened," she said fiercely. Oh, but she was. More frightened than she'd ever been in her entire life. "I just don't want you to hold me anymore. I don't need you. I don't need anyone."

"Don't you?" he murmured. "Somehow I got an entirely different impression a few minutes ago. Why won't you let me comfort you? I'm not going to hold a momentary weakness against you."

"I'm not weak!" she said, her voice vibrating with the force of the words. "I'll never be weak, and I'll never be dominated. Not by you or anyone else."

"Why do you think I'm trying to dominate you?" he asked, his lips twisting in a wry smile. "I don't think I've exhibited any overwhelmingly domineering proclivities in our relationship to date, and you certainly seem well able to hold your own."

"The strong will always dominate," she said. "It's a natural instinct to hunt out the weaknesses of those around them and use them to conquer."

"You're wrong," he said gently. "Strength doesn't always have a component of ruthlessness, as it did in your father's case, Tania."

"Perhaps not, but it's too dangerous to chance." Her dark eyes were glowing feverishly as she moistened her lips. "But why should we be talking about it anyway? There's no question of your ever being in a position to dominate me. This is an isolated situation that will never reoccur."

"Why do I have the feeling that our truce is now at an end?"

"It would never have worked anyway. I must have been crazy even to agree to try it." She tossed her head. "It must have been the full moon. It's said to do strange things to sane people."

"So we're back to square one?"

She rose lithely to her feet. "I've found that you can rarely go back. That leaves only forward, doesn't it? But whichever way it is, it'll be my way, Jared. It will always be my way!"

Then she was gone, streaking toward the distant chateau through the ghostly trees like a slender shadow.

Tania slammed the door of her room and leaned

against it for a moment, breathing hard, her heart a rapid
throbbing in her breast. She knew there'd been no
pursuit. Jared had merely watched her flight with that
quiet, resolute patience that characterized his every
move. There was no reason for this panic she was
feeling, and it had been a mistake to run away from him.
Those keen gray eyes seemed to know everything about
her, and there was little chance that he'd not interpret
her action for what it was. She would *not* be afraid of
him—there was no way he could reach her if she
remained firm. She was just as strong and determined as
he, wasn't she?

Oh, Lord, she hoped so. Tonight, for the first time
in her life, she'd experienced doubts on that score.
During that moment in Jared's arms she'd wanted to flow
into him, become a part of him, share that cherished
privacy that she'd never relinquished to anyone.

Why had she yielded to the impulse to confide in
him, when she'd never discussed that part of her past
with anyone, not even Marguerite? If anything signaled
how dangerous Jared was to her, that confessional
monologue surely did. All he had done was hold her in
his arms and listen with the powerful intensity inherent
in him, and he'd seemed to draw her to him with
magnetlike force.

She unzipped Jared's jacket and took it off, wanting
nothing to remind her of that momentary weakness. She
strode briskly toward the bathroom, tossing the jacket
carelessly on the chair as she passed. It was a mistake she
mustn't repeat. She couldn't risk losing even a particle of
her individuality to Jared. Though he'd never shown any
ruthlessness toward her, she knew it was there in spite of
what he said. She'd learned to trust only herself, and she
wasn't about to let herself be beguiled into entering a
relationship that would endanger not only her emotional
stability, but her very independence.

She opened the door of the bathroom, unbuttoning the mandarin collar of the yellow brocade tunic as she did so. No, she couldn't take that chance, she thought as she turned on the shower and quickly stripped off her clothes. And she certainly couldn't continue the sexual intrigue she'd indulged in with Jared these past two weeks. Now that she recognized how vulnerable she was, it would be the height of foolishness. The only sensible course would be to bring this episode to a swift summation.

Escape.

She stepped beneath the shower, letting the spray cascade over her in a soothing stream. It was the only answer to a dilemma that was becoming more serious than any she'd encountered. She must put an end to these playful attempts at escape she'd regarded as almost a game and concentrate all her efforts on her objective, to get away. She had an idea that she didn't have much time to accomplish the goal if she were to withstand the pull Jared was exerting on both her emotions and her senses. To give in on one front would be to lose on both, and she wasn't about to do so. No, it must be escape, and very soon.

Tania's decision was actively reinforced the next morning when she arrived at the gym for her usual five hours of practice at the barre. Edward Betz, dressed in a dark T-shirt and trunks, was slowly and methodically chinning himself on a bar on the far side of the room. She stopped abruptly, and the heavy door closed behind her with a dull thud. At the sound, Betz looked over his shoulder with the swift wariness of a startled animal. The wariness was replaced immediately by his usual impassivity as he dropped from the bar with surprising litheness. His physique, now that it wasn't concealed by the dark, conservative suit, was also a surprise. There wasn't an ounce of flab on his square, solid body. His short legs were corded with muscle, and his chest and shoulders were equally powerful. Only his plump face and brown, Basset-hound eyes reflected any hint of humanity, and that was nullified by their distant expression.

"Good morning, Miss Orlinov," he said. "I understood you didn't start your practice until seven. I hoped to be through here and out of your way before that time. I'll leave at once."

"I'm a little early," she answered tersely. "I had trouble sleeping." Her shock at seeing him was rapidly being superseded by anger. He was being so damned courteous—as if he hadn't arranged the kidnapping that had brought her here! The man was completely unbelievable. "But why should you let my presence bother you? I didn't notice that you had any hesitation about interfering in my life."

"You're still annoyed with me," he observed slowly. "I'd hoped you'd be resigned to the situation by this time." He leaned down to pick up a hand towel on the floor by the bar. "But from what my subordinates tell me, you haven't even tried to adjust." He patted his forehead with the towel. "You're a very difficult woman, Miss Orlinov."

"Difficult? Because I object to being kidnapped, drugged, and carried off to some chateau in the wilds by a man who has the morals of a procurer for a bawdy house?"

"It was necessary, Miss Orlinov," he said, wiping his neck. "I only do what's necessary. I did try to persuade you first, if you remember. The use of force is always regrettable."

"Yet you had no hesitation about using it," she said, her eyes flashing fire. "And certainly no moral reservations."

He looked up, his brown eyes steady. "No, I had no moral reservations, Miss Orlinov. It might be wise if you realized that fully. I really can't afford to have morals at all." His smile was almost kind. "You see, I'm not a terribly clever man. I'm very slow, and it takes me a long time to comprehend things that more intelligent people understand immediately. I have to work extremely hard even to stay level with those people." Beneath the impassive features, she was suddenly conscious of a current of power. "You may not be aware of it as yet, but I'm tremendously ambitious. I have no intention of giving up the position I've reached by such hard work because I've failed to please the senator in this matter." He shook his head. "No, I definitely can't afford to quibble about morals."

Good Lord, and to think she'd taken the man so lightly that first day in her dressing room. She could feel his determination as almost a living force. He might have been as slow as he said, but that calm, ruthless obstinacy was still an element to be reckoned with.

"I'm sorry you thought my presence was required for your purpose," she said caustically, ignoring the shiver of apprehension that realization had brought. "Because I'm afraid you'll have to make other plans. I have no intention of remaining here."

"So I understand," he said. "Your escape attempts have been brought to my attention." There was a flicker of impersonal admiration in his face. "Some of them were quite inventive. You're to be congratulated. You really kept my men on their toes."

"I wasn't conducting a training exercise for your security team, Mr. Betz."

He shrugged. "It doesn't matter. The results were the same." He frowned. "But you came extremely close once or twice. I think it's best that you cease these attempts."

"I imagine you would," she said with saccharine sweetness. "But I have no intention of obliging you, and one day quite soon I'll succeed."

"That's what I'm worried about," he said. "I couldn't tolerate that possibility, you know." His brown eyes were mournful. "As I said, you're a very difficult woman, Miss Orlinov. According to the information I've received, you haven't even fulfilled the purpose for which I brought you here."

"Not by any fault of yours," she said bitterly. "You certainly believe in hedging your bets, don't you? Kidnapping wasn't enough—you had to give me that damned injection!"

"The paradynoline?" His brows lifted in surprise. "I thought you'd realize it was required in that situation. It was essential that Dr. Ryker be kept contented in my absence."

"Well, I'm happy to say that your little plan failed miserably," she said between her teeth. "I can assure you that Ryker has been far from content since you've been gone."

"Yes, you've not been occupying his bed, I understand." He was frowning in perplexity. "I didn't count on Dr. Ryker's not insisting on it once I'd arranged things so efficiently. It was quite a surprise to me." His expression cleared. "However, you appear to have kept things interesting enough to hold his attention even without a physical involvement. So bringing you here was definitely the correct move. Now that I'm back I can take care of any adjustments that need to be made."

"Adjustments?" Her expression was blank with surprise.

"Well, you can't expect a man with Dr. Ryker's physical needs to continue like this indefinitely," he said calmly. "It's been over four weeks since Dr. Ryker's had a woman, and we have to assume he's very much on edge.

There's even a possibility that he may become impatient and restless again if the situation's not fixed soon. That can't be allowed, of course."

"And just how do you intend to 'fix' it?" she asked, her fists clenching unconsciously at her sides. "Another injection of paradynoline, perhaps?"

"I'll have to think about that," he answered thoughtfully. "It didn't seem too effective the first time, but that could have been because the dosage was comparatively light. I'll have to discuss it with Dr. Jeffers before I come to a decision. There don't appear to be many other avenues to explore. It's an exceptionally touchy problem to handle, considering Dr. Ryker's aversion to using force in your case."

Her question had been sarcastic, but the man was actually serious! She felt a shiver of heat run through her as she recalled those hours of mindless sensuality she'd known the morning in Jared's arms. Combined with the powerful natural attraction she'd admitted to herself, she'd be no more than a puppet whose strings were pulled by Jared . . . and the man standing before her. She couldn't even bear to think about it. "No," she said, her eyes wide and frightened in her suddenly pale face. "No, you wouldn't do that to me."

"What?" he asked, his face still clouded with absorption with his "touchy" problem. "Oh, no final decision has been made. I thought I'd made that clear. I'll get back to you later on it." He turned toward the door that led to the sauna area. "Now, I know you want to start your practice, so I'll leave you to get on with it. I apologize again for interfering with your time here." He turned back, and there was again that flicker of admiration on his face. "I understand those practice sessions aren't only long, but require an amazing amount of stamina and self-discipline. Those are qualities that I admire very much, Miss Orlinov. Very much indeed."

For fully half a minute after the door closed behind him she continued to stare at it in bewilderment. It was hard to believe that their conversation had actually taken place. Betz seemed a villain straight out of the funnies, but no cartoon character could ever be this frightening. She hadn't the slightest doubt that once his decision had been made, only something resembling an earthquake registering eight on the Richter scale would keep him from carrying out his plan. And if those plans included her willing presence in Jared's bed, he'd use any method he saw fit to effect that end.

Paradynoline. That threat had frightened her even more than she'd let him see. She closed her eyes and drew a deep, steadying breath. She couldn't let her will be tampered with again like that. Even though she was certain Jared would have nothing to do with Betz's plan, that didn't mean he could prevent her being given the drug. She'd been injected with it once before against his will, and what was to prevent its happening again? A determination on the scale of Betz's was as difficult to fight as a tidal wave moving slowly and inexorably toward shore.

Her lids flew open, and she moved automatically toward the barre, her mind churning furiously. There was no way she could afford to let herself be given that drug. But with Betz back at the chateau, it was a very real possibility. She automatically assumed first position and began *grand pliés*. As always her gaze was fixed on her reflection in one of the mirrors attached to the walls around the barre. That gaze was entirely lacking its usual critical study of the position of her body; in fact her actions were mechanical, her attention far removed from ballet exercises.

She'd already resolved that her next escape attempt must not only be successful, but executed very soon. Now, that timing had to be accelerated by the urgency engendered by Betz's arrival. Tonight. It must be tonight.

Once the decision was made, she felt her spirits lift and the fear ebb out of her. Yes, tonight would not only satisfy the urgency she felt, but quite possibly it would catch Betz's men off-guard. They wouldn't expect an escape attempt so soon after yesterday's fiasco. Well, they'd get a little surprise, wouldn't they? She grinned at her reflection in the mirror. Now for the escape route itself, she thought.

The road. Here, too, the element of surprise might be on her side, and now that she knew the location of the checkpoint, there was every chance that she'd be able to circumvent it without being observed. She'd be on foot this time, and, she hoped, they wouldn't expect that either. It was about three miles to the checkpoint and Lord knew how many more to the valley below. She was going to need all her strength to make that journey at a pace that would assure her of finding a town or a farm before Betz was aware of her disappearance and on her trail.

She'd reached the section of barre exercises devoted to the strenuous *grand battement*, the rapid raising of the leg to its greatest height and its controlled return to the floor. She lowered her pointed toe. She wouldn't go all out, as she usually did. She would conserve her energy, for she would need all the energy she could muster . . . tonight.

Chapter 8

Damn this moonlight! Was it only last night she had blamed the full moon for her temporary madness? She was going to blame it for considerably more than that if those clouds didn't oblige. She needed the cover of darkness to cross the courtyard and get around the curve in the road before the guard completed his rounds.

She shrank against the stone wall, deep in shadow. Her gaze was fixed worriedly on the sky, watching the clouds; they approached the moon with a laziness that stretched her nerves to the limit. The guard should be back around to the courtyard in another four minutes, according to her calculations. She'd spent three hours here in the shadows four nights ago, observing and timing the guard's movements. If she hadn't had an opportunity to sneak into the back of the van, she'd wanted to be prepared to go out on foot, as she was doing now . . . as she *would* be doing now if those clouds would just cover the moon. She bit her lip in frustration. She didn't dare leave the shadows until the moon was obscured, and she must at least be across the courtyard before the guard rounded the north wall. She could chance his being in the courtyard for the short time it would take her to get around the curve of the road.

Only three minutes to go. With one hand she tugged at the collar of her turtleneck sweater beneath the dark jacket while she clutched a coil of rope in the other. Move, damn you, she commanded the clouds. With maddening slowness, they drifted across the bright sphere, bringing the welcome darkness.

She flew out of the shadows like an arrow shot from a battlement in the chateau long ago, the rubber soles of her tennis shoes skimming over the rough cobbles with sure swiftness. By the time she reached the road she had only one minute to go before the guard would reappear, and already those blasted clouds were rolling through the skies as if fleeing the moon.

She streaked down the road, her braid flying out in back of her and her breath laboring in her lungs as she raced the cloud that could mean her escape or capture. She lost. She was a full fifty yards from the curve in the road when the moonlight suddenly flooded the road with the clarity of daylight. She felt the remaining breath leave her body, and she hesitated for a moment, as if that moonlight were an actual blow striking at her. Lord, it was as bright as a spotlight, and the guard should be rounding the wall right now.

She hadn't thought she could go any faster, but the sudden burst of adrenaline that panic released proved her wrong. Let him be late, she prayed frantically, or let him be thinking of something else. Let him stop for a cigarette, or be looking anywhere but at the road. At any moment she expected to hear a shout and the sound of feet pounding heavily on the cobblestones behind her, but there was no sound except the sharp gasps of her own breathing. Then she'd rounded the curve in the road and was out of sight of the chateau!

Relief washed over her with a force that made her head swim. The first difficulty was overcome and she was on her way. She slowed her steps and then came to a complete halt. Her heart was pounding painfully in her breast and her knees felt weak as butter from reaction. Now that the first bit was out of the way she had to regain control of her nerves, quiver from the tension produced by the precarious cloud cover. There was still the checkpoint to get past and the rest of the road to the valley to cross before she was free.

She drew several deep, slow breaths and then set out at a deliberate steady trot, covering a great deal of ground without feeling the same physically exhausting effect of her sprint from the chateau.

Her escape plan had formed the morning she'd found two key pieces of mountain climbing gear in the back of a closet in the gym. Now she carried those items: a coil of rope and a grappling hook. Her gaze never wavered from the road ahead. Her mind firmly shut out all fears and worries that could weaken her.

The rock-strewn road was rough under her feet and the crisp autumn breeze cool on her warm cheeks. This was far different from the last experience she'd had with a mountain. It should be a piece of cake in comparison, she assured herself staunchly. Well, perhaps it wouldn't be that simple. Though the physical conditions were certainly easier, she had the more dangerous human factors to contend with . . . and one of those human factors should be in evidence just around the next curve.

Her pace slowed to a walk, and she hugged the inner side of the road, taking as much shelter as she could from the foliage on the side of the cliff. Heaven knew there was little enough to hug, she thought dispiritedly. The road seemed to be cut out of the mountain itself here—a bluff on one side, a sloping verge of perhaps five or six yards on the other side. From the edge of the verge it was a sheer drop to the valley below.

But the verge was the key to her escape. She'd noticed there was a sparse straggle of trees on it near the checkpoint. With any luck she'd be able to use them as cover to slip past the chain link barricade across the road. Despite the moonlight, they should provide enough shadow for her to avoid being seen if she were careful. But that steeply sloping terrain was going to prove tricky. On her previous reconnaissance she'd detected little or no ground cover on the verge, and keeping her footing on an incline that steep until she reached the stand of pines was going to be nearly impossible. Her lips curved in a wry smile as she recalled her words to Jared only two weeks ago. Surefooted or not, she might well fall off this bloody mountain.

Well, that was why she'd brought the rope and the grappling hook, wasn't it? She could secure the rope around her waist and use the grappling hook on the trees, working her way from one to another across that sloping verge until she was past the checkpoint and it was safe to crawl back up on the road.

She'd been expecting it, but her heart still lurched when she came around the bend and saw the brilliant glow of the Coleman lanterns about fifty yards ahead. She instinctively shrank closer to the bluff while her gaze swiftly searched the scene ahead for an alternate route that wouldn't be as risky.

Two steel posts anchored the chain barrier stretched across the road. And the two guards who patrolled it were lounging on the bluff side of the road playing cards, leaning against the padded seats of their overturned motorcycles. She could hear their voices in the clear mountain air, and it gave her a little shock. They sounded so close she might have been right next to them. At least their lanterns were on the bluff side of the road, and if their game was interesting enough, it might take their attention off any noise she might make as she crawled past them. It was difficult to tell from this distance, but she didn't think they were the same guards who had brought her back to the chateau yesterday. In fact, neither one was familiar to her, and she'd thought she'd run across every security guard on the place at one time or another in the past two weeks.

Well, she couldn't stay here all night gawking at them. It was obvious the physical setup hadn't altered, and she was just going to have to keep to her original plan. She took the rope and grappling hook from her shoulder and checked the knot she'd tied in the steel loop of the hook to make sure it was tight, then dropped the grapplng hook on the ground while she knotted the other end about her waist with equal care.

There was a burst of laughter from the men playing cards, and it caused her to jump with surprise. She drew a deep breath and forced herself to relax. Easy. This was just a piece of cake, remember? She was going to have to be very cool and certain in the next few minutes, and unsteady nerves would not help her.

She picked up the grappling hook and waited patiently until the clouds once more obscured the moon before dashing across the road and crouching on the edge of the verge for a moment. Then she slowly slid down onto the verge itself, carefully holding on to the trunk of the tree closest to the road. Oh, Lord, it was going to be worse than she'd thought. The earth slid out from under her, and she had to clutch desperately at the pine to keep from sliding with it. The ground seemed to be composed of nothing but loose dirt and shale—it was a wonder it even supported the scraggly pines that bordered the road. Still holding the trunk of the tree with one arm, she cautiously brought the grappling hook into play, reaching as far as she could and fastening it to the tree nearest her. Thank heaven the distance between most of the trees wasn't over two or three feet. It was a relatively simple matter to slip the hook around each slender trunk and then pull herself painstakingly hand over hand to the tree itself.

Once she became accustomed to the tempo of the procedure, her progress was much more rapid, and if she hadn't needed to be stealthy, she'd have been able to cover the fifty yards or so in a relatively short time. As it was, it took her almost twenty minutes to draw even with the barricade. She paused for a minute to catch her breath and wipe her chafed hands on her jeans before taking a fresh grip on the rope. With only the width of the road separating her from the two guards, she could feel her breath constrict in her lungs and the muscles of her stomach knot with tension. She could practically hear them breathe, she thought nervously. One false move and they'd be sure to hear her and react with the efficient swiftness Betz's men always displayed.

But there wasn't going to be a false move. All she needed to do was to continue as she'd started, and in a few minutes she'd be safe. With the utmost caution she negotiated the next two trees, and she was past the checkpoint! Only a few yards past it, but it was a victory nonetheless.

Her swift surge of triumph was abruptly stemmed as she disengaged the hook and prepared to move on. The closest pine was over four yards away! The shock and dismay she felt almost caused her to let go of the tree she was clinging to. There was no possibility she'd be able to lean that far to slip the hook around the trunk. Damn it, just when she was almost home free. She bit her lips, anxiously trying to think of a way out. There was only one, and it was so risky that she hesitated to attempt it. She'd have to toss the hook and hope to encircle the base of the pine. In the darkness her chances of succeeding weren't all that great, and even if she did, the noise might give her away. Well, she really had no choice. She just wished that she'd paid more attention when Tyler had wanted to teach her the fine art of pitching horseshoes, that weekend at the farm.

Her eyes straining in the darkness to gauge the distance, she balanced the hook in her hand as if it were a boomerang. Then, with a murmured prayer on her lips, she let the hook fly through the air. Had she made it?

But suddenly it no longer mattered. If the loud clang as the hook hit the shale hadn't given her away, the minor rockslide that resulted certainly had.

"Sweet Jesus! What the hell was that?" One of the guards jumped to his feet, grabbing for a lantern.

There was nothing left to do but run for it. Her hands ripping frantically at the knot at her waist, she scrambled to her feet and lurched forward, trying desperately to regain the road.

Strangely, she didn't hear the crash of the shot until after she felt the first burning pain rip through her. She knew an instant of wild regret, more poignant than anything she'd ever experienced. Then there was only stark terror as she pitched forward, rolling like a broken toy down the sloping incline and off the edge of the cliff into the darkness beyond.

"Dr. Ryker, are you awake? It's essential that I speak to you." The knocking on his door was repeated with a persistence that belied the politeness of Betz's words.

How the hell could he help but be awake? Jared sat up in bed and leaned over to the bedside table to switch on the lamp. He'd just dropped off when Betz had started that damned knocking, and being awakened didn't improve a disposition that was on the raw anyway. "Come in, Betz. It had better be damned 'essential.'"

Betz opened the door and approached cautiously. He was dressed in his usual dark Brooks Brothers suit. Did the man sleep in his suit, for God's sake? Jared wondered.

"I think you know by now I'd never disturb you for anything that wasn't extremely important." There was a touch of indignation in that ponderous voice. "I believe your privacy has been guarded with the utmost care since you've been here."

"Get on with it, Betz," Jared said wearily. "You're here now. Let's have it."

"I'm afraid you may be quite upset, Dr. Ryker. There's been a slight difficulty regarding Miss Orlinov."

The impatience and annoyance vanished as the anxiety that was always latent in him these days surfaced rapidly. "Slight difficulty?" His voice was carefully neutral, his gaze sharp as a laser. "And just what do you consider 'slight,' Betz?"

"She's been shot." Then, as Jared inhaled sharply and his face turned white, he continued hurriedly. "It's only a flesh wound in the shoulder. Liston assures me there was no serious damage done."

Jared threw back the covers and leaped out of bed, his every move charged with electricity. "Where is she?" His tone was clipped. He stepped into his pants. "And who the hell is Liston?"

"He's a new man I brought back from Washington with me. I decided the chateau needed a change of personnel, as I detected evidence of softening in the attitudes of the other guards toward Miss Orlinov." He frowned. "He's really a very good man, you know. He didn't intend to hit her—it was only meant to be a warning shot. He was startled when she appeared so suddenly at the checkpoint."

"The checkpoint? Is that where she is?" Jared thrust his feet into a pair of brown loafers. Why the hell hadn't he realized she'd try something like this? She'd been almost feverishly gay at dinner that evening, and that should have signaled him that she was hiding something. He'd thought to give her a little time after last night so she could re-erect some of her defenses and feel more secure with him. Now she'd been hurt, and who knew how badly? A security guard wasn't qualified to make the judgment that a wound was superficial. My God, what if the bullet had severed an artery? She could bleed to death before he could even get there. What if there was nerve damage?

Betz was nodding. "Liston radioed word to me from the checkpoint by mobile phone and I dispatched the van to bring her back to the chateau." He paused. "I told them to wait to transport her until you arrived on the scene, however. Since you have a medical degree, I thought you'd prefer to examine her before she was moved." His brow arched enquiringly. "I hope that was in order, Dr. Ryker?"

Jared grabbed a shirt and jacket from the armoire. "I'll need the medical bag you'll find in the closet in the bathroom," he said crisply. "You have the jeep waiting?"

Betz moved obediently toward the door of the master bath. "Yes, of course. I also sent someone to awaken McCord. His experience in the Peace Corps provided him with a certain amount of expertise in medicine that I thought might prove helpful. He'll be waiting for you in the courtyard." He stopped at the door. "This is all very regrettable, Dr. Ryker. It *was* an accident, you realize."

"It may be more regrettable than you know." Jared's

voice was icy, but there was sheer savagery in his granite-hard face. "Because if she's really badly hurt, I'm going to throw your 'good' man, Liston, off this son of a bitch of a mountain. I just may do it anyway. And then I'll start on you, Betz." He turned and left the bedroom, striding through the corridors and down the stairs.

Kevin was waiting by the jeep in the courtyard, as Betz had promised. His jeans and checked flannel shirt had obviously been thrown on hurriedly, and he was shrugging on a sheepskin jacket. His red hair was rumpled, and he was frowning with concern. "Lord, I'm sorry, Jared. This never should have happened."

"You're right, it never should have happened," Jared said grimly as he swung up into the passenger seat. "As you said, nervous men can be dangerous." He drew a deep, calming breath. He mustn't give in to this rage that was tearing through him. He'd need all the cool steadiness he could muster when he saw how badly she was hurt.

Kevin climbed into the back seat. "No one wanted to see her injured, Jared."

"She could have been killed." Jared's voice was ragged in spite of his effort at control. "For all I know, she may be critically hurt, and all because of some maniac with a spastic trigger finger. Don't talk to me about accidents, Kevin."

Betz came hurrying out the courtyard door, carefully placed the brown cowhide medical bag he was carrying in the back beside Kevin, and slid into the driver's seat. "Sorry to have kept you waiting. I took the precaution of asking Dr. Jeffers to fly in immediately in case he was needed."

Jared tensed. "You told me it was only a flesh wound."

"I'm sure it is," Betz said quickly as he started the

engine and put the jeep in gear. "It's just a precaution, Dr. Ryker."

"It'd better be, Betz," Jared said softly, his tone as menacing as a cocked pistol. "If I were you, I'd be praying very hard that it is."

The security man shrugged. "I understand your concern. You needn't emphasize it by threatening me. Liston is a very reliable operator, as I told you. If he says the wound is minor, then I'm certain Miss Orlinov isn't in danger." He reversed the jeep with precision and drove out the arched gate of the courtyard. "In a few minutes you'll be able to judge for yourself."

The checkpoint was teeming with activity and lights when they rounded the curve. Not only were there several men milling around the area, carrying lanterns that cast a glow over the entire scene, but the dark green van itself was parked diagonally across the road, its headlights glaring.

Betz halted the jeep directly before the van and was immediately approached by a tall young man in a leather jacket who burst hurriedly into speech. "It wasn't our fault, Mr. Betz. She hopped up out of the trees and surprised us. We didn't even know who she was. All we saw was a shadow."

"And do you always shoot at shadows?" Jared bit out.

The man moistened his lips nervously as his gaze took in Jared's taut face and blazing eyes. "Not always, sir. But in this case we were told to shoot first and ask questions later, because your safety was paramount. We were only following orders, Dr. Ryker."

"Where is she?" He had to make sure that Tania was all right before he gave himself the pleasure of taking the man apart limb from limb.

The man answered quickly. "We've put her in the

back of the van. I've rigged up a bandage for her shoulder, and the bleeding has stopped. She's unconscious now, but she fainted only when I was applying the bandage." He turned. "I'll take you to her."

"Let's go," Jared said crisply. He got out of the jeep and strode rapidly toward the back of the van. "Bring my bag, Kevin."

"Right." Kevin's hand closed on the handle of the cowhide medical bag, and he shot a glance at Betz. "If I were you, I'd get that particular man as far away from the chateau as I could send him. I don't think he's going to be safe within a thousand miles of Ryker."

"I'd already deduced that," Betz said. "Dr. Ryker doesn't appear to be at all reasonable when it comes to Miss Orlinov." He shook his head morosely. "Pity. Liston is a very valuable man."

When Kevin reached the back of the van, one glance told him that Betz's very valuable man was extremely close to being permanently mutilated. He'd never seen anything resembling Ryker's savage rage as he looked down at the supine figure of Tania Orlinov on the bare metal floor of the van. "My God, her clothes are torn to shreds. What the hell have you done to her? You lying bastard, if I find out you've raped her, I'll chop you into little pieces." He dropped to his knees beside Tania. "Where did she get all of these bruises?"

Liston had gone pale and showed surprising discomposure for the cool operator of Betz's description. Maybe it was not so surprising, Kevin thought as he watched Ryker parting the torn remnants of Tania's sweater to reveal a lurid bruise encircling her midriff and red welts and scratches along her rib cage. Ryker was more dangerously intimidating at that moment than any man he'd ever known.

"We didn't touch her," Liston protested desperately.

He swallowed hard and then proceeded more calmly. "Those are rope burns. When she was shot, she rolled down the incline and over the edge of the cliff. She'd been using a grappling hook on the trees, to inch her way past the checkpoint, and the rope was still knotted about her waist when she rolled over the edge of the cliff. The rope kept her from falling to the valley below, but naturally the jerk bruised her quite a bit." He tried to smile. "Donalson and I tried to be as careful as we could when we pulled her back to the verge, but there wasn't any way we could prevent her from getting a little scraped. She was lucky as hell to come out of it as well as she did."

Lucky. Jared felt the muscles of his stomach tighten at the vivid picture Liston's terse words evoked. Tania dangling hundreds of feet in the air from a slender rope and two trigger-happy idiots the only hope she had of survival. It made him sick even to think about it. Lord, yes, she'd been lucky.

"You say she was still conscious when you were bandaging her wound?" Jared asked thickly. He hoped not. It must have been sheer hell for her if she'd been totally aware during that nightmarish experience.

Liston nodded eagerly. "She was conscious the entire time until we were trying to get her jacket off. She was even able to help a little while we were hauling her up the cliff." He knelt beside Ryker and pushed aside the torn sweater to reveal a crude bandage fashioned of brown plaid flannel, obviously torn from a shirt. "See, the bleeding's stopped entirely. The bullet just grazed her shoulder, clean as a whistle."

"Get your hands off her!" Liston jumped as if he'd been flicked with a whip and backed hurriedly away. Jared drew a deep breath and tried to submerge the anger that had suddenly exploded. "Just get out of here, Liston. Now!"

The guard didn't have to be told twice, and Kevin had to step aside hastily in order to avoid being trampled as the man jumped out of the van. Ryker didn't give him a second glance, his gaze fixed intently on Tania's shoulder.

"Clean as a whistle," he repeated disgustedly. "She'll be lucky if she doesn't get blood poisoning from this damned makeshift bandage. Get in here with that bag, Kevin."

She was so little. He hadn't realized until this moment just how tiny, how delicate, she really was. She was lying there like a broken bird, her lashes casting dark shadows on her pinched cheeks, and the rich olive of her skin was pale and sallow.

"She's awfully still." Kevin's voice in his ear was anxious. He'd opened the bag and extracted a pair of surgical scissors that he passed to Jared. "If the wound isn't that serious, why hasn't she regained consciousness?"

"Loss of blood and shock, probably," Jared said grimly, carefully cutting away the flannel bandage. "I hope to hell that's all. God knows that's bad enough." His hands were remarkably steady, he noticed absently. It was a wonder, when he was shaking so inside. He hadn't felt as helpless as this since the night Lita died. But he wasn't helpless now. He had knowledge and experience on his side. He had to remember that. He hadn't been able to help Lita then, but he could help Tania now.

He soon discovered Liston was right. Though the wound looked ugly and inflamed, the bullet had just grazed the fleshy part of the shoulder. He breathed a sigh of relief as he quickly removed the bandage and reached for an antiseptic. He carefully cleaned the wound before rebandaging it with sterile gauze and taping it firmly.

"That's all I can do for her now. I'll give her a shot to ease the pain, and antibiotic and tetanus injections. After that it's up to Betz's doctor to do his stuff."

Betz himself spoke from just outside the open door of the van. "You seem to have done everything that's required." His brown eyes were speculative. "Perhaps we won't have to have Dr. Jeffers treat her after all. Senator Corbett usually finds him very cooperative, but he might balk at treating a gunshot wound without reporting it."

"Wrong." Jared's tone was crisp and emphatic. "You'll not only get the best doctor available to care for her, but you'll fly in a competent plastic surgeon to stitch the wound. I don't want even a hint of a scar to remind her of this. She's a dancer, and she'd hate to have her body less than perfect."

"But I really think—"

"Then, stop thinking, Betz," Jared said as he inserted the hypodermic syringe filler with pain-killer. "Your track record doesn't show much promise in that area. I may have a medical degree, but I haven't practiced since my internship, and I'll be damned if she won't get the best there is. I don't care what diplomatic problems you have with Jeffers, just get him here."

"If you insist," Betz said reluctantly. "But it may prove extremely awkward."

God, he might murder the man before the night was over! "Bullet wounds have a habit of being awkward," he said caustically. "You might remember that the next time you're giving orders to those apes who work for you." He tossed the disposable hypodermic needle back in the bag. "Now let's get her back to the chateau. Tell the driver I want the ride to be pure velvet. If he jars her even a little, I'll break his neck. Understand?"

"You needn't worry. I've already warned him to be

most careful." Betz disappeared from view, and a moment later they could hear his voice at the front of the van.

Kevin was climbing out of the van. "I'll ride back with Betz and get on the phone to arrange for the plastic surgeon to come for a preliminary examination. I'll also have to call the senator and tell him what's going on, so he can start smoothing ruffled feathers." His lips twisted. "It's one of his great talents."

"So I've heard," Jared said, taking off his jacket and putting it carefully over Tania. He barely heard the van doors close as he drew her into his arms so that she was lying across his lap and cradled against the cushion of his shoulder.

She was very light, yet there was a solid warmth about her that was vaguely comforting. It reminded him of the vitality and strength that usually glowed from her like an aura, and God knew he needed that memory now. His arms tightened about her protectively as the driver started the engine and then drove slowly and cautiously up the road toward the chateau.

It was strange to experience this feeling of belonging to another human being after all those years of standing alone. Strange and a little painful. He wasn't sure he liked it. The emotion had too many sharp edges, and it would probably take time to round them off before he'd feel comfortable with it. Well, he had all the time he needed, and he'd better start adjusting now, because he knew it wasn't going to go away.

He had called it an obsession, and it certainly had been that. She had amused and challenged him at every turn, sparking off him like a small firecracker, arousing him to sexual frenzy one moment and touching off that melting tenderness in him the next. He hadn't really allowed himself to think beyond their time together at

the chateau. Perhaps he'd been a little afraid to face the
commitment he'd seen glimmering on the horizon the
first night he'd met her. Now that commitment wasn't on
the horizon, it was here in his arms. The knowledge had
exploded within him with the same force as the bullet
that had struck her, destroying all the unessentials as if
they'd never been.

"Jared."

It was a mere ribbon of a whisper, but he heard it,
and his gaze flew down to meet the brilliant darkness of
her own. The vitality of her expressive eyes made the
fragility and pallor of her face even more apparent, and
he felt a thrill of fear course through him. "Are you in
any pain?" he asked quickly.

She thought a moment. "A little."

"I've given you a shot. You should be more comfortable very soon."

"I'm comfortable now." She nestled closer to him. "I
feel so warm and safe." She shivered. "I was frightened,
Jared. I don't think I've ever been as frightened in my
life." Her words were becoming slurred as the sedative
took effect, and they were spoken with a childlike
simplicity. "Hanging there in the darkness knowing—"

"Don't think about it," he said huskily. "It's over and
you're safe." His arms tightened about her. "You'll
always be safe now."

Her lids were slowly closing. "Yes, I'm safe now,"
she said drowsily. Then her lashes flew up to reveal her
blazing dark eyes. "Jared!"

"Yes, love?"

"I positively *hate* mountains."

In the next few days Tania came to hate mountains
even more, for they figured in dozens of fevered
nightmares that dominated her existence. If she wasn't

dangling over a precipice in an agony of suspense and fear, she was actually falling . . . trailing through fire, her lungs bursting with pain, falling through ice and snow that froze her to the marrow and caused shudders that wracked her body.

And through it all she was vaguely aware that Jared was always there. It was his strong hands holding her own that stopped the rope from breaking. The cool silver of his eyes kept the fire from burning, and only the warmth of his arms kept her from the cold.

She would wake to find him lying beside her, his hand gently stroking her hair, or feel a cool cloth on her forehead, and knew without opening her eyes who handled it with such deftness. At first it troubled her in some vague fashion that she was so dependent, but it seemed impossible to summon the energy to fight. She let herself flow with the tide, flow with Jared caring for her. It was what she'd wanted all along anyway, wasn't it? She'd wanted to flow into him, seeking out all the dark corners and making them her own. Now, to her relief, she found that depending on him was not only possible, but the supremely natural thing to do. All that was necessary was to accept his gift of warmth and gentleness and suddenly that other knowledge would be hers also.

Like a hundred tiny tributaries that wound their separate paths to the sea, that knowledge filtered through the levies of distrust and anxiety she'd erected, as if they didn't exist.

There was nothing in the man who cared for her so tenderly to fear or distrust, so why shouldn't she give him that acceptance? Though he remained an enigma, it was no longer one that represented danger to her. In these days of pain and nightmare, she'd come to this realization and it filled her with a serene sense of well-being.

The dark green velvet canopy above her bed was familiar, but everything else in the room seemed strangely unreal, when she opened her eyes two nights later. The light of the exquisite crystal lamp on the bedside table cast an intimate glow within its narrow perimeter that included the figure of Jared Ryker, sitting in the tapestry wing chair beside the bed. His face looked taut and drawn, the broad cheekbones more prominent than ever, but his silver eyes were swift and alert in the darkness of his face. They zeroed in immediately on Tania, though she was sure she hadn't made any conscious movement.

"Hello," he said quietly, his hand reaching out to close tightly on hers. "It's about time you came back to me. I was beginning to get a little worried."

Come back to him. Somehow those words sounded so beautifully right, she thought dreamily as her own clasp tightened around the warmth of his hand. Just as it was beautifully natural to wake up and see him sitting there. Dressed in jeans that hugged his slim hips and the muscular line of his thighs and a collarless pearl-gray shirt that made the bronze of his skin gleam darker in contrast, he had his usual air of leashed power and strength. She'd fought that strength for so long and with such skill. Now it was even difficult to remember why it had been so important to resist him.

"Hello," she answered softly. "I think this is where I came in." Her dark eyes started to twinkle. "Though I hope this time I haven't been plied with aphrodisiacs."

There was a flicker of surprise in Jared's face. "I'm glad to see you're in such good spirits," he said. "But perhaps I'm a bit premature. You haven't been given paradynoline, but you're still under the effects of sedation. Once you've come out from under it completely, you'll probably be mad as hell."

Now that he mentioned it, she could detect the

signs of that sedation in the languor she was feeling in every limb, but somehow she didn't think this feeling of security was drug-induced. If Jared had sedated her, he must have had a very good reason, she realized. She should really make the effort to remember what it was.

"I fell off the bloody mountain, didn't I?" she asked.
"You were afraid that I would." She felt a chill of pure panic run through her, and she instinctively shied away from that memory, which was a nightmare in itself. "Did I ever tell you that I didn't like mountains?"

"Innumerable times," he said, leaning over to pull the satin sheet higher over the fullness of her naked breasts. "It seemed to be your prime obsession in the past two days. Not that anyone could blame you." His lips tightened grimly. "An experience like that would cause most people to have a nervous breakdown, not just a few nightmares."

"More than a few," she said, her voice shaky. "I was there, remember?"

"Yes, more than a few," he agreed quietly, his gaze holding hers with steady forcefulness. "And I was there too. We beat them together, Tania. I won't promise you they won't come back, but there's nothing we can't do if we work at it together." A sudden teasing grin lit up the gravity of his face. "What are nightmares to a woman with *erö?*"

"Nightmares are a piece of cake," she said lightly. The phrase inevitably brought back a fragment of memory. That was what she'd told herself her escape would be. She shifted uneasily, and a sharp, jabbing pain in her shoulder caused another recollection to pierce the veil of languor. "I was shot," she said, her eyes widening incredulously. "They actually *shot* me."

"It was a mistake," he said quickly, his hand tightening around hers with bone-crunching strength.

"God, that sounds feeble, sweetheart. Betz had imported a couple of trigger-happy new men, and they were so jumpy they were shooting at shadows. They didn't realize it was you." He was suddenly sitting on the bed beside her, and gathered her other hand in his as well. "It *was* an accident, Tania. Betz may be something of a fool, but he knows I'd murder him if anything happened to you. For that very reason, he discreetly transferred the man who shot you back to Washington while I was occupied with taking care of you. Your wound isn't that bad, Tania. The only reason you went into a tailspin was the shock, and the plastic surgeon assured me that after a few months the scar will hardly be noticeable."

"I take it you're apologizing?"

"I'm not doing very well, am I? I suppose I'm a little rusty at it." His eyes darkened soberly. "Yes, I'm apologizing most humbly, little Piper. Will you forgive me for letting this happen to you?"

She cocked her head consideringly. "I'll have to think about it. I've never had anyone apologize for shooting me before, so I can't be certain you're doing it properly." She grinned. "I must admit I'm tempted to make you suffer a little before giving in. It just might temper that strain of arrogance I've noticed in you."

"No one could do it better," he said huskily. "You're an expert at making me suffer." He lifted her hands and kissed each palm lingeringly. "What would you like me to do? Get down on my knees and plead?"

"Would you?"

"Yes," he said simply. "If that's what it would take. Would it please you to see me like that, sweetheart?"

It would hurt her unbearably, she knew suddenly. She didn't want to see him humbled and beaten, even by her. She shook her head. "No, it wouldn't please me," she said lightly. "Because we both realize it would just be a matter of form. Even while you were saying the words, I'd know I hadn't really won a victory. You're a man of steel, Jared Ryker."

"Nope, that's Superman. And I'm definitely not that where you're concerned. I'm discovering new vulnerabilities all the time." He smiled gently. "I'm getting to the point where it doesn't even bother me anymore."

"I find that hard to believe." She was experiencing an odd sensation that had nothing to do with the sedative and everything to do with the man sitting beside her. "I think you would shore up a weak defensive area so quickly it would make my head swim."

He frowned. "I think your head is swimming at the moment anyway. You're remarkably lighthearted for someone who's just regained consciousness after suffering a gunshot wound." He released one of her hands to place his fingers lightly on her forehead. "No symptoms of fever, or I'd think you were a little delirious. Why the hell aren't you more upset?"

She was a bit confused on that score herself. Why was everything colored with a rosy glow? She had an idea that the answer had something to do with the tentative trust she'd learned to place in him in the past weeks, but she couldn't put a label on the other feeling she was experiencing, and she didn't even want to try. It was too gossamerlike an emotion at this point. She didn't want to share it with anyone, not even Jared, who inspired it. It was a lovely secret that she could hug close to her like a child with her favorite toy.

"Perhaps it's the sedative," she said, a tiny enigmatic smile on her face. "Maybe tomorrow, when my thinking is clearer, I'll take a more logical view of the situation. Yes, I'm sure I'll be quite sensible tomorrow." She closed her lids, but she could still see him sitting there looking down at her with those puzzled eyes. Such lovely silver eyes. "But I think I'd like you to kiss me good night right now. Will you do that, Jared?"

She heard his sharply indrawn breath, and the sound caused that delicate budding to push out new slips of brilliant life. "My pleasure," he said huskily. Then she felt the warm, sweet cleanness of his breath and the touch of his lips on the curve of her cheek. "Definitely my pleasure, love."

Then he was moving, his weight shifted off the mattress, and she could hear him settle once more in the chair beside the bed.

She smiled contentedly, tucking her palm over her cheek to hold captive that lovely treasure of tenderness. He was wrong, she thought drowsily. It was definitely her pleasure too.

Chapter 9

The man sitting in the chair when she woke up wasn't Jared. The fact registered at once, but it took her a moment to realize just who the stranger was who'd invaded her bedroom and possessed such an air of casual élan as he waited for her to awaken. Sam Corbett.

There wasn't a chance of not recognizing a politician so powerful, a man so famous, especially to the hundreds of thousands of women voters who idolized him. His handsome face, with a cleft in the strong chin, was boyish. The lock of gray-streaked brown hair that was allowed to fall over his forehead was boyish, too—but there was nothing boyish about his hazel eyes. They were more a clear green than brown, and revealed a startling directness and a keen intelligence.

Those eyes were regarding her with an alertness that changed immediately to warmth when he realized she was awake. "I must apologize for barging in on you, Miss Orlinov. I'm Sam Corbett," he said with an apologetic smile that lit his tanned face and caused laugh lines to fan out around his hazel eyes. "And that is, I know, the least of my transgressions against you. You've really been treated outrageously by everyone involved in this project since you entered into the picture."

She tried to sit up and he was instantly at her

164

bedside to help her, arranging the pillows behind her with practiced courtesy. She was still naked beneath the sheet, and while she hadn't felt the least bit awkward about that fact with Jared, she now clutched the sheet to her shoulders as it started to slip.

His gaze ran over her with an expression that was distinctly appreciative without being in the least lascivious. "Lovely as you are, I felt you'd be more comfortable while we talked if you were wearing this." He reached down to the foot of the bed and picked up a pink pleated bed jacket that was fashioned like a cape.

"I can put it on," she said.

He gingerly drew the bed jacket over her shoulders. "Allow me. I'll be very careful not to hurt you."

He glanced up with a quick grin as he fastened the first button. "My last report on the situation here stated that you were a very independent woman, Miss Orlinov, but surely it won't bother you to accept a little help under the circumstances. After all, we're the ones responsible for your being hurt." His deft fingers fastened the last of the tiny pearl buttons down the front of the bed jacket and his expression quickly sobered. "A fact I regret exceedingly, I might add. It was totally unforgivable of Betz to let this happen. I flew here from Washington as soon as I heard you'd regained consciousness, to assure you that I'll personally see nothing like this will occur again while you're at the chateau."

"It was unforgivable," she agreed, her dark eyes steady on his. "But this entire charade falls in that same category. I find it incredible you could be involved in something like this, Senator. From what I've heard, kidnapping and shooting innocent women isn't precisely your cup of tea."

He grimaced. "Believe me, it's not, Miss Orlinov. Betz took matters into his own hands regarding you. He can be a little overenthusiastic about his work at times."

"Overenthusiastic!" she echoed, her eyes flashing. "What a euphemism! We're speaking of criminal acts of violence, Senator."

"I'm fully aware of that, Miss Orlinov," he said soothingly as he stood up and moved the few steps to the bedside table and picked up the thermos carafe of coffee on the tray beside the lamp.

"Let me get you a cup of coffee and I'll try to explain my actions more clearly. You may not be sympathetic or forgive the course we've been forced to follow, but you'll at least understand." He poured the coffee into a delicate hand-painted cup. "You take it with cream, don't you?"

"That's right."

It seemed that the senator was very well informed, and exceptionally retentive of even the smallest detail.

He was quite tall and fit. Tania knew he was in his early fifties, yet he looked at least ten years younger in the casual gray flannel slacks and lemon-yellow crew-necked sweater he wore. He'd finished pouring his own coffee and returned to hold her cup out to her. "I thought it best to dispense with a saucer. It would be difficult to manage with only one good arm, and Jared tells me it will probably be painful for you to move that arm for a few more days."

She accepted the cup of coffee. "Jared knows you're here?"

He sat down on the wing chair and stretched his legs before him. "My dear Miss Orlinov, Jared knows everything that goes on in this sickroom; he watches over you like the proverbial hawk." He smiled. "I understand he didn't leave your side until you were entirely out of danger. I had to use all my powers of persuasion to get him to let me take his place even for this short time it will take for me to apologize."

"I find that a little hard to believe," she said, taking

a sip of her hot coffee. "From what I hear, your powers of persuasion are very impressive indeed."

"I'd be overly modest if I didn't admit that was true. Rhetoric is a very useful tool in my profession, and I use it to the limit of my abilities. But don't sell our friend, Ryker, short. He's a very determined man." He raised an inquiring brow. "But perhaps you've found that out?"

"You might say so. He's certainly an unusual one."

"Most geniuses are," Corbett said, and shrugged. "But not all have as strong a will as Jared. However, he probably wouldn't have accomplished what he has without it. A good deal can be forgiven a man who has gifts to give on the scale that Ryker has."

"I've heard that before," she said impatiently. "It's a wonder the man isn't completely impossible, what with everyone afraid of making one false step and offending him."

"Yet you're obviously not finding Jared totally outrageous, despite the trials you've had to undergo because of him. He must be making more progress than I've been led to believe."

She stiffened, and her eyes narrowed intently on his face. "I think my attitude toward Jared Ryker is irrelevant, Senator Corbett. It has nothing whatever to do with the moral issue."

"You're wrong, Miss Orlinov," he said gently. "Nothing concerning Jared Ryker can be considered irrelevant. Everything is of the utmost importance. That's why we've had to be so unreasonable about your release." His gaze dropped to the cup and saucer in his hands. "And that's why I'm going to violate Jared's wishes in this matter and give you an insight into just why I've become a party to this. I think we owe it to you after all the mental and physical pain we've inflicted on you." He glanced up and darted her a quick warm smile. "I'm surprised you've displayed so little curiosity about it to date. You're a very unusual woman in a number of ways."

"My attention was otherwise engaged. I was trying to negotiate an escape from this charming hideaway of yours."

"Oh, yes. And in quite a few refreshingly innovative ways, I hear," he said, his eyes twinkling. He took a sip of his coffee. "I understand that you're studying for your citizenship test, Miss Orlinov. That includes a good deal of American history. How much do you know about Ponce de Leon?"

What on earth did this off-the-wall question have to do with anything? "An explorer," she replied. "Fifteenth century. Florida, I think."

"Very good. But not quite the thorough answer I was looking for. Ponce de Leon explored great tracts of land in Florida, but that wasn't the main purpose of his expedition. He failed totally in his prime objective." He paused. "A quite similar objective to one that Jared has had for a number of years. The only difference is that Jared didn't fail. Old Ponce de Leon would be wild with envy."

"And that objective?" she asked slowly.

"A fountain of youth, of sorts," he said softly. "Jared has developed a method for intervening in the body's aging process . . . and virtually shutting it off. Can you imagine the implications of such a discovery, Miss Orlinov?"

She shook her head dazedly, feeling more stunned than when the bullet had struck her. "I thought he was working on some kind of weapon," she said numbly. "I can't quite take it in."

"We all had the same problem. But I asure you that the breakthrough Jared has made is legitimate; the proof he's given me is quite convincing. His discovery should extend the present life-span to at least four hundred years." He smiled as he saw her eyes widen even more. "And Jared hypothesizes that further refining of his technique in manipulating genetic material may result in extending the life-span even more."

"Eternal life," she whispered.

"Perhaps," he answered, and for an instant there was a flicker of exictement in the depths of his eyes. "Certainly a life-span beyond anything we've ever conceived of. Would you like to live forever, Miss Orlinov? Jared may be able to give you immortality. He can certainly give you, me, all of us, hundreds of years of life of high quality."

"I've never even imagined such a thing," she muttered. Her thoughts were churning wildly. My God, she thought, no wonder security was so tight around Jared! The value of his discovery was beyond price. She stared at the senator. "Jared has done this work under government sponsorship?"

Corbett's lips tightened. "No. Independently. He's even such a maverick that I can't persuade him to let the government control the project now. He won't agree to relinquish key information to anyone," he said tersely. "He tells us he's even destroyed vital parts of his basic research. It's all in that brain of Ryker's. And until we get his knowledge on paper, he's the single most important man on the face of the earth. Even after he shares the method, his ability to continue the research is absolutely necessary if we're to gain the optimum effect." Corbett's voice was emphatic. "He must be protected at all cost."

"I can see that," Tania said faintly. "But I still don't understand from whom you're protecting him. He's done the impossible. He's given every human being a gift so precious it's difficult to imagine. Why should anyone want to hurt him?"

"Why?" His lips curved cynically. "For any number of reasons. It's a gift wrapped in thorns. Think about the ramifications of Jared's discovery." He sighed wearily. "Hell, I can even sympathize with a few of the fanatics who'd snuff out Ryker without a second thought. In the past few weeks not a day has gone by that I haven't identified yet another host of changes and problems that such radically increased longevity brings with it. Maybe Ryker's discovery ought to be deep-sixed."

"You can't mean that," she whispered.

"No, I don't mean it," he said with a reassuring smile. "The advantages far outweigh the problems involved. I guess I'm just tired of beating my head against the system. Some of those bureaucratic arguments are beginning to sound like gospel to me."

"For instance?"

"Where would you like to start?" he asked dryly. "Perhaps you'd like to consider the question of overpopulation. Our civilization depends on the death cycle to maintain life for the rest of us. How will we produce enough food to feed these millions who'll still be around for the next four hundred years? Think of the problems of famine that exist now in the Third World. What kind of reaction do you think leaders in those countries will have when Ryker's discovery becomes known?"

"Explosive."

"Right," he said. "Now think about the economic effect. Social security, which is already tottering, life insurance, pensions, employment. Our system of government will almost certainly prove ineffective. Most sociologists say that the only form of government control that could possibly survive would be patriarchy." His words were coming out with the rapidity of machine-gun fire. "Education will have to be completely overhauled and extended, not merely to keep the young out of the job market but to prepare them for a more sophisticated and learned society. Attitudes toward families and intimate relationships such as marriage will certainly change. How do we keep the boredom factor from triggering more violence and increasing the crime rate?" He paused, one brow arched inquiringly. "Shall I go on? I haven't even scratched the surface yet."

She shook her head. "No, you have my head whirling as it is. I think I get the general picture. The ramifications are . . . are overwhelming. One can scarcely think them through."

"Ryker did. That's why he came to me, Miss Orlinov. He thought I'd have enough clout to cut through red tape and get an international forum established to work on these problems and handle the distribution of his knowledge in an equitable way." His lips twisted. "Unfortunately, Ryker's a very impatient man and has given me only twelve weeks to work out such a plan before he takes an alternative course." He ran his hand through his hair. "He has no conception of what a massive can of worms he's opened or perhaps he'd be a little more merciful. I've been working eighteen hours a day since he came to me seven weeks ago, and I haven't made what he'd consider real progress."

"I haven't found him to be all that impatient," she said slowly. "If he knows how hard you're trying, I think he'd allow you the additional time you need."

"He doesn't like to have his personal freedom curtailed," Corbett said. "I can't say that I blame him, but he should have realized such restrictions go along with his special territory."

"Kevin said he had a totally innovative mind," she murmured thoughtfully. "If that's true, he wouldn't be able to tolerate the bureaucratic squabbling you're speaking about."

"Well, he'd better get used to it," Corbett said grimly. "That's the reality of our social system."

"As it stands now," she said softly.

There was a flicker of emotion on his face that was

curiously enigmatic. "As it stands now," he agreed smoothly, standing and placing his cup and saucer on the bedside table. "That's all we have to work with at the moment. I hope with your help I'll be able to convince him to give me an extension on that time limit. I'm going to need all the support I can get. Jared can be a very determined man."

"My help?" Tania's eyes widened in surprise. "I have nothing to do with this, and I certainly have no influence over Jared Ryker."

"I'm not at all sure about that," he answered. "Naturally, I'm aware that you're not on terms of physical intimacy."

Everyone at the chateau seemed to be aware of that fact, she thought crossly. Were there hidden cameras in the bedrooms, for goodness' sake?

"Nevertheless," Corbett continued, "Jared has displayed an unusually strong interest and concern in regard to you." His look was openly speculative. "It might be that you already hold a position of influence with him."

"A position of influence?" she repeated with a distasteful moue. "What an abominable phrase. It reminds me of the courtesans in the royal courts. No, thank you, Senator Corbett, I have no desire to attain that kind of 'position of influence' with any man."

"Don't be too hasty in rejecting the idea. Being the 'courtesan' of one of the most powerful men in the world could be very rewarding," he said quietly. "There isn't anything you couldn't have, just for the asking. Power radiates a golden aura. Wouldn't you enjoy having kings and heads of state begging you for favors?"

"No, I wouldn't," she said bluntly. Then her gaze narrowed on his face, which once more held that element of excitement. "Would you, Senator?"

"What?" The question seemed to have caught him

off-guard. Then that charming smile was firmly fixed on his face once more. "I'm only too human, I'm afraid," he said ruefully. "A little power can be very heady to us politicians, Miss Orlinov. I'll enjoy the hell out of sharing Ryker's glory." He sighed. "But that's in the future. At the moment, we have a few thousand problems to solve. I won't ask for any commitment of support from you, Miss Orlinov. I realize that it will take time to absorb the implications of what we've discussed. I just hope that when you've thought about it, you'll come to realize that all of us need one another's help on this project." His hazel gaze sharpened to razor keenness. "I can be a very good friend to have. You might remember that."

"I'll remember," she said coolly. He made her vaguely uneasy. "But you're quite right—it's far too early for me to comprehend fully all you've said. Perhaps we can have another discussion at a later date."

"Yes, of course," he said briskly. "Now, I really must go and let you get some rest." He grinned with winning boyishness. "Jared will have my head if I've exhausted you. I'll give orders that you're to be served breakfast in an hour, so that you can nap a little before then." He turned and said over his shoulder as he headed for the door, "That will give me time to talk to Jared before I fly back to Washington. Otherwise he'll be camping in your bedroom like a mother hen." He paused at the door to give her one last flashing grin. "It's been a pleasure meeting you, Miss Orlinov. I hope this will be the beginning of a very promising relationship for both of us." The door closed softly behind him.

Betz was waiting patiently in the foyer when Sam Corbett reached the bottom of the stairs, a worried frown on his usually impassive face. "You can see the woman is recovering, Senator. You needn't have put yourself to the trouble of flying up here. We took care of everything, just as I assured you we would."

"You mean you bungled everything." Corbett's usually mellow voice was a whiplash. "You've not only involved me in a criminal act, in kidnapping and shooting Tania Orlinov, but you've succeeded in antagonizing Ryker in the process. I told you he was to be handled with kid gloves, damn it."

Annoyance flickered for an instant in the depths of Betz's brown eyes before they resumed their doglike passivity. "You told me to protect him," he said steadily. "I did what was necessary."

"And I may find it 'necessary' to replace you, if you continue to botch things," Corbett said, his lips tight. "I have enough on my plate without handling your end too."

"Do you want me to take her back to New York?"

"Hell, no, I can't afford to have her making waves at the moment. Matters are delicate enough without that." Corbett frowned. "Besides, I may be able to make use of her if things escalate the way I hope. She definitely stays here."

"Whatever you say. The shooting may have been a mistake, but it still may discourage her from further escape attempts."

"Perhaps. Where is Ryker now?"

"He's in the gymnasium, working out with Mr. McCord. Would you like me to tell him you want to see him?"

Corbett shook his head. "You have all the finesse of a bull in a china shop," he said caustically. "You don't send for a man like Ryker and expect him to come running. I'll go to him." He was already moving across the foyer. "Go tell the helicopter pilot I'll be ready to leave in forty-five minutes."

When he opened the door of the gymnasium, it was

to see both men in the traditional loose pants and tunic top of karate *gi* engaged in a workout that was both intricate and potentially deadly. He stood quietly watching for a moment until McCord noticed he was there and backed quickly away from Ryker.

He threw up his arms, a broad grin on his face. "You've come to save me, Senator? You couldn't be more welcome. I think I was about to receive the *coup de grâce*."

"You seemed to be holding your own very well, Kevin," Corbett said genially. "I had no idea you were so good."

"He gets better every session," Ryker said as he stooped to pick up his towel from the floor. "He's a remarkable man."

McCord shrugged. "I learn from experience." His blue eyes twinkled. "And battling Jared is definitely an experience."

"I'm sorry to interrupt you, but I've got to fly back to Washington at once, Jared. I wonder if I could have a word with you before I leave."

"I think that's my signal to head for the showers," McCord said, starting to turn away.

"They're getting the 'copter ready now," Corbett said. "I hoped I could persuade you to walk me out to the pad."

"Why not?" Ryker asked laconically, his dark face impassive. "I have a few things to discuss with you as well." He strode over to the side of the gym and thrust his feet into a pair of thongs. "You don't mind if I stop in the hall to get a jacket?"

"Of course not. We wouldn't want you on the sick list, too."

"No, you certainly wouldn't want that. It's been brought to my attention that my continuing good health is of primary importance around here, even to the point of shooting down a helpless woman." He slung a towel around his neck and strolled over to Corbett, standing by the door.

The senator allowed Ryker to precede him. "I thought my famous charm had succeeded in pacifying you a bit." He fell into step with him. "It appears I'll have to redouble my efforts in the brief time I have left."

"Don't bother," Ryker said tersely. "I'm a little short on time myself. I should be getting back to Tania, if you've finished trying to make excuses for the inexcusable."

"You needn't run right back. When I left her, Miss Orlinov was just settling down for a nap. And in the short interval I was with her, the lady impressed me as being anything but a helpless female. I think she can survive without your presence for the next thirty minutes or so."

They had reached the foyer, and Ryker opened the closet door and pulled out his dark blue jacket and slipped into it. "Can she?" he asked bitterly. "She seems to need all the protection I can give her here at the chateau." He paused. "I want her sent back to New York."

"You know that isn't possible," Corbett said softly.

"The hell it's not! You can surround her with an army of security men and she's bound to be safer than she's been here."

"That's possible," Corbett admitted as he opened the front door. "But I'm afraid that's not the point, Jared. We can't allow anyone with knowledge of your work to have access to anyone who isn't involved in the project. It wouldn't be safe for you."

"What the devil are you talking about?" Ryker's eyes narrowed. "She doesn't know anything about my work. I've made damn sure of it."

Corbett glanced away, obviously uncomfortable. "She does now. I felt it only fair to fill her in, after all she's been through. How was I to know you'd want to send her away?"

A gust of chilly wind lifted the dark lock of hair on Ryker's forehead, but it was no colder than the glance he shot at the other man. "I think you knew that might well be my reaction. You're an extremely perceptive man, Corbett," he said slowly. "I find it very interesting that you immediately took the only action that would make sending Tania away completely unfeasible."

Corbett's brisk pace across the courtyard slowed, and his forehead knotted with a frown. "Nonsense. What possible purpose could I have in keeping her here?"

"You tell me," Ryker asked. "I do know that you never do anything without a purpose. I studied you a long time before I selected you, Corbett."

"You make me sound like a choice cut of sirloin. I think I deserve more than that from you, Jared. If you don't trust me, how do you expect me to protect you?"

"I trust you." A faint, cynical smile touched his lips. "Within certain limits. And I have no objection to accepting your protection, as long as it's also kept within bounds. I'm well able to look after myself in the general course of events."

"I think McCord would testify to that," Corbett agreed. "However, a black belt in karate wouldn't help if you were overpowered and taken. Can't you see how stupid it is not to furnish us with written information? As long as you have sole knowledge, you're a walking target." His voice deepened persuasively. "There are drugs that can make a man tell everything he ever knew, Jared. They'd empty your mind before six hours were up."

"I think not," Ryker said grimly. "I'm a chemist, remember? Do you think I'd be fool enough not to fortify my body against the use of those particular kinds of drugs?" His lips twisted mockingly. "And self-hypnotism can be a very valuable tool for shutting out pain, so I think torture would be equally ineffective. I made sure that I wasn't completely vulnerable before I left the island."

"So it would appear." Corbett was silent for several seconds. "I suppose it's useless to try to make you see reason. The only thing I can do is to take every precaution to protect you." They stopped several yards from the helicopter pad on the lonely promontory at the rear of the chateau. Still, the wash of the propellers ruffled their hair and clothing. Corbett turned to Ryker and thrust out his hand. "I'll be in touch, Jared," he shouted over the roar of the helicopter's engine. "Lord knows I'm doing everything I can to keep that blasted deadline you gave me."

Ryker's handshake was perfunctory. "I'll be waiting to hear from you." He stepped back and watched quietly as Corbett walked to the chopper and climbed into the passenger seat.

The yellow helicopter kicked up a miniature cyclone as it lifted from the pad like an awkward hummingbird. Corbett waved at Ryker, who stood watching his departure, an aloof, perhaps disdainful expression on his face. The senator felt a sudden surge of annoyance. The strong wind whipped Ryker's clothes, and dust swirled around his body, yet he still emanated an aura of power and control. There was no reason for that, Corbett thought. No reason at all.

The door had no sooner closed behind Corbett than Tania tossed the covers aside, sat up, and swung her feet to the floor. She reached over and put her nearly full cup on the bedside table, ignoring the sudden wave of dizziness the movement brought. She wasn't about to lie back tamely and take the nap the senator had prescribed. It was obvious the man was accustomed to

having people bend to his will. It would probably
surprise him, she thought, to discover she hadn't
followed his directions.

She sat on the edge of the bed for a moment more,
gathering strength and waiting for that slight dizziness to
pass. The dizziness wasn't all physical, she realized. Her
mind and emotions were whirling from Corbett's revela-
tions of the last half hour. She couldn't begin to sort all
the implications, but one thing was shining brightly
through the chaotic haze: Jared was terribly, achingly
alone. What must it be like to bear such a responsibility
and be able to trust only yourself? Throughout those last
moments before Corbett had left the room, she'd
scarcely been able to restrain her impatience. She had
wanted to run to Jared, touch him, speak to him,
anything to alleviate his loneliness.

The urgency of that desire was still with her, but her
body wasn't responding to the directives of her heart and
mind. Jared had said the wound was just a scratch, yet
her shoulder was so sore it was agony even to move it.
When she tried to get to her feet, she found her legs
were rebelling against her will. They had all the firmness
of wet spaghetti, she thought disgustedly as she tottered
toward the bathroom. Her limbs were scarcely in better
shape when she returned to the bedroom wrapped in a
towel. She'd had only the strength for a brief wash and
the brushing of her teeth, but not for fixing her hair. It
would just have to remain in its braid until her shoulder
had healed enough for her to brush and arrange it.

She sank onto the bed and leaned back against the
headboard, her breath coming in harsh gasps. There was
light perspiration dewing her forehead, she realized
indignantly. Good Lord, five hours of straight practice
had never produced such a debilitating effect! She
mustn't give in to it or she'd probably collapse back on

that inviting pillow and take the nap Corbett had ordered. She had to see Jared.

A sudden surge of adrenaline gave her the strength to finish dressing. But once out of her room, the corridor seemed to stretch forever.

Forever. Strange, how often the word came to mind in any number of connections. Yet no one really thought about its true meaning. Well, everyone would have to start thinking about it very soon, she realized. But she couldn't do so at the moment. She had to concentrate on getting to Jared. One step at a time.

Great journeys were accomplished one step at a time, Jared had told her, and she'd found it true herself. So all she had to do was to think about that next step and she'd make it through the blasted corridors and down the horror of a staircase. Yet the last step proved almost too much, and when she reached the end of the staircase, she sank down on the bottom stair and closed her eyes. She leaned her head against the curved bannister post and drew several deep breaths. In just a minute she'd get up and go on, but right now she'd give in to weakness. It would do no good to try to renew her strength, she thought wryly. She had absolutely none left.

"What in God's name are you doing here?"

The words were more of a shocked imprecation than a question. Tania opened her eyes to see Kevin kneeling in front of her, a worried frown on his face. He was dressed in jeans and a blue plaid flannel shirt, and his red hair was a little damp, as if from the shower.

"Hello, Kevin." Her voice was as weak as her knees, she noticed with annoyance. "I wanted to see Jared. Do you know where he is?"

"In the shower at the gym. He came in just as I was leaving." Then, as she started to get to her feet, he pushed her firmly back down. "Stay where you are.

There's no way you could make it another step. You're white as a sheet."

Her chin lifted defiantly. "I can make it," she said indignantly. "I'm just resting at the moment."

There was a fugitive twinkle in Kevin's blue eyes. "Right. Well, suppose you come along with me to the library and rest there. Unless you'd prefer to scrub Jared's back and help him dress, you're not going to get much accomplished until he gets out of the shower."

He was probably right. She wouldn't be able to talk to Jared under those circumstances, and the gym seemed a thousand miles away at the moment. "All right," she said resignedly. "I'll wait for him in the library."

"That's very good of you, princess," Kevin said, his lips twitching. "Now, if you'll allow me to help you into said library, we'll have it made." Without waiting for her to reply, he scooped her up in his arms and carried her across the foyer to the library.

Tania clutched his massive shoulders. "This isn't at all necessary, you know," she said haughtily. "I'm perfectly able to walk."

"I'm beginning to believe that you're perfectly able to do anything you set your mind to. But give me a break. I'm a man who likes to feel needed." He gently deposited her in the easy chair by the fire. He scooted the ottoman closer and arranged her legs carefully on its cushion before dropping down on it to face her. "There. Indulging me wasn't all that difficult, was it?"

"I suppose not." The cushioned chair certainly was more comfortable than the step, she had to admit, and it was impossible to resent Kevin's action, when it was accompanied by that beguiling grin. "Though I did feel a little like a piece of pirate booty," she said tartly. "Didn't anyone ever tell you that women don't like to be treated that way in this day and age?"

"Many times," he said lightly. "But I've found that I just have to ignore them if I'm to fulfill my prime directive."

"Prime directive? That sounds like something out of a science fiction novel."

"Which should put me right at home with the company I'm keeping. It's not as farfetched a concept as it sounds, you know. We all have a prime motivation that guides all our actions in one way or another. Sometimes we don't recognize it, but it's there nevertheless."

"And what is your prime directive, Kevin?" she asked, her gaze on his blunt, craggy face, which was surprisingly serious.

He shrugged. "I'm a throwback to another century, I guess. I can't identify with the modern philosophy of living only for one's self. I want to help people." He paused before ending simply, "I *like* the human race, Tania. I think we're all worth giving a helping hand."

She felt a warm surge of affection for the big man. "Is that why you went into government work?"

He nodded. "It doesn't give me the personal contact I prefer, but you can accomplish considerably more on the federal level." The seriousness vanished from his demeanor as he rose to his feet. "Now, why don't you let me exercise my directive even more fully and order you some breakfast?"

"No, thank you." She leaned her head weakly against the high-cushioned back of the chair. "I'm not hungry. I'll just rest here until I can see Jared."

"I should really bundle you back upstairs to bed. Jared is going to climb the walls when he finds you're out of bed and wandering around the chateau."

She was no longer listening, her gaze wandering to the Adam mantle, where the openwork clock was once more ticking with abrasive loudness. "Someone must have started it again," she said absently.

"What?" Kevin asked. Then, as his gaze followed hers to the clock, he said, "Oh, I did. Someone must have turned off the mechanism."

"I stopped it." A tiny smile tugged at her lips as she remembered something else. "Jared said he'd stopped a clock once too. I didn't understand then what he meant."

Kevin went still, his eyes narrowed intently on her face. "But you do now? Someone told you about his work, didn't he? Was it Jared?"

"Senator Corbett." A cynical smile touched her lips. "He said he thought I deserved to know."

Kevin's lips pursed in a soundless whistle. "That's not going to please our resident genius even a little bit. I wonder why the senator did it. He must have known it would upset Jared."

She didn't want to think about that at the moment. In fact, she didn't want to think about anything. She'd thought a brief rest would rid her of the weakness that touched every part of her body, but instead the exhaustion seemed to be growing. "Perhaps he was sincere about what he said." She wished Jared would hurry. It was becoming difficult to concentrate, and even more difficult to speak. "He appeared genuinely concerned about Jared's safety."

"He should be," Kevin said grimly. "Jared's life is on the line. There aren't many men who believe in something so much they're willing to risk what Jared has. You have to admire his courage." His expression became thoughtful. "I've often wondered if doing his research has been Jared's prime directive all these years since his sister, Lita, died. If so, then where does he go from here? He'll be damned lost until he finds something to replace it."

She'd been letting his words flow over her, but something had caught her attention. A spark of interest lit her eyes. "His sister, Lita?"

"The senator didn't tell you about her?" When she shook her head, he said quietly, "She died when she was twelve of a very rare disease, an extreme form of hypercholesteremia that causes an accelerated aging process. It's an inborn error in metabolism and biochemistry in which the body produces incredible amounts of cholesterol that are deposited in tissues throughout the system. Arteriosclerosis and other symptoms begin in early infancy, and by the time adolescence occurs, the victim literally dies of old age."

"My God! Oh, my God!" Her eyes widened with shock. How agonizing it must have been, not only for Jared's sister, but for him, to see that rapid disintegration taking place before his eyes. "Wasn't there any cure?"

"None," Kevin said. "It was all the more tragic because Jared and his sister were so close. Evidently he had sole care of her almost from the moment she was born. His father was their only support, and spent most of his time in either the mines or the neighborhood tavern, and their mother had left them shortly after Lita was born. Jared was only about ten years old then. You can see why he felt a driving passion that channeled his work in the direction it did."

"Yes, I can see that." She could see more than that. She could see the pain and frustration of a sensitive boy unable to help a loved one and could feel once more Jared's terrible loneliness. "It must have been horrible for him."

"Probably more than we can possibly realize," Kevin said gently. "It's no wonder he's not eager to let anyone too close to him."

"What the hell are you doing down here?"

Startled, they both turned toward the doorway. Jared was dressed in worn, faded jeans and a gray sweatshirt with the sleeves pushed up to the elbow. His expression was definitely stormy.

"That's what Kevin asked when he saw me," Tania said, trying to smile. It wasn't a very successful attempt. Her initial exhaustion had been augmented enormously by the shock of what Kevin had told her, and she felt weak as a day-old kitten. "I'd think it would be obvious what the hell I'm doing here."

"She wanted to see you," Kevin put in quickly.

"Then why the devil didn't you take her back to bed and send for me?" Jared growled as he strode swiftly across the room. "Just look at her. She's going to collapse any minute. Haven't you got any sense at all, Kevin?"

Kevin's mouthed I-told-you-so from where he stood behind Jared brought a reluctant smile to Tania's face. "It wasn't Kevin's fault," she said, wishing her voice were less shaky. "I do what I wish to do."

"So do I," he said. "And what I wish to do at the moment is take you back to your room and put you to bed." He scooped her up from the chair. "Any objections?"

If she'd had, it wouldn't have done her any good, she thought crossly. This seemed to be her day to be toted about by arrogant men. She had to admit, however, that it was very pleasant to be held close to Jared's warm strength and lean her head against the soft, fleecy cotton of the sweatshirt stretched across his broad chest. "No objections," she said meekly.

There was a moment of surprised silence. "She must be worse off than I thought," Jared said dryly. Then he was moving across the study. "Order her a light breakfast, Kevin. She hasn't had anything substantial to eat for two days."

"I'm not hungry," she repeated stubbornly. Why did everyone insist that she eat, when all she wanted to do was relax here in Jared's arms and go to sleep? He smelled deliciously of soap and something slightly musky that was very intriguing. "I won't eat."

"You'll eat," he said flatly. He was rapidly mounting the stairs. "Every single bite, and then you'll sleep all day, and we'll hope that you'll escape the results of your stupidity without a setback." He was striding down the corridor to her room. "I should have known better than to leave you alone. You think you're ten feet tall and built like Kevin, damn it!"

"I may not be ten feet tall, but that doesn't mean I'm not as tough. I have—"

"*Erb*." He finished it with her. "I'm beginning to wish I'd never heard that word. If you weren't so blasted determined to prove yourself a lady Atlas carrying the world on your shoulders, both our lives would be a great deal less difficult."

He negotiated the opening of the door of her room and crossed the Aubusson carpet with four long steps. "I know what Corbett told you upset you, but why couldn't you have waited, like a sensible person, until I came to you?"

Despite the exasperation in his voice, his hands were gentle as he put her down on the bed. They were also very deft as he unbuttoned the tiny pearl buttons of the bed jacket she wore. It was only when he opened the jacket to slip it off that he hesitated, his gaze on the naked swell of her small, perfect breasts.

"What's wrong?" she asked, puzzled.

He shook his head as if to clear it. "Not a damn thing," he said huskily. "I just feel as if someone had kicked me in the stomach. God, you're lovely."

She could feel a warm tingle in the pit of her stomach. "It's not as if it's something you haven't seen before," she said shakily. "I've obviously been stark naked for the last two days."

"Hell, I don't know why it came as such a shock," he

said, his gaze fastened on the dark pink of her nipples, which were suddenly flowering into hardness. "I guess there's something about taking off a woman's clothes that provokes all the sexual urges." He ran his tongue over his lips. "Before, I was thinking of you as my patient, a child clinging in the night. Suddenly it's not that way anymore."

"It's not?" She could see that it wasn't. It was evident in the pulse that was pounding in his temple and the tension that was tightening the muscles of his shoulders.

His hand went to the single side button of her wraparound skirt. "I think I'd better get you into bed and get out of here," he said grimly. "If I don't, I'm not going to care whether you're injured or not. I'm getting damn close to that point now." When he opened the skirt, she could see the pulse jump in the hollow of his throat, and he drew in a long, ragged breath. No underwear. "Well, at least I can't accuse you of wasting much energy getting dressed." He slipped the shoes from her feet and pulled the satin sheet over her with careful gentleness, despite the slight tremor of his hands. "Remind me to order you some granny nightgowns to wear during the next few days." He leaned forward to press a light kiss on her forehead. "Go to sleep. I'll wake you when your breakfast arrives."

She was already half asleep as her head touched the pillow. There was something she wanted to say to him, but she couldn't remember what it was. Then it came back to her. "I'm so sorry, Jared."

"Sorry?" Jared's face was puzzled.

Sorry for the pain he'd known, sorry for the loneliness she could sense deep inside him even now. She was much too tired to tell him all that, so she merely said, "Your sister, Lita."

His expression hardened. "Corbett really did fill you in on all the details, didn't he?"

"It was Kevin who told me about your sister," she said, trying to clear her head of the clouds of sleep that persisted in descending. "It must have hurt you very much."

He shrugged. "It was a long time ago. It's not wise to dwell on past pain." One soothing finger stroked the winged line of her brow. "I'll tell you all about it some other time. Go to sleep now, love."

And within seconds she'd followed his injunction.

Chapter 10

"Checkmate," Tania said, lying back against the pillows with a triumphant chuckle. "I did it. This isn't such a difficult game, Kevin. I don't know why it took me so long to learn it."

Kevin sat back in his chair and smiled at her. "Five days isn't a lifetime, you know. Though I must confess I'm very glad you had a few problems with it. It wasn't too damaging to my ego to be beaten unmercifully by Jared at poker, since I'm something of a novice, but chess I consider *my* game."

"You play it very well." The mention of Jared had momentarily obscured her feeling of triumph, and she moved restlessly, pushing the chessboard aside and sitting up straight in bed. Then a thought occurred to her that caused her dark eyes to narrow suspiciously. "Perhaps *too* well to allow yourself to be beaten by a beginner. Did you let me win, Kevin?"

"I know better than that, princess. You wouldn't thank me for that kind of victory. You won fair and square. Besides, why should I let you win, when it's the only form of ego-stroking I get around here?"

"Perhaps you wanted to pacify me?" She swung her feet to the floor and stood up, her expression revealing clearly the discontent she felt. "That's why you're here, isn't it? To keep me amused and out of Jared's way?" She walked swiftly toward the French doors. "Well, you've done a very good job, Kevin," she said bitterly as she opened the door to let a gust of fresh, cold air into the bedroom. "Jared should be very pleased with you."

Kevin's gaze followed her, his expression troubled. Her small form, silhouetted in the late-afternoon sunlight, was charged with restlessness. He'd expected this outburst and was surprised it hadn't come earlier. There had been an almost feverish tension about Tania for the last two days. "Yes, that was my job," he said quietly. "One that I've enjoyed very much. I'd hoped that you'd found the last five days at least tolerable, too, Tania."

She drew a deep breath, the cold air searing her lungs, her gaze on the mountains that were being touched by the first rays of sunset. It wasn't fair to take out her frustration on Kevin, she thought remorsefully. He'd been an angel of patience and good humor, and she probably would have gone totally insane without his efforts to keep her happily occupied.

Her hands clenched unconsciously as she remembered the morning when Jared had carried her back to this room and she'd gone to sleep with his hand stroking her so gently. When she'd awakened two hours later, that gentle touch was gone. In Jared's place was a very apologetic and appealing Kevin McCord, who had been her constant companion ever since. She hadn't even seen Jared since that moment she'd dropped off to sleep five days ago. It had been Kevin who changed her bandage, saw that she ate every bite of the meals that were brought to her, and kept her from going crazy with boredom from the unaccustomed inactivity, which Jared had insisted upon.

Other than Jared's rejection of her, it was the inactivity that was the most painful. He'd made sure she would be active not only by Kevin's presence during the day, but by posting a guard at her door from the moment Kevin left her until he returned the next day.

"You've been very kind, Kevin," she said wearily, turning toward him. "I suppose I'm just bad-tempered because my nerves are a bit strained." She made a face. "I'm not cut out to be an invalid, I'm afraid. This is all completely ridiculous, you know. I'm perfectly well now."

"Jared wanted to be sure. Shock can do funny things to your nervous system. The additional rest didn't hurt you, and built up your resistance to infection and virus."

"It didn't hurt me!" she exclaimed. She tightened the belt of her robe and marched over to stand before him. "It's driving me out of my mind, not to mention making me lose muscle tone by keeping me from practicing. A dancer can't afford such inactivity, damn it! Obviously, Jared doesn't care that it's going to take me two weeks of hard work just to get back to normal."

"He cares. You wouldn't doubt it if you'd seen the way he gives me the third degree every time I leave you in the evening. I have to give him a report that includes everything from your mental state to the tragic development of a hangnail. He knows very well how you feel. Why do you think he set the guard over you? He's afraid you'll be tearing all over the chateau and exhausting yourself."

"Curiosity doesn't necessarily mean concern," she said, careful to keep the hurt from her voice. "The man hasn't even had the courtesy to pay me a visit for days."

"It doesn't make sense to me either," he said with a helpless shrug. "But I'm not about to question Jared, considering the mood he's been in lately. I feel like I'm walking a tightrope between the two of you now. Just be patient—"

"I've been patient long enough," she interrupted. "He needn't think I'm going to bother him by inflicting my presence on him. I've no intention of even going near him, but there's no reason I shouldn't be permitted to leave my room now. You can tell him I won't stand—"

"You can tell me yourself." Jared stood in the doorway. He looked self-possessed and very attractive in dark cords and a black, long-sleeved shirt that gave his slender, whipcord body the appearance of a vaguely sinister strength. He sauntered toward them, pausing for a moment to toss the large box he was carrying on the bed. "I'm not going to give you any argument. You can leave your room any time you wish. House arrest is officially over."

She tried to stifle the sudden leap of joy she'd known at the sight of him. She hadn't realized how achingly she'd missed him until he'd walked through that door. "I'm surprised you came to deliver the message yourself," she said caustically, her dark eyes flashing. "Why didn't you just send me a telegram or have that behemoth of a guard tell me?"

"Yes, I'd say you are definitely well on your way to recovery. Has she been giving you hell, Kevin?"

Kevin stood up. "She's been very good, actually. You can't blame her for coming a little unglued, under the circumstances. You'd be going crazy by now, Jared."

"I'm well aware of that," Jared said, his eyes on Tania's flushed, tense face. "I'm considering having the senator put you up for a medal for tolerating both of us."

"Well, if anyone could swing it, you could," Kevin said lightly. "I gather I'm a fifth wheel?"

"At the moment," Jared agreed, his gaze still not leaving Tania's face. "I think I can handle things from here."

"Well, if you can't, feel free to ask me at any time," Kevin said breezily as he strolled toward the door. "I'm sure we can manage between us. We might not even have to call Betz's boys for help."

"Don't count on it," Tania said tartly as the door closed behind him. "Have I ever told you how much I detest being spoken of as if I weren't here?"

"Judging by what I heard when I came in, you're in a mood to resent anything I'd say," he replied calmly. "Not that your attitude is completely unexpected."

"No wonder you decided to release me," she answered caustically. "If I'd known my assurances not to bother you would have that effect, you'd have gotten them five days ago."

Ryker's expression turned stormy. "I expected you to be impatient," he said deliberately. "I didn't expect you to be stupid. You're too intelligent a woman to jump to inane conclusions."

"Inane!" Her eyes were blazing. "How can you say that, when you—"

She broke off as he put his hand firmly but gently over her lips. "Let's start over again," he murmured. "I have no intention of letting you goad me into a quarrel. My temper is just as edgy as yours, after this week, or I'd never have responded like that. Maybe you actually don't know why I stayed away from you for the last five days. Though God knows how that can be true."

Then, as she continued to glare up at him with mutinous eyes, he shook his head in exasperation. "Do I have to spell it out for you? I want you, damn it! I knew I couldn't see you every day without taking you or going through an inferno more blistering than any you've been putting me through since you appeared on the scene. My control wasn't strong enough to resist so much temptation."

For a moment it didn't sink in; then her eyes widened as she felt an exuberant singing somewhere deep inside. Her lashes lowered as she reached up to pull his hand away from her lips. "You could have told me," she said shakily. "How was I to know that you hadn't gotten bored with our little game and opted out?"

"It's never been a game. Not even in the beginning. It was too late to opt out from the first moment I saw you. I don't see how I could have clarified what the problem was without actually climbing into bed with you." His lips twisted. "And I knew I hadn't the right to do that yet."

"Right?"

"I had hurt you. Not only physically, but psychologically. It may not have been my hand that did it, but it was certainly my responsibility. I didn't have a right to ask anything of you until I'd healed that hurt." He paused. "That's why I'm here right now. I want you to come with me. Will you do that, Tania?" His eyes were holding hers with a steadiness that was almost mesmerizing.

It was odd how she'd first thought those eyes were ice-cold. Now they seemed to hold all the warmth in the world. "I don't understand," she said huskily. "Where do you want me to go?"

"Don't ask questions. Just come, okay?"

Dazed, she nodded, still gazing bemusedly into his intent face. "Okay."

She was rewarded by a smile that was so brilliant it took her breath away. "Good," he said softly. Then he was briskly turning away and moving toward the bed. "Where we're going you'll need something a little warmer than the robe you're wearing, so I came prepared." His hands were reaching for the large box he'd tossed on the bed when he'd first come into the room. "I think this ought to fill the bill."

When the lid was lifted and the delicate tissue paper pushed aside, it revealed a white fur so lustrous and soft that it seemed to radiate light all over the room. Tania stroked it. "It's magnificent. What is it?"

Jared's hands were at the belt of her robe. "Ermine." He pushed the satin robe from her shoulders and let it fall carelessly to the carpet. His gaze ran lingeringly over the graceful figure in the clinging peach nightgown. "I never did send for those granny gowns, did I? I was wiser than I knew, to stay away from you." Then he took the white fur out of the box and draped it over her shoulders. It was an evening cape of such luxurious richness that her breath caught in her throat. It billowed behind her in a graceful little train, the hood making a perfect frame for the golden duskiness of her face. Jared's hands slowly fastened the two buttons at her throat, his eyes locked with hers in the same hypnotic intimacy. "You look like a little empress, proud and lovely and free. I knew you'd look like that when I ordered it from Athens."

Her hand touched the fur with a fairylike gesture. "It's too much!" she said, trying to control the trembling of her voice. "It must have cost the earth. I can't accept it."

"You have no choice. It's yours now." He leaned forward to brush her lips with a tenderness that caused an ache to start in her throat. "Besides, you'll make Betz most unhappy if you refuse. He was practically ecstatic when I told him I wanted him to get it for you. He thinks I'm at last yielding to the temptation he so efficiently put before me." His lips brushed hers again. "He's right."

Her laugh was shaky. "Well, we wouldn't want to disappoint Betz."

"Which shoes are you wearing?" He pulled aside the skirt of the cloak to reveal the low-heeled satin slippers. "Those will be all right for the little distance we're going," he decided as he took her hand in his, pulling her with insistent gentleness toward the door. "Come on, we have to hurry. It's almost time."

She almost had to run to keep up with his long-legged stride as he hurried her through the chateau and courtyard and on to the formal garden. The air was crisp and cold, and the dwindling ray of sunlight cast a mellow glow over the barren orderliness of the hedges. She felt the same mellowness pervading every atom of her being as she walked beside Jared with her hand clasped tightly in his in a joining that seemed oddly timeless. He hadn't put on a jacket, she suddenly noticed with a frown. He'd decked her out with the most magnificent fur imaginable and hadn't even bothered to slip on his old flight jacket. She was about to insist that they go back to the chateau, when she heard it.

It started as the merest breath of sound, like the misty wisps of which dreams are woven. The silvery music that was surely the most evocative and beautiful in the universe.

Her eyes flew to Jared's. "Wind chimes?" she asked wonderingly.

He nodded, his eyes fixed on her face, drinking in every fluctuation of emotion he found there. "Wind chimes."

Then the music was growing like a magic symphony, and her bewildered gaze followed the sound to its origin in the birch grove just ahead of them. "Oh, my God!" It was more prayer than imprecation. She stopped stock-still in the path, feeling as if a hand had been laid upon her heart.

The setting sun was behind the trees, and the slender white trunks of the clustering birches looked fragile and graceful bathed in its rosy glow. Yet it wasn't the lovely symmetry of the trees that had caused the singing deep inside her suddenly to burst into joyous song, but the branches. The bare branches that had looked lonely and stark against the skyline were now decked with hundreds—no, thousands—of wind chimes. Hanging on every branch from the very highest to the lowest reaches were exquisite crystal-and-silver prisms that reflected the setting sun in a rainbow blaze of color, like the icicles of fairyland.

"I can't believe it," she whispered. Her senses were dazzled, assaulted by color and beauty and sound whose quantity and quality were almost too intense to bear. Then she was running, flying down the path and up the hill until she was among the trees. The hood had fallen back from her head as she raced, and her dark silken braid danced against the soft white fur as she spun in a circle, her arms outstretched and her face more luminous than the setting sun. The wind chimes cast rainbow shadows on the earth carpet on which she moved, and to the man who stood quietly watching her at the edge of the trees, she seemed a mythical princess from ancient Atlantis, lightly skimming the waves of brilliant textures, yet making them part of her.

The fragile silver carol seemed to be interwoven with the color, filling her, intoxicating her with beauty until the tears were brimming in her eyes. She finally stood quite still and let that beauty flow into her. "It's too lovely," she whispered over the painful tightening of her throat. "It's so lovely that it's hurting me."

"That wasn't the idea." Jared's voice was gentle. "It's supposed to heal you. I remembered what you said about the wind chimes healing your hurt when you were a child. I figured there couldn't be too much of a good thing." He came forward and took her hand. His slender, black-clad figure was a dark flame against the rainbow-dazzling aura surrounding them, and his expression was grave. "I want to heal all the pain you ever knew, little Piper. Will you let me do that?"

He was drawing her with him to the edge of the

cliff, his hand warm and secure around her own and his eyes holding hers with that same loving steadiness. He stopped when they were under the birch tree where he'd been sitting that first day. It clung to the very edge of the precipice, and it, too, was covered with wind chimes that sang in the brisk breeze that whipped across the mountain.

Jared slipped an arm around her waist and stood with her only inches from the drop to the valley below. "Remember this, love." His voice was a husky murmur in her ear. "Remember the color and the wind song. Remember the beauty. How could fear and ugliness exist in a world this lovely? It was all a bad dream and now the nightmare is over, never to return. Whenever it tries to come back, you'll remember the beauty and the wind song and it will go away again." His lips brushed the delicate veins at her temple. "All you have to do is accept it to make it so, Tania."

She *was* accepting it, she discovered with a little tingle of incredulous joy. The ugly memory of that horror when she'd dangled helplessly in an agony of fear was being released and floating away as she stood there. She was being healed by the enchantment of the world Jared had created for her, and it was the act of creation itself that was the most effective balm. That he'd cared enough to go to these gloriously extravagant lengths to help her was the most magical wind chime of all.

She turned to him, her magnificent dark eyes blazing and her lips trembling with a vulnerability that brought her no sense of shame. "Thank you," she said simply. No words were adequate at the moment. "I will remember forever, Jared."

Forever. Again that word, but this time she knew she spoke only the truth. No matter how far their forever stretched, she would remember the bright radiance of this instant.

He inhaled sharply and took an impulsive half-step forward. He halted abruptly. There was a pulse pounding erratically in the hollow of his throat, and his silver eyes were glowing with a deep, burning flame. He closed his eyes and made an obvious effort at control. He deliberately released her, his arm dropping from her waist as he stepped back. "That's all that's important," he said quietly. Then, incredibly, he was turning to leave!

"Jared?" Her eyes were wide and questioning.

"Stay here," he said gently. "It will be good for you to be alone for a while."

"You're leaving?" she asked disbelievingly.

"I find I'm not quite as self-sacrificing as I'd thought. I don't want to blow the whole purpose of the exercise by grabbing something for myself." One finger reached out to feather the curve of her cheek. "This is for you, little Piper." Then he was gone, striding swiftly through the rainbow-dappled grove like a dark, powerful shadow.

She gazed after him until he disappeared from view. He had lavished a multitude of gifts upon her this day, and not the least of them was that generosity of spirit which had prompted his departure. She knew he'd wanted her with an intensity that had nearly broken his control only a few minutes before, but he'd given her the gift of his restraint as simply as he'd wrapped her in the warmth of this magnificent ermine cloak. There was no question in her mind which was the more valuable present.

She leaned against the slender column of the birch tree, her eyes on the fiery sphere that was sinking behind the dusky purple-violet of the mountains. She felt almost affectionate toward those towering peaks, she realized with amazement. Jared had given her that also, and the knowledge caused that tentative budding she'd experienced the night of the shooting to begin to unfold its petals in a poignantly beautiful blossoming.

Was it love? She didn't know and really didn't care. How could she put a label on something she'd never experienced? It was enough to feel this overwhelming desire to give and take, to belong to another human being on levels she'd never conceived possible. She had received precious gifts today that she must return in kind. It was how those gifts should be presented that she must decide. For a moment she felt an odd rush of shyness, before she quickly smothered it. She lifted her chin proudly, her eyes on the moon, which was gaining glittering prominence now that the sun had gone down. There was nothing to be shy about. She was the Piper, wasn't she?

Her sudden joyous laughter echoed on the clear night air as she began to make her plans. She stayed there a long time while the moonbeams turned the wind chimes to silver tears and the breeze played mysterious melodies in the branches of the trees.

The moon was high in the heavens when she quietly opened the door to Jared's room a few hours later. The heavy velvet drapes on the French windows across the room were drawn back and the moonlight was streaming in, revealing the outlines of the heavy antique furniture in the master suite.

"Welcome home, sweetheart." The voice came from the confines of the huge canopy bed in the center of the room. "Do you know how long I've waited for you to walk through that door?"

"You were expecting me?" She glided forward, the white ermine cape billowing gracefully out behind her. She could dimly discern his lean, shadowy form on the bed, several pillows propped up against the headboard behind him. "If I'd known that, I wouldn't have kept you waiting," she said teasingly. "You could have let me know, Jared."

"Not expecting," he said quietly. "Hoping, love."
She was close enough now to see the polished bronze of
his naked shoulders and the dark curling thatch of hair
on his chest, which narrowed to a thin line where the
satin sheet was pulled carelessly over his flat stomach.
"There's quite a difference. I'd never insult you by taking
you for granted."

She could feel her heart hammering against her ribs
as she slowly unfastened the buttons of the cloak. "I'm
afraid I've committed that particular faux pas already,"
she said a trifle breathlessly as she shrugged out of the
cloak and draped the lovely thing on the back of the chair
a few feet away. "Should I have waited for an invitation?"

"You know better than that," he said gruffly, his pale
gray eyes glistening in the darkness of his shadowed
face. "I've wanted you here in my bed for at least an eon
or two."

"Good." Her hands were swiftly unbraiding her
hair. "I'm glad you're going to support my seduction of
you." She ran her fingers through her long tresses, and
he had a fleeting memory of her small, vibrant figure
clothed in scarlet chiffon, preparing for the tempting of
the piper.

"Is that what you're doing, seducing me?"

She was still. "I thought that was what you wanted."
There was a frown of uncertainty on her face as she
peered at him through the dimness of the moonlit room.

"With utmost fervor, love." There was a reassuring
thread of humor in his voice. "But that's not enough, not
any longer. I feel I have need for the solace of the spoken
word. In short, I want to know why, Tania. Why are you
willing to come to me now?"

"What if I said it was lust?" she asked softly. "What if
I said I didn't care what you thought or what you were,
as long as you could give my body the pleasure you gave

it that first morning I was brought to the chateau? Would you still invite me to your bed?"

"You're damn right I would." He chuckled. "And then I'd do my very best to make you take back every word before morning. I've made a study of you, remember? I know that, as beautifully passionate as you are, you wouldn't be here if you didn't feel something else as well. What I want to know is, what is that something?"

She shrugged helplessly. "I just don't know," she said with bold honesty. "I've never felt like this before." She ran her tongue nervously over her lower lip. "It's strange. . . ."

"I wouldn't want to include that eloquent avowal in a testimonial," he said dryly. "It might sound as though you're coming down with a rare tropical disease."

She laughed shakily. "Do you want promises? I can't give you that. It's all too new."

For a moment there was a flicker in his face that might have been disappointment, before he held out his hand to her. "No promises," he agreed quietly. "Perhaps that's the safest road for both of us. We'll just play it by ear."

"One step at a time," she said softly, placing her small hand in his and letting him tug her toward the bed.

She paused with one knee on the mattress, resisting the pull that would have brought her down into his arms.

"There's something you should know," she said, her voice hesitant. "I'm a virgin." She saw the shock that tensed his body, and rushed on. "Probably not in the physical sense. Ballerinas rarely are. But I've never known a man. If that turns you off, I'll understand."

"Windloe?"

"My friend," she answered with a little shrug that was awkward for someone so innately graceful. "At first I think he wanted to be something more, but in time he accepted that I couldn't be for him what he wished."

His gaze was narrowed intently on her face. "And why couldn't you do that? Your father?"

"I don't know," she whispered, her dark eyes wide and vulnerable. "It might have had something to do with it."

"And why do you feel differently now?"

Why was he asking these questions that she couldn't answer? "I just do." She threw out her hands in helpless frustration. "I trust you, Jared. I think if you'd asked me to jump off that cliff tonight, I'd have done it. Is that enough?"

"It's enough, love." His voice was husky. "For now, it's more than enough." With one strong tug he pulled her down into his arms.

His flesh was so firm and warm against her own that for a moment she couldn't breathe for the delicious shock of it, the heady scent of soap and musk surrounding him. She could see the molten gleam of his silver eyes as he looked down at her. "You don't mind my being a virgin, then?"

His lips nuzzled against the side of her throat. "It may present a few problems." He bit the lobe of her ear gently. "But nothing we can't overcome."

Her hands moved up to the smoothly corded muscles of his shoulders. "I like to touch you," she said softly. "You feel like steel sheathed in silk." Suddenly she frowned. "My own body isn't very pretty right now. My shoulder isn't altogether healed, and there are still bruises from the rope. I can't be very appealing. If you'd rather wait . . ."

"I wouldn't rather wait," he assured her, an amused smile tugging at his lips. "I'll close my eyes so that I won't see all your many imperfections, sweetheart. Now, is there any other horrible surprise lurking for me, or may we proceed?"

"There are my feet," she said seriously. "I have very

ugly feet. Dancers do, you know. I can't even promise that will get better."

He shook his head in amusement. He couldn't believe this. Where was the sensual siren who'd been driving him insane for the last three weeks? She was like an earnest little girl as she anxiously cataloged all her faults, and an aching tenderness tore at his heart strings. He tried to keep the huskiness from his voice as he said lightly, "Well, that's another matter entirely. I think I'm going to have to examine these monstrosities before we go any further." Then he was moving away from her, down her body, pushing up the satin of her nightgown and taking one small foot in his hand. "Yes, I can see why you felt you had to warn me," he said with a solemn frown. "Callouses"—his thumb lightly massaged the arch—"muscles, and I even detect a few tiny scars." He bent his head and lightly kissed her instep. "It's incredible that such ugly feet could produce magic like the Piper."

She felt a little shock run through her. The Piper. She'd let her inexperience and insecurity temporarily make her forget who she was. She wasn't a child, she was the Piper, and the tolerant amusement in Jared's voice must be changed to something more respectful of her status. She took her foot away and sat up in bed. "Perhaps I can do something to overcome that revulsion and make you forget how ugly I am," she said. "Let me think for a minute." Almost absently she pulled the nightgown over her head and threw it casually aside. She was totally naked now, her silky dark hair cascading over her shoulders and the exquisite line of her back. She heard him inhale sharply and felt a thrill of satisfaction run through her. "Let's see, I don't think you expressed any aversion to my breasts. Perhaps concentrating on them would distract you." She got to her knees so that she was facing him, and edged closer until the rosy tips of her nipples were grazing his chest. "They're a bit on the small side, but you seemed pleased with them before." Her lips brushed the hollow of his throat, where the pulse was throbbing jerkily. "Do you like my breasts, Jared?"

"Yes, I like your breasts." They were exquisite breasts, he thought, perfectly formed, with sweet, perky nipples that blossomed passionately when he touched them with his lips and tongue. He wanted to touch them now, but he was afraid she'd revert back to that uncharacteristic insecurity. He'd not even considered the possibility that she was a virgin, and the primitive surge of pleasure he'd known had been followed by concern. He'd wanted their joining to be everything it could, and now he was going to have to move very carefully. He didn't want her uncertainty to cause her to lose even a minute portion of the pleasure that was to come. He'd hoped his teasing amusement would snap her into this aggressive vitality that was an integral element of her personality. The confidence that being in charge would give her would help ease her triumphantly into this new experience, but it was going to prove more difficult than he'd imagined to play a semipassive role, when all he wanted was to be inside her. He made a deliberate effort to steady his breathing. "They're very lovely breasts."

"I'm glad you think so," she said, rubbing them back and forth across his hair-roughened chest like a sinuous little cat. "I like yours also." She leaned forward to nibble at a tiny male nipple. "It's very satisfactory that we're so different there, isn't it?"

"Very satisfactory," he said in a strangled voice. Her hair smelled faintly of wild flowers and was silky soft as it brushed against his chest. Oh, Lord, he didn't want to lose control and reach out for her. "We have several other satisfactory differences as well."

"I've noticed." One small hand reached out to brush the most prominent of those differences with a teasing gesture that caused his hips to jerk forward in explosive reaction. "Do you like me to touch you there, Jared?"

"Yes, I like it," he said thickly. "I like your hands on me, I like your lips on me, and I'm absolutely insane about what your tongue does to me. I'd like to spend the next hundred years or so just letting you perfect your technique with all three. Would you like that, too, little Piper?"

"It would take much less time than that," she scoffed, grinning at him impishly. "I learn very quickly, Jared." She was finding that teasing Jared was very exciting. It was completely different from the frustrating enticement she'd meted out as punishment during their dual of wills. Knowing the pleasure she was going to give him made these anticipatory moves like a *pas de deux* that preceded the explosive finale. She could feel the tension in him like a dark, dangerous current, and that river of strength was even more thrilling because it was leashed. She hadn't realized until now how much she'd hated being sexually dominated by Jared when she'd been under the influence of the paradynoline. It was comforting to know that she had a certain amount of power also in this most intimate of conflicts. "Would you like to see how quickly I learn?" Her legs parted and then closed upon him, capturing him between her thighs. He felt so warm, so hard, so right against the sensitive center of her womanhood that she felt a surge of explosive heat rise within her that was dizzying in its intensity. She abruptly forgot all about conflicts and power struggles as she clutched desperately at his shoulders. "Jared . . ."

The rest was lost as his lips closed over hers in a savage hunger that he quickly softened into an equally urgent sweetness. He hoped to hell she was ready, because he didn't think he could wait much longer. God, he loved the taste of her. His tongue explored the smoothness of her teeth, the side of her cheek, savored the texture of her tongue, in a kiss that ravished and entreated in one. He could feel her thighs tighten around him, and he gave a low groan that was almost a gasp. The erotic feeling of flesh against flesh was too close a parody to the real thing for his self-control, and he moved away from her with a wrench that caused the muscles of his stomach to knot painfully. "The step you just took was more of a quantum leap," he said huskily, his chest moving rapidly from the harshness of his breathing. His hand moved between her thighs in an exploring caress that caused her to stiffen with an electric shock of pleasure. He smiled with relief as he felt the welcome evidence of her arousal, but he had to be sure. She was so tiny, and even if there was no barrier, her virginity would doubtless cause her to be tighter than any woman he'd ever had. He'd better take more time to be sure she experienced no pain at all. Just the thought of her in pain filled him with an aching empathy greater than any he'd ever known. "Why don't you just rest on your laurels now and let me help?"

Her nails bit into his shoulders as one of his hands slid around to cup her buttocks while the other began a rhythmic thrusting that caused her to arch against him with a little guttural cry of need. He paid no attention, his fingers delving and rotating with a skill that was causing lightning flashes of sensation to pour through every vein. There was a frown of intense concentration on his face, and she could hear the painful rasp of his labored breathing. She could feel his hunger like an invisible force, and it fed her own desire until she was moving against his hands and pressing against him with an urgent rhythm of her own.

He closed his eyes, his face flushed and heavy.

"Would you like me inside you?" he asked thickly. "Do you want me to fill you with every bit of me? I want to invade you and make you mine, little Piper. Would you like that too?"

"Yes." Her affirmation was more like a moan as another finger was added to the rhythmic sorcery he was performing on her body. "Oh, yes."

He pushed her gently on her back and moved over her, parting her thighs and slipping swiftly between them. It was all done with such skill and deftness that before she knew it she was lying looking up at him bewilderedly in the most vulnerable position known to woman.

It brought her a sudden shock of uneasiness that must have been reflected on her face, for his eyes suddenly narrowed. "What's the matter?" he asked quickly, his hands moving caressingly on the softness of her belly. "What's wrong, love?"

She shook her head in confusion. "I don't know," she whispered. "I feel so . . . helpless."

He seemed to understand at once. "It's only an illusion," he said quietly. "You're not being dominated, Tania." His hands were gently preparing her once more, easing the tenseness. "It's only that it will be easier for you this way." He moved closer. "There's no reason for you to worry about domination or conflict, because there isn't going to be any." She felt the warm hardness of him begin to enter her. "No one is going to lead and no one is going to follow. We're traveling along this road together." He was pushing gently, carefully, his face taut with pleasure and self-restraint, until suddenly she was surrounding all of him in an unbelievable closeness. "All the way."

His breath expelled sharply in a little burst of relief. Oh, Lord, she had taken all of him, and there was no sign of pain or discomfort on her face. There was only glazed pleasure and a childlike wonder. Her breasts were moving as she breathed in little pants, her eyes wide and dark in her flushed face, her lips parted in a delicious invitation that he couldn't resist.

He bent forward to take her lips, content for the moment to just fill her, to be joined to her in this incredible tightness. His tongue entered to move and probe with a freedom he would not yet allow his body.

Her fingers curled in the hair at his nape to bring his head closer. The double impalement was unbelievably erotic, and unconsciously she suddenly thrust her hips upward to take more of this blinding sensual pleasure. The movement brought a molten sensation that caused her eyes to widen and a little gasp to break from her.

He tore his lips from hers. "No," he whispered urgently. "It'll hurt you. Let me do it." His lips brushed her cheek in a kiss so beautifully tender that it made her throat tighten. "I couldn't bear to hurt you, sweetheart."

"You aren't hurting me," she said. "You feel wonderful. I just want more." Her lips rose to cover his with loving sweetness. "Please give me more, Jared."

He felt something inside him explode into a million shimmering pieces that he wasn't sure could ever be put together again. He wanted to give her everything, every part of his heart and soul, his memories, all of his future, but the only thing he could offer her in this moment of poignant intensity was his body.

"I will, Tania," he said, his voice a throaty murmur. "Whatever you want, sweetheart." He started to move with painstaking care, but the silken friction was a provocation that couldn't be denied, and his thrusts gradually escalated to a fiery intensity, until they were both riding the tide of feeling, moving with frantic urgency, reaching for that ravishing beauty.

And it *was* beauty, she thought, a beauty so strange and all-encompassing that everything else faded in comparison. It was like the wind chimes, whose music tantalized and satisfied at the same time, whose silver-and-crystal loveliness could be pristine or reveal a rainbow spectrum of brilliance. The music was surrounding her, enfolding her. The rainbow was setting her on fire with sensation while still wrapping her in the bands of loving protection.

Then Jared was garlanding all the branches of her spirit with rainbows, as he had decked the forest of white birches, and the song of the wind chimes echoed in every corner of her heart and body.

Jared's finger was gently stroking the dark wing of her brow, his other arm cradling her close in an embrace that was lovingly possessive. "What are you thinking about?" he asked lazily.

What could she answer? she wondered. Her thoughts were so confused and fragmented that her usual mental incisiveness was a mere phantom. I'm thinking I've never known a human being so passionate and loving, that you've just left me and I want you to come into me again, that you've touched me on a thousand different levels that I never knew existed. How could she tell him that, when they'd agreed a short time before that there were to be no promises, no commitments. "Wind chimes," she said softly. "I'm thinking about wind chimes."

He chuckled, his arm bringing her still closer, his hand tucking her head in the hollow of his shoulder. "That seems to be something of an obsession with you. I thought I'd given you enough of them in reality to keep them from claiming your daydreams as well."

She nestled closer, her fingers tangling in the thatch of hair on his chest. "You did. You gave me all the wind chimes I ever wanted, Jared." Wind chimes of beauty, of healing, of passion. "I thank you with all my heart."

A look of swift concern replaced the amazement on his face at the slight break in her voice. "Hey!" he protested, tilting her face up so that he could search her expression. "They were supposed to make you happy, not cause you to cry."

"I'm not crying," she denied quickly. "I never cry." Her dark eyes were suspiciously bright and her dignity very fragilely balanced.

"Forgive me," he said, his eyes twinkling. "I'd forgotten what a wonder woman you are. You couldn't possibly shed a tear. "You have er*b*, right?"

"Right," she assured him. She'd never admit how close she'd come to weeping all over him or how grateful she felt that he'd let her retain her control in this when she'd lost all semblance of it in any other area. "It's perfectly natural that I should be grateful to you, but I haven't cried since I was a very little girl."

He didn't ask what had brought her to tears then or what traumatic experience had made her build that fierce wall of reserve. There were surely a hundred answers, and he wanted her only to forget that pain now. It hurt him even to think about it. Strange how this bond of empathy was growing between them. Strange and quite possibly very dangerous. But he wouldn't think of that now. It was worth any risk to feel this golden completion and know that she was drawing closer to him, edging like a cautious little bird ever nearer to the warmth he wanted to give her. "You're very welcome, sweetheart," he said gravely. "The wind chimes were my pleasure."

She suddenly burst into laughter, and when he gazed at her, puzzled, she laughed again. "You use that phrase so often, but this time you're wrong, Jared," she said, her dark eyes dancing. "They were *my* pleasure." Her lips caressed the flesh beneath his shoulder blade. "And I think I'd like to hear them again now."

"Now?" he asked blankly.

She chuckled. "Now," she said firmly. Then, as he continued to stare bemusedly at her, she pulled his head down for a kiss of heated sweetness that was an explanation all its own. "Never mind," she whispered. "I'll tell you all about it later."

And she set herself to the delightful task of weaving a glittering new garland of rainbows around her wind chimes.

Chapter 11

She woke, as she always did, when the first gray morning light began to filter through the French windows. It was a lovely, hazy light, she thought sleepily, making the room seem unreal. There was nothing the least unreal, however, about the arm that was a heavy band about her waist or the feel of the naked chest against her back. Jared's embrace was endearingly protective . . . secure.

Protective. The thought caused her lids to flick open in sudden wariness. She had no need for protection. She certainly wouldn't invite protection, so why was she lying here in his arms as complacently as a well-fed kitten? It was indicative of how far she'd come into Jared's sphere of power that it felt the supremely natural place to be.

She slipped from beneath his arm and began to inch quietly and carefully away from him. She was off the bed in one lithe movement. He was sleeping deeply, his breathing regular, and he didn't stir as she glided toward the chair where she'd draped the ermine cloak. She mustn't give in to the impulse prompting her to stay in that bed with Jared. The experience she'd known last night had been so beautifully moving it could well be addictive, and she couldn't afford a passion as consuming as this one promised to be. It would weaken her, make her vulnerable in ways that she'd never tolerate.

Already she felt that some small part of her personality had flown out of her to merge in a mysterious alchemy with that of Jared Ryker. The trust she'd felt for him was too fledgling, this emotion too explosive for her to embrace without reservations. She must move very slowly.

The wariness couldn't stop the sudden melting warmth she knew as she paused a moment beside the bed before leaving the bedroom. The misty gray light softened the harsh, powerful planes of Jared's face, and sleep had removed the hard edge of cynicism. He looked almost boyish lying there with his hair rumpled and the piercing silver of his eyes masked by his closed lids.

But he wasn't boyish, she reminded herself as she turned and walked quietly toward the door. He was mature, totally in control, and perhaps the strongest man she'd ever met. Even his lovemaking had reflected that control. In the heights of passion, when she'd been as mindless and weak as a puppet, he'd been able to subdue his own rocketing emotions and guide them both to ecstatic completion. She'd been grateful for that control at the time, but now it filled her with a nagging anxiety. It was a weapon she didn't possess and made her doubly vulnerable to him.

When she reached her own room, she headed straight for the shower. An hour later she'd finished showering, washing, blow-drying, and braiding her hair, and slipped on her black leotard, leg warmers, and slippers. It was time she reasserted her priorities and resumed her own responsibilities. She was quite well enough to begin her practice again. She was a dancer with a career, not Jared Ryker's mistress. She might well become that as well, but it would never be her primary occupation. She was her own person, with her own goals, and she must keep that firmly in mind.

She'd been doing warm-up exercises for perhaps fifteen minutes when Kevin walked into the gym. He stopped just inside the door, his brows lifted in surprise. His lips pursed in a soundless whistle as he strolled toward her. "This is a surprise. I thought I'd have the gym to myself this morning."

"Why?" she asked as she dropped to the floor to begin her sit-ups. "You heard what Jared said before you left my room last night. I'm officially off the sick list. There's no reason I shouldn't start to get into shape again."

He sat down beside her and crossed his legs tailor-fashion, looking a little like a king-sized leprechaun, in his dark green sweat suit. "I don't think Jared had this particular degree of exertion in mind. Does he know you're here?"

"No." She'd reached one hundred and she sat up again, reaching for the hand towel on the floor beside her. "But he couldn't have stopped me. I know my body's limitations better than he does. I've already lost too much time." She wiped the back of her neck with the towel. That fact was becoming very obvious to her, she thought grimly. She was feeling weak as a baby after only this pitifully brief workout, and her shoulder was beginning to throb with a deep heat that was becoming hard to ignore. She'd gotten just as soft as she'd feared. "A dancer can't afford this kind of self-indulgence."

"I admire your dedication, but don't you think it's a little out of proportion? Could a few more days of rest hurt?"

"A few days can become very precious when you consider how short a ballerina's career can be," she said, rubbing her shoulder. "I'm twenty-four years old, Kevin. I don't have many more good years left." She glanced at him a trifle indignantly as he gave a shout of laughter.

"Sorry," he said, still chuckling. "It just struck me funny to see you sitting there looking about thirteen and talking like a little old lady." He shook his head, his blue eyes twinkling. "Did it ever occur to you that you may not be a has-been in ten years, Tania? Think about what Jared's work is going to mean to you . . . its impact on your career."

She dabbed at the sweat on her forehead, her dark eyes stunned. She hadn't thought at all about the personal impact of Jared's discovery. She had perceived only the universal significance. Now it came home to her that it could make drastic changes in her own life as well. Instead of the bright flame of a career quickly extinguished that she'd had to accept as her destiny, she could look out on a whole new horizon. She would be able to dance as long as she wanted; she would be limited only by her desires. She felt a rush of pure joy, and her expression became luminous.

"How marvelous! How absolutely marvelous!" She stopped short. "Marguerite. She'll be able to resume her career after all."

"Marguerite?"

"My friend Marguerite Montclair," she said excitedly. "She gave up dancing when she gave birth to Barry. It was a terribly difficult choice. She knew that her best years would be over by the time Barry didn't need her anymore. Now she can have it all." She threw her arms out exuberantly. "Every woman can have it all! A career, children, whatever she wants. Isn't it wonderful?"

"It's wonderful for your friend Marguerite," Kevin agreed hesitantly. "Do you like children, Tania?"

She nodded. "I love them," she said eagerly. "You

should see Barry. He's only five, but he's so bright, and he has a polite, old-world courtesy that—" She broke off as she saw the sympathetic, almost pitying look on Kevin's face. "What's the matter? Why are you looking at me like that?"

"Jared's breakthrough is a double-edged sword, Tania," Kevin said gently. "One of those cutting edges carries with it some bitter wounds. There will almost certainly have to be a legally mandated zero population growth."

"What are you talking about?"

"I'm talking about birth control," he said quietly. "And in case of accidental conception, abortion. Perhaps sterilization for the entire population."

"No!" Her eyes widened in horror, and she felt suddenly sick to her stomach. "They can't do that!"

"It's bound to come, Tania." His voice was soothing. "It's best that you come to grips with the idea and accept it."

"No more babies," she said dazedly. "A world with no more children. How can I accept that? How can anyone accept that?"

"It will be necessary to insure survival for the rest of us."

"It's ugly." Her voice was shaking with the violence of her feelings. "It's monstrous." She jumped to her feet, her hands clenched into fists at her sides. "And I won't accept it! If I live forever, I'll never accept it!"

She threw the towel on the floor and ran from the room. She ignored Kevin's worried voice calling after her as she streaked down the corridor to the front door and out across the courtyard. She had no conscious destination, but it didn't surprise her that she was suddenly leaving the formal garden and running into the birch grove. Today it was cloudy and the wind chimes weren't rainbows, they were shimmering mother-of-pearl, but their music was just as healing. The Lord knew that she needed healing now.

She threw herself on the ground beneath Jared's favorite tree. She was vaguely aware of the feel of the cold ground through the thin material of her leotard and the stinging whip of the early-morning breeze against her face, but it made no real impression. A world without babies. She couldn't believe it. She was never going to have a little boy like Barry. She'd always taken it for granted that someday she would have a child, someone of her own to lavish all her love and attention upon, and now it was never going to happen. She felt as if she'd been robbed of something very precious. As if her child had already been torn from her womb, as Kevin had assured her it would be. A child like Barry. She blinked rapidly, her eyes stinging with tears she wouldn't permit to fall. Perhaps she *should* cry. Someone should cry for all those children never to be born into the world, never to be held close and sung lullabies to, never to . . .

"There'd better be a damned good reason for this idiocy, Tania." Jared's voice was grim, but no grimmer than his expression. He was standing only a few feet away, dressed in jeans and a navy windbreaker and carrying a sheepskin jacket over his arm. "I should have known better than to assume you'd have the sense to opt for moderation. First Kevin tells me you were half killing yourself in the gym earlier, and now you're running around outside in practically nothing. Do I have to keep a watchdog on you all the time just to make sure you're not doing something crazy?"

"But you did have a watchdog on me, Jared," she said bitterly, sitting up very stiff and straight. "I'm surrounded by watchdogs, remember? Even Kevin, charming as he is, acts as your eyes and ears when the occasion calls for it. You wouldn't be here if he hadn't come running to you."

"He was worried," Jared said gently. He knelt beside her and draped the sheepskin jacket around her, fastening the first two buttons. "He said the two of you had been talking and suddenly you got upset and ran out of the chateau like a wild woman. What the devil's wrong with you?"

"Nothing's wrong with me," she said, her eyes on a point past his left shoulder. "I just started to think of this wonderful world you're going to create for all of us, Jared." Her lips twisted bitterly. "I'm not sure it's a world I want to live in." There was a flush on her cheeks, and she was speaking with a feverish rapidity. "Do you know that I've never found the idea of being a little old lady even the slightest bit sad? I liked the idea of being able to say the most outrageous things . . . and do with perfect impunity any eccentric thing that took my fancy. Old age grants us a certain grace and privilege." Her voice was fierce. "You've robbed us of that, Jared. You're going to populate the earth with a race of healthy, sterile robots."

There was a flicker of raw pain on his face before it became coolly impassive. "If I have, then I'll accept the responsibility," he said. "Everything has its price. I just happen to think that this advancement is worth nearly any price we have to pay." His smile was a little forced. "If you want to be a little old lady, I'll buy you a white wig and a theatrical makeup kit and you can play dress-up, pixie."

"It's not funny," she said between her teeth. "And some prices are just too high, particularly when we have no choice about paying them." She jumped to her feet and backed away from him, her dark eyes blazing in her white face. "Damn your discovery, Jared Ryker!"

"Why are you so upset?" His gray eyes were narrowed on her face. "What's at the bottom of this, Tania? All this talk of spunky old ladies and robots is evasive. How can I reason with you when you won't bring the real problem out in the open?"

"That's what you're best at, isn't it, Jared? You're always so coolly reasonable and in control." Her voice broke. "Well, I'm afraid I won't fit into your neat little plans. I'm not at all like you, Jared. I have emotions, and sometimes they're not under control at all."

"That's quite obvious." He was a little paler than before. "But I'm still curious as to just why your emotions are running so high. Why the hell are you turning your knife in me, Tania?"

"Because of the children," she shouted, her dark eyes wild and blazing. "Because you've taken away my babies." Her words were a harsh cry of pain. "And I don't think I'll ever forgive you, Jared Ryker!" Then she turned and ran away from him toward the chateau, like an animal in pain hunting a lair in which to tend its wounds.

Jared's eyes followed her until she disappeared from sight, his hands clenched into fists at his sides and his body rigid. She had called him "coolly reasonable," he thought dully. It would be funny if it didn't hurt so much. He'd never felt less mechanical or controlled in his life than in this moment. Capsules of pain were exploding inside him with every breath. He was trying to reason, to empathize with her, but he couldn't get past that wall of agony she'd built with those words she'd hurled at him.

Last night he'd held her in his arms and thought all the years of loneliness were behind him. Now, with a shocking suddenness, that certainty had vanished. He was once more alone, and he began to feel a deep, burning resentment toward her for hurting him like this. No, damn it, he wouldn't let her snatch the gift away from him. He couldn't go back to experiencing such loneliness. She was his now, and he'd keep her any way he could.

There was no knock on the door, but Kevin's voice boomed out. "Open the door, princess. My hands are full."

Tania moved quickly to unlock and throw open the door. Then she stepped aside as Kevin strode into the room, a covered rattan tray in his hands.

"I've brought you a light supper," he said as he crossed the room to deposit the tray on the bedside table. "It's only soup and sandwiches, so you needn't scowl like that. You didn't show up for dinner and you refused the tray George brought you, so I had to take matters in my own hands." He grinned. "I couldn't let you start skipping meals and undoing all the progress you've made. After all the time I've spent with you in the past week, I definitely have a vested interest."

"Thank you for thinking of me, Kevin," she said quietly. She tightened the sash of her red chiffon robe and leaned against the door to regard him with wry exasperation. "But really, I'm not hungry."

"Eat anyway. You've been closeted in here all day without touching a bite. Come on, princess," he coaxed, "I know I'm the one who made you come apart this morning. I always did have a tendency to put my foot in my mouth. You wouldn't want to give me a king-sized guilt complex, would you?"

No, she wouldn't want to do that, she thought wearily. None of this was his fault. He'd only been trying to be kind, preparing her for what was to come. How could he have known it would cause such an explosion of pain and anger deep within her? Nevertheless, she was fleetingly surprised that Kevin had blundered so cruelly. Before this, she had found him almost exquisitely sensitive to the feelings of others.

"No guilt complexes," she said. Her smile was a bit forced. "You did what you thought was right, and that's all any of us can do. Leave the tray, Kevin. I'll eat something later."

"Great." His blue eyes were concerned. "Why don't you make it an early night? You look a bit frazzled."

"I'll do that." She wished he'd leave. She was more than frazzled, she was confused, and there was a raw ache in her breast that had something to do with the memory of the pain on Jared's face this morning when she'd been striking out at him. "Don't worry about me, Kevin. I'll be fine in the morning."

"I hope so. It's not at all comfortable being the catalyst for all this turbulence. Not only are you hurt and upset, but Jared's a menace! I've never seen him in such a savage mood."

"I wouldn't be overly concerned," she said with a sad little smile. "His mood may be savage, but Jared's always in control. He'll never let his temper get beyond the limits he sets for it."

"I'm glad you're so confident," Kevin said dryly. "I'm not nearly as sure, and I don't think you would be either if you'd seen him at dinner. He's been in the library all day just staring into space, and I don't think he likes the pictures he's seeing. He reminds me of a delayed explosive, with the timer primed and ticking. I don't know what went on between you two this morning, princess, but whatever it was, it had a highly dangerous effect. It would be wise to be very careful around him for a while." He moved toward the door. "Now that I've delivered both physical sustenance and dire warnings, I think it's time for me to leave you in peace."

She automatically moved aside as he opened the door. "Good night, princess." His index finger gently touched her cheek in a gesture that was a near-caress. "You're a very special lady, and I like you very much. I can't tell you how I regret hurting you." Before she could speak, the door had closed behind him.

She turned away and walked slowly over to the table where Kevin had set the tray. She lifted the domed aluminum cover and gazed at the sandwiches on the delicately flowered plate for a moment before replacing it with distaste. Perhaps later she'd be able to eat a little, as she'd promised Kevin. Now she felt even the vegetable soup wouldn't slide down her throat. Maybe a little fresh air would help. She'd been so upset she hadn't even noticed how stale the air was in her room.

She wandered over to the French doors and stepped out on the balcony, leaving the door open so the icy wind could curl through the room behind her. The sharp cold was oddly welcome as she stood staring out into the darkness. It gave her something more substantial to struggle against than the emotional phantoms that had been plaguing her all day. With a little shiver, she folded her arms protectively across her breasts as a particularly piercing gust of wind struck through her gossamer scarlet chiffon robe. It must be close to freezing, she thought absently. The weather had been very mild for autumn in Canada, where heavy snows were commonplace at this time of year, but there was a moist chill in the air, indicating that Indian summer was now a thing of the past.

Indian summer. Such a bittersweet phrase for the golden period preceding the frosts of winter. Her time in Jared's arms last night had been her own Indian summer. She just hadn't thought that the frost of reality would bring the season to so swift an end.

"Are you planning to jump off the balcony or do you think catching pneumonia will accomplish the same end?" Jared asked caustically from behind her. "Suicide is one way of assuring you don't have to live in a sterile world, but it's not one I'd think you'd choose." Before she could answer, his hand on her arm was guiding her forcibly back into the room and closing the balcony door with a decisive click.

Her surprise was swiftly superseded by anger. "I'm growing a little tired of your interference, Jared. I've taken care of myself for a good many years without your help, and I don't need it now or in the future."

"You made that more than clear this morning," he said tersely. He released her arm and stepped back from her. He was dressed casually, as usual, in dark cords and an olive-green sweatshirt, but there was nothing casual about his demeanor. He was as charged with electricity as a lightning bolt, his face taut and lean with tension and his silver eyes burning fitfully. "You don't need any help from robots or icemen, right? I'm the villain of the piece, who is going to destroy all your plans for the future."

"I lost my temper. I shouldn't have said all those things," she said, frowning. "Not that they weren't true, but voicing the obvious doesn't help anyone. It certainly won't change what you plan on doing."

"You're damn right it won't change my plans," Jared said, blazingly angry. "Because I happen to believe in what I'm doing. I'm not going to deny that there will be a hell of a lot of problems to overcome, but if I didn't think it worthwhile, do you think I'd be willing to take on the whole world? Do you think I'd be here on this god-awful mountain wasting my time, when I could be working, if I were the destroyer you think me?"

"I didn't say you were a destroyer."

"No, it was closer to baby-killer, wasn't it?" he said

bitterly. "Forgive me for paraphrasing you. Let's see. Robot, baby-killer, robber. Have I left anything out?"

Had she said all that? She'd been so upset, she might have accused him of almost anything, but she couldn't believe she'd been so viperish. "No, I guess that about covers it," she said wearily. "I don't remember everything, but I imagine that comes pretty close." She started to turn away. "Now I wish you'd leave, Jared. This conversation isn't going to lead either of us anywhere we want to go."

His hand snaked out to close on her wrist and whirled her back to face him. "The hell it's not," he said between his teeth. "It's going to bring us exactly where we want to go. I admit I'd hoped for a great deal more, but we can't have everything. I'll just have to make do with what you're willing to give me. Who cares about trust and understanding, anyway? I've done without them all my life and haven't suffered any major traumas."

Not even loneliness? The thought was so ephemeral that it was gone before she was conscious of it. "I'm not willing to give you anything," she said, trying to shake off his hand. "Last night was a mistake that won't be repeated. We're too far apart in every way that matters, Jared."

"I wouldn't say that." His lips curved cynically. "What happened in that bed last night mattered more than you're willing to admit. They say good sex is ninety percent of any relationship, and you can't deny that we were fantastic together. Besides, I may be the only man who can give you what you want, so don't be so eager to show me the door."

"And what do I want?" she asked sarcastically. "You?"

"I wouldn't flatter myself," he said. There was a flicker of remembered pain in the depths of his eyes.

"No, I'm referring to the reason for this rhubarb you've been throwing. I gather from your rather inarticulate raving this morning and what I found out later from Kevin that my primary sin in your eyes concerns the birth-control factor. You want to have a child, and you aren't going to be able to have one."

"How coolly you say that," she said bitterly.

"But then, what would you expect from a robot?" he asked smoothly. "I'd hate to disappoint you." He paused. "But you won't be disappointed, will you, Tania? Because I'm going to give you that baby you're so crazy to have."

"What?" Her eyes widened in shock.

"Isn't that what you want?" he asked, pulling her unresisting body into the circle of his arms. "You want a child to love. A child is safe. A child won't demand more than you want to give. He'll love you all your life and never expect you to be more than a nurturer and friend." His arms tightened around her. "That's much safer than letting yourself be committed to me, isn't it? Because I'd ask that you give me everything you are—now and in the future. I wouldn't be interested in halfway measures."

"You're not making sense." She was struggling to free herself, her hands pushing against his chest. "You don't know anything about the way I feel."

"That's right. I don't have any feelings myself, so how could I hope to understand your sensitive, maternal yearnings?" His face was granite-hard, and for the first time she felt a twinge of fear. "But it doesn't necessarily require emotion for the process of procreation, so that shouldn't be a drawback. You might even enjoy it. I didn't hear any complaints last night."

Then he was lifting and carrying her to the canopy bed across the room. For a moment she was too stunned to struggle. "I can't believe this," she said. "This isn't like you, Jared."

"I should think you'd be grateful. You presumably believed every word Kevin told you about the horrors of the repercussions of my work. Poor unsuspecting society! You didn't come to me and ask my opinion or what I intend to do. You just judged me and tried to throw me out of your life."

"You mean it won't happen?"

"I hope to God it won't," he said. "I'm going to do everything I can to prevent it, but I can't give guarantees." He placed her on the velvet counterpane. "And that's what you want, isn't it?" He sat down beside her, his hands pinning her shoulders to the bed. "Don't worry, Tania. I'm going to be the king of this brave new world, remember? They need me to make all the clocks of the world stop. Everyone knows that a king has to have an heir, so your baby will be safe. It's all very neat and tidy in my sterile robotic world."

She was staring up at him with compulsive fascination. She'd never seen him with that look of bold recklessness on his face. His eyes looked almost feverish, and there was a ferocity about him that appeared dangerously close to release. "Don't do this, Jared," she said quietly. "I'll fight you, and if you do succeed in raping me, I'll never forgive you."

He'd released one of her shoulders, and his hand was swiftly unfastening the tiny buttons of her scarlet negligee. "It won't be rape. You're a very passionate woman, and I have a great deal of patience when it suits me. Remember? It's going to be a very educational night for you, Tania. You're going to find out that it's possible to want completion so much you're even willing to ask a monster like me to give it to you." He had unfastened the last button and was opening the scarlet negligee and slipping it off her shoulders and down her arms to reveal the matching silk gown beneath it. "I like this gown. It reminds me of the costume you wore the first time I saw you. You looked like a lovely flame maiden." He thoughtfully rubbed the material of the low bodice of the nightgown between his thumb and forefinger. "I watched you dance, and all I could think about was how much I wanted to do this." With one lightning movement his hand clenched the neckline and jerked downward, ripping the gown from bodice to hem.

She gasped, her hands flying out instinctively to cover herself. "Are you crazy?" she cried, her dark eyes blazing up at him.

"Why no, Tania," he said mockingly. "I'm just being the man you think me. I wanted you naked in the fastest possible way, and I wanted to point out the difference between the act of rape and seduction." He was removing the tatters of scarlet silk from beneath her body, and he held them up like a teacher with a scientific specimen. "That was an act of violence, a preliminary to rape." He tossed them carelessly aside. "Lesson one. I will now proceed with the seduction."

"The hell you will." Her hand cracked against his cheek with all the strength she could muster, the impact sounding like the snap of a whip. At the same time she rolled with frantic speed to the other side of the bed and was on her feet and racing toward the bathroom. She was only halfway there when she felt Jared's arm encircle her from behind and jerk her back. He picked her up kicking and struggling frantically and carried her back to the bed.

But this time she wasn't stunned or bewildered into a semblance of meekness. She was angry. She felt as if every breath she was drawing should have been steaming with the fury that was coursing through all her veins. Her fists were striking at him with each step, and when he bent to lay her on the bed, one hand grabbed his hair and pulled with all her might. When the flash of surprised agony caused his grip to loosen, she rolled away and aimed a lethal kick at his solar plexus with her hard dancer's foot. He gave a grunt of pain that made her smile with savage satisfaction, and she was scooting to the end of the bed before he could fully recover.

Then she heard a low, muttered curse behind her and the mattress dipped under his weight as he dove after her, just managing to grab her hips as she was slipping off the bed. His powerful hands dug into her soft flesh as he jerked her back on the bed, and she gave an involuntary cry of pain.

"Damn it, see what you've done," he said raggedly.

"What *I've* done?" He was the one who'd injured her, she thought furiously. He still wasn't being any too gentle as he dragged her up to the center of the bed until her head was on the pillow. He swiftly straddled her, using just enough weight to keep her immobile, the rough denim of his thighs rubbing against her naked hips, his chest moving rapidly with the force of his breathing.

He was staring down at her, and if there had been leashed savagery in his face before, it was blazing open and free now. His dark hair was wild and tousled, and the livid mark of her hand was still visible on his cheek. Her fist swung up in an attempt to give him a matching blow on the other cheek, but he caught her wrist before it connected.

"What the hell do you think you're doing?" he grated out as he pinned both her hands above her head. "Do you want to hurt yourself?"

"I told you I'd fight you!" Her eyes were flaming with rage. "I don't want you, and I don't want your crown prince of a baby. You'll have to hurt me, and I don't think you'll do that, Jared."

"I won't hurt you," he promised grimly. "But I see right now that I'm going to have to do something to keep you from hurting yourself."

He caught both wrists in an iron grip and stretched sideways, his other hand searching while his gaze remained fixed warily upon her. It was a few moments before he found what he was searching for and straightened. He had the silk rags of the torn nightgown in his hands, and he released her for the briefest moment, while he tore a long, narrow strip before tossing the remnants of the nightgown aside. Then she realized what he was going to do.

"No!"

Her hands reached out like claws to tear at him, but he grabbed them both, and a moment later they were firmly trussed together with the scarlet silk and he was bringing her arms over her head to tie the silken rope to the cherrywood column supporting the canopy.

"Let me go, Ryker," she said between her teeth. "I won't let you do this to me. I won't be tied up like some lowly slave for your pleasure."

"If I let you go, you'll begin to fight me again and probably hurt yourself." He smiled bitterly. "And then you'll blame me for that too."

He pulled the olive-green sweatshirt over his head and threw it carelessly on the floor beside the bed. "You're so afraid of being dominated, you're willing to give up everything we might have together." His hand was on her braid, deftly loosening the tresses before combing his fingers through it, letting the satin strands run between his fingers with a frankly sensual pleasure. "Well I'm not about to permit you to do it, pretty Piper. I'm going to keep you any way I can, and I'll use lust or need or even that domination you're so frightened of to do it."

She tugged futilely at the silken bonds, twisting her head back and forth to try to avoid Jared's hands in her hair. She felt so helpless that a surge of panic pierced the anger that electrified her. She was more vulnerable than she'd ever been in her life, and the man astride her wasn't the patient, gentle lover who'd brought her such a rainbow of ecstasy the night before. He was a stranger with blazing silver eyes and a hard, bitter mouth and words that hurt her even while they filled her with rebellion. "You're wrong," she spat out. "You'll never dominate me, Jared. Not you or anyone."

"I think I will." He swung off her supine body, stood up, and began to unfasten his belt. "I never wanted to, you know. You never believed that, but it was quite true. I wanted a partner, not a slave." He was quickly stripping off the rest of his clothes. "Well, I'm not going to have that, but I'll salvage something for myself."

He was naked now as he came back to the bed and sat down beside her. His hand gently cupped one small breast. "You have such lovely breasts, sweetheart. Shall we start with them?"

She glared up at him with silent defiance. His hands were moving to the sides of her breasts, pushing gently inward to bring the mounds into swelling prominence, then his head was bending with deliberate slowness until his lips were just a breath away from one taut rosy peak. "So pretty," he said thickly. With every word, she could feel a little burst of warm breath against the sensitive nipple. "And so responsive. See how beautifully the little bud is beginning to blossom?" His tongue brushed her, and she inhaled sharply at the jolt of fire that light touch sent spinning through her. How could her body be this treacherous? He was stroking the nipple with his warm, skillful tongue while his thumb gently rubbed the other into engorgement. "Think about the baby I'm

going to give you, love. Think about how he'll love these
sweet breasts when they're full of milk. Will his lips feel
like mine, Tania?" Then his mouth was enveloping her
with a strong, gentle suction while his hand kneaded and
teased the swollen mound. She was unable to suppress a
gasp as the evocative words followed by the erotic pull of
his lips combined to cause a flood of heat to every part of
her body. She didn't know how long his lips continued
their sensual play with her breasts, alternating from one
to the other, stroking, sucking, nibbling. It seemed like
forever in the delirium of desire he was invoking within
her. Her body was becoming excruciatingly sensitive,
stretched taut and helpless by the silken rope, while his
lips and teeth engendered a feverish heat. She felt each
caress as a little shock that was almost painful.

Her head moved back and forth on the pillow. "No."
Her voice was a choked moan. "No, Jared."

His head lifted, his eyes glazed. "Too much?" he
asked huskily. "Then we'd better move on, hadn't we?"
His hand slid down her body to gently rub the softness of
her belly. "Will you like having my baby tucked in here,
soft and secure? It's such a lovely, tiny haven. It's hard to
imagine that it could hold a life." His hand moved
caressingly down over her soft flesh to the juncture of
her thighs. "But you can take a great deal, Tania. I found
that out last night. Open your thighs, sweet."

"No." Her whisper was a mere breath of sound. "I'll
never give you anything willingly, Jared."

He was moving astride her, his own hands parting
her legs. "Yes, you will," he said grimly. "Give me
another hour and you'll be more than willing. Like I
said, you're a very passionate woman, Tania." Then he
set to work, his hands as devilishly skilled and sensual as
she remembered. Probing, stroking, rotating until she

was moving helplessly against them. He'd said he was a very patient man, and he demonstrated that patience now. He brought her to the very edge of release any number of times, only to jerk her back from the precipice. He would soothe her, stroking her with hands and words, and then begin the fiery arousal of her senses once more.

He'd said to give him an hour, and at the end of that time she couldn't have said whether it had been a moment or a decade that had passed. Her breasts were heaving from the tumult of her breathing, and her dark eyes were fever-brilliant in her flushed face. Only one thing was important in the universe, to assuage the aching emptiness that seemed to encompass her entire body. She was almost mindless with the need he'd provoked so skillfully, and the muscles of her stomach clenched painfully as he reached around to knead her buttocks with gentle hands.

He smiled down at her, his gray eyes noting the reflex with tiger-bright alertness. "I think you're ready, sweetheart," he said softly. "I think you're ready to ask me to give you what you want." His fingers gently compressed her flesh. "What you need. Just one sentence, that's all it will take. Just say the words."

Oh, God, she couldn't, she thought dazedly. She had to hold out or something inside her would be lost forever. Yet how could she not, when nothing seemed more important than receiving the completion that Jared was withholding from her? She felt as if she were being ripped apart, and suddenly she was unutterably weary of fighting her own body as well as Jared. Her lashes slowly closed, and she wasn't even conscious of the two tears that brimmed over and slowly rolled down her cheeks. She opened her lips to speak.

"No!" Jared's voice was almost a shout. His hand

swiftly covered her lips. Her lids flew up in shocked surprise to see Jared's face above her, a twisted mask of agony. Suddenly the stranger was gone, but she almost wished she had him back. He would have been easier to face than this haggard, pale-faced man, whose silver eyes looked as if they'd gazed into hell. His hand moved from her lips to tenderly stroke the silky wings of hair at her temple. "It's all right, love," he said quickly. "I know you'll never give in." He gave her a pained travesty of a smile. "You'll always be the Piper. I guess I'll just have to dance to your tune one last time."

Then he was plunging within her, thrusting with a wild force and passion that was everything he'd teased her with, giving her the full vibrance of himself in a cascade of skilled movements that caused her to catch her breath with the sheer power of it. In a matter of minutes she'd received an explosive completion that left her shivering and weak.

She was so dazed and shaken that she barely felt the brush of Jared's lips on her forehead or the tug of the silken bonds as he swiftly released her. Then he was slipping off her and getting up. She lifted heavy lids a moment later, to see him fastening the snap at the waistband of his jeans. He was bare to the waist, and the low-slung jeans clung closely to his slender hips and the powerful column of his thighs. His face was dark and shadowed with the same pain she'd glimpsed before. He turned away from the bed without another glance at her and strode across the room to the French doors, thrusting back the curtains to stare sightlessly out into the darkness. His spine was straight and rigid, and she could see the coiled tension in every muscle in his naked back.

She sat up sluggishly and pushed her mass of dark silky hair away from her face. She felt so dazed and bewildered that for a moment she wasn't able even to begin to comprehend what had transpired in those last incredible moments. She shook her head as if to clear it, her gaze on the taut figure of the man across the room.

Chapter 12

"*I* 'll call Corbett in the morning." Jared's voice was harsh with strain. "I'll tell him that I won't have you here any longer. It won't be possible to send you back to New York, but he'll find a place where you'll be safe and comfortable until we can release you. I promise that you won't have to put up with my presence for more than a few days at the longest."

It was such a complete reversal that for a moment Tania was breathless. "You're sending me away?"

"I think it's more than time, don't you?" His voice held all the weariness in the world. He continued to stare blindly into the darkness. "Maybe Corbett and Kevin are right after all. They say we're still too close to savagery to make any revolutionary transition easy. Well, I certainly proved that tonight. Perhaps I am the thief and destroyer you think me." He laughed mirthlessly. "You might add rapist to that list."

There were waves of such intense agony emanating from him that she could feel them across the room. It started an echoing ache somewhere deep within her, and instinctively she tried to make an attempt at assuaging both. "You didn't rape me," she said huskily. "Toward the end I wanted it just as much as you'd said I would." It

236

didn't bother her a bit to admit it, she found to her amazement.

"You're very generous." She could see his hand clench the velvet drapes until the knuckles showed white. "We both know that only made the offense more despicable. I tried to steal something from you that was a hell of a lot more important than the pleasure of your body." He added quickly, "I didn't succeed, of course."

But he had succeeded. Everything was suddenly coming into focus. She'd been stripped of her defenses and made to admit defeat for the first time in her life. She had opened her lips to say the words that would give him final victory, but he'd known even before that he'd won. Yet he'd defaulted at the last minute, denied his victory and tried to give her back the confidence in her own supremacy that he thought was necessary to her. And he was still insisting she'd bested him even while she sensed the pain and self-disgust tearing at him. He was trying to protect her shield, not realizing it was no longer there.

The knowledge came to her with the simplicity of unquestionable truth. She would never lift the shield against Jared again. Not because she was defeated, but because it was no longer necessary. Last night she had told him she trusted him, but it hadn't really been true. There had remained an ember of suspicion, quickly fanned into flame by dissension.

Her lips curved in a smile of almost maternal tenderness. It was strange to learn ultimate trust from a situation so fraught with violence and anguish. She'd been forced to admit to herself that Jared *could* dominate her, and then in the same moment she'd realized he never would. Even in his pain and anger, he had cared enough to stop before she'd been subjugated. If she could trust him at such a moment, she could trust him at any time.

And with trust came the final golden flowering she'd been refusing to acknowledge, even to herself. Like a phoenix rising from the ashes, spreading its wings until it seemed to encompass everything she was, came the realization. How odd and new it felt.

"I'm not going to ask you to forgive me," he said quietly. "Some things are beyond forgiveness and understanding." He shook his head incredulously. "I can't understand it myself. I've always prided myself on being so civilized and logical. Yet I find I'm as much an animal as if I'd just crawled out of a cave. Not a very pleasant thing to discover after living thirty-eight years."

"And why did that control break tonight, Jared?" She got slowly off the bed and crossed to the large armoire against the far wall, pulled a tailored white wool robe from a padded hanger, and slipped it on. "What made the difference?" She walked toward him.

"I'm not going to make any excuses," he said harshly. "There aren't any that would be worthy of the name. I was frightened and in pain and I acted like any other savage and struck out." His voice broke. "My God, I tried to hurt *you*."

His back was still toward her, and she didn't see his face until she was right next to him. Then she caught her breath. She'd been so dazed before he'd left her that she'd been only subliminally aware of his expression of torment mingled with self-disgust. She immediately averted her eyes, not wanting to see his suffering.

"It's starting to snow," she murmured, watching the first pristine flakes gently drift against the pane. What could she say to him that would ease that pain? There was no question that she wanted to do so. It was sheer self-defense . . . for she felt his pain as her own. Would it always be like this now? She'd been so caught up in a virtual hurricane of emotions in the past hours that she wondered for a moment if she could put aside her own selfish need for comfort to give to him. Then she discarded the thought impatiently. Of course she could do it. Jared had given her back her strength, and now she must use it to soothe his pain.

"Don't worry, it shouldn't interfere with your leaving," he said, still not looking at her. "There's no major snowstorm forecast, and this flurry will probably have stopped by the time Corbett can make arrangements."

She moved closer. "I'm not worried," she said softly, "because I'm not leaving, Jared."

He stiffened as if an arrow had pierced him, and he slanted a glance at her. "What did you say?"

"You heard me." Suddenly a gamin grin lit her face. "You needn't think I'll let you whisk me away out of sight so you won't have to remember how you've abused me. I'm going to stick so close to you, you'll have to wear me like a hair shirt."

"You're laughing," he exclaimed.

"What did you expect, weeping and wailing? I'm not saying that what you did was right. It was very wrong. If anyone else had done the same thing, I'd probably be planning his murder." She scowled. "You mustn't ever do anything like that again, Jared. It causes far too many problems."

"Problems?" His laugh was sharp with bitterness. "You call what I just did to you a 'problem'?"

She nodded. "That's why you mustn't do that again. We're going to have enough problems adjusting, without your causing more." She stepped even closer. Her arms went around his waist, and her head nestled on his chest as if she were a trusting little girl. "There are several other things you have to understand, Jared."

She could feel his body freeze, until even his breath seemed to stop in his chest. "Understand?"

"That I must be allowed my own career, that's most essential. That you be honest with me at all times." She rubbed her cheek against his chest like an affectionate kitten as she continued. "That you give me the baby you spoke of so eloquently. Last, but not least, if you're going to be any kind of monarch, it had better be as a monogamous king, not a sultan. I think I could become quite fierce if you suddenly decided you wanted to have a harem."

He had released the curtain and his hands were hovering above her shoulders as if afraid to touch her. "You're going to stay with me?"

"For a genius you really can be very thick, Jared." She sighed. "What have I been telling you? Of course I'm staying until it's safe for you to leave the chateau. It would be unreasonable for me to do anything else. But then I think you should insist they arrange quarters for you in New York instead of Washington. That's where *my* work is." She glanced up at him mischievously. "After all, you can be a king anywhere. Okay?"

"Okay." His voice was still dazed. "Oh, God, yes, it's more than okay." His hands touched her shoulders hesitantly, as if they were very fragile. Suddenly he was laughing freely, joyously. "New York instead of Washington, a baby, a career, anything you want. I'll even give up the harem." His arms went around her, and he crushed her to him. "I'll give up the whole damn world."

"That won't be necessary. Depriving yourself of the harem will do."

He buried his face in the loose hair at her temple. "I thought I'd lost you," he said huskily. "I *should* have lost you. Why didn't I, sweetheart?"

"Because I'm a very clever and self-serving woman who refuses to give up what she wants just because you did something stupid," she said lightly. "To even things out, though, I should really insist you permit me to tie you down and let me drive you crazy." She tilted her head consideringly. "I think pink satin bonds would be quite attractive on you."

He sifted through the nonsense to what was important to him. "And what do you want, Tania?"

She looked up at him, her dark eyes glowing. "You, Jared Ryker," she said simply. "I think there's every possibility that I feel something very special for you. I've never cared for anyone this way before, so I can't be certain. But whatever it is, I think it may last as long as the time that your work is going to give us."

He went still. "You mean that?" There was an uncertainty in his expression that she found very endearing in a man as usually composed as Jared. He shook his head incredulously. "There can't be another woman like you in the entire universe. Do you know that you've totally committed yourself to me without even demanding any vows of undying devotion in return?"

"It would be nice if you'd say something lovely and meaningful, but it's not really necessary," she said gravely. "I'm a very determined woman. If you don't feel that way about me now, then I'll just have to work much harder until you do." She paused. "But I think you do feel something pretty close to what I want, Jared. Am I wrong?"

His hands reached up to frame her face. "No, you're not wrong. I think if you ever left me, I'd go a little crazy." His eyes were shining with a warmth and joy she'd never seen there before. "It would leave an aching gap the size of the Grand Canyon." His head bent and his lips touched hers with a warmth and solemn sweetness that caused a lump to form in her throat. "I want you by my side and in my bed for the rest of our lives. Is that close enough to what you want?"

"Close enough." She was blinking rapidly. "Isn't it foolish—I suddenly feel ridiculously weepy. I never cry."

For the first time he realized she'd not even been

aware of those tears that had run silently down her cheeks and broken him into a million pieces. His lips lightly, tenderly brushed each lid. "No, you never cry," he agreed gently.

She pushed away from him and stepped back. "Now that we've indulged in all the proper sentimental avowals, I think it would be very helpful if we talked." Her voice was shaky, but she didn't really care.

She took Jared's hand and led him to the bed. There was a bemused smile on his face as she pushed him briskly down on its cushioned softness. "This isn't an invitation to lechery, you understand," she said with mock sternness as she flicked out the crystal lamp on the bedside table. "But there's no reason we can't be comfortable." She lay down beside him. "Hold me."

"Delighted."

His arms enfolded her, holding her close for a moment before turning her so that her back was to him, spoon fashion. She wriggled against him contentedly, and his arms tightened. Lord, she felt sweet and warm, filling his arms, filling up all the empty places he'd ever known. "You're not talking," he observed.

"I know," she said dreamily. It was blissfully tranquil just lying here wrapped in the security of Jared's arms. The dimness of the room, the falling snow that was forming Currier and Ives etchings on the panes of the French doors, the soft velvet canopy above them all wove a silver mesh of intimacy that was poignantly beautiful. "Words don't seem very important right now."

He kissed her ear. "There's no hurry. Later."

She shook her head. "No, I want it to be tonight." There had been too many misunderstandings already between them. "You said earlier that I hadn't come to you to ask the questions I should have. Well, I'm coming to you now, Jared."

"I know what's bothering you the most, of course," he said quietly. "The children."

She nodded. "I love them. I don't think it's the selfish ego trip you accused me of. I think some women need motherhood to complete them and that I'm one of them." Her voice became strained. "But I'm not the only one who will suffer. There's an entire world of women out there who are like me, Jared."

"It's not an ego trip at all," he said gruffly. "It's as beautifully natural as you are, sweetheart. I must have gone a bit insane to rip at you like that." His cheek rubbed caressingly against the curve of her lower jaw. "Like I said, I can't give guarantees, but I don't go along with Corbett and Kevin in believing compulsory birth control, sterilization really, is inevitable. There are other roads we can travel. Hydroponic agriculture, farming the sea—improvements are increasing our food supply all the time. With a multi-national effort that will certainly take place, we should be able to produce enough to last for the time we'll need it."

"For the time we'll need it?" Tania asked, puzzled.

"Until we branch out to other planets," he said calmly. "It's the only real solution to overpopulation. We'll have to explore and colonize new worlds."

"You say that so lightly." She chuckled. "Kevin said he should be right at home with science fiction ideas, considering the company he was keeping. I'm beginning to see what he meant. Is it really possible?"

"Not at the moment. There are a few ideas on the drawing boards that look promising, but it would take a breakthrough to be able to colonize planets or create space stations of any size." His gaze was fixed thoughtfully on the falling snow. "That breakthrough will come, though. It took us only ten years to reach the moon once we made it a national priority. Think how much more could be accomplished with every major country in the world cooperating. Longevity will help there, I think. Who knows how many advancements have been lost to civilization because a life was cut short? I think that you'll find most of the killer diseases will soon be conquered. The work in genetics, the understanding of immunologic systems in humans, the ability to intervene with DNA—all that was basic to my own discovery—is rapidly eradicating cancers and heart diseases."

"Utopia?"

"I can't promise utopia," he said gravely. "The problems Corbett and Kevin mentioned are just as real and difficult as they told you. I recognize that. The only difference is that I don't think any challenge is insurmountable for the human race. I don't believe we're going to blow each other up or cut each other's throats for the last grain of wheat. I think that when it comes down to choices, we'll make the right ones and work together."

"I hope you're right," she said, her expression troubled. "It's a frightening responsibility you're facing, Jared."

"Do you think I don't know that? Do you think I don't have doubts and insecurities like any other person?" He drew a deep breath. "Why do you think I reacted so strongly when you went for the jugular this morning? I believe what I'm doing is right, Tania, and I can't afford to have that belief shaken. Without it I'd have to admit to being the monster you called me."

She felt a swift pang of remorse for her vitriolic attack. Perhaps Jared's actions tonight were even more understandable than she'd thought. She must have struck him to the heart in any number of ways. "You've got to admit that your reaction was a bit extreme," she said softly.

"I was frightened," he said, with a simplicity that caused her throat to tighten with unshed tears. "Last night you gave me everything I'd ever wanted sexually in a woman; before you'd shown me all the qualities of your heart and mind that I'd dreamed of finding. Then you were taking all of yourself away from me. I thought I had lost you." His arms tightened around her. "I couldn't take our separation, little Piper."

"Neither could I," she said huskily, one hand lifting to gently cover his. "I don't think I'd be able to stand the loneliness without you. I never thought about loneliness until I met you. I don't think it really ever existed for me."

"And I never knew anything else."

She'd known that instinctively since the moment she'd met him. "Not even with Lita?" she asked gently.

He shook his head. "I loved her, but it didn't help the loneliness. I knew I'd only have her for a little while." His voice deepened from pain. "The hellish thing was that she knew it too. Her disease caused premature aging, but not senility. She could see what was happening to her body, but she didn't understand it. She was a pretty little baby when she showed the first symptoms. By the time she died she looked as if she were ninety." His voice was fierce. "And she was only twelve years old, damn it. Only twelve."

"Jared—"

"No one else is going to have to go through that. Do you know how tragic it is to see someone you love lose everything that makes life worth living for them? It's happening all the time, all around us, to everyone. But not anymore. Not now!"

She could feel the passion in him reach out as a vibrant, living entity. She wanted to take away his pain, but she could only tighten her hand on his. "No, not anymore, love. You've stopped all the clocks. It can't happen now."

She wasn't sure he'd heard her. His gaze was still on

the snowfall, which was gradually growing in intensity. "When I was a boy, I read a book called *Childhood's End*. That title has stayed with me all my life. Our lives are so pitifully short that we scarcely leave adolescence before our minds and bodies begin to deteriorate. It's such a heartbreaking waste. God, I hate that waste."

"*Childhood's End*," she repeated thoughtfully. "It's such a sad little phrase."

"It doesn't have to be that way," he said. Suddenly the bitterness was gone from his tone of voice, replaced by a pensive quality. "It could mean something entirely different for us if we let it. It could mean mankind's entering into the maturity it's entitled to, ready to put aside toys of war and shackles of ignorance and reaching instead for peace and knowledge. It could mean that, Tania."

She nodded but didn't answer, her throat tight and her hand clasping his. He fell silent, too, and they lay there with their eyes on the flakes drifting earthward while their thoughts dwelt on Childhood's End.

Tania very carefully formed the snow into a hard-packed ball, aimed it with all the precision of a major league pitcher, and let it fly. It landed with a very satisfactory thunk on the nape of Jared's neck.

"What the hell?" The imprecation was followed by several more that were considerably more obscene as Jared whirled from his contemplation of the valley below with a wariness that vanished immediately when he saw Tania standing a few yards away, calmly making another snowball, a mischievous grin on her face.

"I should have known," he said, shaking his head. "You not only keep me waiting out here in the cold until you finish practicing, but you have the nerve to add assault to your sins."

"I couldn't resist! You were much too solemn

standing there." She weighed the snowball in her gloved hand. "In fact, you've been taking yourself much too seriously all this past week. I thought it was time I took you down a peg."

"Oh, you did?" he asked silkily. His eyes narrowed dangerously and he glided toward her with a pantherish stride. "Life isn't just fun and games, pixie. It's time you developed a little respect for my worth. I've been letting you get a little too uppity lately."

She backed away, her dark eyes sparkling. "I'd forgotten your kingly destiny, O Honorable Master." She pressed her hand to her heart in mock horror. "What punishment are you going to mete out to me?" Quick as a flash her expression changed to deviltry. "Oh, well, I might as well be hung for a sheep as for a lamb." She threw the snowball in her hand with lightning swiftness. She didn't wait to see it hit his cheekbone with a soft splatt but turned and streaked away through the birch grove with a shout of laughter.

She could hear him pounding after her, his feet crunching the snow, and his exultant laughter. She didn't realize how close he was, however, until she was brought down by a neat tackle worthy of an end for the Pittsburgh Steelers. She was swiftly rolled over on her back and he was astride her, his hands pinning her shoulders to the snow-blanketed earth. "Now," he said, looking down at her with supreme satisfaction. "What were you saying about punishment?" His face was lit with mischief, and he looked more boyish than she'd ever seen him. Her heart lurched with the queer melting tenderness that was almost always with her now.

He swiftly opened her tan sheepskin jacket. He gathered a handful of loose snow in one hand and gazed appraisingly at the open throat of her tailored blouse. "I think I have a few ideas on that score," he said teasingly.

"No! You wouldn't put that down my blouse," she

protested, her laugh bubbling. "I'll get you for this, Jared Ryker. That's cruel and unusual punishment."

"Still unrepentant?" He shook his head disbelievingly. "Not only that, but actually threatening. I'm afraid something definitely has to be done. But I wouldn't think of dumping this down your blouse and getting it all wet. You might catch cold." He released her other hand and was swiftly unbuttoning her blouse. "We couldn't have that, now, could we?"

"Jared!"

His hands were swiftly parting the material. Suddenly the teasing mischief died as he looked down at her. "Naked and lovely and ready," he said thickly, his gaze on the swelling perfection of her breasts.

"Not ready for this," she choked out breathlessly, her eyes wide and startled. The exuberant playfulness of the previous moment was fading before the languid heat that was beginning to surge through her. It was oddly erotic to be here in the icy snow with her breasts bare beneath the hot kindling of Jared's gaze.

"I think perhaps you may be," he drawled. "Let's see, shall we?"

The hand holding the loose snow slowly moved over her, and he let it flow through his fingers like sand, over one taut breast.

She inhaled sharply. The shock of cold against her warm flesh caused a burning sensation that was electrifying. "Kinky. Very kinky," she pronounced.

His gaze narrowed on her face. "But I think you like it," he murmured, "which is all that's important, love. All I ever want is to give you pleasure." His gaze held hers compulsively. "Do you want more?"

He didn't wait for an answer, but scooped up more snow with both hands. This time, instead of letting it drift down upon her, he kept it in his hands, with which he encircled one breast.

"Roses in the snow," he said softly, his smoky gaze fastened on her bare skin.

She was gasping when his lips descended on the engorged crest of her nipple. She groaned as she felt the wildly arousing contact of the frigid snow and the hot, moist warmth of his mouth and tongue teasing and tugging at the distended tip. Her back arched like a bowstring and her hands reached up to tangle in his hair and bring him closer to her. The strong suction increased, until her hips were thrusting and rubbing against him with mindless urgency.

He broke away from her with a gasp, his head lifting to reveal a face flushed and heavy with need. "I think we'd better call a halt," he said hoarsely. "Otherwise, I'm afraid you're going to end up totally naked in a bed of snow. We'll be much more comfortable back at the chateau." He gently brushed the snow from her breasts before buttoning up her blouse. He swung off her, stood up, and stretched out a hand to pull her to her feet. He brought her close for a quick kiss. "If I can wait that long."

His hands were shaking slightly while he fastened the wooden buttons of her jacket, and she stood as docilely as a child, accepting his ministrations. He linked his hand in hers and started back toward the distant chateau.

"Oh, I'm sure you can wait," she said impishly. "We all know what an iron man you are, Jared." Her eyes were dancing. "Besides, a man of your experience shouldn't become rattled by a little erotic foreplay, kinky though it may be." She arched a brow inquiringly. "Do you know any more interesting little variations, by the way?"

"Hundreds," he assured her blandly. "That little example was purely impromptu. As you say, I'm a very experienced man. Would you like a demonstration when we get back to the chateau?"

"Demonstration?" she asked warily. There was a flicker of mischief in Jared's eyes that boded no good.

"Actually, I was thinking of those pink satin ropes you were threatening to use on me," he said, his lips twitching. "Let's see, if we tied each of your ankles to the bedposts and . . ." He broke off as her elbow landed in his midriff with a force that belied its playfulness. "I gather you don't like the idea." He chuckled. "I guess I'll have to think of something else, though that one did have a certain appeal. Think about it, love. You stretched out so beautifully open and welcoming, with me bending over you, going in and out and around. Moving slowly, then—"

"Jared!" She found she *was* thinking about it, and it made her knees feel weak as melted butter. And judging by that mischievous glint in his eyes the maddening man knew exactly what she was feeling, damn it!

He gave a whoop of laughter and scooped her up in a bear hug, whirling her in a circle. "Sorry, sweetheart. I couldn't resist." His lips covered hers in a kiss that was honey-sweet and infinitely loving. When he raised his head, she caught her breath at the clear, glowing joyousness in his eyes. "We don't need that kind of titillation," he whispered gently. "We don't need anything but this."

He was right, this golden radiance of warmth and beauty was all they'd ever need. Her arms slipped around his waist, loving the hard, supple feel of his smooth, corded muscles. Loving the gentleness and the strength.

"Uh-hum!" The cough was discreet. "I'd diplomatically disappear, but I have a message for you, Jared," Kevin said from behind her.

Tania started to turn, but Jared's arms tightened

possessively, and he spoke over her head to Kevin. "So give it to me," he said lightly.

"The senator will be arriving this evening for dinner. He wants to talk to you." Kevin's voice was grave. "It sounded as though it might be fairly urgent."

"Really?" Jared's face was suddenly an impassive mask. "I can't say it comes as a surprise. I've been expecting him to make a move since the last time we had the pleasure of his company. It will be interesting to hear what he has to say."

Kevin's voice was cautious. "Move? That's rather cryptic. I'm not sure what you mean."

"Don't worry about it, Kevin. I have an idea everything will be clarified for all of us very soon." He slowly released Tania and stepped back.

As she turned to face Kevin, she caught an odd expression of regret on his face. Regret? Then he smiled, and she thought she must have been mistaken. "I never worry," he said lightly. "I have it on the best authority that worry gives you terminal acne."

She chuckled. "What authority?"

"My teenage sister. She should know. The poor kid has more spots than a leopard."

Jared had a faraway expression on his face. "Tania, why don't you go back to the chateau with Kevin? I think I'll go for a walk."

"Do you want company?"

He shook his head, and when he saw her look of hurt surprise, he dropped a light kiss on the tip of her nose. "I have some thinking to do, and that can be pretty difficult with you around, pixie. Go with Kevin." Then he was turning and walking swiftly away, his hands jammed in the pockets of his jacket.

Judging by the remoteness of his demeanor, he'd probably forgotten about her already, she thought, puzzled and exasperated. She hadn't seen that look of cool absorption on his face since that first afternoon, and it filled her with a vague unease. He'd changed from passionate lover to almost complete stranger in the space of a few minutes. Why should Corbett's arrival have such a radical effect on him?

She was frowning as she fell into step with Kevin. "Do you have any idea why Corbett is coming?"

"I can make a few guesses, just as Jared can," he admitted frankly. "But I haven't been taken into the senator's confidence, if that's what you're hinting at. He's prone to play his cards very close to the chest, and I'm just a lowly aide, remember?" His glance was speculative. "There's every possibility that his visit concerns you, however."

"Why do you say that?"

He shrugged. "Just guessing. I do know he's been closely monitoring your relationship with Jared since you were shot. Betz's reports have been very detailed and complete on that score."

Tania felt a flush mount in her cheeks that was more from annoyance than embarrassment. "You mean he knows that we're sleeping together," she said crossly. "There's something obscene about all this curiosity concerning Jared's sex life."

"He knows you're sleeping together, eating together, spending every moment in each other's pockets. Neither of you has exactly made your association top secret. You've been the most blatantly in love couple that I've ever seen."

They'd been so absorbed in each other that they hadn't given a damn who was aware of it. "That should have made Betz positively ecstatic," she said caustically. "I'm right where he originally intended me to be, in Jared's bed, keeping his charge contented."

"Oh, you've been doing that, all right," Kevin said,

a gentle smile on his face. "He lights up like neon whenever he looks at you. I never thought I'd see Jared Ryker in such a reckless state of euphoria. It makes one a believer in the old maxim about the world's being well lost for love."

"I don't know what you're talking about," she said with indignation. "Reckless? Everyone has been nudging me toward Jared with all the diplomacy of a bawdy-house madam, and now you're hinting that it's somehow dangerous!"

"Did I give you that impression?" he asked ruefully. "I didn't mean to frighten you, princess. I've never been known for my silver tongue. Of course there's nothing for you to worry about. I suppose I'm so used to political shenanigans that I get a little uneasy when I see an absence of intrigue."

"If there's nothing to worry about, then why is Jared acting so strange?" That bothered her more than any of Kevin's hints. Their relationship was still too new for her not to question any fresh nuance.

"I imagine we'll find out when Jared chooses to tell us. By the way, the senator prefers that we dress for dinner, so you're going to have the opportunity to dazzle us."

Chapter 13

Several hours later, as she walked gracefully down the staircase, Tania was a dazzling sight. The uneasiness that had started as a whisper had been growing to a shout as the day wore on. Jared hadn't come back to the chateau until it was almost time to dress for dinner, and even then he'd retained an air of abstraction. He'd quickly showered, dressed, and left the suite to join Corbett in the library for drinks before she was out of the shower. That he hadn't waited for her signaled that she might need all the reinforcement she could muster, and she'd dressed accordingly.

Her velvet gown was of a rose so vibrant, it was almost red, with a high-waist regency cut that was very flattering to her petite figure. It left her upper breasts bare, and the graceful little train made her feel splendidly regal as she swept into the library like a young czarist empress.

"Enchanting!" Sam Corbett rose to his feet, sleekly impressive in his black tuxedo. "I see that you're beautifully recovered, Miss Orlinov." His smile was charming. "With special emphasis on the adjective." He turned to Jared, who was leaning against the mantle with a cocktail glass in his hand. "It's not often that this chateau has housed such a ravishing lady, even in the olden days. It makes one want to cherish such a lovely captive, doesn't it, Jared?"

The words were spoken lightly, but Jared stiffened imperceptibly, and his eyes narrowed. "A curious choice of words, Corbett. I'm sure you're aware that Tania is no longer a captive, but a guest."

"So I understand," Corbett said genially. "A circumstance that we're all exceptionally happy about, I'm sure. You mustn't take umbrage at my every verbal faux pas, Jared." For a moment there was a flicker of mockery in his hazel eyes. "I have a very romantic soul, and the idea of a castle with its own resident captive princess has a certain appeal."

"Fantasy is fine in its place," Jared said with equal smoothness. "It's only when it intrudes upon reality that it can become dangerous."

Kevin had come forward from the bar across the room and handed her the Perrier and lime he knew she preferred. "Speaking of princesses, I like your hair in that coronet of braids," he told her lightly. "You look quite regal."

"Thank you, Kevin. This is all quite flattering, but so many allusions to royalty are making me a little uncomfortable. I may be a capitalist by choice, but my Bolshevik upbringing still gives me an occasional twinge." At least Kevin was directing his conversational gambit at her, she thought grimly. She was well aware that the interchange between Jared and Corbett had as many dangerous undercurrents as the river Styx.

"Then we'll change the subject at once," the senator said with a flashing smile. "We wouldn't want you to suffer even the slightest pain or discomfort." He turned to Jared. "Isn't that right, Jared?"

Jared returned his challenging look coolly. "That's right, Corbett." Carefully he put his cocktail glass down on the mantle. "I suggest we go in to dinner now. Tania can bring her drink. I think we're eager to get the amenities over with so we can proceed to our discussion."

"An excellent idea," Corbett said heartily. "I've always admired your incisiveness, Jared. It saves so much time."

During dinner Tania was sure that neither Jared nor Corbett was aware of what they ate or of the elegant accoutrements provided. The candles in their antique silver holders spread a mellow glow on the delicate Sèvres china. George, in his black jacket, moved silently in and out of the room, serving each course. The muted colors of the ancient tapestry on the far wall enhanced the scene. It all reminded her vaguely of a Rembrandt painting, with its richly contrasting light and shadows.

Jared and Corbett, except for their modern evening clothes, might have come from the same dangerous era as that old master, she thought with a chill of fear. They reminded her of duelists involved in a preliminary engagement designed to test out each other's weakness. Their verbal exchange was just as full of barbs and double entendres as the conversation in the library, and she found herself eventually falling silent to watch them with a growing sense of alarm.

There was an air of exultant triumph about Corbett tonight, together with a reckless boldness that was foreign to the smooth politician she'd first met. Though she couldn't understand exactly what was going on, she did realize that it was the senator who was on the attack, and Jared who was quietly defending his position.

The dessert course had just been served when Jared decided to bring the initial skirmish to an end. He pushed back his chair and got to his feet, tossing his napkin on the table. "I don't think either one of us is in the mood for anything else, Corbett," he said with a thread of irony in his voice. "Particularly a sweet. I believe your appetite at the moment is geared more toward rich red meat. You have a lean and hungry look."

"Ah, you're fond of Shakespeare," Corbett said silkily, pushing back his own chair and standing up. "He's a particular favorite of mine. He understood human nature so well. Much better than you do, Jared." He smiled. "And if that reference to Cassius is supposed to be an insult, you failed. I find the character very admirable in many ways."

"I thought you would," Jared said coolly. He gestured mockingly. "After you, Corbett. It's time we had our little talk. I believe the ides of March is at hand."

Tania waited until the door had closed behind them before she shook her head incredulously. "Why do I suddenly feel as if I've become invisible? Do you think they even knew we were in the room?"

Kevin leaned back in his chair and reached for the crystal wine decanter. "Oh, they knew you were here, all right," he said as he refilled his glass. "I got the impression that you were very much the focus of their attention. I was the forgotten person." He shrugged. "I'm sure we'll be brought back into the picture once they've finished their little contretemps. There's nothing we can do but wait. Would you like more wine?"

"No, thank you," she said, her brow knitted in a frown. "And what was all that about Shakespeare? What was the ides of March?"

Kevin hesitated an instant in the act of setting the decanter back on the table. "You're not familiar with Julius Caesar?"

She shook her head.

Kevin put the crystal stopper carefully back into the

decanter and picked up his glass. "The ides of March was the day of betrayal. The day Caesar was assassinated."

"Let me get you a drink," Corbett said cheerfully, moving across the library to the bar against the book-lined wall. "There's no reason our discussion can't be a sociable and civilized one. Brandy and soda, wasn't it?"

"Yes, but just brandy now." Jared watched quietly as Corbett poured three fingers of brandy into a snifter before preparing his own scotch and water. "By all means, let's observe all the appropriate rituals." He smiled faintly. "I wouldn't want to spoil your enjoyment."

"I'm afraid you couldn't if you tried." Corbett strode to where Jared was half sitting, half leaning on the massive oak desk and handed him the snifter. "You'd have to be in control to do that, and I'm the one who's holding the reins at the moment." He strolled to the Queen Anne chair by the fire, dropped into it, and propped his feet lazily on the ottoman. "But feel free to try if it amuses you."

"It doesn't." Jared took a sip of his drink, his gaze narrowed on the senator's face, which was flushed with a reckless excitement. "I don't find anything about your subtle little threats amusing. I like to have all the cards on the table. I gather I've made a mistake in judgment in your case, Corbett. The past weeks have been an elaborate stall, then?"

Corbett nodded. "Almost from the beginning," he admitted. He took a sip of his scotch. "For a while I was tempted to go along with your idealistic dream of eternal life for the masses. I rather fancied a golden halo around my distinguished head. But that didn't last long." He laughed. "I decided I'd prefer a golden scepter instead. Yes, you definitely made a mistake in judgment, Jared."

Jared shrugged. "I always knew there was that possibility. It was the chance I took." He lifted his glass to his lips, regarding Corbett steadily over the rim. "I realized you were an ambitious man, but I hoped you'd settle for less than the big apple."

Corbett shook his head. "I found the idea of standing in your shadow while you tossed pearls before swine very distasteful, Jared. Your way never would have worked anyway. Our world is too corrupt to accept a revolutionary advancement like this. It will require careful guidance to handle a problem this massive."

"Your guidance, I assume," Jared drawled.

"My guidance," Corbett affirmed. "Why not? I'm well qualified for the job. I've known I was heading in this direction since I was a kid. I just didn't realize it would be on quite this grand a scale."

"Emperor of the world instead of just President of the United States?"

"I found that expanding my horizons was no real problem," Corbett agreed. "Of course, that's quite a distance down the road. For some time I'll be working behind the scenes to form a network that will support my plans. I think I'll find it ridiculously easy to obtain whatever I want from the powers of any nation once they know what I have to bargain with."

"You're talking about a highly selective use of my work, with you playing God, of course."

"It's the only sensible course for me to follow initially," Corbett said. "Once I'm in total control I may set up a special clinic for those individuals whose accomplishments have proven them worthy of an extended span."

"Very condescending of you," Jared said dryly. "I have an idea that group would be very small indeed."

Corbett nodded. "It's the rarity of any commodity

that makes it valuable." He smiled mockingly. "Surely you can see that, Jared?"

"No, I can't see that," Jared said grimly. "And I doubt if it matters to you whether I do or not. Would you care to tell me where you've decided to position me in your hierarchy?"

"Oh, very prominently, Jared," the senator assured him. "You'll be essential to my operations for some time to come. Even after you furnish me with the information I need, you'll still be required for the follow-up work. You needn't think I'm going to allow you to fade into oblivion just because I'm planning on changing the scenario a bit." He gazed down at his scotch thoughtfully. "Naturally, I'll provide you with every physical comfort, just as I have over the past few weeks. Of course, I can't allow you the freedom you seem to desire, but I'm sure you'll get used to that. You're going to have a great deal of time in which to do it." He raised his gaze, and there was malice in the hazel depths of his eyes. "It's really all I can do. You're not a man I can trust to recognize the realities of the situation. You're an idealist, Jared, and that makes you very dangerous to me."

"So I'm going to be the resident Merlin in your Camelot," Jared said, his face impassive. "What brand of magic were you intending to use to accomplish all this, Corbett?"

"Do you want me to put it into words?" Corbett asked softly. "I think you're aware of the nature of the mistake you've made. Not that I'm ungrateful you didn't prove as invulnerable as I feared you would. I was getting pretty frustrated waiting for something to break that I could get a handle on. You'd built some very efficient defenses, you had no family or close friends I could use, and I couldn't risk damaging you in any way. I could only play for time and hope that you'd furnish me with enough ammunition to blow you out of the sky." He smiled with smug satisfaction. "Which you were obliging enough to do."

"Tania?" Jared kept his voice coolly impersonal. Corbett already had a dangerous degree of insight into his feelings for her. He refused to give him any more to work on.

Corbett nodded. "It was really very stupid of you to develop such a weakness at a crucial time like this. From the reports I've had, you've become passionately attached to her." He shook his head reprovingly. "She's quite charming, but is she really worth giving up your dreams for? Because that's what you've done, you know. You're a hard man, Jared, but I don't believe you're tough enough to withstand the pressure we can put on you now."

"And the nature of that pressure?"

"Why, pain, of course," Corbett said softly, his gaze fixed hawklike on Jared's face. "Miss Orlinov is a very lovely, vibrant woman. One gets the impression that she would experience every sensation with great intensity." He paused. "Emotional and physical."

"Spell it out, Corbett," Jared said crisply. "I know you're getting a great deal of enjoyment out of this, but I'm a little tired of the game."

"Very well," Corbett said. "You give me what I want or you stand by and watch some very talented gentlemen go to work on your pretty ballerina." He smiled faintly. "I'd give orders that she not be physically marred in any way that might spoil your pleasure, but I can promise that she would suffer excruciating pain for a very extended period. Do you think you could take that?"

Jared felt an explosion of rage so savage that for a moment he went berserk. The picture Corbett's words evoked of Tania suffering while he stood helplessly by was unbearable. Hell, no, he couldn't take that! Not without killing any son of a bitch who laid a finger on her. It took him a moment to realize Corbett was watching his reaction with a look that mirrored both hunger and satisfaction. He was playing right into the bastard's hands by letting him see the emotional response his words engendered. With no little effort he forced his features back to their former impassiveness.

"We'd have to see, wouldn't we?" He lifted the snifter and drained it. He set the glass down on the desk and lifted his gaze to meet Corbett's. "Do you think I'd let a woman I've known only a few weeks stand in the way of a project to which I've devoted most of my adult life? Would you, Corbett?"

For a moment there was a flicker of uncertainty on the senator's face. Then it was gone. "No, I wouldn't," he said as he pushed the ottoman aside and rose to his feet. "But, then, we have a different set of priorities. I think you'll find it very difficult to resist the persuasion I have in mind for Miss Orlinov." He set his glass on the end table beside the chair. "I'm not going to rush you. I'll let you have a few days to think about it." He strolled toward the door, but paused with his hand on the knob. "I'll be back from Washington at the end of the week, and I'll be accompanied by those talented gentlemen I mentioned." He smiled. "Don't make me use their services, Jared."

As he closed the door behind him and strode briskly toward the staircase, Corbett's smile widened. It had been a very satisfactory interview on the whole, and Ryker had revealed more vulnerability than he usually permitted himself. His face brightened still more when he saw Tania Orlinov approaching from the direction of the dining room, a worried frown on her face. The timing couldn't have been better if he'd staged it. Her appearance immediately after that eloquently brutal picture he'd drawn for Ryker would be most effective.

"Ah, Miss Orlinov, you've been positively angelic, putting up with our neglect of you this evening," he said, smiling with boyish charm. "But now Jared and I have finished our discussion and he can devote the rest of the evening to you. Why don't you join him?"

"I think I will," she said slowly, moving toward the door of the library. "Kevin asked me to tell you he'd gone to his room to work on those dispatches you brought, in case you inquired."

"Thank you," Corbett boomed genially. "Kevin is such an industrious young man. I feel very lucky to have him. Well, I think I'll call it a night." He started up the stairs. "I want to get an early start in the morning. Good night, Miss Orlinov."

"Good night, Senator," she answered quietly. The anxiety she was feeling was escalating in leaps and bounds. Sam Corbett was a little too sleek and well satisfied for her peace of mind.

She opened the door of the library and immediately forgot about everything but the horror that met her eyes.

Jared was lying crumpled on the carpet in the center of the room, his powerful body ominously still!

Tania wasn't even conscious of the scream that tore from her throat as she ran forward and sank to her knees beside Jared's frighteningly immobile body, or of the startled exclamation from Corbett, on the stairs behind her.

The only thing that she was aware of was Jared's white, drawn face and an exotic odor as she lifted his head on her lap to cradle him fiercely in her arms. He was so pale, so still, that he looked as helpless as a little boy struck by some deadly virus. Deadly.

"Oh, no." Her cry was an agonized moan. "Oh, God, no!" He couldn't be dead. Death couldn't come this quickly, this mercilessly. Not to Jared. But he was so still.

She could hear someone cursing, his voice violent and angry, and she was vaguely conscious that it was Corbett. Then the senator was kneeling on the other side of Jared, bending over him, his hand searching frantically for a pulse. Her eyes wide with fear, she waited in an agony of suspense.

"He's alive, but his pulse is very slow. I don't know how much time he's got." His hands were running rapidly over Jared's body. "No obvious wounds. What the hell weapon did they use?"

"Weapon," she repeated dully. She hugged Jared's head to her breast. "What are you talking about? What's wrong with him?"

"Quite possibly poison." Corbett's eyes were narrowed keenly on Jared's face. "But what kind?" His face was flushed with exasperation. "God damn it! He can't die! I won't let him." Then he was standing up and moving swiftly to the library door. "Betz!" he roared. "Get Betz here on the double."

She was vaguely conscious of a tumult in the hall, the sound of several voices, and the pounding of feet running on the polished wooden floors. Poison. How could anyone have poisoned Jared? He was all gentleness, strength, and bright, clear visions. Couldn't they see how valuable he was?

Then Corbett was back and Betz was with him. Betz went immediately to the phone on the desk and dialed a number while the senator knelt once more beside Jared, his hand going immediately to his pulse. "Still alive," he said grimly. "I've sent for McCord. He has some medical background. We're trying to get Dr. Jeffers on the phone, though I don't know what the devil he can prescribe long distance, when we don't even know what Ryker was given!"

She barely heard more than the first two words. He was still alive, but for how long? "He's so cold," she said, rubbing her cheek against his as if to warm him. She was conscious of that same exotic odor on his breath. He must have had a liqueur instead of his usual brandy. "He smells of almonds," she said numbly.

"Almonds!" Corbett leaned forward to sniff. "It is almonds." He swiftly rose to his feet and crossed to pick up the brandy snifter on the desk. He passed it beneath his nose, and his face darkened grimly. "Almonds. They must have put it in his brandy."

She was staring at him in confusion. They? Almonds? She couldn't put any of it together. What did it matter? All that was important was that Jared live. Then Corbett was taking the phone from Betz and speaking rapidly into it.

"Is he still unconscious?" She glanced up to see Betz standing next to her, a surprisingly anxious expression on his face. His eyes were fixed on Jared's face with a compulsive intensity, as if he'd literally will him out of that comalike state. "He mustn't die, you know. Dr. Ryker mustn't be allowed to die."

Of course he mustn't, she thought bitterly. Betz might be blamed for the lapse in security that had permitted this horror and lose his precious job.

She looked down at Jared and gasped. A slight grimace had appeared on his lips. "You're not going to die," she said fiercely. "I won't let you."

Then Kevin was in the room. He was still dressed in his black tuxedo trousers and shirt but had removed the jacket and tie. His face was almost as white as Jared's as he came toward her.

"God, I'm sorry, princess," he said quietly, his blue eyes bright with pain. "What can I do to help?"

Her dark gaze clung to his desperately. Thank God Kevin was here. Kevin would help Jared. "Poison." It was hard to get the words past the tightness in her throat. "They think it's poison. He can't die, Kevin." Her face was a naked mask of pain. "Please don't let him die."

He knelt beside her, his hands closing bracingly on her shoulders. "I'll do everything I can," he said simply. "You know that, princess."

Corbett was replacing the receiver and coming toward them. "Jeffers says it's almost certainly cyanide. That almond odor is very distinctive. We'll have to work fast. He'll be here as quickly as he can, but it will be too late for Ryker if we don't instigate emergency measures at once. Cyanide produces respiratory failure, and it could come at any time," he said crisply. "Betz, you're to begin artificial respiration at once." He consulted the scratch pad in his hand. "You'll also have to set up an IV with ten-milligram injections of sodium nitrate at two- to four-minute periods."

"Where the hell are we supposed to get all that?" Kevin asked, frowning. "The first-aid room is equipped with IV equipment, but I don't know if we have the rest of the stuff."

"Jeffers said we did, and he should know. He's the one who stocked the first-aid room for me." Corbett was walking toward the door. "I'll take a couple of men and hunt up what we need while you and Betz spell each other on the artificial respiration. Get cracking!"

Betz was already taking off his navy blue coat and dropping to his knees beside Jared, his hands reaching out to move Ryker from Tania's arms.

"No." Her arms tightened around him, and she shook her head. "Tell me what to do and I'll do it."

"We don't have time, princess," Kevin said gently. "Let us help him."

How could she let him go? she thought dazedly.

Who could she trust in a world that would do this to Jared? The ides of March, the day of betrayal. "No, I can't let you take him."

It was Betz who shocked her into awareness. "If you don't, he'll most certainly die in your arms," he said curtly. "And you'll be guilty of murdering him yourself. Do you want that responsibility, Miss Orlinov?"

Her low cry was answer enough, and when her arms loosened, Betz smoothly grasped Jared's limp form and laid him on the carpet. He loosened his clothing, slipped his hand under Jared's neck and arched his throat to open the air passage, and began to administer mouth-to-mouth resuscitation. She felt Kevin's hand on her elbow gently pulling her to her feet.

"You can't do any more here, Tania," he said, his voice soothing. "We'll take care of him now. Why don't you go to your room? I'll let you know as soon as he's conscious."

She gazed at him as if he'd gone mad. "I'm not leaving him," she said flatly. "I'm not leaving this room until I know he's going to be all right."

"I didn't think you would, but it was worth a try," Kevin said resignedly. He led her to the Queen Anne chair across the room and pushed her gently down on the cushioned surface. "Stay here, then. Just don't get in the way while we're doing our best to save him, okay?"

"Okay," she said absently, her eyes glued anxiously on Betz, across the room. "I'll stay here."

In the hours that followed, that promise became very hard to keep as she watched the men frantically working to keep Jared alive while she sat helplessly doing nothing. The room was seething with activity as Betz's men came and went. The IV was set up and the medication was administered at regular intervals. Jared was watched with the sharpness of desperation by every person in the room.

When Dr. Jeffers walked into the room three hours later, the short, balding man looked as beautiful as an archangel to Tania. He went immediately to Jared and knelt to examine him briefly. "I think the crisis is past," he said tersely. "He's beginning to stabilize. Let's move him to a bedroom, and I'll begin gastric lavage."

"He's going to live?" Corbett said sharply.

"Unless complications set in," Jeffers said cautiously. "But I see no reason why that should happen. In a day or so he should be pretty well recovered."

Tania felt almost limp with relief. She expelled a breath she hadn't even been aware she was holding. Thank God. Jared was going to be all right. She leaned her head back against the high back of the chair, suddenly conscious that it was swimming with dizziness. Oh, thank God.

"Why hasn't he regained consciousness?" Corbett asked with a frown. "Is he in a coma?"

"He's suffered a very serious shock to his system," Jeffers said patiently. "He may remain unconscious for some time." He turned to McCord, who was standing by the IV. "You've done an exceptionally good job of regulating those injections, McCord."

"Shall I keep them on the same schedule after you leave?" Kevin asked, wearily rubbing the back of his neck.

"That won't be necessary," Jeffers said as he stepped aside so two of Betz's men could lift Jared's body and put it on a stretcher. "Senator Corbett has asked me to stay until Dr. Ryker is entirely out of danger. I'll be supervising the IV and will put him in an oxygen tent for tonight, at least."

Betz's men were moving toward the door, carrying Jared on the stretcher, while another followed closely with the IV. They were taking him away, Tania thought with a thrill of panic. She mustn't let them do that. She must go with him, protect him, take care of him. Nothing like this must ever happen to him again.

She struggled to her feet and strode toward the door, firmly fighting off the odd weakness in her knees.

Kevin stepped forward, his face concerned. "Call it a night, princess," he urged softly. "He doesn't need you now."

"No?" She drew a deep breath. "Perhaps not. But I need *him*. I need to be with him, and no one is going to stop me. He's mine, Kevin."

She turned to follow the stretcher out of the library.

Chapter 14

$\mathcal{T}$ he light, tantalizing fragrance of wild flowers pierced the shifting mists of darkness that surrounded Jared. Tania?

She was sitting in the chair next to his bed, still wearing the rose velvet gown, and there was a charged tension about her that seemed to reach out to him, dispersing the fog that was clouding his faculties. Her hand was tightly clasped in his, as if she were a small child afraid of the dark, and she was instantly aware of the moment when he opened his eyes.

She drew a deep, steadying breath. "They said you were going to be all right, but I was beginning to think they were wrong," she said, and gave him a shaky smile. "You took so long to wake up—it's been twelve hours. It was most contrary of you, Jared." She reached over to the bedside table and picked up a plastic cup with a curved plastic straw. "Jeffers said you'd want a drink to soothe your throat. He had to put a tube down to wash all the poison out of your system."

Poison! As he sipped the cold water, he forced his mind to focus in its usual keen fashion. That last dizzy moment in the library before the mists had closed in on him, he'd been conscious of something very wrong. Poison, of course.

"How?" he asked quietly.

"Cyanide in the brandy. That sounds like the title of an Agatha Christie thriller, doesn't it? Someone substituted the bottle you were drinking from before dinner with another one doctored with cyanide. Not very efficiently, thank heavens. It wasn't laced heavily enough to kill you immediately."

"Who was it?"

"Corbett doesn't know. He thinks there was a leak and one of Betz's team was bribed to do it." Her laugh was mirthless. "Betz is denying it, of course. He says his men are all good, loyal men, totally incapable of being corrupted." She rubbed her forehead wearily. "I just don't know. Maybe it was Corbett himself."

He shook his head. "Corbett has too much to lose by my death at this point. He has a vested interest in keeping me very much alive."

"Kevin said yesterday was the day of betrayal. He also said that all the verbal fencing concerned me." Her eyes were feverishly bright in her strained face. "And the poisoning, Jared? Did that have something to do with me too?"

"God, no, sweetheart." His hand tightened on hers. "None of this was your responsibility. Corbett's trying to use you as a lever, yes." He smiled grimly. "The bastard's trying every dirty trick in his repertoire to get what he wants. It seems our charming senator has a chronic case of megalomania."

"It doesn't really surprise me," she said slowly. There had been enough signals last night to make her suspect something of that nature. "He's going to force you to turn over your work to him?"

"He's going to try," Jared said quietly. "He's not going to succeed. There's no way on earth I can let him get hold of it." He paused, and for a moment there was a haunted, pained expression on his face. "Even if it means putting you in danger to keep him from doing it. Can you understand that, Tania?"

She could see by the uncertainty in his face that he didn't think she could. He wasn't sure he could inspire that kind of loyalty and commitment in her, she realized in amazement. He wasn't certain she would be willing to run any risk to keep his dream intact. She lifted her chin proudly. "No one manipulates me, Jared, not even you. There's no way you could put me anywhere I didn't want to go." Her lips curved in a tender smile. "I'm the Piper, remember?"

He was silent a long moment before he lifted her hand to his lips to kiss it gently. "How could I forget?" he asked huskily, his eyes suspiciously bright. "You're going to be around to remind me for the next millennium or so."

"I'm glad you realize that," she said, her throat suddenly tight and aching. "And there's one more thing you'd better put on that list I gave you besides the baby and the New York residency requirement."

"What's that?"

"You are *never* to come even close to leaving me again," she said, her tone fierce. "You're never to catch a cold or trip on a step or get a cramp when you're swimming. Nothing, you understand?"

His lips twitched. "I'll do my very best to oblige. Anything else?"

"Yes." Suddenly the tears that had been brimming were rolling silently down her cheeks. "You must promise that you won't die before I do. That's absolutely required, Jared. I won't go through life without you. I can't do that now."

"Yes, you could," he told her with gentle raillery. How could he promise her that, when next week might be the most hazardous of his life? Yet she must survive, even if he didn't. "You have *er'b.*" His fingers traced the path of her tears down one cheek. "You never cry."

She nodded. "I never cry." The tears continued to pour down her cheeks. "After tonight." She bent and nestled her damp cheek against his shoulder. His naked flesh was warm and vitally alive. He was alive. "Tonight even a woman with *er'b* has a right to cry."

"Come to bed, love."

She didn't resist as he shifted over on the mattress and lifted the sheet to bring her under its silken protection. She should get up and take off her clothes, she thought vaguely, but it was too much bother. She didn't want to leave Jared even for the short time it would take to accomplish it. She never wanted to leave him again. As long as she was beside him, she could watch over him, protect him.

Yet it was Jared's arms that were enfolding her in a blanket of protectiveness, his hands that were loosening the coronet of braids before pulling her into the comfortable hollow of his shoulder, his lips that brushed her temple with poignant tenderness. "I shouldn't be here," she said wearily, her arms curving around his waist. "You've been ill."

"All the more reason," he said lightly. "I've always known you were the most potent of medicines." His lips touched her brow. "Not to mention your distinctly addictive properties. Now, hush up, and let me hold you. Sick men should be humored."

She gave a sigh of contentment and nestled closer. Why was she arguing, when she was just where she wanted to be?

"What are we going to do about Corbett?" she asked lazily. It was impossible to take anything seriously at the moment. She was feeling too secure and full of thanksgiving that Jared was still alive and able to hold her like this. "He left for Washington early this morning, but he said he'd be back in a few days."

"Much as I know you'd enjoy it, we're not going to launch a full-scale attack, pixie," he said. "I think we'd better opt for discretion, and just try to escape with our skins intact. That should be enough of a challenge even for you, particularly as I'm sure Corbett left instructions with our friend Betz to tighten security."

A frisson of fear closed along her spine. "Will we be able to do it?"

"We have no choice. We'll do it." He smiled faintly. "Besides, I have a few surprises up my sleeve that our lovable senator isn't aware of yet. I'm not such a fool that I'd allow myself to be completely boxed in without a way out."

"What do you mean?"

"Never mind." His strong but gentle hand was massaging the muscles at the nape of her neck. "It's best that we don't go into it at the moment. We've got to assume that surveillance has already been tightened."

"You mean—?"

"I don't know," he interrupted, "but it's safer not to discuss anything but the weather until we get out of here."

The sharp wind blew through the birches, touching the wind chimes and causing them to make their familiar music, but for once Tania paid no attention, her eyes fixed on Jared's face.

"It doesn't make any sense," Tania said. "Nothing at all has changed. It's as if the poisoning had never happened, as if Corbett had never been here. From what you said, I expected hidden microphones in every room and a security man dogging our footsteps at every turn. Instead we're still being allowed the run of the chateau as if there weren't even a possibility that we'd want to escape."

Jared nodded, his eyes fixed thoughtfully on the valley below. "I saw Betz before I left the chateau to meet you here, and his primary concern seemed to be whether I was warmly enough dressed to withstand the rigors of a short walk so soon after I got out of the sick bed." He shook his head, a faint smile touching his lips. "He was like a mother hen with its first chick. I almost expected him to zip up my jacket and tuck a scarf around my neck."

"Betz?" she asked incredulously. Then she moved a step closer and turned up the collar of his flight jacket. "Why didn't you wear a scarf?" she asked, frowning. "You can't be at death's door one minute and two days later expect to bounce back to normal."

"I assure you I'm not even close to bouncing," he said dryly, "and the only part of me that's like a rubber ball is my knees. I'd love to earn your respect and admiration by my stoic endurance, but you made me promise always to be honest with you." His eyes twinkled. "Besides, I may need you to hold me up before we get back to the chateau."

Despite his joking, he was paler than she'd ever seen him and there were mauve shadows beneath his eyes, she noticed worriedly. "You should be back in bed."

"Presently," he said. "I wanted to talk to you away from the chateau. I'm afraid I don't entirely trust this obvious absence of surveillance either. I'm sure security should be tighter than this, after that assassination attempt. It's almost as if they are inviting someone to have another go at me."

Tania felt a chill of panic. "Then we've got to get out of here right away," she said quickly. "Tonight."

He shook his head. "Not tonight. Tomorrow. In

broad daylight. We're going to walk out of this trap as if we're just taking a Sunday stroll."

"What?" Her eyes widened. "Are you crazy? Do you want to get caught?"

"Somehow, I don't think it will work that way," he said slowly. "I think all this freedom was meant to be an open invitation to more than the killer. I have an idea that Corbett wants us to try to escape."

"Why should he do that?" Tania asked. "That cyanide must have damaged your mental processes. The man wants to lock you up and throw away the key, remember?"

He shrugged. "Perhaps he's playing a cat-and-mouse game with us. It's the kind of thing he'd enjoy. He might want us to get to the brink of escape and reel us in again. A defeat like that would certainly put us in a more receptive mood for the pressure he intends to apply when he comes back with his goon squad."

"You think he's going to let us walk down that road without trying to stop us?" she asked skeptically. "And how far will he let us go before he slams the door of the cage shut?"

"Far enough to give us the start we need, I hope." He smiled tigerishly. "I think I can safely assure you that I can take care of the two men at the checkpoint. All we need to do is reach the valley. After that we've got it made."

"If you say so." Tania made a face. "I could have used a little of your self-confidence on my little jaunt across the Andes. I'd guess we might expect a few problems in avoiding pursuit and arranging transportation to get us to safety."

"We have transportation," he said coolly. "I was willing to trust Corbett only so far. When he told me where he was planning on quartering me, I took a few safety measures to insure I wouldn't have to rely on his goodwill in case it suddenly dried up."

"Such as?"

"I leased a vacant farm a few miles from the village. It's just a few acres and some outbuildings, but the barn was large enough to house a helicopter."

She gazed at him for a stunned moment before she started to laugh. "I don't know why I'm so surprised," she said. "It's just the sort of thing you'd do. My mind doesn't work on such a grand scale—I'd have had a jeep standing by, not a helicopter." She arched a brow inquiringly. "Where did you learn to fly a helicopter?"

"I lived on an island for four years, if you recall," he said, gazing at her bemusedly. God, he loved to hear her laugh. Until now, he hadn't realized how tense and anxious she'd been looking. "And I'm known to get seasick in a bathtub."

She threw her arms around him and hugged him exuberantly. "Don't worry, I'm a very good sailor. Between us we'll rule the sky and the waves."

His arms closed around her. "It's everything in between that we have to worry about," he said wryly. With the sweet weight of her in his arms he couldn't deny that worry. They had no choice but to attempt to escape now that Corbett knew how vulnerable he was where Tania was concerned. The threat to her here was greater than if they were on the run, but he wasn't stupid enough to minimize that danger. The only thing he could count on was that Corbett wouldn't eliminate Tania if he could help it. She was far too valuable a tool to use against him. He had to believe that or go a little crazy thinking of the risk he was exposing her to. "But we'll muddle through, pixie."

"Jared, what about Kevin?" She raised her head to meet his eyes. "Surely we could trust him to help if he knew that Corbett was planning—"

"No," he interrupted firmly, "we can't take the chance." He gave her a quick, hard kiss. "I know you're fond of him, but you've got to remember he's in the enemy camp." He paused before continuing deliberately. "And I'm not at all sure he hasn't figured out what's in the air."

"I can't believe that," she said. Not Kevin. Gentle Kevin, with his warmth and friendship. "You've got to be wrong."

"I hope I am," Jared said quietly. "I've grown closer to him than I'd have believed possible. I'd like to think I could trust him, but there's no way I'm going to put your safety on the line by banking on an unknown quantity." He shook his head. "We go it alone."

"But I told you how hard he worked to save you the night you were poisoned," she protested, troubled.

"From what you said, Corbett and Betz were just as concerned, and I strongly doubt either one of them had my well-being at heart," he countered. He pushed her away and turned her toward the chateau, his arm still about her waist. "Now, I think it would be a good idea if you took me back and put me to bed for a nap."

"You're feeling worse?" she asked anxiously. "I knew you shouldn't have gotten out of bed so soon."

"I'm feeling stronger every moment," he lied. He was still damned weak, but there was no use worrying her, when she had tomorrow to face. "I just want to cuddle you." His lips brushed the tip of her ear. "You're an eminently cuddly woman, little Piper."

Jared insisted on coming downstairs to dinner despite her protests, and she was given an example of Betz's weird maternal protectiveness when they reached the bottom of the staircase.

Betz came padding forward, an anxious frown on his face, his brown eyes narrowed on Jared's pale face. "You shouldn't have come down, Dr. Ryker. Dr. Jeffers said you should take it easy for a few days, and you've already taken that long walk to the grove. I really think you should let us serve you something in bed and make it an early night."

The grove. So surveillance hadn't been as careless as it appeared, Tania thought. And now that she thought about it, Betz had been hovering in the halls whenever she'd left Jared's room during the past two days. Not obtrusively, nor vigilantly, just there.

"Do you, Betz? But then, we've already discussed your failings in that department. I have no intention of returning to my room." His gray gaze sharpened. "Unless you'd care to try to enforce Dr. Jeffers's instructions?"

Betz's frown deepened. "I told you, I only use force when it's absolutely necessary," he said slowly. "I thought you understood that." He sighed morosely. "You're going to be a very difficult charge, Dr. Ryker." He turned and walked away.

"Charge." Jared's lips curled disgustedly. "He makes me sound like a schoolboy under a tutor's care. I think I preferred the old polite menace to this."

"He's right, though," Tania said as she slipped her arm through his and drew him toward the library. "I hate to agree with Betz about anything, but you're definitely overdoing it on your first day up." She lowered her voice. "Particularly considering what you're planning for tomorrow. You should be mustering your strength, not expending it."

"You wouldn't care for a karate match, by any chance?" Kevin asked cheerfully as he rose from the padded executive chair behind the desk and came toward them, a warm smile lighting his face. "I think I just might beat you." He slowly shook his head. "You look like a sick cat, Jared. You should have stayed in bed."

"Thank you. That seems to be the consensus around here. It's enough to make a man feel unwelcome. Not that I didn't before. Cyanide in the brandy has a tendency to quash thoughts of winning popularity contests."

"I can see how it would," Kevin said, his expression somber. "I didn't have a chance to do more than pop in occasionally to see how you were doing, but I think you know how sorry I am that such a thing happened, Jared. Corbett took the bottle back to Washington to have it dusted for fingerprints, but it was clean. He's doing an independent security check on all Betz's men to see if he can come up with an association with any groups that might be hostile."

"It's very comforting to know that," Jared said ironically. "But Corbett always did have my interests at heart." He looked steadily into the other man's eyes. "Didn't he, Kevin?"

"What do you want me to say?" Kevin asked with a shrug. "I think you realize that I suspected the senator's motives weren't the purest from the beginning. I've gotten to know him moderately well over the years. I hope you'll believe that I wasn't absolutely certain until quite recently." He turned to Tania. "You know me well enough to realize I'm not that good an actor, princess."

"And now that you do know, what do you intend to do about it?" she asked quietly. "We can use all the help we can get, Kevin."

"I wish I knew," he said, frowning. "I told you I disliked being a catalyst, and the situation is shaping up just that way. I have to admit to mixed feelings."

"Mixed feelings!" Tania exclaimed. "When you know what Corbett is planning on doing?"

"I'm able to do a great deal of good in the position

I'm in now as the senator's aide, Tania," he said earnestly. "Corbett may be corrupt, but with his power he can move a mountain of red tape. He enjoys having a philanthropic image, and I can use that."

"I can't believe it," Tania said slowly. "You're telling me that you'd sanction Corbett's actions against Jared and his misuse of his work in the name of the 'greater good'?"

"I think you know I don't altogether agree with Jared's view on the long-range value of the formula," Kevin said. "So it shouldn't surprise you that it's going to come down to a choice." His face clouded. "One I'm going to have to make in very short order. I received a call from the senator just before you came in."

"So?" Jared's eyes narrowed warily.

"He's sending the helicopter for you two tomorrow morning. He wants both of you brought to Washington right away."

"Why the change of plan?" Jared asked. "He seemed to relish keeping us on tenterhooks, waiting for his visit."

Tania could feel her throat tighten with fear. How could Jared be so cool, when this might be the end of any hope of escaping? Suddenly she realized how weak and ineffectual that thought was. She'd never been afraid of facing a challenge before, no matter how dangerous. It was only now, when Jared shared the danger, that she was experiencing this sick anxiety. She unconsciously squared her shoulders and lifted her chin defiantly. Jared's strength could only enforce, not weaken, her.

Kevin shrugged. "Who knows why the senator does anything? All I know is that the helicopter will be landing sometime after midnight and you're both to be brought to the landing pad for takeoff at seven tomorrow. Two of Betz's men will accompany you."

"Then you have a decision to make." Tania's eyes

met his soberly. "And I hope for all our sakes that it's the right one."

"So do I, princess," Kevin said, his face grim. "Now, if you'll excuse me, I think I'll skip dinner tonight and go for a walk instead." He smiled ruefully at Jared. "If it helps you to think, maybe it will do the same for me." He turned, but glanced back over his shoulder to say, "I think you should know that Betz will almost certainly double the guards tonight." He walked swiftly out of the library.

"Do you think he'll help us?" Tania asked, frowning.

"Who knows?" Jared asked as he propelled her gently out of the library and across the foyer toward the dining room. "I'd have felt a little more confident if he'd decided to have dinner with us, though."

"Why is that?"

"Kevin has a curious sense of values that's almost medieval," Jared answered. "I don't think he'd feel comfortable eating at the table of an enemy."

"But we're not his enemies," she protested.

"That remains to be seen," he said dryly. "We'll know at seven tomorrow morning, at any rate."

"We're not going to try to escape tonight, then?"

"You heard him, security is sure to be tightened. We'll have to take our chances in the helicopter tomorrow."

"With two of Betz's men in attendance?" she asked uncertainly. "That will make our chances of succeeding pretty slim."

He smiled reassuringly. "We'll have to play it by ear, but then, we've both done that before." He planted a kiss on the top of her head. "I'm not worried."

"Why not? I certainly am."

"But then, you've only got me to protect you," he said lightly, "while I've got the Piper in my corner."

During dinner Jared remained insouciant and refused to discuss any but the most trivial of subjects. Even when they returned to the master suite, he maintained that maddeningly carefree façade, which grated on her nerves like sandpaper.

Irritated, she followed him into the room and slammed the door decisively behind them. Marching over to where Jared was standing in the middle of the room, she planted her hands on her hips belligerently. "Are you quite through playing Pollyanna now?" she asked tartly. "You've been so soothing and nauseatingly cheerful, I may have a problem keeping down my dinner."

The surprise on Jared's face was quickly superseded by amusement. "Sorry," he said calmly. "I believe it's traditionally called keeping a stiff upper lip. I didn't see any need to be unnecessarily pessimistic."

"You mean you were treating me as patronizingly as a grown-up giving sugar-coated medicine to a sick child," she said. "Don't you think I know how poor our chances are going to be tomorrow if Kevin refuses to help us? I'm not a complete fool, you know."

No, she was brave and beautiful and so damn lovable that he could feel his chest tighten achingly. She looked so small and fragile standing there with her head thrown back and her eyes blazing up at him. He wanted to protect her from the whole damn world. He would have liked to lock her up somewhere where nothing could touch or hurt her again. Instead he could only offer her danger and a chance of survival that was probably even slimmer than she imagined.

"No, I don't think you're a fool. I think you're as wise as a seer and as sweet as honey. I suppose I was just trying to keep your mind off tomorrow." Suddenly there was a flicker of mischief in his eyes. "I should have known the only way to distract a little fireball of energy like you was to keep you busy." He tilted his head consideringly. "Yes, I believe that's the only solution."

"What are you talking about?" she asked in exasperation.

"I have to keep you occupied," he told her, his lips twitching. "I'm prepared to make the supreme sacrifice." His voice softened to a seductive murmur. "But you have to remember I'm not entirely recovered and I may need a little help."

"Help?"

"Undress me, pixie."

She gazed at him with annoyance that faded as swiftly as it had come. She'd thought for a moment that this was the ploy with which he'd teased her, that he was still offering her that patronizing comfort. But there was none of that in Jared's face as he looked down at her. There was only tenderness and humor and something else that made her catch her breath and take a step closer. Something wild and sad, yet so loving that it flooded into every corner of her being.

"You want me?" she asked.

"I'll always want you." His gaze was holding hers with a look that was almost a joyous benediction. "I'll want your laughter, your strength, and your zest that turns every moment into an adventure. I'll want your courage and thirst for knowledge that will make you even more tomorrow than you are today." He drew a deep, ragged breath. "Yes, I want you, my love."

Her lips parted in surprise, and she experienced a sweet, heady joy that was like no other she'd ever known. She'd expected desire and had received something infinitely more precious. She tried to laugh, but it came out husky and uncertain. "That wasn't what I meant."

"I know." He took a step nearer, and his fingers were deftly unfastening the cloth-covered buttons of her tailored silk blouse. "But the other goes without saying.

There isn't a moment I'm with you that I don't want to ravish your beautiful body." He pushed the edges of the material aside and slipped his arms around her waist, his thumbs rubbing sensuously at the hollow of her spine. "You should know that by now." He pulled her closer to bury his face in the fine silky hair at her temple. Her bare breasts brushed against the rough wool of his crew-necked sweater, and she felt a mist of heat start to envelop her. "So don't react as if this is a love snatched from beneath the shadow of the sword or some such nonsense."

She went still. "Love? You were talking about wanting."

"Love," he said quietly. "I'm tired of using all the pat, safe euphemisms we've been hiding behind." He lifted his head and looked down at her. "It's time we took another step forward, Tania. I'll go first, if you like. I love you, and I believe I always will." His expression was grave. "I don't know if marriage as we know it will exist in the future, but I think there will always be a ritual of commitment in which two people who love each other can state their love. I want that with you, Tania Orlinov." He kissed her gently on the lips, and it was as sweetly solemn as the ritual of love he'd been speaking about. "Will you belong to me until beyond childhood's end, as I will belong to you, little Piper?"

She nodded, her dark eyes shining with tears. She felt as if her heart were swelling with such emotion that it was in danger of exploding. Oh, Lord, how beautiful and moving were those simple words. "I want to belong to you," she said, burrowing her head in his chest as her arms went around him and she hugged him fiercely. She wanted to be so close to him that she was actually a part of him. "Until beyond childhood's end."

She heard his chuckle reverberate beneath her ear. "Trust you never to do things in the accustomed order, sweetheart. Now that we've made the commitment, will you please tell me you love me?"

She opened her lips to give him what he wanted and suddenly felt her throat close with panic. Of course she loved him. She'd known that for some time. It filled her whole world and colored everything in it with rainbows. Why couldn't she say the words?

He must have felt her stiffen. "Tania?" He pushed her away a little to look down at her searchingly, effortlessly reading the panic and tension in her expression. There was a flicker of disappointment in his face that was gone the next instant. "Not yet?" he asked softly. "Don't worry about it, love. I know what you're feeling. It was a little hard for me too."

But far harder for her to take that final important step toward total commitment, he thought pityingly. Considering her background, it was a miracle she'd been able to come to love him at all. She'd given him so much that he had no right to push her into a corner just to obtain a verbal acknowledgment he didn't really need.

"Jared, you know . . ." Her dark eyes were enormous in her troubled face.

"Shhh." He put his finger over her lips. "Easy. Don't force it. It will come when the time is right. I don't feel cheated." His fingers moved caressingly over the fullness of her lower lip. "I have everything I want. More than I ever expected to have."

Oh, God, she did love him. How could she help but love him, when he seemed to know her every thought and feeling and treated each one with the most exquisite delicacy? Suddenly the intense emotion she was experiencing seemed too much to bear, and she had to lighten it or see it splinter.

Her teeth suddenly closed on his fingers and nipped them teasingly. "I don't think you have quite everything you want," she said, her eyes sparkling impishly. "Not at the moment, anyway. What did you say about wanting me to undress you?"

His smile lit the somberness of his face. "I've changed my mind," he said, his hands moving to push the silk blouse from her shoulders. "I think to celebrate our new commitment, it should definitely be a mutual effort. Besides, it will be much faster if we each contribute our bit."

It was faster, and in minutes they were slipping into the king-sized bed and into each other's arms. He was so deliciously hard and firm, she thought, running her hands over the supple, whipcord muscles of his shoulders. She should have been familiar with the lovely feel of him now, but every time they were like this, flesh to flesh, it was as fresh and new as if she'd never touched him before.

"You're so strong," she murmured, her lips moving over the pulse point just below his chin. "I love to feel that surge of power beneath the sleekness." She shook her head wryly. "Some convalescent."

"It's always nice to be appreciated," he answered as he suddenly rolled her over on top of him. "But I fully intend to exercise my sick-bed privileges and let you do the work tonight, love." He lifted her to a sitting position, so that she was astride him, and grinned up into her surprised face. "I'm waiting for the music to begin, little Piper."

"Are you indeed?" she asked silkily, gazing at him from beneath her lashes. After the first moment of surprise, she found she very much liked the feeling of being in control of their lovemaking tonight. The edginess of apprehension at what lay before them tomorrow had sharpened her emotions to fever pitch. It helped soothe away her feeling of frustration and helplessness to have command of something involving the two of them. Did Jared know that about her as well? It was more than likely, when he seemed to know every other nuance of her personality. Once again he was giving her what he thought she needed. He was always giving to her, she realized with a sudden pang of tenderness.

"I'll play your music, Jared." Her eyes were glowing softly in a face illuminated with the love she found so difficult to express in words. "I'll weave you a melody that will call you down from your mountain and bring you home to me."

The melody begain as a faint overture of haunting chords as she slowly bent her head to kiss his lips with lingering sweetness. Then she began to build on the basic theme with hands and tongue in a slow teasing arousal that caused Jared's chest to labor harshly with the force of his breathing. She could see the look of glazed pleasure on his face as her hands plucked delicately at his tiny nipples. He still made no move, but merely accepted, though she could see his fists clench involuntarily with the effort to keep from reaching out for her.

She adjusted herself and slowly, carefully surrounded him with her warmth, until she felt that every cell of her body was full of the glorious abundance that was Jared. Her breasts were heaving and she could feel that brand inside her burning and melting everything in its path. She gazed down at him and smiled lovingly. "If I remember correctly, at this point a *pas de deux* is artistically required," she whispered. "Do you know the steps, Jared?"

"God, yes!" He groaned as his hands flew to her hips. "I was only waiting for an invitation." His hips lunged powerfully upward while his hands pressed her down to him. She gasped and clutched desperately at his shoulders as she took more of him than she would have believed possible. Then she was lost in a fiery rhythm of thrusts and withdrawals that indeed was like the intricate moves of the most passionate of dances. But it was more exciting than any dance she'd ever known, she thought hazily, more intense, more meaningful, more . . . Then she couldn't think anymore as they took the *grand jeté* that was like an exultant leap for the stars.

Her heart was still pounding with a jerky cadence that matched Jared's when he carefully rolled her over so they lay facing each other, his hands cupping her buttocks so that she remained locked in their enchanted union. She felt his chest heaving against her own and the dew of perspiration on the shoulders where her cheek was resting. Her lips brushed his flesh with a kiss that was redolent of tenderness and gratitude. It was strange to be able to feel gratitude untainted by resentment or wariness, she thought dreamily. Another gift.

"It gets better all the time," she murmured with a contented sigh. "Yet it's always different. Isn't that wonderful?"

"Wonderful." His hand was stroking her temple with mesmerizing gentleness, willing her to sleep before the tension and apprehension returned to disturb her. Lying relaxed against him, she felt as light and small as a child, and he knew that swift surge of aching tenderness that was a familiar part of his love for her. "Now, go to sleep, sweetheart."

"Soon," she said drowsily, nestling closer to him. "Will it always be like this, Jared?"

"Different?"

She nodded.

"I think we have every chance of its staying that way as long as we both continue to change and grow." He kissed the top of her head. "And I have no intention of standing still no matter how many years the future encompasses. I wouldn't dare, with a little dynamo like you to keep up with."

No, Jared would always be moving forward, she thought, her heavy lids closing. It would be she who'd be hard-pressed to keep up with his pace. But it would be a challenge she would embrace with eagerness and joy. She could hardly wait to . . .

He could tell by the deepening of her breathing that she was asleep, and he drew her gently closer with instinctive possessiveness. Thank heaven she'd drifted off so easily. She'd surely need all the strength she had tomorrow. God, he'd do anything to be able to protect her from that danger. At moments like this, she seemed so endearingly dependent and helpless that he almost forgot how strong she really was.

There was no question but that they'd have to make the attempt to escape, no matter how hazardous it proved to be. That bastard Corbett! Escape was the only answer, and Jared wasn't nearly as confident of their chances of success as he'd pretended.

It was over two hours later when he, too, fell asleep.

Chapter 15

*H*er shoulder was being shaken gently but firmly. "Come on, princess, we have to get this show on the road."

She opened sleepy lids to see Kevin's bright blue eyes only a few feet away and immediately was jerked into full consciousness. "Kevin!"

"None other," he said with a grin. "I decided I couldn't chance Jared's trying to hold out alone against Corbett's men. Not with your safety in the balance."

"You're going to help us?" she asked eagerly. She sat up hurriedly, holding the sheet up to her chin, and for the first time noticed that Jared wasn't in bed beside her. Her alarmed glance flew back to Kevin's face.

"He's in the bathroom getting dressed and taking all the wonder drugs from his medical bag," Kevin said reassuringly. "He wants to be prepared for any emergency. You're bound to be on the run for a while before Jared can arrange a permanent safe haven for the two of you." His lips tightened grimly. "The senator's not one to give up easily, and you can bet he'll have everyone from the FBI to the CIA looking for you on some pretext or other."

"What time is it?" The room was lit by the bedside

lamp, and one quick glance revealed only darkness beyond the panes of the French doors.

"Only a little after three," he said as he picked up her robe from the chair beside the bed and crossed the few paces to hand it to her. "Jennings flew in at about one, and I invited him into the library for a friendly drink together with the two guards who patrol the rear of the chateau." He politely turned his back as she tossed back the covers, jumped out of bed, and quickly slipped on the robe. "Unfortunately, they all felt the sudden need for a little siesta," he said cheerfully. "They're all napping as peacefully as newborn babies, but I can't guarantee how long they'll sleep. I burgled the first-aid room for the sedatives I put in their drinks, but there weren't any instructions on the bottle about how to use them as knockout drops. Very remiss of the pharmaceutical company, don't you think?"

"Yes, very remiss," she agreed, chuckling, as she moved swiftly across the room to the bureau and quickly extracted underthings, a dark, bulky ski sweater, jeans, socks, and then moved to the armoire to grab her tennis shoes. "You plan for us to steal the helicopter, then?"

He nodded. "It stated in Jared's dossier that he could fly one, and it seems the safest way for you to exit the scene. You'll have to ditch it as soon as possible, though. Corbett will have the registration number and be able to track you."

"We will," Jared said as he came out of the bathroom. He was dressed in jeans and a black wool turtleneck sweater and suede desert boots and was carrying a small pigskin valise. "Get moving, sweetheart. I'll throw a change of clothes for you into my case while you dress."

"Right." She strode briskly into the bathroom and closed the door behind her.

She took only enough time to hurriedly throw on

her clothes, run a damp washcloth over her face, brush her teeth, and thrust a few pins in her hair to hold it away from her face. When she returned to the bedroom, Jared was waiting for her with her sheepskin jacket in his hand. He'd already put on his old navy flight jacket, and he helped her into hers with an economy of motion.

Kevin was picking up his plaid car coat from the back of the chair and shrugging into it. "With any luck, there won't be a problem until you actually take off. Betz said he was going to increase the guards outside, but not in the chateau itself. He didn't regard it as 'necessary.' We should be able to get to the landing pad without any trouble, but the sound of the engine is bound to bring somebody running." He retrieved two flashlights from his voluminous jacket pockets and handed one of them to Jared. "There are lights at the landing pad, but I've turned them off at the main switch box."

"What about the guard in the courtyard?" Tania asked, preceding them into the corridor. "He makes a complete circuit of the chateau once an hour."

Kevin shook his head wryly. "I should have known you'd be well versed on the security routine, given your experience. Maybe I should have let you plan the escape. You'd probably even have known how many of those sleeping pills constitute a mickey."

"Perhaps you should have," she answered. "I couldn't have judged the dosage, but I'm sure Jared would have been able to. Together we could have managed quite well."

"Together you could probably rule the world," Kevin drawled.

"The guard," Jared prompted impatiently as he took Tania's arm and they started down the stairs.

"Oh, yes," Kevin said. "There'll be no problem there. Since all the guards outside have been doubled, they'll be stationary. Again, a patrol isn't 'necessary,' according to Betz."

"How very convenient," Jared said dryly, his keen gaze scanning the empty foyer. "Almost too convenient. Betz may lack imagination, but he's damn good at his job. I find it difficult to believe he'd make it so easy for us."

"As you say, he lacks imagination," Kevin said. He paused at the door of the library. "I think I'll just take a look at our sleeping beauties to make sure they aren't on the verge of waking up, to cause us any more problems. Why don't I meet you at the old scullery door in a few minutes?" Without waiting for them to agree, he opened the door and entered the library.

"Do you really think it's all a little too pat?" Tania asked, biting her lower lip nervously. Now that she thought about it, there *was* something a little peculiar about Betz's laxity.

"Let's just say I'll be glad to get that helicopter off the ground," Jared said grimly. He propelled her swiftly through the corridors and down the short flight of stairs that led to the unused scullery. Now that they'd left the brightly lit foyer, it was almost pitch-black, and Jared was forced to flick on his flashlight to negotiate the winding stairs. Their steps echoed eerily on the stone, and ominous shadows seemed to press at them from all sides as they made their way carefully across the cavernous room. Why did it seem so sinister now, since she had found it merely an interesting anachronism when she'd explored it before? She let out a sigh of relief as they reached the brass-bracketed oak door at the far end of the room.

Jared flicked off the flashlight and opened the door. It swung open on rusty hinges; its creak sounded as loud as the whine of a rifle on the still night air. "I feel like I've been transported onto the set of a Dracula movie," he said lightly as he nudged her forward into the recessed alcove of the stoop. "I think we'll just leave the door open until Kevin joins us. That inner-sanctum-type creaking can probably be heard for some distance. We wouldn't want to call attention in case Betz isn't quite so dense as Kevin assumes." His gaze narrowed as it tried to pierce the darkness before them. "Still, it all seems deserted so far."

"How can you tell? You can hardly see your hand in front of your face. We'll be lucky if we don't wander off the edge of the bloody cliff."

It wasn't really that bad, but it came fairly close. There was just a sliver of crescent moon tonight, and even the shining yellow metal of the helicopter a few hundred yards away could only be discerned as a shimmering, ghostlike blur.

Jared's arm pulled her close for a quick reassuring hug. "No way," he said. "Whatever else may happen, I promise you I'll make sure there won't be any cliff acrobatics involved."

"I guess I should be grateful for small favors," she said, "though I can't say that 'whatever' qualification is exactly bolstering my confidence." She wrapped her arms around herself in a little shiver. "I wish Kevin would get here."

"Presto! Just rub your Aladdin's lamp and all things come to pass, princess." Kevin's voice came cheerfully out of the darkness behind them. As they turned they could see the brilliant beam of his flashlight, but it appeared to be suspended in mid-air in the stagnant blackness of the scullery. "They're still dozing, but I think we'd better move fast. Jennings was beginning to stir a bit as I was leaving the library." He was beside them now. "You lead the way, Jared. I'll be right behind with Tania." He switched off his flashlight. "We don't want any more light than we absolutely need. If you turn on yours, we should be able to see well enough."

Jared stood quite still for a moment, and Tania could sense the sudden tension that gripped him. She glanced up at him in surprise, but couldn't read his expression in the darkness. Then he was turning away. "Very well. Keep close, so you don't stumble." His flashlight flicked on and he strode swiftly toward the helicopter, his tall, slender figure silhouetted clearly against the halo of light.

Kevin's hand closed on her elbow, and he urged her forward, his long legs setting a pace that she had difficulty keeping up with. He'd fallen suddenly silent. She could feel the taut intensity that emanated from him like a wave of pure electricity, and his shadowy features in the faint light looked as brutal and blunt as an Easter Island statue. Brutal? Why had that thought occurred to her, when there was nothing in the least brutal about gentle, sensitive Kevin McCord? Yet there was something indisputably different about him tonight.

That strangeness kept drawing her glance away from the path, where her attention should have been riveted. If she hadn't experienced that uneasiness, she never would have seen the stealthy movement of Kevin's left hand toward the voluminous pocket of his jacket. Then he was withdrawing it with smooth dexterity and his hand was gripping something metallic. Another flashlight? she wondered. He was raising the metal barrel of the object, his gaze narrowed on Jared's back, outlined as clearly in the halo of light as a target in a shooting gallery.

Shooting gal—Oh, my God, it was a gun!

"Kevin, no!" It was a frantic half scream, half moan. She leaped wildly for the pistol and out of the corner of her eye saw Jared whirl to face them, the strong beam of his flashlight pinning their struggling figures in the pool of light. They weren't struggling very long, though, as Kevin swiftly pinned her to his side with a bone-crushing grip of his right arm, freeing his left hand to lift the gun and point it with cool steadiness at Jared.

"Don't move, Jared," he warned softly. "I don't want to hurt her, but I know how lethal you can be at close quarters, remember. I'll use her to protect myself if I have to."

"I'm not moving," Jared said, his voice calm and almost soothing. "And I know that you have no intention of harming Tania. You've told me any number of times how much you like her, Kevin. She's no threat at all. Why don't you let her stand aside while we get on with it?"

"Sorry, Jared." Kevin shook his head regretfully. "I wish I could do that, but there's too much at stake. She'll have to stay until it's all over."

Over? What a casual euphemism for murder, Tania thought dazedly. She felt as if she were in the midst of a familiar nightmare, only this one was more terrifying, for it was Jared dangling over the precipice.

"Kevin, this is crazy," she cried. "You can't do this! Why?"

"Because I can't let him go ahead with this life-extension business," Kevin said simply. "And I know Jared well enough to realize the only way to stop him is to kill him. When I first came to the chateau, I realized that possibility existed, but I hoped I'd find an alternative." He shrugged. "I didn't."

"You've been planning this all along?" Tania asked, stunned.

"Since the moment Corbett told me about Jared's work." Kevin's smile was bittersweet. "I had an idea that the senator would try to grab the information for himself, but even if he'd succeeded, the danger still would have been there. He might have been able to limit the use of

Ryker's techniques for a while, but a discovery like that can't be suppressed indefinitely. There'd be too many people clamoring to get control of it. Eventually it would come down to the same thing anyway."

"It was you who switched the brandy bottle?" Jared asked.

"It was easy enough to do while you and Corbett were playing word games." Kevin's lips twisted. "I didn't get the dosage right, evidently. I told you I'm an amateur at these kinds of high jinks."

"But you were working so hard to save him," Tania said incredulously.

"I imagine," Jared said, "that was because, with Betz and Corbett on the scene, he couldn't do anything else without immediately being under suspicion. Isn't that right, Kevin?"

"That's right." There was an expression of regret on Kevin's face. "I didn't want to do that, you know. I like you, Jared, and I respect you more than any man I've ever met. I hoped like hell I'd find a way to keep you from going forward with your plans without resorting to violence. I've been wondering lately if that inadequate dose of cyanide was a Freudian slip."

"But one you're ready to correct now," Jared said ironically.

How could he be so cool? Tania wondered wildly. She couldn't see his face, he was merely a dark shadow behind the flashlight, but his voice was as calm as if he was discussing the weather, not his own murder. "Kevin, you said you didn't want to do it," she said pleadingly. "It's against everything in your nature. Can't you see what a mistake you're making?"

He shook his head. "You're wrong, princess," he said sadly. "It's precisely because it is my nature that I have to do it. Remember what I told you about my prime directive? I know what a three- or four-hundred-year life-span could do to the human race. I spent two years in India and Bangladesh." His blue eyes were bright with pain. "I know what hunger can do to people. I've seen a father sell his daughter into prostitution for a meal that wasn't fit for a dog. I've had a child die in my arms who looked more like a twisted skeleton than a human being." He drew a deep, ragged breath. "That's what your life extension would do to the world, Jared. I can't let you do it."

"It doesn't have to be that way, Kevin." Jared's voice was almost gentle. "I've tried to tell you."

"I'm afraid I've seen too much bureaucratic hypocrisy to believe you," Kevin said. He laughed mirthlessly. "Corbett and I are in complete agreement on that score. At any rate it's not worth taking the chance."

"You're talking about taking a life," Tania said. "How can you possibly justify your actions?" She tried to wriggle out of his firm grasp, but he was unbelievably strong. "You'll have to murder both of us, you know," she said fiercely. "Because I'll kill you myself if you harm Jared."

"No!" Jared's cry cut like a knife.

"Don't worry, Jared." Kevin's voice was unutterably weary. "I don't think I could force myself to kill again even in self-defense. After I've done what I have to do I can't say that I care what happens to me."

Tania felt her heart lurch sickeningly as she saw him start to raise the gun. Oh, God, it couldn't be happening. "Kevin, please, no," she whispered. "He mustn't die."

"He must, princess. It's the only way." There was a faint ominous click as he cocked the pistol.

The explosive sound of the shot tore through the night. It was followed by her piercing scream of raw agony. "Jared!"

Her eyes were glued to that shadowy figure beyond the light, waiting in a horror of suspense for him to fall, and then she felt Kevin's arm loosen from around her and she broke free and ran forward. "Jared!"

She wasn't aware of the low groan Kevin gave as he slowly sank to the ground, unconscious, behind her. She brushed the flashlight aside, her arms going around Jared's slim waist. "Are you hurt? Where did he shoot you?"

Jared's arms went around her with blessedly reassuring strength. "Easy. I'm not hurt at all," he said quietly. "Kevin was the one who was shot." He turned her around to face the helicopter. "And if I'm correct the shot came from there." He raised his voice. "Isn't that right, Betz?"

The door of the helicopter swung open. "That's right, Dr. Ryker." Betz's voice was as coolly expressionless as always. "I thought it was time. You were almost certain to make a move at any second, and I was afraid you might be harmed if I allowed any type of scuffle to take place."

He jumped to the ground and reached into the helicopter to bring out a Coleman lantern. He lit it carefully, and suddenly the landing pad was bathed in a pool of light. "That was to be avoided at all costs, of course."

He was dressed in his customary impeccable dark suit, and his hair was combed with its usual meticulousness. He'd just shot a man, and there wasn't even a hair out of place, Tania thought numbly as she watched him pad toward them.

"I find it quite interesting that you knew it was I who shot McCord," Betz said mildly, crossing to kneel beside Kevin. Dispassionately he lifted the unconscious man's lid before searching for a pulse in his wrist. "He's still alive," he said carelessly. "I didn't think I'd killed him." He looked up at Jared curiously. "How did you know the shot was mine?"

"Guesswork," Jared said tersely. "The whole setup was off kilter. Your security measures left much to be desired."

"Yes, they did," Betz admitted calmly. "I was hoping you'd notice that, Dr. Ryker. I thought it quite likely you would. You're such a clever man."

"Jared said it was almost like a written invitation to escape," Tania said thoughtfully.

Betz permitted himself a faint smile. "A very clever man," he repeated admiringly. "That's exactly what it was. You could have walked out of here any time you chose in the last two days and none of my men would have lifted a hand to stop you."

Blood was spreading in an ever-widening stain on Kevin's plaid jacket, and Betz opened his coat to examine the wound. "Upper chest," he said. "Not necessarily fatal, I think, though there's quite a bit of blood."

Jared was releasing her and going over to join Betz at McCord's side. "For God's sake, are you going to stand by and let him bleed to death?" he asked impatiently. "Fix him a pressure bandage."

"I don't believe the bullet severed any arteries." Betz was obediently extracting the pristine white handkerchief from his front pocket. "And may I call your attention to the fact that the man was attempting to kill you only a few minutes ago? Quite premeditatedly, too. When he told me last night that the senator was sending a helicopter to pick you up, I took the precaution of checking on it. It was McCord who ordered the helicopter, not Senator Corbett."

Jared took the handkerchief, wadded it up, and pressed it hard against the wound in Kevin's chest. "Hold this steady," he ordered. He took his own handkerchief out of his pocket, pressed the folded square over the first bandage, and put Betz's hand firmly over both.

"Is all this really necessary?" the security man complained. "We'd be much better off if McCord did die, you realize. He's a very tenacious man, and he's bound to cause us a good deal of trouble in the future."

"Us?" Jared's brow arched in surprise.

"Us," Betz said firmly. "I thought I'd made that clear. Why do you think I took such pains to make sure you'd escape?"

"I thought it might be a cat-and-mouse game Corbett was playing," Jared said slowly. "You're telling me you did all of this on your own initiative?"

"Yes, of course," Betz said with a satisfied smile. "I'm not without that capacity, you know. It takes me a good deal longer to make up my mind than most people, but I have no hesitancy about acting once I've decided what course to take."

"And in this case you've decided to act against Corbett's orders?"

"I considered all my options most carefully," he said earnestly. "Breaking with Corbett was a very difficult decision I was forced to make. I had a great deal to lose, you see." He sighed. "But I finally realized I would have to transfer my allegiance. It was necessary."

"Necessary?" Tania asked. That seemed to be the watchword by which he lived.

"Why, yes, Miss Orlinov," he said. "I told you that I was a very determined man, a very ambitious man. I'm slow, however, and it takes me more time than it would a more clever man." His brown, Basset eyes were serene in his plump face. "But give me that extra time and there's nothing I can't accomplish. I can be anything I want to be. Dr. Ryker's breakthrough is going to give me that time. That's why it's very important that he get a chance to release it, because that's the only way a man in my position will get a chance to use it." His smile faded. "Senator Corbett would never have considered me a candidate for his privileged little group of Methuselahs. He wouldn't have thought me 'worthy.' But give me enough time and I'll travel farther than the senator ever dreamed."

Tania could believe it. Such obsessive determination and self-discipline would be as irresistible as a riptide, and just as deadly.

"I trust you're going to help us escape, then?" Jared's eyes narrowed on the other man's face.

Betz nodded. "The helicopter will be much more convenient than ground transport. I think we should take advantage of Mr. McCord's perfidy, under the circumstances. You and Miss Orlinov can find a place that's fairly safe and then notify me of your whereabouts. I'll come at once and take measures that will insure your security." His face had a childlike gravity. "I'm very good at my job, Dr. Ryker. You won't be disappointed."

"I'm sure I wouldn't, Betz," Jared said dryly. "But I don't think we'll require your services after you help us escape. We'll be able to handle everything ourselves from that point on."

"You won't be letting me know where you are?" Betz sighed gloomily. "I always knew you were a very difficult man, Dr. Ryker. Now I'm going to have to waste a great deal of valuable time tracking you down." His jaw set doggedly. "But I *will* find you. You've got to be kept safe. It's absolutely necess—"

Jared held up his hand. "Yes, I know, Betz," he interrupted. "Unfortunately we don't agree on the importance of your presence in maintaining that safety." He shrugged. "Not that I believe it will deter you from trying to find us. I'm surprised you're not insisting on coming with us right now."

Betz shook his head regretfully. "I thought about it, but decided it would be better for me to join you later. I have some loose ends to tidy up here." His gaze rested thoughtfully on McCord's unconscious face. "Yes, I'll definitely have to take care of a few other things first."

"Like removing the pressure bandage and letting Kevin bleed to death?" Jared asked grimly.

"I didn't say that." Betz's face was impassive. "I can't understand why it should matter to you one way or the other. As I said, McCord is something of a fanatic, and could prove a threat to us."

"Kevin may be a fanatic, but he genuinely believed what he was doing was right." Jared's voice was weary. "And he was willing to risk everything to do it."

Tania moved to stand beside them. "He tried to kill you," she said fiercely, "and he'll try again, damn it."

"So we're to go on demanding an eye for an eye?" Jared shook his head. "No, Tania, we can't live like that anymore. We've got to start somewhere, and it might as well be here."

She stood looking up into his silver eyes, and suddenly she understood what he was trying to tell her. "Childhood's end?" she asked softly.

"Childhood's end," he affirmed, smiling gently.

"Dr. Ryker, I'm afraid you don't—" Betz began.

Jared pulled his gaze from Tania's, and suddenly his face was no longer gentle. "McCord lives," he said crisply. "You're going to take very good care of him to insure that, Betz. Because if you don't, even if you do track me down, I promise you won't stand a chance in hell of changing my mind about accepting your services." He smiled grimly. "You'll find just how difficult I can be. Do you understand?"

"Oh, yes, I understand." He looked wistfully down at the pressure bandage. "McCord will live," he said reluctantly.

"Good." Jared rose to his feet and took Tania by the arm. "Now I think it's time we left. I'd like to say goodbye, but I'm very much afraid it will be *au revoir*, Betz."

He was propelling her swiftly toward the helicopter, and as he opened the 'copter door and lifted Tania into the passenger seat, he heard Betz's colorless voice behind him. "I said you were a very clever man. *Au revoir*, Dr. Ryker, Miss Orlinov."

Betz watched tranquilly as the rotors began to whirl, starting a minor hurricane, and then the helicopter lifted off the pad, making a hundred-and-eighty-degree turn before it started to climb. One of Betz's hands calmly smoothed his hair back into orderliness, while the other held the pressure bandage on McCord's chest.

It was going to be very inconvenient being tied to the chateau until McCord was well, he thought with a troubled frown. There was no doubt that it was going to interfere with his tying up the loose ends he'd referred to in his conversation with Dr. Ryker. It was fortunate that Ryker had assumed he was talking about McCord, or he'd probably have wrung another promise from him about Corbett. He shook his head in bafflement. Dr. Ryker's reasoning was totally incomprehensible. Couldn't he see that when a danger presented itself, it was only logical to remove it?

Well, he'd made no promises regarding Corbett, and he had every intention of making sure the senator would present no future threat to Dr. Ryker. That was absolutely necessary. Certainly luring the senator to the chateau presented no real problem. Ryker's escape and McCord's shooting would accomplish that. Now all he had to do was adjust his plans to encompass the delay McCord's convalescence would entail and then proceed. . . .

The huge, many-turreted chateau towered on the top of the mountain with a dark and pompous grandeur. As the helicopter gained height, it seemed to shrink into a cozy, postcard stereotype of Disneyworld, except for the tiny pinpoint of light on the landing pad that was Betz's lantern. There was nothing in the least cozy about the man they'd just left kneeling beside McCord, Tania thought with a shiver.

She glanced at Jared at the controls next to her, and was unsurprised to see his gaze on that little flame of light also. "Betz is a very dangerous man," she said soberly. "Give him the time he needs to develop and we'll have another Corbett." She grimaced. "And one Corbett in the world is more than enough."

The dim lights on the control panel illuminated the curious smile on Jared's face. "Perhaps. We'll have to wait and see what the next fifty years bring. He said he could be anything he wanted." He darted her an amused glance. "Evidently we're going to have him in our corner whether we want him or not. Maybe we can convince him it's 'absolutely necessary' that he become a saint."

"Somehow I doubt that," Tania said dryly. She leaned back on the padded seat and tried to relax. Everything had happened so fast that she could still feel the adrenaline sweeping through her. "Where do we go from here?"

"We'll land at the farm in the valley and change helicopters," he answered. "Then it will probably be best if we spread a false trail by zigzagging across the country before we zero in on our ultimate destination."

"And where is that?" She should have known that Jared would have everything planned in advance.

"I've developed a fondness for islands over the past four years," he said with a smile. "When I sold the one I had in the Caribbean, I bought another in the south Pacific in case I needed somewhere to go to ground. I made sure the sale was drowned in an avalanche of red tape and paper work and the deed issued in another name." His hand reached out to squeeze her thigh affectionately. "There are a few hills, but no mountains, I promise you, sweetheart."

"That's something, I guess." She sighed. "I suppose this means that the New York residency requirement I gave you is down the drain. There isn't, by any chance, a resident ballet company in this pagan paradise?"

"I'm afraid not, little Piper. And it won't be safe for you to perform in public for some time to come."

"I suspected as much." She was silent a moment, trying to smother a disappointment that was heartbreaking. "Well, what's on the agenda for the next few years?" she asked, keeping her tone light with no little effort.

"We establish a base on the island and form our own network for using my work." His eyes were narrowed in thought. "I'd still like to find a way to set up an international body to avoid the turmoil that's bound to erupt, but I'm a little wary of trying to find an intermediary, after our experience with Corbett." He shrugged. "If I can't find a person whom I can trust, I'll just send a release to all the newspapers in the world, and we'll sit back and see what happens. Either way, we go public on the process for life extension."

"If you follow the second course, we may need Betz after all. We're going to be awfully vulnerable on that island, and you'll be the most wanted man in the world for one reason or another."

"With the most wanted woman," he said lightly, his hand rubbing her thigh in a gentle caress. "I'll always be in the very best company."

"And what will you be doing while we're sitting back watching the fallout?" she asked, covering his hand with her own. "Working on the refining of the process?"

He shook his head. "I have plenty of time for that. I thought I'd start working in a new direction entirely, on something a little more urgent." He grinned. "Something our friend Betz would thoroughly approve of, by the way."

"And what is that?"

"Mind expansion. At the present time we're using only one tenth or less of our potential intelligence. There should be some way to tap that great reservoir. We're going to need every bit of our mental resources if we're to go interplanetary before conditions become critical."

She started to laugh, and when he looked at her inquiringly, she shook her head. "You're utterly incredible, do you know that, Jared Ryker?" Her dark eyes were dancing. "You're not satisfied with making all of us Methuselahs, we're going to have to be Einsteins too!"

He smiled. "Why not? It's all out there, just waiting for us." Then his face clouded with concern. "I've got my work cut out for me, but you've been robbed of yours. God, I'm sorry, love."

"Who says I've been robbed?" She lifted her chin defiantly. "I still intend to be the best ballerina on the face of the earth. I'll just have to delay it a little while. I'll still maintain my practice and work on new choreography." Her spirits were rising even as she spoke. "And there are other subjects I can study and master while I'm waiting." She darted him a challenging glance that was brimming with mischief. "Who knows? I may decide to give you some competition in your own field, or I might take over the dissemination of the process."

"No one could do it better." The look he gave her was so full of pride and love that it started a joyous singing inside of her more beautiful than any wind chimes on earth. "Thank you, little Piper."

"Because I'm being so marvelously philanthropic and fantastically generous?" she asked teasingly, and when he nodded, she said lightly, "But you should have expected it, Jared. It's the traditional attitude for a woman in love." She felt his hand tense beneath her own. She continued clearly, "And I do love you, Jared. Now and forever." It seemed so easy to say, she thought wonderingly. Why had it been so difficult before? Perhaps the experiences they'd undergone tonight had broken the final bonds and set her completely free.

His hand under hers turned palm upward and laced her fingers in his warm, secure clasp. "Then, nothing else is important," he said huskily. "And thank you for that, too, sweetheart."

She smiled serenely at him and deliberately used the phrase she'd heard him say so frequently. "It's my pleasure, love."

And it would be her pleasure and delight for as long as they lived, she knew with surety. No matter what the future held for them, what challenges they would have to meet, they would face them together. They would walk their path hand in hand, one step at a time, from here to the horizon, from now until beyond childhood's end.

FROM THE BESTSELLING AUTHOR OF
THE PROUD BREED

W I L D
S W A N
by Celeste De Blasis

Sweeping from England's West Country in the years of the
Napoleonic Wars when smuggling flourished and life was led
dangerously, to the beauty of Maryland horse country—a
golden land already shadowed by slavery and soon to be
ravaged by war—here is a novel richly spun of authentically
detailed history and sumptuous romance, the story of a
woman's life and the generations of two families interwoven by
fortune and fate, told as it could only be by the bestselling
author of THE PROUD BREED.

Don't miss WILD SWAN, available in paperback July 1,
1985, from Bantam Books.

THE LATEST BOOKS IN THE BANTAM BESTSELLING TRADITION

SPECIAL
MONEY SAVING
OFFER

Now you can have an up-to-date listing of Bantam's hundreds of titles plus take advantage of our unique and exciting bonus book offer. A special offer which gives you the opportunity to purchase a Bantam book for only 50¢. Here's how!

By ordering any five books at the regular price per order, you can also choose any other single book listed (up to a $4.95 value) for just 50¢. Some restrictions do apply, but for further details why not send for Bantam's listing of titles today!

Just send us your name and address plus 50¢ to defray the postage and handling costs.

DON'T MISS
THESE CURRENT
Bantam Bestsellers

☐	23994	**THE OIL RIG #1** Frank Roderus	$2.95
☐	23117	**RAIN RUSTLERS #2** Frank Roderus	$2.95
☐	24499	**VIDEO VANDAL #3** Frank Roderus	$2.95
☐	24595	**THE TURNOUT MAN #4** Frank Roderus	$2.95
☐	24706	**THE COYOTE CROSSING #5** Frank Roderus	$2.95
☐	23952	**DANCER WITH ONE LEG** Stephen Dobyns	$3.50
☐	24257	**WOMAN IN THE WINDOW** Dana Clarins	$3.50
☐	24363	**O GOD OF BATTLES** Harry Homewood	$3.95
☐	23823	**FINAL HARBOR** Harry Homewood	$3.50
☐	23983	**CIRCLES** Doris Mortman	$3.50
☐	24184	**THE WARLORD** Malcolm Bosse	$3.95
☐	22848	**FLOWER OF THE PACIFIC** Lana McGraw Boldt	$3.95
☐	23920	**VOICE OF THE HEART** Barbara Taylor Bradford	$4.50
☐	23638	**THE OTHER SIDE** Diana Henstell	$3.50
☐	24428	**DARK PLACES** Thomas Altman	$3.50
☐	23198	**BLACK CHRISTMAS** Thomas Altman	$2.95
☐	24010	**KISS DADDY GOODBYE** Thomas Altman	$3.50
☐	25053	**THE VALLEY OF HORSES** Jean M. Auel	$4.95
☐	25042	**CLAN OF THE CAVE BEAR** Jean M. Auel	$4.95

Prices and availability subject to change without notice.

Buy them at your local bookstore or use this handy coupon for ordering:

Bantam Books, Inc., Dept. FB, 414 East Golf Road, Des Plaines, Ill. 60016

Please send me the books I have checked above. I am enclosing $_____
(please add $1.25 to cover postage and handling). Send check or money order
—no cash or C.O.D.'s please.

Mr/Mrs/Miss_____

Address_____

City_____State/Zip_____

FB—4/85

Please allow four to six weeks for delivery. This offer expires 10/85.